MW00583440

EAGLE ROCK

ALSO BY IAN K. SMITH

FICTION

The Overnights: An Ashe Cayne Novel

Wolf Point: An Ashe Cayne Novel

The Unspoken: An Ashe Cayne Novel

The Ancient Nine

The Blackbird Papers

NONFICTION

The Met Flex Diet

Plant Power

Burn Melt Shred

Fast Burn

Mind over Weight

Clean & Lean

The Clean 20

Blast the Sugar Out

The SHRED Power Cleanse

The SHRED Diet Cookbook

SUPER SHRED

SHRED

The Truth About Men

Eat

Happy

The 4 Day Diet

Extreme Fat Smash Diet

The Fat Smash Diet

The Take Control Diet

Dr. Ian Smith's Guide to Medical Websites

EAGLE ROCK

An Ashe Cayne Novel

IAN K. SMITH

AMISTAD

An Imprint of HarperCollins*Publishers*

This is a work of fiction. Names, characters, places, and incidents are products of the author's imagination or are used fictitiously and are not to be construed as real. Any resemblance to actual events, locales, organizations, or persons, living or dead, is entirely coincidental.

EAGLE ROCK. Copyright © 2024 by Ian K. Smith. All rights reserved. Printed in the United States of America. No part of this book may be used or reproduced in any manner whatsoever without written permission except in the case of brief quotations embodied in critical articles and reviews. For information, address HarperCollins Publishers, 195 Broadway, New York, NY 10007.

HarperCollins books may be purchased for educational, business, or sales promotional use. For information, please email the Special Markets Department at SPsales@harpercollins.com.

FIRST EDITION

Library of Congress Cataloging-in-Publication Data has been applied for.

ISBN 978-0-06-325375-9

24 25 26 27 28 LBC 5 4 3 2 1

To Damian Cherry,
a lover of all things Ashe Cayne, the Kansas City Chiefs, and Keno. Long live the power of Grayskull. Luvya, cuz!

1

"What the hell are you doing?"

I was still fumbling to get the phone to my ear, but I knew right away it was Commander Rory Burke. His cantankerous growl was unmistakable even when I was coming out of a deep sleep.

"I'm doing what any sane person north of thirty would be doing at two in the morning," I said. "Trying to finish a damn good dream."

"Get your ass outta bed," Burke grumbled. "You have a case."

"Since when?"

"Since Elliott Kantor was found dead, tied up to a four-poster bed with women's panties on and a leather dog collar around his neck."

That sat me up. Elliott Kantor was one of the richest men in Chicago, next to the real estate titan Randolph Gerrigan. The two had made a sport of alternating the top spot on the *Forbes* list of the wealthiest Chicagoans. Kantor had built his fortune in textiles. Last I had checked, he was beating Gerrigan by a mere hundred million, give or take.

"Are you shittin' me right now?" I said.

"Stupid question," Burke said. "It's two o'clock in the morning. You think I have time for games at this ungodly hour? I'm at the Manor apartment building in Lincoln Park. How long before you get here?"

"Thirty minutes."

"Make it twenty. I need to get his body out of here ASAP."

THE AFFLUENT LINCOLN PARK NEIGHBORHOOD was a straight shot north of where I lived in downtown Streeterville. There was barely anyone on Lake Shore Drive that early in the morning, so I reached the Fullerton Parkway exit in five minutes, and after a few more minutes traveling west from the lake, I could see the enormous rectangular landmark building that I had passed hundreds of times but had never entered. My realtor friend had once told me its story as I hunted for an apartment to purchase once I separated from the Chicago Police Department. The building had been erected in the early 1920s to house the Fullerton State Bank, but then the Great Depression hit, and it closed. The Perfection Burial Garments, a company that made inexpensive clothing to drape over corpses before they were buried, took over the building. That's why there was still the word *PERFECTION* carved into the stone underneath the *F* logo that had been preserved from the building's former life as a bank. Now it had been gloriously and expensively renovated into eight huge, extremely private apartments.

I noticed several unmarked cars, a wagon, and only one patrol cruiser sitting outside the southern entrance of the building. All of their lights were off, and they were parked orderly, not haphazardly at different angles like they normally parked at a crime scene. When I worked as a detective for CPD, this was how we arrived when we didn't want to arouse unnecessary attention, quietly present but not intrusive.

Burke stood inside the massive lobby, looking impatiently at his watch as I entered. His eyes were red and irritated, the bags underneath badly swollen.

"We need to move quickly," he said. "Not a lot of time."

"What's going on?" I asked.

"Follow me."

We walked through another set of glass doors, then down a small hallway to the right and around a sharp corner. An impressive amount of marble and limestone had been meticulously laid on the floor and along the walls. The enormous windows several feet above our heads allowed ambient light to rush in and boost the dim glow from the gold sconces perched high on the otherwise barren walls. A plainclothes officer stood guard outside of a wide black door with a shiny brass *1W* centered above an ornate design. He opened the door for us to pass. We stepped inside, and immediately I was struck by the sheer immensity of the apartment. Voices from the other end of the dark hallway softly echoed in our direction.

"A call came into the district that an older man was unresponsive in his bed and likely needed assistance," Burke said. "They gave the address and apartment number, then hung up. A patrol car was dispatched. It took the officer several minutes to gain access to the building, but another resident eventually buzzed him in. He arrived at this ground-floor apartment and found the door slightly open. He knocked and called out, but no one answered. He entered and walked around and finally located the primary suite, where he found the deceased. He'd been dead for some time. No chance of reviving him. He found the man's pants on the floor, retrieved his wallet, and called in the name. The patrolman who found him was young. Didn't recognize Kantor's name, but someone on the desk did. Everything went into hyperdrive. I got the call from HQ to get over here, take care of things, and keep a lid on it. Kantor was one of Bailey's biggest donors."

I wasn't surprised. Mayor Bailey's political allies were as varied and rich as his list of enemies. This was how he conducted business: intervening at will, never afraid to ignore protocol or ethical guidelines, circumventing the law when it served his purposes. In his mind, the police force worked for him first, then the good of the city afterward.

"All makes sense," I said. "So why am I here?"

"The son wants to talk to you."

"I didn't even know he had a son."

"He wants to hire you."

"To do what?"

"I'll let him talk for himself. He's downstairs waiting for you in the wine cellar. But I want you to see the body first. They're almost done processing the scene, then we're getting him out of here."

"Where you taking him?"

"To his estate up in Kenilworth. For the purposes of the media and everyone else who's not here, that's where he died."

I followed Burke through the large rooms that had been sparsely but expensively decorated. They were dark and cold, as if an interior designer had gone about their work for the sole purpose of being featured in a design magazine, without any regard for the practicality of someone having to live there. The primary suite sat in the back of the apartment. An officer gave us booties and gloves to put on just before we entered. We walked through a carpeted sitting room with a couple of matching chairs, a large chaise lounge, and a television monitor the size of a billboard. We passed through a set of wide double doors and into a barrage of camera flashes that popped every few seconds. Three officers stood along the perimeter of the room. A massive bed stood in the middle of it all, underneath a domed ceiling with a colorful fresco painted underneath it. We approached the foot of the bed. Kantor was stretched out in the center of the bed, his hands and feet individually spread, each tied to a post. Besides the ruby-colored women's panties, he was completely naked. A forest of unruly curly gray hair worked its way across his sagging chest and downward until it stopped just above his protuberant abdomen. His legs were those of a prepubescent boy: completely shaved, very white, and skinny. His face had fallen to his left side, his eyes partially open. A yellowish fluid had dried around his lips and pooled on the white satin sheets. His horseshoe smattering of hair had been neatly trimmed, and his bald dome had a couple of small older scars where it looked like he had been nicked while shaving.

Kantor bore no resemblance to the powerful and vibrant man who, despite reaching his upper seventies, remained a social bon vivant, donating generously to almost any charity that asked, and a fixture at sporting events around the city. The newspapers loved him because he always had a good quote at the ready, and he was a fierce defender of Chicago, constantly calling it the greatest city in the country, even lauding it above his native New York. How in the hell did he end up here? How in God's name did he end up like this?

I took out my cell phone and walked the perimeter taking snaps of the scene. One of the techs stepped in to stop me, but Burke waved him off. Beyond the panties and Kantor's being tied up, it didn't feel right. I couldn't exactly put my finger on it, but something was amiss. I zoomed in and snapped his feet then his neck. The studded leather collar was loose enough against his neck for me to slide at least two fingers between the leather and his skin. I photographed the rest of the room, but there wasn't much. A pack of opened condoms and a small plastic bag with a couple of blue pills sat on the nightstand. A tall dresser stood against the wall opposite the foot of the bed. I opened the drawers in succession and found that only three had anything in them. One drawer had a stack of underwear and T-shirts. Another drawer had a few socks with tags still on them. A third drawer had several Chicago Bears shirts and two Chicago Bulls jerseys—Michael Jordan and Derrick Rose, who had made it to the NBA after growing up playing street ball just ninety blocks south.

Two officers entered the room with a stretcher and body bag. Burke approached me.

"They're taking him out the back, through the garage," he said. "Let's go talk to the son."

I took one last look at Elliott Kantor. I had been to many gruesome crime scenes with all the gore of amputated limbs and exposed organs, but not even they had moved me like the sadness of this indignity.

Burke led me through several more hallways.

"This place is a damn maze," I said.

"Rich-people shit," Burke said.

"The son?"

"Name is Simon Kantor. He's downstairs in what used to be the vault when this place was a bank. I wanted you to talk to him down there so you could have privacy."

We descended a wide set of steps, took a couple of turns, walked through a personal gym, then found ourselves standing at a gigantic, polished steel door.

"You can see your way out when you're done," Burke said. "I've gotta get back and wrap this up. And just so you know, all reports are coming to me first before going into the CHRIS system. I have to keep a lid on this as best as possible."

CHRIS was the computer system cops used to enter the general case report and any additional reports that were filed as an investigation progressed. Anyone could access the reports as long as they knew the case RD number. This was why it had long been standard practice on special heater cases like this to have the reports run through a commander or another higher-up first before being entered into the system. Once reports were in CHRIS, thousands would have access, which in a high-profile case like this almost guaranteed leaks. So everything would run through the commander first, and it wasn't uncommon for the reports to be strategically edited before being uploaded into the computer.

I walked into the wine cellar, which was bigger than any I had seen, even at some of the city's nicest restaurants. A man with dark hair that had been cut into a bob and pulled behind his ears sat at a long, elevated table. He wore a bright blue polo shirt and knee-length shorts. His leather driving loafers with bright blue stitching matched his shirt, and an enormous gold Rolex with an emerald green face occupied most of his narrow wrist. He looked like he had been crying.

"I'm sorry about your loss," I said, extending my hand.

"Thank you," he replied, accepting my shake. His hands were soft, almost feminine.

I sat in a chair facing him.

"My father was a good man," he said. "No way he deserved to go out like this. I want you to help me find who did this to him."

"You have more than thirteen thousand men and women in blue who can find out what happened," I said. "You don't need me."

"I do. We do. Me, along with my younger sister and brother. I was told you work quietly. Effectively. Most of the time you figure out what happened."

"I have my own style," I said. "Not exactly orthodox, but I get results. And not most of the time. All the time."

"We'll pay you whatever you want."

"I'm not going to take your money."

"We don't want you to work for free."

"I'm sorry this happened to your father, Simon, but I'm not going to take this case."

"Why?"

"No disrespect, but I don't know if there really is a case or if your father was having a bit of fun and just got unlucky in the privacy of his own bedroom. But more importantly, I'm taking the entire summer off."

He didn't disguise his confusion.

"I thought you did private investigative work?" he said.

"I do. But I'm also a degenerate golfer, and the last two years I've been promising myself that I am going to spend an entire summer working on my game and nothing else. This happens to be that summer."

"Dad was a golfer," he said. "Not a good one, but he liked to go out and swing the clubs with his friends or clients who flew into town."

"Where did he play?"

"Chicago Golf Club."

I wasn't surprised. It was the most exclusive club in all of Chicago and believed to be the first golf course in the entire country. I had played it once with my billionaire friend, Penny Packer. Her family had been charter members when it opened in the 1800s.

"What do you think happened upstairs?" I asked.

"Someone killed him."

"Was he into kinky sex?"

"He's my father. We didn't talk about things like that. But based on how he was found, I can't just outright deny the possibility."

"When was the last time you talked to him?"

"Yesterday afternoon. We talked several times a day. He was leaving the office and heading to the family house."

"This isn't the family house?"

"No, he lived up in Kenilworth. This was just a little place he bought when he wanted to stay in the city."

"Does your mother ever stay here?"

"My mother died two years ago from breast cancer. Dad bought this place several years before she died. She never knew he owned it."

"I'm sure you know I was a detective with CPD before I became a private investigator," I said.

He nodded.

"I've handled lots of cases in my career. Some of them garden-variety robberies or homicides. But there have been many that were complicated, some gruesome, and some downright strange. I guess I'm telling you this to say that I've seen a lot in my career, and what I just saw upstairs, I've never seen before."

"Is that why you don't want to take the case?"

"No. I don't want to take the case because often people think they want to know the truth, when really they're better off just leaving things alone."

"That's my father," he said with a tinge of indignation. "Of course I want to know the truth."

"Many people say that, but when secrets are laid bare, they fold."

"I'm not many people. I'm a Kantor."

I looked directly into his eyes, then said, "The city's richest man is upstairs hog-tied to a five-thousand-dollar bed with a leather dog collar around his neck and wearing red panties. Who did that and why they did it could lead anywhere and reveal anything. What you need to think about is whether digging up those answers is really worth it to you and your family and the memory of your father."

I turned and walked out of the vault and up the wide stairs that had brought me down just minutes ago. As I navigated the dark maze of hallways, I saw them slowly rolling a now-bagged Elliott Kantor underneath his multimillion-dollar paintings out the back of the mansion apartment and into the cold, dark garage.

2

Two days later, I got up and headed out for an early run. We were easing into the first week of May, and the city was in its last phase of our spring thaw. We could almost count on it that snow would no longer be in the forecast and the rains over the last few weeks would give way to a much-needed sun and clear skies. More birds began chirping and singing early in the morning, which was a telltale sign that warmer temps were on the way. I walked toward my starting point by the lake, stretching my arms and legs along the way. I could see the sun behind the edge of the water, just peeking above the horizon. Runners were already out in force and most of them were heading north, so I took a right and headed along the southern path, which I had not been on in a while. It was quieter and more scenic and would carry me by the yacht club; Soldier Field, where the Bears played football; and the grasslands past the city's gigantic convention center.

I had an easy day lined up: first, breakfast with my father at his house, then a round of golf with my friend Penny Packer an hour northwest of the city at Bunker Hill Farms, an invite-only course that was so exclusive it didn't have any members. Not only did you have to be specially invited, but only one group played the entire course at a time. An invite to play was a rare treat, but it helped that Penny's surname had been carved into more buildings than Chicago's city seal.

I finished my five-mile run in just under thirty-four minutes, jogged back home to walk my dog, Stryker, then quickly showered and changed before driving down to my father's house in Bronzeville. He was watering his plants in the sunroom when I entered. He wore a pale blue dress shirt with a perfectly knotted red-striped tie and navy blue gabardine trousers. Dr. Wendell Cayne had retired from his work as a psychiatrist more than ten years ago, but he still woke up every weekday morning and got dressed as if he were going into the office to see patients.

We went upstairs to the second floor, where his housekeeper, Pearline, had set up a table underneath the large bay window that overlooked his backyard and the expansive park a block away.

"You look good," he said. "Have you been working out a lot?"

"I never stopped," I said.

"Your face seems thinner, your shoulders a little wider."

"I'm doing the same routine. Nothing's changed."

"Maybe nothing's changed, but you haven't bothered to see me for two weeks and four days," he said. "But who's keeping track?"

"Dad, you say the same thing every time I visit you. If you want to see me more often, why don't you just pick up the phone and call me?"

"Because a father shouldn't have to beg his son to come and see him."

This was a recurring argument that I had no chance of winning, so I had learned a long time ago to find a fast way out.

"Are you back on the tennis court?" I asked. Tennis was his second favorite topic to discuss, after his issues with my fabricated negligence.

"My knee is strong again," he said. "That arthroscopy they did a few weeks ago really worked. They cleaned out the joint, and I can feel a real difference. My weekly game is back on."

"Which tournaments are you going to this year?"

"Probably the French and US Opens. We were able to score good seats at both."

My father never knew what a bad seat was, because he only went to sporting events if he could be so close to the players, he could hear them burp. Pearline served us a plate of veggie omelets, pancakes, and bacon. We dug right in.

"Awful news about Elliott Kantor," my father said between bites. "No sickness or any warning. Just drops dead of a heart attack."

"Where did you hear that?" I said.

"All over the papers and the news."

I took out my phone and opened up the *Chicago Tribune* site. There it was in the top headline. "Billionaire Elliott Kantor Dead at 77." I quickly read the article, which mostly focused on his business success that had started in New York then moved to Chicago when his wife wanted to live closer to her family. It covered his prodigious philanthropy around the city, his love of Chicago sports, and his several failed attempts to get the owners of the Bulls and Bears to sell their beloved teams. There were only two sentences at the end of the article that talked about him dying in his sleep of a suspected heart attack in his Kenilworth manse. I couldn't help but smile.

"What's so funny?" my father asked.

"Nothing."

"You smile at things that aren't funny?"

"I'm laughing at how different things are for the rich," I said.

"You say that as if it's a new concept," my father said. "Always been like that. Always will be. They play by a different set of rules. Held to a different standard."

I told him about the night I was called to Kantor's apartment and what I saw. I shared the conversation I had with the son and Burke's role in keeping everything quiet as they got the body back to Kantor's Kenilworth estate.

"Nothing surprises me when it comes to those people," my father said. "The rules weren't meant for them. They were made for the rest of us."

I opened up my phone and showed him the photos I had taken.

"Interesting," he said, studying the photos.

"What is?"

"The way the scene was set up. It doesn't strike you as contrived, like someone arranged it?"

"It looks to me like he was in the middle of kinky sex with someone half his age and something went wrong."

My father shrugged. "You could be right," he said. "But I see it differently."

He handed my phone back to me and took another bite of his omelet. After he took a sip of coffee, he said, "Those photos send a message. It's all about context. You have one of the richest, most powerful men in the city, a man who has commanded a vast fortune and business empire, here in a submissive and weakened state. He's gone from being powerful to being dominated. All of the things that were likely important to him have been stripped away and his vulnerabilities laid bare. Whoever did this wanted him to be found in this particular way. They wanted him exposed."

"What about the red panties?" I asked.

My father nodded pensively. "That part is gonna take a little more thinking."

I MET PENNY PACKER AT the heliport situated behind the Costco on the West Side. She didn't want to make the hour-long drive, so she ordered up her helicopter for the fifteen-minute trip by air. She informed me this was how most people who played Bunker Hill arrived at the course. Penny was in a jovial mood as we boarded the chopper. Her great-grandfather had started a small cosmetics manufacturing company that had grown into a sprawling international conglomerate. Penny had won an internal family power struggle and now occupied the chairman's seat on the board, the first woman in the family to ever do so. She had just closed a deal to purchase her biggest US competitor, which would give the Packers a large bump in their market share and put them right on the heels of industry-leading L'Oréal.

"You're really gonna love this round," she said. "Bunker Hill isn't the most difficult of courses, but it's one of the most difficult to get on. I've played it several times, and the more I play it, the more I like it."

"Is it really true they only allow a couple of hundred rounds per year to be played there?" I asked.

"Some years less than that. The most exclusive clubs around the city play that many rounds in one summer weekend. The family who owns it is very quiet and doesn't like to make a big fuss."

It felt like no sooner had we gotten going than the pilot informed us we were about to land. The golf course suddenly came into view, bordered on one end by an expansive lake and the other sides fortressed by long ridges of towering trees. Even from several thousand feet in the air, the lushness of the fairways was vibrant and inviting. We landed on a manicured lawn, where we were met by a small team of people who immediately handed us cool mint-scented cloths to wipe our hands. Others began unloading our golf bags and driving off to the clubhouse as Penny and I were whisked away in the back of a separate cart.

After a quick bite and a few practice swings at the driving range, Penny and I walked up to the first tee with two caddies trailing us, our bags strapped across their shoulders. The sun sat perfectly above the thin clouds, warming up the air enough so we didn't need our light jackets. There was no one else on this sanctuary of 450 acres except for the staff and families of wild animals minding their own business while tolerating our temporary intrusion. We both teed off with our drivers, and our balls landed safely in the fairway. Our round had officially begun.

"Did you know Elliott Kantor?" I asked her as we crossed a small rock bridge and walked up the fairway.

"Very well," she said. "He and my father sat on many boards together. Elliott was a good man. Started his business fresh out of college with a small loan from his grandmother, who had survived the Holocaust. He built it up to the empire it is today. He was a bit on the quirky side, but lots of fun."

"What do you mean by 'quirky'?"

"He had his way of doing things. He was a creature of habit. His trainer came to his house three mornings every week for a five-thirty workout. By six thirty he was in the car, and his driver drove him down into the city, where he'd get a shave and trim from his barber every morning, then head over to his offices on Wacker. He always ate breakfast at his desk, had two young male assistants who tended to his every whim and demand, then spent all day in and out of meetings, growing a business that had already made him one of the wealthiest men in the country. Elliott had more energy in his seventies than three men half his age combined. The city's gonna miss him."

We arrived at Penny's ball first. She had about a 150-yard shot to the center of the green. She asked her caddie for a six iron, then stepped up to the ball and unleashed her textbook-perfect swing, sending the ball high into the air before it landed softly on the right side of the green and settled twenty feet from the flag.

"Did he have any enemies?" I asked as we walked to my ball twenty yards ahead. A small family of deer that had been grazing in the rough scattered into the trees.

"Of course he did," Penny said. "We all do. It's inevitable. I'll never forget my father once telling me, 'You don't get this rich without making enemies along the way.' The building of wealth is never without controversy. Part of the deal."

We reached my ball, and I chose a pitching wedge for the 130-yard shot. I knew by the sound of the clubface contacting the ball that I would like the result. I watched patiently as the ball landed past the flag, then quickly spun back and rested just several feet from the hole. Penny nodded approvingly and gave me a fist bump, and we trudged toward the elevated green.

"Simon Kantor wants to hire me," I said.

Penny suddenly stopped. "Hire you to do what?"

"Figure out what happened to his father."

"He wants you to figure out what made his heart go bad in his sleep? You're good, Ashe, but you're not a miracle worker. And last I checked, your father's the doctor, not you."

"He didn't die in his sleep, nor in his bed," I said. "At least not the bed in his Kenilworth house like the media reported."

By the time we had finished our putts and had teed off on the second hole, I had told Penny the entire story, her astonishment growing with each detail.

"To be honest, I'd heard some things," she said as we resumed our march up the fairway. The caddies stayed a respectful distance behind. "But you never know what to believe."

"What kinds of things?" I asked.

"Elliott took his wife's death really hard. Tore him apart. He was a real mess for a couple of years, sort of retreated from social life. No one heard anything from him for a while. No one saw him out. Then all of a sudden he was back. I'd heard plenty of rumors. He was spending a lot of money, donating money, front and center again at all the sporting events. He buzzed his hair, started dressing better, even lost weight. Some said he was hanging out with a young set. Girlfriends. Trips to private islands. Supposedly, he flew in all these athletes so they could party together, have a good time."

"You believe he was really doing all of that?"

"I know he was."

"How?"

"Because Elliott had two body men. One worked the dayside; the other worked the night shift when he would go out to events. My chef's cousin dated the night man. She said some of what Elliott was doing was even stranger than the rumors."

"Would she talk to me?"

"I don't see why not. Are you planning on taking the case?"

"I don't know. But I sure as hell can't stop wondering what Kantor was up to."

3

The next afternoon, I had just finished working the heavy bag at Hammer's gym in the basement of Johnny's Icehouse when my phone rang. I didn't recognize the number.

"This is Simon Kantor," the caller said. "I want to meet you as soon as possible and talk about you taking on my father's case."

"If nothing, you're persistent," I said.

"I am. Can you meet this afternoon?"

"I'm hitting balls for an hour. I can meet you at my office after that."

We arranged a time, and I jumped in my car and headed to the Jackson Park Driving Range situated just off Lake Michigan on the South Side. The temperatures were already hovering in the mid-sixties, which meant thousands of golf bags were being pulled from the back of cold garages and meticulously cleaned for the earnest start of a new season. At the end of last season, I had finally achieved a single-digit handicap, something that had taken me the last five years to achieve. Now the real work had begun—keeping it there.

My phone rang just as I had set up my clubs and a bucket of balls. It was Burke.

"You're taking the case?" he said.

"'Secrets travel fast in Paris,'" I said.

"You're in Chicago, smart-ass."

"Yes, but Napoleon was talking about Paris when he said it."

"Jesus Christ," he said. "Are you taking the case or not?"

"I'll know for sure in a couple of hours."

"What's stopping you?"

"The size of their bank account," I said.

"Meaning?"

"It always seems to work out that the richer the client, the more headaches and complications."

"You took on the Gerrigan case a couple of years back."

"And look how much of a pain in the ass they were."

"Simon Kantor is pretty much a straight shooter," Burke said.

"And his dad?" I said.

"He had his secrets."

"Care to share?"

"We haven't confirmed anything yet, but we're hearing whispers about his nighttime extracurriculars. He didn't exactly behave like you'd expect a seventy-seven-year-old billionaire with five grandchildren would."

The first thing that came to my mind was drugs. "Was he a user?"

"Not of drugs," Burke said. "But of people."

"That's surprising?"

"No, but who they're saying he was using might raise a few eyebrows."

"My eyebrows are waiting."

"Young foreign nationals."

"Girls?"

"Boys and girls."

My eyebrows stretched upward.

"Any specific geography?"

"They were mostly Asian and South American."

"Are you telling me that Elliott Kantor was caught up in sex trafficking?"

"We're still digging for confirmation, but there's some noise."

I had very little experience in the world of sex trade. That was mostly handled by the Special Investigations Unit, and I had worked robbery and homicide. But what I had come to learn over the years was that not only was sex trafficking growing in this country but the perpetrators were rarely the creepy neighbor who drove an old tinted-window van and gave out full-size candy bars on Halloween. In fact, the most common procurers of these sexual services were normal-appearing, well-employed men who sat in boardrooms and looked into microscopes in acclaimed research laboratories. They taught high school science and held elected seats in statehouses. There wasn't any singular type. These depraved and craven men came from all walks of life and every corner of society.

"Do you think the family knew about any of this?" I asked.

"I don't know," Burke said. "But you'll have an opportunity to ask when you finish whacking around that stupid little white ball."

"You should see my five iron. I'm hitting it almost two hundred yards, a hundred and eighty all carry."

"Is that supposed to impress or surprise me?"

"When was the last time you were surprised?"

"About an hour ago, when I learned Kantor had purchased that apartment under the name of a woman who works in his company's mail room and lives in a one-bedroom apartment in Pilsen with three kids under the age of seven. She had no idea her name was on the title of a four-million-dollar Lincoln Park address."

FIVE MINUTES AFTER I HAD settled behind my desk and opened the window shades to allow a generous view of Buckingham Fountain and Grant Park, my buzzer sounded. I had installed this security system a few months ago, after some unwelcome guests had broken in and rummaged through my desk, though there hadn't been much for them to find. My Walther PPQ 9mm was always locked in a secret compartment, and they would've needed ten sticks of dynamite to blow it open.

Simon Kantor walked in wearing tennis whites, as if he were about to jump into a convertible and head to the country club. His hair looked wet, as if he had just stepped out of a shower and hadn't had time to towel off. He had a different Rolex on than the one he wore the night we had met in his father's wine cellar. This one was rose gold with a blue face and diamond bezel. We exchanged pleasantries, he took a seat, and we got down to business.

"My father had a great heart," he began.

Not according to the papers, I thought, but respectfully didn't verbalize.

"My mother was the glue to our family," he continued. "But Dad became the center once she died. We weren't always super close to him. He spent most of his time working or attending dinners and events. But the last couple of years, we really got a chance to come together. Finding out what happened to him will never bring him back, but it will at least help us get some closure."

"Closure is something that happens at the end of real estate deals," I said. "You don't find it after a relationship ends badly, and definitely not when it involves the murder of a loved one. You might get answers, and those answers might help you better understand what happened and why, but that doesn't mean you have true closure."

"Fair enough," he said. "We want answers. We want to know who took our father away from us and why."

"I really don't know how to put this delicately, so I'm just gonna shoot straight. Often in life we want answers, but sometimes the unknown is better for us than the known. What we hope to get from knowing only deepens whatever pain or anxiety we were feeling by not knowing."

"You sound more like a psychologist than a private investigator."

"That's what happens when you grow up with a psychiatrist for a father."

"I have a hard time taking no for an answer," Simon said. "I need you to agree to find out what happened."

"That's why we're sitting here."

"You'll do it?"

"'Many strokes, though with a little axe, hew down and fell the hardest-timber'd oak.'"

He looked at me quizzically.

"Shakespeare," I said. "His way of saying persistence overcomes resistance."

"I was told you like to quote Shakespeare."

"Marvin Gaye too."

Simon smiled, flashing a perfect set of veneers. "So how do we start?"

"By you honestly answering some indelicate questions."

"I'm ready."

"Who would've wanted your father dead?" I asked.

"You mean a specific person?"

"Yes."

"No one. My father had a lot of friends. He was good to many people. He was well-liked. Everyone loved him."

"Maybe someone got the short end of a business deal and didn't want to forget about it."

"Par for the course. My father was tough. A master negotiator. He won a lot more than he lost. But he wasn't ruthless. He didn't try to hurt people. He just knew what he wanted, and he went for it."

"Did he ruin anyone? Destroy anyone's business?"

"Not that I know of, but I didn't work that closely on his side of the business. I handled more of the customer accounts. He dealt with the manufacturing side. He spent a lot of his time over in Asia, working with our factory partners."

"Who worked closely with him?"

"His two assistants and Peggy."

"Peggy?"

"She managed his business relationships. She made sure the trains ran on time and stopped at the right stations."

"Have you talked to the three of them about how and where he actually died?"

"It's too embarrassing. I don't want them to remember my father that way."

"What did your father do in that apartment?"

"He stayed there when he was too tired to go back home."

"He had a driver around the clock. If he was tired, he could sleep in the back of the car on the ride home. Give me a better reason."

Simon sighed softly then said, "My father was very depressed when my mother died. There was a time I thought he was going to take his own life. We asked him to talk to a professional, but he refused. He stayed home. He refused to go out. He would only speak to a few people. He went to work, came to see us, and that's it. Then he went away for two months to the Bahamas. When he came back, he was a new person."

"What do you mean 'new'?"

"He had his energy back. He was smiling and laughing again. He still talked about my mother, but it didn't make him cry anymore. He became social again."

"Was he dating?"

"I don't know if he was dating, but I know he had women."

"Women as in more than one?"

"Yes."

"Did you ever meet them?"

Simon shook his head. "He would never let that happen. He would find that disrespectful to my mother's memory."

"So how did you know about the women?"

"His assistants told me. They were worried."

"Worried about what?"

"He was spending a lot of money on them. Flying them all over the world. Buying cars, jewelry, handbags, all kinds of expensive gifts. They didn't want him to be taken advantage of."

"Do you know what kind of women they were?"

"I don't. I didn't want to know, so I didn't ask. No one wants to think about their father having sex, especially as old as he was."

"Were you surprised he was tied up and wearing women's panties?"

"Very. Who expects to see their father in panties? He was always a man's man."

"Was he into young women?"

"I don't know. If I were his age and had his money, that would be my preference."

"Do you think your father cheated on your mother?"

"My father loved my mother more than anything in this world."

"That might be, but you didn't answer my question."

"I believe he had friends," Simon said. "He was very quiet about it, but I think he had company."

"Thus the apartment in the city."

"Have you ever been married?"

"Close once, but no Cohiba."

"My parents were married for fifty-seven years. Relationships change when you've been together that long. Things that once were important don't seem so important when you get to a certain age.

What my father did on his own time was not a reflection of what he thought about my mother. The fact that he went to such lengths to be discreet about it was a real testament to how much he loved her."

"Your father died tied up with a leather dog collar around his neck and wearing red panties," I said. "I'm not making any moral judgment or even calling that strange. Plenty of people are into that kind of stuff. But what does strike me as just a little strange is that a man your father's age and establishment enjoyed bondage and gender transposition."

Simon noticeably winced.

"I can't explain it," he said. "I guess he liked to kink it up. I honestly don't know what else to say."

"Was your father bisexual?" I asked.

Simon stared at me as if I had smacked him in the face. The question had not only rattled him but also seemed to offend.

"Totally out of the question," he shot back indignantly. "My father loved women. He would never think about being with a man. He would never find another man attractive like that. Don't get me wrong. He wasn't against homosexuality and people making their own choices, but he was old-school. That's just not something he'd get into. It's not who he was or who his friends were."

Listening to Simon and watching how vehemently he shot down the possibility instantly made me think of the old *Hamlet* line: *The lady doth protest too much, methinks.*

4

Once Simon had left an extremely generous retainer check and departed for the country club, I looked out the window toward Buckingham Fountain. The water jets had been turned back on for the season, and tourists had taken up their customary positions along the fountain's enormous lion-headed basin, posing for selfies and tossing coins. I was always amused that it had been recognized as one of the world's largest fountains, yet it only took in about two hundred dollars a year in tossed coins, while Rome's Trevi Fountain hauled in over a million.

The deep blue water of Lake Michigan remained calm as runners jogged along its edge and cars zipped along the drive. Watching ordinary people carrying on with the simple activities of life made me think how inconsequential we all really were when it came to the seemingly infinite landscape of time. For many years, the rich and powerful Elliott Kantor had sat on top of Chicago's business world as well as the city's complicated social pyramid, revered and untouchable. Suddenly, in the darkness of an ordinary night, he was gone, swallowed into the deep history of formers, his memory kept alive only by—except for those who knew him—the buildings where his name had been carved for posterity. But they too might one day be destroyed and swallowed into the bottomless well of antiquity.

There was something about Simon's visit and his demeanor that bothered me. He spoke lovingly of his father, but there was also a discernible detachment, as if he were speaking about a man he really didn't know. I was more than familiar with the tensions that could arise between a father and son, as my father and I had survived many storms. But this was different. Simon wasn't at odds with his father; rather, Simon saw him from a distance.

My cell phone's ring interrupted my thoughts. It was Burke.

"Learn anything from the son?" he said.

"Other than the fact that his watch collection is probably worth more than what the average person will earn in his entire lifetime?"

"Yes, other than that."

"There's something that's a little off, but I can't totally wrap my head around it. Maybe it's the money thing. Rich families have strange dynamics. They relate to each other differently. There's this coldness to it all. Simon and his father didn't go fishing together on Saturday afternoons."

"Maybe not, but Simon probably spent more time with him than the other kids," Burke said. "He was in the business. The younger brother and sister wanted nothing to do with it. The brother is an artist, and the daughter runs a cattle ranch out in Montana."

"I think the old man had a wild side that he kept well hidden from most, but I think Simon knew about it. Some of Kantor's staff were worried enough about it to tell Simon. I get the feeling they believed Kantor was walking too far on the other side. If they found my father like that, you'd have to help me off the floor. But now with Simon. He doesn't seem really surprised. He just wants to know how it happened. Very transactional."

"We've talked to the old man's two assistants," Burke said. "Nothing jumped out at us. They're being pretty tight right now. We didn't want to push too hard too fast. Bailey is keeping tabs on everything that happens. Maybe you can get more from them."

"Does Bailey know I'm involved?"

"Of course he does. He signed off on it."

That was odd. Bailey and I despised each other. He was a dictatorial, corrupt megalomaniac, and those were my good thoughts of him. He had summoned me to the fifth floor when I refused to go along with the cover-up of the shooting of an unarmed Black man who had been shot in the back seven times, all caught on bodycam. Edging perilously close to threatening me if I didn't fall in line, he dismissed me from his office with the warning that this was *his* city and that his reach was as long as his memory. My father found a law firm that wasn't in bed with the city, and in a matter of months, an extremely substantial settlement had been reached, and I had joined the illustrious ranks of former CPD detectives.

"What's Bailey's play?" I asked.

"You're asking me to figure out what goes on in that man's head? Hell if I know. The word came down and I made the call."

Bailey's involvement definitely added another prickly layer for me to wade through. There was nothing innocent or coincidental when it came to him. He was a very intentional man, always playing the angles.

"The assistants were next on my list," I said. "Simon gave me their contact info. What about the autopsy?"

"Medical examiner said he died from a massive heart attack. Several welts and small scars on his ass, as if he had been beat."

"Were they fresh wounds?"

"No. They were described as old."

The way he had been tied up had all the markings of BDSM—bondage, discipline, dominance and submission, and sadomasochism. I knew the perfect person who could help me unpack it all.

"What about the blood and urine tests?" I said.

"Should be back in a couple of days."

"And the person who called it in?"

"Dead end. They didn't call from a regular phone line. They used one of those free internet numbers, and the voice was likely disguised. The cyber team has tried everything so far. Completely untraceable."

"I need to go back and take a look at the building layout."

"Not a problem. I can arrange that with the management company."

"What about footage from security cameras?"

"That's why I called you. We have several hours of it. They had six cameras. I can get you the raw footage tomorrow. We've been able to identify one person seen entering the building just after eleven. She leaves exactly fourteen minutes and twenty seconds later. The call came into the desk just a few minutes after she left the building."

"Who is she?"

"Young Asian girl who lives in Wicker Park."

"What does she have to say?"

"Come find out yourself. We're interviewing her in two hours."

MANY THINGS HAD CHANGED SINCE I left the department. As always, every change had been preceded by grandiose promises of the positive impact it would have on making the department more efficient and the city safer. The city's detectives had been divided up into three areas—Area North, Area Central, and Area South. I had worked out of the South District over on Seventieth Street and

Cottage Grove, across from the city's biggest cemetery, Oak Woods. Now the three detective areas had returned to five, and they were numbered accordingly. Burke commanded Area Three, which housed homicide detectives on the second floor of a rambling brick station on the northwest side of the city.

One of the guys working the desk recognized me and pointed upstairs. Burke was in the hallway talking to a suit as I approached. He ended the conversation and signaled me to follow him down a bright corridor.

"Her real name is Su-Wei Hsiah, but she goes by the name of Jenny Lee," he said.

"Does she have a two-handed forehand?"

"What the hell is that supposed to mean?"

"Tennis. Does she hit her forehand with two hands or one?"

"What the hell is the difference?"

"A two-handed forehand is extremely uncommon in the professional ranks. Ninety-nine percent of professional players use a single-handed shot."

"How the hell am I supposed to know if she even plays tennis?"

"You said her name is Su-Wei Hsiah."

"So."

"That's the name of a famous Taiwanese tennis player."

"What the hell are we even talking about right now? She's not here to discuss tennis or how she swings a racquet. She was in Kantor's building the night he died, very close to the time the call came in. She's a person of interest, smart-ass. I'm sure this girl is not a famous tennis player."

We walked over to a small row of large computer monitors that had been set up against the back wall. Another officer—I assumed a detective working the case—was seated in front of the middle monitor, which showed an extremely attractive Asian woman with straight shoulder-length hair, bright red lipstick, and a top that barely contained her ample bosom. She was tapping furiously on her phone. The door opened and a short, redheaded plainclothes officer entered. He wore tortoiseshell-framed glasses and a dress shirt open at the collar. He could've easily been an accountant. He smiled as he sat.

"Ms. Su-wei," he said, opening up his folder.

"It's Lee," she said, putting her phone in her purse.

"I apologize. Ms. Lee, my name is Detective Gallagher. I appreciate you coming in and talking to me."

She nodded.

"We wanted to talk to you about your activities on Thursday night, the second of May."

"Are you accusing me of something?" she said.

"Not at all. Just trying to understand what you were doing that evening."

"Why is that any of your business?"

"We're in the midst of an investigation where someone died under suspicious circumstances. You happened to have been in the area of the deceased."

"Where was that?"

"The Manor apartment building on Fullerton Avenue."

Lee thought for a moment, as if weighing her options.

"Okay," she said. "What does that matter?"

Gallagher opened his folder, took out an enlarged black-and-white photograph, and slid it across the table. It was a picture of Elliott Kantor.

"Do you know this man?" he asked.

Lee quickly looked down, then back at Gallagher, and shook her head. "I've never met him before."

I studied her body language. Something changed. She was less expressive. She stopped talking with her hands. I also noticed she didn't answer Gallagher's question directly. He had asked if she knew the man in the photo. She carefully chose her words and said that she had never met him. It didn't mean she didn't know him.

"Can you take another look at the photo?" Gallagher said.

Lee looked down again for about the same amount of time as she did previously, then said, "My answer doesn't change. Is there a reason why I should know him?"

Gallagher looked down at the pad in his folder. "I just thought it possible you might've seen him, since you were in the vicinity of his apartment at eleven fifteen the night of May the second."

"Where did you say the address was?" she asked.

"1425 West Fullerton Avenue."

"I travel all over the city," she said. "It could be possible."

Gallagher nodded and softened his face. "Do you travel around for work?" he asked.

"I travel around because I enjoy the city and all the neighborhoods. There's lots to do in Chicago. I like to take advantage of it."

"Are you still in school, out of school?"

"I went to college for a year in California, then I moved here for a change of pace. One of my good friends lived here. I came out to visit her and liked it, so I stayed."

"Must've been tough getting used to our winter," Gallagher said, sitting back in his chair. "For Californians a sprinkle of rain sends them into hysteria. Can only imagine what snow would do."

Gallagher was good. He was getting familiar, relaxing her. He was doing what we called in boxing "the roll counter." He rolled away from her punches, then when he was clear, he would come up and counterpunch.

Lee smiled. "We Californians are definitely spoiled when it comes to the weather. Took a while for me to get used to the freezing cold."

"So, what kind of work do you do?" he asked.

"I work up at Rivers," she said.

"Never been to that casino," Gallagher said. "I usually go to the boats over in Indiana. You a dealer?"

"I'm a beverage server," she said. "Just something temporary to hold me over."

"They tip well up there?"

"Depends on how much they've had to drink. Once you loosen them up a little, then the tips grow."

"Must get pretty annoying sometimes. I'm sure a beautiful girl like yourself gets bothered all the time by guys looking for more than a cocktail."

"Comes with the turf," she said with a shrug. "You get used to it after a while. Most of them are just looking for some attention. Bad marriages. Controlling girlfriends. Lonely. They just wanna flirt a little and feel alive."

"You ever go out with any of the good tippers after work?" Gallagher said. "Meet up for drinks or something?"

"Never," she said. "You go out with one guy, the others find out about it, and they'll never leave you alone."

"Maybe you recognize the man in the photo from the casino?" Gallagher said.

"I see hundreds of men in just one shift," she said. "No way I can remember everyone I've served."

"Understood," Gallagher said. He reached into his folder and pulled out two more photographs and slid them across to Lee. "Those photographs are of you entering and leaving the Manor apartment building. You were there for a total of fourteen minutes and twenty seconds."

The counterpunch.

Lee looked down at the photographs, then back up at Gallagher.

"The man in the photograph, who you said you've never met, lived in the same building you entered," Gallagher said. "His name was Elliott Kantor. If you don't mind me asking, who were you visiting in the building?"

"I don't know that name, and I really don't want to talk about this anymore," she said, gathering her purse. "Are you making me stay here?"

"Not at all," Gallagher said. "You're here voluntarily. I was just trying to understand what you were doing in that building. That man was found dead in his bed about ten minutes after you walked out the front door of the building."

Lee stood. "Like I said, I never met him before," she said. "And I'm leaving now. My shift starts in an hour."

Burke looked at me and said, "She also works for a high-end escort service run out of Ukrainian Village. Her professional name is Destiny Blue. She charges three thousand dollars an hour. Her specialty is whips and leather."

5

Dr. Olivia Kenicott sat in a metal and leather aviator chair, looking like she was ready to crush a thousand hearts. The slit in her dress showed just enough to get the imagination started, and her tapered blouse showed more than enough to get the imagination finished. Years ago, she had been one of my father's star psychiatry residents. I'd met her at one of the annual dinners he hosted at our house for his medical staff. She had been equally alluring back then, even in her weathered scrubs and bruised clogs. I had followed her career online and through her occasional television appearances. She had become a noted sex therapist and worked for several years at the sex clinic at Loyola before opening her private practice downtown.

"Should I consider this visit official or unofficial?" she said as I got comfortable in a padded wing chair. The window blinds were fully open, allowing the sun to add warmth to her otherwise austere office.

"Totally unofficial," I said.

"Great. Then I won't start the clock." She smiled, and I wondered how many of her patients came to truly get help or just be in her radiant presence.

"Introduce me to the world of BDSM," I said.

"As a participant or an observer?"

"Neither. Let's start with becoming an understander."

"It's a pretty big topic," she said. "Definitely one I can't cover in just thirty minutes."

"Only thirty minutes?"

"You said this was unofficial."

"I'm working on a case where a man was found alone in his bed late at night, strapped to the bedposts, with a studded dog collar around his neck. He also sported red panties."

"Cause of death?"

"Right now, it looks like his heart gave out. But all the labs aren't back yet, so the final isn't in."

"You expect foul play?"

"I think he was too old to do what he was doing, and his heart couldn't keep up. But you never really know until you know."

"You'd be surprised," Olivia said. "People mistakenly believe this type of sexual play is only for the young and adventurous. It's been trending a lot with older men. They're the growing demographic."

"How does all of this work?"

"Depends on who it is and what they're into. There's no set way or pattern. It can be a very customized experience. Many first believed this type of sexual role-playing represented some type of underlying psychopathology. But as researchers dug more into it, they realized that the participants were normal, psychologically healthy adults who simply wanted to venture beyond the normal confines of traditional sexual interplay. There's definitely no one-size-fits-all. People experiment until they find what they like."

"So what exactly are people doing during this interplay?"

"It's a pretty big list to choose from," Olivia said. "But role-playing is very popular, as people act out fantasies in a private environment where they feel safe being vulnerable. In most scenarios, one person assumes a dominant role while the other person becomes the submissive.

The dominant partner is called the 'dom,' and they control the action. Accordingly, the submissive is called the 'sub,' and they willingly give up control to the dom. Most of the time, people have a preferred role they like to play, but then you have some people who like to switch between roles. They're called 'switches.'"

"And what about the leather accessories?" I asked.

"Sometimes it's leather; sometimes it can be ropes or chains. Depends on an individual's fetish. In general, some type of physical restraints is involved as well as some degree of humiliation and power dynamics. Sometimes the session might involve pain, but that's not a requisite. It really depends on what the sub likes."

I thought about the welts and old scars the medical examiner found on Kantor's bottom.

"Help me understand the panties thing," I said. "That really strikes me. I can't make sense of it."

"Because you, like most men, have been conditioned to only see things within the narrow boundaries around masculinity and heterosexuality that society has set."

"As a heterosexual man, it's never crossed my mind to wear my girlfriend's panties."

"Would you wear them if she asked you to?"

"I can't imagine her asking me to do that. Why would she want me to wear her panties?"

"Let me give you a number to remember," Olivia said. "Around ninety percent of men who enjoy women's clothing are heterosexual. They are not gay, and they don't have any desire to be gay."

"So why are they wearing panties?"

"Lots of reasons."

"Such as?"

"I had one patient come in a couple of years ago. He was a former Marine, happily married to a woman he was deeply in love with. One night, he had to attend an event dressed in uniform. He had gained a few pounds and was having difficulty getting into his trousers with his boxers. He couldn't get them to zip up. He could get them on without underwear, but he was nervous that if his pants split for some reason, he'd be exposed. So he went into his wife's drawer and pulled out a pair of her silk panties, put them on, then pulled up his trousers. It worked. He never told his wife he had done it, nor did he want to admit to himself that he actually enjoyed wearing them. Not only did they feel good but they also enhanced his arousal. So he would often go into his wife's drawer or clean laundry and swipe a pair, wear them around the house when she wasn't home, then return them without her knowing. One weekend, his wife's girlfriend came over to spend a couple of nights. He found himself sneaking into her suitcase and snatching a pair of her panties and wearing them while his wife and her girlfriend went out shopping. That night he had barely gotten them back into the suitcase before they returned, and he spent the entire weekend panicking that the girlfriend would notice someone had disturbed her undergarments. He came to see me and wanted to know if he was weird or if he was homosexual and just didn't know it."

"What did you tell him?"

"That he was neither. Millions of men are walking around right now wearing women's panties, and the vast majority of them are straight and very normal. Some men do it as a fetish. Others actually do it because their girlfriends or wives find it a turn-on when they wear them during sex. Some men simply like to wear them because they're softer and more comfortable. None of these reasons are pathological nor should they be a source of embarrassment, but because larger society regards this as abnormal behavior, it's something that's not openly discussed."

My mind flashed back to the Oscar De La Hoya scandal. De La

Hoya, also known as the Golden Boy, was arguably one of the greatest boxers of all time, the first to win titles in six different weight classes. The world was stunned when photos of him wearing a fishnet bodysuit, women's panties, and heels had been leaked by a mistress looking for a multimillion-dollar payday.

"I can't help but think of the boxer De La Hoya," I said. "After years of denial, he finally admitted that it really was him wearing women's lingerie in those photos."

"If I remember that case correctly," Olivia said, "he claimed drugs and alcohol are what drove him to cross-dressing. But make no mistake that while intoxication can lead people to do things they otherwise would not have done, the underlying desire to do many of these things is already there. The substance abuse only unlocks the door, but what's inside is already there."

"This case I'm investigating involves a very successful, very powerful man," I said. "If I'm understanding what you've said so far, I'm still left wondering why a man so formidable and in control in his real life would take on the role of a submissive in his sexual life."

"You answered your own question," Olivia said. "It's very common for alpha men, who are accustomed to being in control, to take on the sub role in this kind of interplay. Recent data shows that as many as thirty-four percent of men prefer to be subs. They want to be dominated. They get a high from giving up control."

"Do a lot of people die from these activities?"

"Despite what they like to portray on TV, most participants are not doing extreme things that would lead to death. The play can get a little rough, but most of these people are experienced, and they know just how far they can take it. Occasionally, there's an accident, but those are the rare cases."

"What about rich men? Are they any different?"

"A lot of wealthy men practice BDSM," she said. "It's almost like a trend with them. They don't talk about it publicly, but many of them are doing it quietly in very closed circles."

"Is it always a one-on-one situation?"

"Not always. Sometimes you have couples that like to do it together, and they switch partners."

"I'm trying to be open-minded, but it's hard for me to understand how a guy can sit there and watch another man fuck his wife or girlfriend."

"It can get even more interesting than that. Sometimes the men will ditch the women and partner with each other."

CAROLINA ESPINOZA SAT ACROSS FROM ME, glowing like she always did, even in the dim lighting of Virtue, a restaurant known for its reinvented Southern fare in the heart of Hyde Park. Foodies from all over the city made the trek south to this neighborhood that sat against the lake and was made famous by the University of Chicago's sprawling campus. We hadn't been seated for more than ten minutes, and I was already making fast work of the homemade butter biscuits with pimento cheese and ham.

"Did you learn anything about BDSM you might wanna try later tonight?" Carolina asked. She had allowed herself half of a biscuit and then pushed the other half to me, claiming she would save her carbs for the banana bread pudding.

"I don't know if it would work for us," I said. "One person is supposed to be the dominant, and the other is supposed to be the submissive."

"That could be a problem," she said. "I guess two dominants wouldn't work. In the spirit of equality, we could take turns."

"That would be called switching. Some people do it that way too."

"Look at you with all your fancy new lingo. You sound so proficient."

"What I am proficient at is tying knots."

"Relevance?"

"I learned how to tie more than twenty knots when I went to summer camp as a kid."

"I didn't know there were so many," Carolina said. "Most people don't even think about knots. Don't they just tie things together?"

"My point exactly. Most people will use a simple knot like the overhand knot used when tying your shoes, or a figure eight when you're attaching something to a tree or post. But the knot used on Kantor was very specific, extremely secure, and not common for the average person. It's called a becket bend. It's used a lot in the military and fire departments."

"Is it hard to tie?"

"Not once you get the hang of it, but it's a knot that takes practice. Most people don't have enough patience or interest to tie a knot like that."

The server appeared with Carolina's gem lettuce salad with radish, slices of hard-boiled eggs, crispy black-eyed peas, and buttermilk dressing. She had asked them to take out the bacon. I prepared to dig into the blackened catfish with Carolina Gold rice and barbecue carrots.

"Were all the knots tied the same way?" Carolina asked between bites of salad.

"That's a good question," I said. "Honestly, I didn't think to look. I saw the knots on his feet and assumed the same for his hands."

"Well, that's why you have me," she said.

"To remind me of the things I've missed or to test my knot skills?"

"Both."

She took a sip of her favorite wine, a Tignanello red.

"So, what do you think happened?" she said.

"I think he was having kinky sex with some young girl, and it got too much for him to handle, and his heart exploded."

"Don't most men say that's the way they want to go?"

"Depends on if it happens before or after the deed is finished."

"Did he finish?"

"Not from what I could see, but they're still testing samples. His panties appeared to be clean."

"What's up with the panties?"

"Sexologist Dr. Olivia Kenicott says the panties are very common in men who are heterosexual and are normal in every other way. For some it's a fetish that produces greater arousal; for others it's comfort. Millions of men are walking around right now, lifting weights in gyms, running the armed forces obstacle course in basic training, sitting ringside at boxing matches, and no one knows they're wearing panties."

"Except their partners, if that's what they're both into. You think this had something to do with why Elliott Kantor died?"

"Honestly, I don't know what to think right now. A young Asian woman who serves drinks up at Rivers but also works for a high-end escort service was seen entering and leaving his apartment building around the time the call came in that Kantor was dead."

"How high is high-end?" Carolina said after taking a sip of wine.

"Three thousand dollars an hour," I said.

"Why does a girl with that size sticker on her cha-cha need to serve drinks to a bunch of bleary-eyed gamblers?"

"That's exactly the question I plan on asking her."

6

I walked into Hammer's gym and immediately heard the loud thud of leather gloves hitting each other. I could tell by the speed of the blows that it could only be one person doing that kind of damage in the ring. Dmitri "Mechanic" Kowalski was a six-foot, hundred-and-ninety-pound killing machine with some of the fastest hands I had ever seen and a dexterity with a gun on par with the most decorated of soldiers in the elite forces. He was fearless and completely unemotional about causing pain when the need arose. For all of the aforementioned reasons, I was happy he had always been a friend and never an enemy. He got the nickname Mechanic growing up in his small Lithuanian neighborhood on the West Side, where even as a young boy, he was known for his ability to fix other people's problems. Hammer, the gym's namesake and a former Olympic boxer, watched from ringside, then turned away when the bell sounded.

"I don't know what's gotten into him," Hammer said as he walked by me. "But I wouldn't go in there with him today. He's fighting like a wild animal."

I approached the ring as Mechanic was stepping through the ropes.

"Not bad," I said. "But you're still dropping your hands on the one-two. If I was in there, I would've tapped you with a counter."

"Assuming my first punch didn't knock you out," Mechanic said.

"There's a first time for everything," I said.

We walked over to a nearby bench and took a seat. He twisted the lid off a water bottle and drank about half of it in one swallow.

"What do you know about escort services?" I said.

"Nothing, because they're too expensive for my taste, and I like to get mine the old-fashioned way."

"There's a company called Karol's Angels that supposedly operates out of Ukrainian Village," I said. "They take the money and supply the women."

"You have a name and address?"

"Just an address on Division Street."

"Let's go knock on the door and see what we find out."

Mechanic quickly showered before we jumped into his black Viper and headed over to the neighborhood where he had earned his stripes as a hard-knock kid. Minutes later, we pulled up to a small row of storefronts. The address belonged to a UPS Store squeezed between a pet store and a Jimmy John's sandwich shop. Mechanic pulled into a parking spot across the street.

"The number 2027 is on the door of the UPS Store, but it could also be the apartments upstairs," I said. "Let's take a look."

We walked across the street. There was no way to get up to the apartments from the UPS location, but next to Jimmy John's we found two identical glass doors a few feet apart from each other. One was 2029, and the other was 2033. Each had a panel of buzzers next to the entryway. These were definitely the entrances to the apartments above the UPS Store. We turned back and walked into the store. A short kid with a buzz cut and glasses stood behind the counter, typing something into a computer. The nameplate pinned to his chest announced him as Enrique.

"Can I help you?" he asked.

"We're looking for a company called Karol's Angels," I said.

"Are you looking to drop something off for them?" he said.

"No, we're trying to get in contact with them."

"Their mail comes here, but the company isn't physically located here."

"Who owns the company?"

"I'm sorry, sir, but I can't give out that kind of information."

"Do you know who owns the company?"

"I'm really not sure. We just accept their mail."

"What about the location of their real physical address?"

He shook his head. "I don't know that either."

"Is there anything you know?" Mechanic said, stepping forward.

"I just work here part-time," he said. "I don't know all these things."

Another guy walked in from the back of the store at the other end of the counter. He had olive skin and black hair that had been gelled and frozen several inches above his head. He looked very professional. His name badge read Ricardo.

"Is everything okay?" he said as he approached.

"Do you own this store?" I asked.

"I'm the manager," Ricardo said. "How can I help you?"

"Who owns this store?"

"The owner's not here," he said. "But is there something I can do for you?"

"I'm looking for Karol's Angels."

I could see him visibly tighten.

"Do you need to leave a package for them?" Ricardo said.

"No, we need to talk to them."

Ricardo looked at Mechanic, then back at me.

"I'm sorry, sir, but we're just a mail-and-shipping service," Ricardo said. "We accept mail or packages for them. That's it."

"Do you know who owns the company?"

"I don't."

"Does your owner know who owns the company?"

"She lives in Atlanta."

"Maybe you should give her a call and let her know she has a customer who runs an illegal escort service and is using her store as their company address."

Ricardo took a nervous swallow.

"If you leave a message, I can get it to her," Ricardo said. He pulled a pad and pen from underneath the counter and handed them to me.

"The message is pretty simple," Mechanic said, refusing the pad and pen. "Tell her the next time we come back looking for answers, we won't be asking our questions so politely."

We turned and left the store. When we got back into the car, Mechanic said, "Don't worry about it. I'll pay them a little visit later."

I knew exactly what that meant.

WHEN I GOT HOME THAT NIGHT, a small manila envelope with no markings had been slipped under my door. I knew it was from Burke. I opened it to find a single flash drive inside with a small note that had three time codes written on it. I refilled Stryker's water and food bowls, promised to take him out for a walk in an hour, then plugged the flash drive into my computer. Three filmstrips ran across the screen. The first was an exterior black-and-white image of Kantor's building. The vantage point looked out onto the sidewalk and street. The second strip was an interior shot coming from somewhere in the lobby and facing the entrance. It caught anyone who entered through the front door. The third strip also faced the street but looked to be from the rear of the building. I started with the first strip, where the time stamp showed 9:47 p.m. I hit the play button.

Several cars drove by over the next couple of minutes, and various people walked by with their dogs on leashes. One car drove up at 9:50 and stopped in front of the walkway. A woman and her small child got out of the back seat of the car, carrying two bags of groceries. They walked toward the camera and disappeared out of view.

9:53 p.m. A blue van with a white Amazon logo that had been painted across the side sliding door pulled up alongside the fire hydrant in front of the building and stopped. A heavyset white man in a dark uniform got out and rolled a large trunk down a ramp extending from the back of the van. It reminded me of one of those trunks that college kids pack when they head off to their first year of college. Once he had gotten the trunk cleared of the ramp and on the ground, he rolled it toward the front door of the building.

9:59 p.m. The deliveryman reappeared with the trunk and rolled it back up the ramp and into the van. He jumped behind the wheel and took off.

For the next few minutes of tape, nothing really happened. An older man with a Cubs baseball cap left the building wearing a light jacket. He lit a cigarette once he was outside, then walked west on Fullerton. More people and their dogs walked in and out of frame. I didn't know so many people were up that late taking their dogs out to do their business.

At 10:05, a black tinted-window Cadillac Escalade pulled up to the hydrant. The driver, a middle-aged white man in a black suit and white shirt, jumped out quickly. He ran around, opened the rear passenger door, and extended his hand to help the passenger out. The older man waved him off dismissively, as if he were annoyed at the offered assistance. It was Elliott Kantor. He was wearing a two-piece suit and a light-colored shirt open at the collar. He said something to the driver, who nodded his head and promptly closed the door. Kantor walked toward the building, and after he went out of frame, the driver hurried back around the car, got in, and drove off. The time code read 10:08 p.m.

I watched the next hour of tape. The old man with the Cubs cap returned. He was still smoking a cigarette, which he discarded and stamped out before walking toward the building. A few people walked by the building, but there was nothing notable or suspicious. I slowed the tape when a woman delivering food arrived at the building a few minutes later. She parked next to the hydrant, flashed her hazards, then walked quickly to the building. She returned three minutes later, counting money before stuffing it into her pocket, jumping in the car, and driving away.

The next person to appear approached the building from the west at 11:09 p.m. She stood on the sidewalk for a moment, looked down at her phone, then back up toward the building, as if confirming she had the right address. When she made her way toward the entrance, I recognized the beautiful Jenny Lee. She walked out of frame at 11:10 p.m.

The tape kept rolling without anyone entering or leaving the building. At 11:24 p.m., Jenny Lee appeared in frame. She ran toward the street and turned west. She was gone in a matter of seconds.

My cell phone rang. It was Mechanic. I stopped the tape.

"Our friends suddenly got their memory back," Mechanic said.

"They're only kids," I said. "I hope you didn't spill blood."

"Didn't have to," Mechanic said. "I just opened up my coat a little so they could see Black Betty sleeping in her holster. Suddenly they had perfect memories."

Black Betty was Mechanic's Smith & Wesson .500 Magnum. Forget about the sound it made when fired and the fact it could open a hole in your chest the size of a basketball—just looking at her was enough to instill the fear of God.

"The owner is a guy named Adam Mickiewicz," Mechanic said.

"You're kidding, right?"

"My Polish isn't the best, but that's pretty much how you pronounce it."

"That can't be his real name."

"Why?"

"Mickiewicz might be the greatest Polish poet to ever write a sonnet. 'Monsters merge and welter through the water's mounting din. All hands, stand fast!' I forget the rest of it, but I always loved those two lines."

"Fuck sake," Mechanic said. "You know Polish poetry too."

"And a few Serbians, but the memory is fading."

"I don't know if this guy writes poetry or not, but he has an address in Avondale and a phone number with a California area code."

"Five to one both of those are about as fake as his name."

"He comes in once a week, usually late Saturday afternoon, to pick up his mail."

"Maybe your new friends at the UPS Store will be nice enough to make an introduction."

"They won't have to. I have no problem handling my own introduction."

Once Mechanic hung up, I went back to the tape. This time I clicked the second strip, the one with the vantage point from inside the lobby. I tapped the play button and watched the activity that mirrored what I had seen from the first video. I saw the woman with her son enter first. They walked straight back into the building and out of frame. Next was the Amazon driver. He entered with the trunk and took a right, which had him walking toward the camera, then out of frame. In less than two minutes, he was back in frame, wheeling the trunk out the door. Next, the man with the baseball cap appeared from across the hall and walked out the door. Elliott Kantor was next. He entered, took a right toward the camera, then moved out of frame. A woman who looked to be Filipino walked into view from the direction the woman and her son had disappeared into. She stopped at the entrance, opened her handbag, then went back in the direction she had come from. I made a note of the time she appeared.

Jenny Lee walked through the door at 11:10 p.m. That matched the time I had written down from the first video. She followed the same path that Kantor had taken. Over the next fourteen minutes, there was no activity at the door or in the lobby. At 11:24, Jenny Lee reemerged, running toward the door. She fumbled with the handle for a couple of seconds in her urgency to leave, then once she got the door open, she ran out and was gone. That time also matched what I had written down from the first video. From this point of view, she looked to be more than in a rush. She looked panicked.

I watched the rest of the tape. I saw the beat cop come in. Twenty minutes later, the two detectives arrived. Ten minutes after that, Burke came busting through the door. They all walked in the same direction that Kantor and Lee had taken. The crime scene techs arrived a few minutes later. The tape ended.

I pushed back from my screen and closed my eyes, trying to let it all settle. Something bothered me about the timeline and Jenny Lee's behavior. Was she running because she was scared, or was she running because she had just done something really bad and was trying to escape as quickly as possible? Jenny Lee knew a lot more than she was letting on. I also couldn't help wondering if she ever got her cut of that three thousand dollars.

7

One of the basic investigative rules is that if an incident occurs at night, then it's always imperative to revisit the crime scene during the day. So with that in mind, I jumped into my '86 Porsche Turbo and headed north to Lincoln Park. I didn't have much reason to visit this heavily residential and yuppified part of the city, but as I drove through the cramped streets and narrow houses, it brought back memories of a girl I had secretly dated one summer whose parents were from Stockholm, Sweden, and thought I was giving their daughter tennis lessons. Little did they know that it was the other way around. I was the one receiving lessons, and they weren't on the tennis court but in the bedroom.

Fullerton Avenue was an east-west street that cuts through the heart of Lincoln Park, running all the way from the lake on its eastern border to the Kennedy Expressway on the west. Starting in the pricey lakefront neighborhood and its multimillion-dollar apartments, the landscape dramatically changed, becoming more commercial and accessible the farther west one traveled. A brush through DePaul University's campus, then several retail blocks before the Manor suddenly appeared like a giant ship that has run ashore. Uncomfortably situated on a corner, the Manor towered imperiously above its squat neighbor to the east, The Warehouse Bar & Pizzeria. On the opposite corner, farther west, was an understated hair salon, and across the street to the north, a suite of offices belonging to an insurance company. A block east of the building sat a Burger King badly in need of some refreshing.

My first thought was how odd it was for one of the city's richest men to have an apartment in this neighborhood. I would expect him to have a private getaway in one of the superluxury high-rises in the Gold Coast, not on a street full of small hair salons and insurance agents sitting behind metal desks. Then I thought about it more and realized this actually was a perfect place for him to have his secret apartment. No one would expect a man of Kantor's stature to spend some of his nights hidden away in this pedestrian block, many miles away from his palatial estate farther north up the lake. I couldn't help but think of the irony that a man with so much money died in his bed in a building that was once a bank.

I sat in my car across the street and observed the building's façade. Two security cameras were positioned on both wings of the building, and one camera was above the entrance. The video I had seen must've come from the camera above the entrance. I snapped a couple of photos with my phone's camera, then got out of the car and walked across the street, toward the building. I continued along the side of the building that faced west, along the side street Janssen Avenue. Unlike the commercial storefronts on Fullerton, this was a small residential street full of narrow houses with shiny windows and freshly painted doors. I wondered why he hadn't chosen to purchase one of these houses, where he would have had complete privacy, rather than an apartment building that had neighbors who might have recognized him.

The back of the building had three garage doors that opened into an alley separating the building from the houses on the other side. This was where they had backed up the wagon that night and taken his body out to avoid the spectacle of carrying him out the front door. I noticed one camera on the eastern edge of the building. That camera's video was not on the flash drive Burke had given me. I walked through the alley, then looked at the side of the building abutting the adjacent bar. There was enough room to walk between the buildings, and two of the upper floors had balconies that looked out over the bar and the back of the building. Not exactly a million-dollar view.

I walked back around the building. There was very little activity on Janssen Avenue, and I expected there was even less late at night, when most of the families were likely sleeping. But Fullerton was extremely busy at all hours, as evidenced in the video, with cars constantly racing by and people walking their dogs at all hours. The Burger King at the end of the block must've contributed its fair share to the activity.

I made it back to my car just as a parking enforcement officer stood looking at the CPD placard sitting in my window.

"Nice car," she said. "You cops must make a lot of money. You drive better cars than the mayor."

"Only when we work a lot of overtime," I said.

She smiled and shrugged, then walked away, searching for her next victim.

I stood and looked across the street again at the Manor. Something wasn't right about the timeline. Jenny Lee had been in the building for no more than fourteen minutes and twenty seconds, and in that short time, she had tied him up, did whatever it is a dom does to a sub, then fled when Elliott Kantor died. I'd heard that some of these women worked fast, but this brought a new definition to the concept of a quickie. I needed to talk to Jenny Lee, and I needed to find out what really happened.

I dialed Burke's number.

"Any updates?" I asked.

"My guys are still working around the clock," he said. "There's just not a lot to go on right now."

"What about Jenny Lee?"

"We're monitoring her, but we don't have enough to bring her in. They've been calling her. She won't return the calls. We got her fingerprints and ran them against what we found in the apartment. No matches. We only have her entering the building and walking down the hall in the direction of his apartment. We don't have anything that puts her inside his apartment."

"What's going on with the rear video camera on the east side of the building? I just took a look and noticed it in the back alley. None of the video you gave me had anything from that camera."

"The management company is working on it," Burke said. "They were having a problem getting the video to download from the cloud. All this fancy shit. That's what happens when everything turns so high-tech. Anyway, we're expecting something within the next forty-eight hours, if not sooner. And I got a call from the ME's office. They're planning on having all the lab results back tomorrow. I'll let you know when they come in."

"Is Bailey saying anything?"

"He's up Fitzpatrick's ass every goddamn day, who then gets up my ass. I'm getting too old for this shit."

"Nothing's stopping you from retirement."

"Trust me. The minute I have enough to buy a place on the gulf, I'm long gone. I'm trading all this shit in for margaritas and tacos."

"You're gonna miss our deep-dish and Italian beef."

"Not hardly. With a credit card and app, anything can be shipped these days. High-tech shit."

JENNY LEE WALKED OUT OF the Rivers Casino employee entrance five minutes after her shift ended at eleven. I had my car positioned so that I could see her pull out of the employee lot. Not long after she walked into the restricted parking area, the electronic arm lifted, and a midnight blue Maserati with tinted windows pulled out into the casino driveway. I slowly fell in behind her and kept a safe distance as she made her way onto River Road and then the expressway to make her trip south toward the city.

Traffic was light at this time of night: mostly passengers who had arrived on late flights at nearby O'Hare, mixed with motorists passing through Chicago to get to Indiana. I kept her in my sights as she changed lanes without using her signal. Not only did I like her ride but I liked that she wasn't afraid to put her foot on the gas. She looked delicate and timid sitting in the interview room in front of Gallagher, but she was anything but that behind the wheel. We made it downtown in just under ten minutes for a drive that typically took fifteen. I followed her off the Ohio Street exit that fed into one of the major arteries running into downtown. Once we had come to the end of the exit ramp, she took a series of left turns, which put us in the trendy River North neighborhood. I wondered if she was going home or going to see a client. She pulled up to a well-maintained mid-rise building at 400 West Huron. She drove past the garage and pulled into a parking spot on the street. I was waiting for her when she got out of the car. She immediately clutched her large handbag when she noticed me standing in the shadows.

"Your bag is the last thing I want, Jenny," I said, stepping under the streetlight so she could see me better. "I just want to ask you a couple of questions."

She scanned around nervously, as if planning an escape route. Then she looked back at me and said, "Who are you?"

"I'm the guy who's gonna help you keep from getting arrested and going to jail."

"Arrested for what?"

"For killing a man you didn't kill."

"I haven't killed anyone."

"I just said that. But the cops don't know that. They think you either killed Elliott Kantor or helped whoever did."

"I don't know anyone named Elliott Kantor."

"You might not know him, but you have his address in your phone: 1425 West Fullerton. He's the dead man strapped in his bed you found a week ago."

A slight relaxation in her face signaled I was correct. She started to walk past me. "I have to go," she said.

"He was already tied up to the bedposts by the time you arrived," I said. "You had been given the assignment to go and see him, much like you're about to do right now."

She stopped, but she didn't turn around.

"When you got into his apartment, the place was so big, it took you a little while to find him. He was already dead when you walked into the room, so you didn't try CPR or anything. He would've had your lipstick all over his mouth. Instead, you shook him once or twice, and his head just fell to the side. You panicked and ran away. You didn't do anything wrong, but they're still gonna keep coming after you, because unfortunately for you, that man wasn't just any client. He was one of the richest men in this city."

She turned and faced me.

"What do you want from me?" she said.

"The truth."

"Are you a cop?"

"I used to be."

"Well, if you're not a cop, why are you here asking me these questions? What business is it of yours?"

"I used to be a detective, but now I'm a private investigator. And I've been hired to help the cops figure out what actually happened in the apartment that night."

"If you're working with the cops, and you know I didn't do anything, then just tell them I'm innocent and leave me alone."

"That's not how this works," I said. "You answer my questions truthfully, then I'll have enough to go back and tell them to leave you alone. You hide anything from me, then sooner or later, they're gonna pick you up in the middle of your shift at the casino and haul your pretty little ass to jail."

She thought for a moment, then walked back toward me.

"What's your name?" she asked.

"Cayne. Ashe Cayne."

"You think all this is funny?"

"No, I think you were unlucky that night. You were in the wrong place at the wrong time. All you have to do is tell me what exactly happened, then I'll get back in my car, and you can go visit whoever it is you're scheduled to see."

"How do you know I don't live here?"

"Because you drove by the garage entrance half a block back, and you put that beautiful hundred-thousand-dollar car on the street next to a fifteen-year-old Honda Accord with missing hubcaps."

She took a beat to process what I had just said then asked, "Even though you're not with the police anymore, can what I tell you be used against me?"

"Depends."

"On what?"

"Did you commit a crime?"

"No."

"Then you'll be fine."

Jenny looked relieved, then took a deep breath. "This is what happened," she began. "I got a text message to go meet a friend at that address. I was running a few minutes late, because I had to get one of the other girls to come in early and cover the last couple of hours of my shift at work, and she was running late. I showed up at the address and rang the button next to his apartment number. A few seconds later, the buzzer sounded, and I went in. I found his place and went to ring his doorbell, but I noticed the door was already open. I knocked a couple of times, but no one answered. I rang the doorbell and waited. Still no answer, so I opened the door and went inside. I kept calling his name, but there wasn't an answer. The place was huge, so I started looking around. I finally got to the primary bedroom, and that's where I found him."

"Was he moving or breathing when you walked into the bedroom?"

"No, he was just lying there."

"Then what did you do?"

"I walked over to the bed and shook his shoulder. His eyes were slightly open. His head fell to the side when I shook him. I knew right away he was already dead."

"My next questions are really important," I said. "I need you to tell me the truth."

She nodded nervously.

"Who sent you to meet him?"

"I don't know the name of the person."

"What's the name of the company that sent you?"

"Karol's Angels."

"How long have you worked for them?"

"I don't work *for* them. They give me assignments. It's been almost two years."

"And they always provide the client?"

"Friend, not client," she said. "We call them friends."

"Really? Someone you've never met and don't even know their name?"

"Friends," she said adamantly. "Prostitutes have clients. I'm not a prostitute."

Now was not the time to debate nomenclature.

"You told the police you didn't know Elliott Kantor's name, but you just told me that you called his name when you walked into the apartment. Which is it?"

"The name they gave me wasn't Elliott Kantor. The message said his name was Vernon."

"No last name?"

"They never give us a last name."

"Was this the first time you were assigned to Vernon?"

"Yes."

"Was this the first time he used Karol's Angels?"

"I don't know. Sometimes they'll say if it's a frequent flier; sometimes they won't. Typically, I get a first name, address, and the friend's preferences. They didn't tell me his status."

"And when you're done with your visit, what happens?"

"I send a text message back that says 'Complete, and the visit is closed out.'"

"Did you send that message?"

"Yes."

"Even though he was already dead when you got there?"

"I showed up. It wasn't my fault he was dead. I missed out on other paying appointments. I need money like anyone else."

"Did you see anyone leaving his apartment?"

"No."

"Were you the one who called 911?"

"No, I was too scared," she said. "That would only make them think it was me who had something to do with it."

"I want you to think really hard," I said. "Was there anything else out of the ordinary? Anything that bothered you besides the fact you found a dead man in his bed?"

Jenny looked up toward the dark sky as she thought.

"There is one thing I still can't figure out," she said.

"I'm listening."

"When I arrived, I rang his buzzer. Someone had to buzz me in. It couldn't have been him. He couldn't buzz me in, tie himself up, then die in just a couple of minutes. Someone was there, and every time I think about it, I get creeped out. If they killed him, they could've killed me too."

"You sure you pushed the right buzzer?" I said. "Maybe you pushed another buzzer, and someone else let you in."

"I'm sure," she said. "1W. It was the top buzzer. They didn't ask me my name. They just buzzed me in."

"Did that strike you as strange when they didn't ask for your name but just unlocked the door?"

"Not at the time. I figured he had seen me on the camera, so he knew it was me. There was no reason to ask my name."

"Do they send the men your photo before you show up?"

"Of course," she said. "The female friends we visit get sent our photos also."

"Female friends?"

"Women use the service too, as much as men do. But I'm not into that, so I don't accept those assignments. I only do single men or couples."

"I believe you," I said.

"Can I go now?" she said.

"One more question. Did you ever get the three thousand dollars?"

"I'm only paid a third of the rate. And no, I never got it. The company gets their money as soon as they make the booking. But I only get paid once the friend sends back confirmation that my visit is complete."

"Just complete, or does it also have to be satisfactory?"

"My visits are always satisfactory."

I watched her walk away and thought about how much fun someone was about to have.

8

The next morning, I called Carolina and asked for help. Her position as the administrative supervisor at the police headquarters in the Bureau of Investigative Services meant she had access to files and information that otherwise would've been near impossible for me to access from the outside. She agreed to run Jenny Lee's license plate number if I agreed to make a sweet potato pie that weekend. I used a recipe that had been handed down from my great-aunt Dora B., who had learned it from her mother and passed it on to her only daughter, who taught it to my mother when she was a little girl.

This spring I had committed to an hour hitting lesson every Friday morning with a man named Eddie "Smooth" McAdoo, who still held the low-round record at Jackson Park at eleven under par. Climbing into his mid-seventies, he didn't hit the ball as long, but his swing was still a work of art. I was already noticing a difference in my ball flight after just three sessions.

Today we would be working on my short game around the green.

Smooth had me hitting short ten-yard chip shots in the grass when my phone rang. It was Burke.

"Are you close to downtown?" he said.

"Not at all. It's Friday. I'm out at Marquette Park hitting balls."

"How do you keep clients when you're always on the damn golf course?"

"They know about my near-perfect close rate. Can't say the same for your men."

"That's a bullshit comparison, and you know it. You get to handpick your cases. We have to take everything that comes across the radio. Anyway, we just got the labs back. Extremely high levels of MDMA, synthetic cathinones, methylone, and mephedrone."

"Kantor was popping Molly?"

"According to the ME."

"That's a kid's drug. What's an old man like Kantor doing popping ecstasy? Who was this guy?"

"Had something else in his system, a sedative called midazolam. Some kind of surgical anesthetic."

"Had he been in surgery?"

"His family and assistants say he had not. His internist says that he never prescribed him anything like that. No one knows what to make of it."

Sometimes the mysterious just gets more mysterious until you dig hard enough to make sense of it all. And if you're lucky, sometimes the answers get tired of hiding and finally show themselves. That, in this business, is the definition of luck. I finished the last fifteen minutes of my lesson, paid Smooth, then jumped into my car. Kantor Textiles occupied the entire thirty-sixth floor of a gleaming skyscraper at 401 North Michigan. After passing through two different layers of security, I was shown to a waiting area adjacent to a row of high-top tables lined with computer monitors. The offices were located in the center, while most of the floor was open space with chairs and meeting areas arranged along the perimeter. There weren't any walls; rather, everything was glass, and the floor-to-ceiling windows offered the most spectacular panoramic views of the city that I had ever seen. A young woman approached me with a bottle of Evian and offered to take me back.

We walked down toward the other end of the floor and turned into an enormous office whose blinds had been closed. Two identical glass-and-chrome desks sat across from each other. A tall, swarthy young man sat at one desk, and an extremely thin young man who was well on his way to losing most of his hair sat at the other. They were dressed casually in jeans and T-shirts. Both had enormous computer monitors in front of them. They stood and shook my hand. The tall one introduced himself as Javier. The shorter one was Pedro. I took a seat in a chair between the desks. Several framed photographs of Elliott Kantor and various professional athletes hung on the walls between framed, autographed sports jerseys. Another attractive woman knocked on the door, walked in, and dropped a folder on Javier's desk, then left.

"Nice place to work," I said. "Everywhere you turn there's a view."

"You get used to it," Javier said, winking.

"I don't want to take up too much of your time," I said. "So I'll get right to it. I read where you both have been with Elliott for ten years."

"Eleven for me," Javier said. "Pedro ten."

"You guys start working right out of high school?" I asked.

"I did," Javier said. "Pedro did a couple years of college before joining us."

A phone started ringing, and Pedro pushed a button to silence it.

"How was Elliott as a boss?" I asked.

"The best ever," Pedro said. "He could be cranky sometimes and talked rough, but he had a great heart and took care of everyone."

"Did everyone get along with him?"

"Who's everyone?" Javier asked.

"Here in the office?"

"Absolutely," Pedro said. "Elliott was like our grandfather. He had his quirks, but that was just him. He liked making money and having fun. He wanted everyone else to have fun also."

"A real party guy," I said.

"Party how?" Javier said.

"Party like men party," I said. "Girls, drinks, lots of laughs. Maybe hit a club now and then."

They both laughed. "Elliott didn't go to nightclubs," Javier said. "He was almost eighty. That wasn't his scene."

"What was?" I asked.

"Elliott was a sports nut," Pedro said. "He worked every day and then went to a game at night. That's what he liked to do most."

"Did you guys go with him?"

"Sometimes," Javier said. "But mostly he took his grandkids or friends in the business. Bulls, Bears, White Sox, Cubs—I love all of 'em, but there are only so many games I can go to."

"You didn't mention the Blackhawks," I said.

"Elliott didn't like hockey," Javier said. "He still had season tickets every year. Went to a couple of the games when they were playing for the Stanley Cup. But he bought the tickets mostly to give away to other people."

"Girlfriends?"

They both smiled.

"Elliott didn't have girlfriends," Pedro said. "He had friends."

I immediately thought of Jenny Lee.

"What kind of friends?" I asked.

"Just because Elliott was old doesn't mean his eyes didn't work," Javier said. "Take any five guys my age, and Elliott had more energy than all of them combined. He was always on the move."

"I heard that about him," I said. "Did he have one special friend or maybe a couple?"

"We weren't involved in Elliott's social life like that," Pedro said.

"We kept his schedule, ran errands, handled things around here in the office. But the girls and stuff like that? Elliott handled that himself."

I half believed him.

"Maybe you remember some names of people he bought special gifts for, someone he took to dinner on Valentine's Day."

"Elliott didn't discuss that with us," Pedro said. "We set up dinners and arranged the plane, but we didn't get into the names of his guests."

"He flew them on his plane?"

"He flew everyone on his plane," Javier said. "Friends used his plane all the time."

"Like who?"

"Name it. Ball players, actors, politicians. Elliott had friends everywhere, and he was good to all of them. He had a hard time saying no to people he liked."

"How did he keep track of his evening activities?" I asked.

"We kept his schedule, printed it out every morning, and gave it to him right before he left the office."

Javier opened a desk drawer, pulled out a stapled packet of papers, and handed it to me. "This is what a typical day looked like."

I scanned the pages. He was busy from seven in the morning until his dinner meeting at nine thirty. Phone calls, in-person meetings, reminders to choose birthday gifts for one of his grandchildren—there was barely any time for him to go to the bathroom.

"Who was with him at night?" I asked.

"Manny," Javier said. "His night driver."

I thought about the surveillance video and his driver letting him out that night at his building.

"Where's Manny now?" I asked.

"Manny only works nights," Javier said. "He's probably home sleeping or doing something with his family."

"Does he have a new job now that Elliott is gone?"

"No," Pedro said. "He still works for the company. We all do."

"Who is he driving?"

"He got reassigned," Javier said. "He worked for Elliott the last ten years, but now he'll drive some of the other executives when they have evening appointments or need rides to the airport."

"How long was Elliott doing drugs?" I asked.

"Whoa, what are you talking about?" Pedro said. "Who said anything about drugs?"

Javier's face tightened.

"C'mon, guys," I said. "Let's not bullshit each other. You both know Elliott messed around with drugs. I'm not being judgmental about it. I'm just trying to find out if it was occasional or if he had a serious problem."

"We didn't party with Elliott like that," Javier said. "He did his own thing at night. That was none of our business. But we never saw or heard Elliott talk about drugs."

"That's well and good," I said. "But you're still not answering my question."

They looked at each other as if trying to decide their next move.

"I'm gonna be perfectly honest," Javier said. "Elliott went through a depression when his wife died. We were really worried about him. He wouldn't eat. He was missing days at the office. He didn't have his usual energy. It got so bad, we thought he might do something to himself. Finally, we convinced him to go down to his place in the Bahamas. He had a big estate on the water in Albany. He flew down there and stayed for two months. When he came back, he was a totally different person. He was happy again, barking orders, going to games. He was fixed."

"What fixed him?"

"We don't know," Pedro said. "He just said he was ready and

needed to go on with his life. Said he couldn't be sad forever, or he would die."

"So everything just returned to normal?"

"Just like old times," Javier said. "He still got sad when he saw pictures of his wife or someone mentioned her name, but he didn't break down like he used to. He traveled a lot, went out almost every night. He said he was feeling thirty years younger."

"Do you have his schedule from the night he died?" I asked.

Javier reached behind him, pulled out a thin folder, and handed it to me. I looked it over, then said, "Have you ever been to the apartment in Lincoln Park?"

"Many times," Pedro said. "We helped with the redesign after he bought it."

"In what way?"

"He bought the apartment on spec before they had rehabbed the building. The architect drew up the plans, but Elliott didn't like them. We talked to the architect and the general contractor to make sure he got what he wanted. Elliott was really particular about how he wanted things done. Cost was never an issue as long as he got what he wanted."

"Did you guys have a key to his apartment?"

"No one had a key," Javier said. "Elliott could never use a key. Just another thing he'd lose. The door has a digital lock that's opened by a code."

"Do you both know the code?"

"Of course," Pedro said. "We needed to be able to get in if he needed us to do something."

"Anybody else have the code?"

"I don't think so," Javier said. "Maybe Simon. I'm not sure."

"What about Manny?"

"He wouldn't have the code," Pedro said.

"And his friends? The girls?"

They both shrugged. "We wouldn't know about that," Javier said. "But it's unlikely he would've given it out."

"What did he say he was doing that night?"

"He had dinner with one of our manufacturers who had flown in from China," Javier said. "They went to eat at RPM Steak. Mr. Min always likes to have steak when he comes to town. There were no games that night, so they were just having dinner."

I looked down at the schedule. He had dinner with Huan Min at eight o'clock. The rest of the evening was blank.

"Did he tell you he was planning on staying at the apartment that night?"

"He didn't say," Pedro replied. "Sometimes he'd make up his mind at the last minute and tell Manny where to take him."

I thought back to the video with him refusing Manny's help from the car, then him walking toward the apartment building's door and Manny pulling off.

"Can you print out his schedule for the following day?" I said.

"No problem," Javier said, quickly tapping his keyboard and bringing the printer to life. He stapled the pages, then handed them to me as I stood to leave.

"So, what will the two of you do now that he's gone?" I asked.

"Simon is going to keep us on," Pedro said. "There's still a lot of things Elliott was involved in that need to get done. We'll keep helping out, and they promised they'd eventually find us new positions in the company."

Javier stood and walked over to a small filing cabinet. He pulled open the drawer and said, "What games do you like?"

"Bulls and Sox," I said.

The entire drawer was full of tickets, organized by teams and bunched together by rubber bands. He pulled out a couple of wads and fingered through them. He counted out eight tickets, then handed them to me.

"Two Bulls games and two Sox games. Two tickets to each. Elliott always had the best seats in the arena. He'd want you to have them. If you need more, let us know."

I looked down at the tickets and saw $3,500 stamped in the corner of each one. The average man had absolutely no idea how lavishly the rich really lived.

9

I decided to have lunch in my office so I could get some work done. I grabbed a couple of slices from Robert's Pizza and barricaded myself in the office with the lights turned off and the sun cutting its way through the window. I opened an ice-cold can of root beer and allowed my attention to drift between Buckingham Fountain, which was now shooting water several stories in the air, and Kantor's schedules that Javier had given me.

I was most struck by how busy Kantor had been for a seventy-seven-year-old grandfather who had enough money to retire on his own private island and never have to worry about another meeting or sales spreadsheet. In the span of forty-eight hours, he had ten in-person meetings; fifteen phone meetings; a call with the former president, who was building his presidential library ten minutes south of downtown; a cancer gala where he served as a co-chair; and a school band performance for his two oldest grandchildren.

I was finishing the second slice of pizza when Carolina called in.

"Is this a bad time?" she asked.

"Have you ever heard me say that?" I said.

"I remember that time I called you while you were on the golf course and just about to swing. You hit a bad shot. You got a bogey or double bogey, and it cost you the match. You weren't very happy."

"That was three years ago. Ancient history. I'll never complain again."

"You have a deal," she said. "But you also have a problem with that plate you gave me."

"What's wrong with it?"

"That car isn't registered to anyone by the name of Jenny Lee," she said. "The registration comes back to Green Nod Holdings, LLC."

"Any idea who owns that?"

"The managing agent is a guy named Monroe Connelly. He's a lawyer with the firm Strook, Connelly, and Levy."

"You can't make this shit up," I said. "A high-end escort who serves drinks on the second shift at a casino discovers the dead body of one of the city's richest men after showing up for a night of bondage and kink. She also drives around in a hundred-thousand-dollar car registered to an attorney at a fancy downtown law firm. And just for good measure, she has almost the same name as a famous Taiwanese tennis player, but spells her name differently by just one letter."

"Which is?"

"An *e* versus an *a*."

"Does it matter?"

"When the name is spelled with an *e*, it means 'pure and clear' in Chinese. Jenny's real name is spelled with an *a*, which has no real translation that I could find."

"Maybe it means 'impure and unclear.'"

"Which, if I didn't know any better, I'd think you came to that biased conclusion based on the delicate nature of her profession."

"According to you, the activities she had planned for Kantor were anything but delicate."

I couldn't help but laugh. "What would my life be like without you in it?"

"Ever try a bowl of warm, soggy cereal that's been sitting on the counter for two days?"

"That's just about right."

MECHANIC AND I SAT IN his two-year-old silver Prius across the street from the UPS Store on Division Street. He only used this car when he needed to blend in with the surroundings. Adam Mickiewicz came every Saturday afternoon between five and six o'clock to pick up his mail. We didn't know what he looked like, but Mechanic had convinced Enrique to text us when the mysterious customer appeared.

"I just get the feeling there's a lot more to this than an old man who overdosed on bad drugs," I said. "There's so much that doesn't make sense to me."

"Like what?" Mechanic said.

"Let's start with Jenny Lee. She gets an assignment with one of the richest men in the city, and she doesn't even know his name or what he does. He's just some anonymous guy who's willing to pay her three thousand dollars to rough him up while he's wearing panties and a dog collar."

"Rich people do weird shit," Mechanic said. "And crazy-rich people do crazy-weird shit. That's what happens when you have everything you want. Nothing is normal anymore."

"It's almost like he was leading a double life," I said. "Business mogul and loving grandfather by day, then at night he was either a sports nut, major philanthropist, or hiding away in his apartment popping Molly while getting tied up and whipped, and who knows whatever else."

"You think his assistants really didn't know about it?"

"They had to know something. They were with him every minute of the day."

"But not at night."

"No, he was only with his driver Manny."

Mechanic's phone vibrated. He opened the message. Blue shirt with a red baseball cap.

We jumped out of the car and quickly made our way across the street. There were three customers in the store. An old woman with a long coat and a small dog in a rolling basket stood at the counter. Mickiewicz stood behind the old woman, and a girl in pink leggings stood behind him. Enrique was helping the old woman. I walked in while Mechanic stayed outside. I stood in line with everyone else. When the old woman was finished, Mickiewicz stepped up, and Enrique turned away from the counter and walked behind the mailboxes. He came back with a large packet of mail, put it in a plastic bag, and handed it over. They exchanged words, Enrique laughed, and Mickiewicz headed toward the door. I let him walk by me, then followed. Once outside, he turned right. Mechanic then followed him as I hung back. When they were halfway down the block, Mickiewicz stopped at a red Audi e-tron SUV. The lights flashed as he got closer. He went to open the driver's door, but Mechanic jammed his hand out to stop him.

"What the hell is your problem?" Mickiewicz said.

"Adam Mickiewicz?" I said, approaching from behind.

He turned and looked at me.

"Who the hell are you?" he said.

"A big admirer of your ride," I said. "Nice color. Three hundred and fifty horsepower, right?"

He looked at Mechanic. "Get outta my way, muthafucka," Mickiewicz said.

"I'm not so sure I'd talk about his mother like that," I said. "That's a sensitive topic. She raised him alone while working two jobs. *And* she's still alive. Which you might not be for much longer if you continue to piss him off."

Mickiewicz sized up Mechanic. The stats were definitely in Mickiewicz's favor. At least on paper. He had Mechanic by about two inches and seventy-five pounds. He was definitely wider at the shoulders, but I could tell his chin was soft, and his legs were like toothpicks. For his sake, I was hoping he chose wisely.

"What the hell is this all about?" Mickiewicz growled.

"Karol's Angels," I said. "Cute name by the way. A nice play on *Charlie's Angels.*"

"Are you a cop?" Mickiewicz said, keeping his eyes on Mechanic.

"I could be," I said.

"What's that supposed to mean?"

"If you don't answer my questions, then I'll make one phone call, and you'll have a bunch of cops crawling all up your ass, and they won't be charging you three thousand dollars. They might charge you with accessory to murder."

"Murder? Are you crazy? I haven't killed nobody. And you guys ain't cops, so back the fuck off before this gets physical."

No sooner had he finished getting that last word out than Mechanic jabbed him under his right rib cage. I could hear the sound of bone cracking. Mickiewicz dropped his bag of mail and bent over. An older woman walking by and pushing a baby stroller shrieked and ran away.

"Jesus Christ," Mickiewicz gasped. "You broke my fuckin' rib."

"You have fourteen facial bones," I said. "His next punch will crack half of them, and you'll be drinking your next birthday cake through a straw."

"Okay, what is it you want?" Mickiewicz groaned. He straightened up and leaned back against the car.

"Does Jenny Lee work for you?"

"She's one of my girls."

"You gave her an assignment about ten days ago over at 1425 West Fullerton Avenue."

"I don't remember everyone's fuckin' assignment," he said. "I have eleven girls. They all are busy."

"She says you texted her the assignment," I said.

"You talked to Jenny?"

"I did."

"So, what are you after?"

"I want to know how that job was set up. Do you use an app or website?"

"Neither one. I get a message from the exchange service, they give me the information, and I assign one of my girls."

"And who collects the money?"

"The exchange."

"How much?"

"What the fuck?"

Mechanic took half a step forward.

"Okay. Okay. They keep a third, and I get two-thirds."

"How do they pay you?"

"They send me the money through Cash App."

"What's their username?"

"Why are you asking so many damn questions?"

"Because I'm a private investigator, and part of my job is to ask shitheads like you questions."

"I'm done answering your questions."

"That's your choice. But it also means you'll be driving this very fancy car with one side of your face two inches lower than the other side and spitting blood like a faucet. Won't be very good for those Corinthian leather seats."

Mickiewicz looked at Mechanic, whose eyes had about as much life in them as a tree stump waiting for the roots to die.

"The username is friendlypartners69," Mickiewicz said. "All small letters."

"Who do you work with at this exchange?" I asked.

"Nobody. They text me the info, and I assign it to one of the girls."

"What's the exchange's number?"

"Won't get you anywhere. They won't answer the phone, and they won't text you back unless they know who you are."

"Thanks for the advice. I'll take the number anyway."

He recited the number.

"Who is Monroe Connelly?"

"Never heard of him before."

"We're gonna check out all you've said, and if some of it doesn't work out, you'll be using diapers the rest of your life."

"I told you all I know," he said. "I'm just a middleman. Whoever these guys are, they don't want to be found out, which is fine by me. As long as I get my money, I don't ask any questions."

"You should give Jenny her money for that job. You still owe her a thousand dollars. It's not her fault the guy was dead by the time she got there."

The look of surprise on his face was authentic.

10

The temperature that night was much warmer than normal for mid-May, so I decided to go out for a quick three miles when I got home. I liked running along the water just after sunset, when there was less noise on the drive and the sounds of the lake moved in on the back of a gentle wind. The path was mostly empty, and I was alone with my thoughts and a full moon lighting my way. I ran all the way to Bronzeville, not too far from my father's house, then turned around and headed back north.

I couldn't help but think about Elliott Kantor. Why would someone want to kill him? Was it over a bad business deal? Was it an accident? Was he just one of seventy thousand other Americans who overdosed each year? But why was Elliott Kantor doing drugs? Molly, of all things. A club drug. Cocaine seemed like it would've been a better fit.

I dialed my father's home phone number. He was one of the last few people in Chicago who still used a landline. He always turned his cell phone off after dinner. He picked up on the third ring.

"I was just finishing up this special by Henry Louis Gates Jr. on PBS," he said. "He's covering the four-hundred-year-old history of the Black church. Very powerful. Very moving. Your grandfather would've enjoyed it."

My grandfather had been a Baptist preacher in a small town called Greenville, North Carolina. I remembered being scared of him when I was a little boy and we'd go down there in the summers to visit. He was a big, dark-skinned man with a deep, booming voice and huge watery eyes. His hands were as big as mitts, and when he swung them in your direction, you best be on the move. He was a no-nonsense man, and excellence in his household wasn't optional; rather, it was obligatory. He was proud that my father had become a doctor and my uncle one of the first Black federal judges, who had been appointed by President Carter. He and my grandmother lived long enough to see both of them at the top of their professions, and he was never afraid to tell anyone who would listen that it all started on the front pew of his tiny church in a tiny Southern town.

"I'm sure they streamed it," I said. "I'll watch it online when I get a chance."

"You'll have to show me how to do that," he said. "The second part comes on in a couple of days. You should come and watch it with me. I'll have Pearline fix your favorite dinner."

I was supposed to have dinner with Carolina, but I knew turning down his invitation would mean several months of him complaining that I gave him very little time since my mother had died a few years ago. My father would never admit that he missed me. Instead, he created narratives, trying to make me feel guilty. We would argue, not talk for a week, and then I would call him to make up. This was the recurring cycle in our relationship. Despite the fact he had spent an entire forty-year career getting others to open up about their feelings, he rarely—if ever—heeded his own advice. Doctors really were the worst patients.

"I look forward to coming over," I said.

"And don't be late," he said. "We'll have dinner downstairs first, then go upstairs to watch the show."

“What do you know about the drug Molly?” I asked.

“A lot,” he replied. “I saw the damage it can cause hundreds of times working the ER.”

“Elliott Kantor had Molly in his system when he died. Does that surprise you?”

“When it comes to drug usage, nothing really surprises me,” he said. “But that’s not the drug I’d expect a man like him to use.”

“That’s what I want you to explain.”

“MDMA really got popular with young people in the nightclub scene,” he said. “It was and still is really big at these all-night dance parties called raves. Typical user is a male between eighteen and twenty-five. Kantor definitely doesn’t fit the profile.

“Older people lean heavily toward alcohol and marijuana. Next in line would be cocaine. But you have to remember that data doesn’t determine how people behave. It’s very possible he was into MDMA.”

“What else should I know about it?”

“User demographics tell us that sexual orientation also influences the usage rates. Gay or bisexual men and women are more likely than heterosexuals to use it.”

“But why would someone choose MDMA over cocaine?”

“They’re both stimulants. They increase the levels of dopamine in the brain. But there are differences. MDMA produces much higher levels of dopamine because the nerve cells respond differently than they do to cocaine. Also, the high you get from cocaine is much shorter, because half of the drug is removed by the body in an hour. It can take up to twelve hours to remove the same amount of MDMA, so it stays around longer, which means the high does too. MDMA is much cheaper, which is another reason a lot of young people use it. Problem is, cheaper often means lower quality, so the dealers mix a lot of fillers with the MDMA, and sometimes those added ingredients can have adverse effects.”

"Does it kill a lot of people?"

"Not as many as you might expect. It can cause all kinds of side effects, like blurred vision, chills, nausea, and sweating, but most people come through it okay. The people who die from it do so because of the other drugs that might be mixed in with it."

"Kantor was seventy-seven. He died from a heart attack."

"Not surprising. His age and all those steak dinners, he probably had underlying heart disease. You put too much MDMA and other drugs on top of an already sick heart, and it's gonna go haywire and give out. If I were you, I'd try to answer two questions: Why did Kantor choose MDMA? And where did he get it from?"

TWO DAYS LATER, OVER A plate of blueberry pancakes and warmed maple syrup, I took a look again at Elliott Kantor's schedules. There was a small entry that simply had the letters *POL*. There was no description or specific time attached to it. I'm not sure what about it grabbed my attention, but I couldn't stop looking at it. Maybe he had a call with a politician or had to attend a political fundraiser. But if either one of them was true, there would be more written, like with the other entries.

It wasn't nine o'clock yet, but I called Simon anyways. After several rings he answered.

"Are you making any headway?" he asked.

"One step forward, two steps backward," I replied.

"Anything you can tell me?"

"I assume CPD told you about the meth and alcohol in his system."

"They did, and I don't believe it."

"You think they made a mistake?"

"I do. Maybe they mixed up his labs with someone else or one of the tubes got mislabeled. I don't know what happened, but there's no way in hell I believe my father had meth in his system."

"Labs make mistakes," I said. "But this isn't the kind of mistake they'd make, especially with someone like your father. They go the extra mile to make sure everything is done to the highest standards. This is not a case they want to get wrong."

"My father drank like any normal adult," Simon said. "But use drugs? Nope. I'm not buying it. I asked them to repeat the lab tests, and I've hired an independent pathologist to do the same."

I understood when family members were surprised by unexpected autopsy findings, but rarely did repeat tests produce different results. He seemed more upset about the drugs than he was with his father being found in a compromised position.

"Do you know what 'POL' means?" I asked. "I saw it on your father's schedule."

"Politician?" he said. "I'm not sure. I haven't seen his schedule in years. The guys at the office kept it for him."

"I have his schedule for the day after he died. There's a small entry at the top of the page that says 'POL.'"

"That's it?"

"Nothing more. Nothing less."

"I have no idea. You'd have to call Javier or Pedro."

"Are they in the office yet?"

"One of them is always there by eight. At least that was their schedule before Dad died. He didn't like being in the office alone."

"Thanks, I'll give them a call."

"Can you prove my father didn't have meth in his system?" he asked.

"I can do a lot of things, but unfortunately, that's not one of them," I said. "Best I can do is have someone else read the report and see what they think."

"If you learn anything, please let me know right away."

I found Kantor's office number and dialed it. Javier picked up right away.

"It's Ashe Cayne," I said. "You're off to an early start."

"Early bird catches the worm," he said.

"And the second mouse gets the cheese," I replied.

"Never heard that before. What does it mean?"

"The first mouse going for the cheese gets stuck in the trap. The second mouse comes along and gets the cheese without getting caught."

"I like that one. Gotta use it sometime."

"I didn't make it up, but feel free. Anyway, I called about the daily schedules you gave me. I noticed for the schedule on the day after he died that the letters 'POL' were at the top of the page. I couldn't figure out what that means."

"'Plane on loan,'" Javier said. "Whenever Elliott loaned out his plane to someone, we put it on the schedule so we could keep track of where it was."

"But it didn't say who was borrowing it or where they were going," I said.

"All of that's in a separate file. Elliott loaned his plane out so much, we had to use another schedule to keep track of it."

"Do you know who used it that day?"

"Not off the top of my head. Give me a second."

I heard him tapping his keyboard. *The problems of the rich*, I thought as I waited. *Needing a separate calendar to keep track of their private planes. You can't make this shit up.*

"Lance Greene," Javier said. "He and a couple of friends used it."

Lance Greene was the former all-pro tight end for the Chicago Bears. He was third on the all-time receiver list and the only Bears player to catch a hundred touchdowns. He retired a few years ago and now co-hosted a radio show on ESPN and a football show on NFL Network. Next to Walter Payton, it didn't get bigger than Lance Greene. He was a god to the fans, and the women couldn't get enough of him. I had seen him once at a restaurant. He was even bigger in person than on TV. Two hundred and fifty pounds of solid muscle.

"Where did they go?" I asked.

"Down to the Bahamas to play golf."

I had heard that Greene was a big golfer. One of the caddies at Medinah Country Club said his handicap was in the low single digits, and he hit almost every drive well past three hundred yards.

"Was Elliott good friends with Greene?" I asked.

"Definitely," Javier said. "They met at a Bears game. Elliott had seats on the fifty-yard line, but he watched most of the games on the field next to the players. Lance used the jet whenever he needed to. He'd come out to the Michigan house during the summer with his girlfriends. He's a good guy."

"'Girlfriends,' plural?"

"Lance is very popular with the ladies. People love him everywhere he goes."

"Where did Lance stay in the Bahamas?"

"Elliott's house."

"Even when Elliott wasn't there?"

"Of course. Everyone used Elliott's house whether he was there or not. Elliott was very generous with his friends."

"Who went with Greene on those trips?"

"I don't know right off, but I could find out. Everyone who travels on the plane has to be listed on the flight manifest."

"Do you keep a copy of all the manifests?"

"Not here in the office, but our management company does."

"I'm a complete novice when it comes to stuff like private planes," I said. "But tell me exactly what a management company does."

"They handle everything related to the plane, like the pilots, flight attendants, cleaning, safety maintenance, flight coordination, and catering. We've used the same company for the last ten years. JetProper."

"Can you get me all the flight manifests from the last six months?"

"I will talk to the company and see what they can send me."

"One more thing," I said. "You and Pedro said that Elliott went into a depression after his wife died, then he went down to the Bahamas for a couple of months and came back a new person."

"Yup. He came back more energized than ever."

"Did you or Pedro go down to visit him?"

"No, he wanted us to stay here and keep everything running in the office."

"Did anyone go down to see him?"

"The kids and grandkids went for about a week, then some of his friends went down to cheer him up."

"Do you know who exactly went?"

"I don't, but Pedro would. He was mostly in charge of Elliott's real estate portfolio."

"Portfolio?"

"Elliott had fifteen houses and apartments around the world," Javier said. "He was really particular about where he stayed. Whenever possible, he'd always choose having his own place or staying with a friend rather than sleeping in a hotel."

"So Pedro was in charge of the apartment on West Fullerton?"

"That's the one residence that Pedro didn't manage."

"Who did?"

"Elliott ran everything there himself."

11

The next day, I got up early, did several sets of push-ups and sit-ups, then took Stryker for a quick walk. The sun was already out and warming up the skies to near-record temperatures for a May morning. After what felt like an endless winter of heavy snow and freezing winds, the city was fully open. The boats returned to the harbors, and hordes of people filled Grant Park to play sports or just enjoy a walk along the lake. Today was my mother's birthday, and as I had done every birthday since she passed, I dressed up in a powder blue shirt (because she said that color always looked best on me), grabbed a bouquet of her favorite flowers (red Peruvian lilies and golden yellow sunflowers), and headed to Oak Woods Cemetery.

My mother had always spoken about her love of Marrakech, Morocco, as it had been the place she first visited on the African continent. While she and my father had visited all fifty-four African nations, Morocco held a special place in her heart because it was the first one they had visited. She wanted her gravestone to reflect the decorative muqarnas she had seen while visiting the famous Saadian Tombs. It took my father the better part of a year, but he finally found a craftsman who could re-create the intricate, colorful honeycomb made of stone and ceramic clay that was typically plastered against a vaulted ceiling.

Once I arrived at her resting place at the top of a small knoll facing the rising sun, I took out a bottle of cleaner and a rag and wiped down her stone. I didn't talk about her much, but she was constantly on my mind. I was always saddened that she never got to see me walk down the aisle and enjoy that dance at my wedding or see the tiny face of her grandchild. But I found comfort in the fact that she knew how much I had loved her and how so much of the man I was today was because of all that she had taught me.

Once I had cleaned her stone, laid down the flowers, and recited her favorite Maya Angelou poem, "Still I Rise," I stood up and looked to the left of her stone, where my father had already purchased his plot so they would be together again. My father was a strong, proud man who protected his innermost feelings behind an ironclad façade, but I knew he missed her deeply, as their marriage and life together had been a true love story. I always made the trip on her birthday alone, and he made his visit on their wedding anniversary in the summer. Every time I came here, I left with the same thought: there was nothing I would not do to get one more day with her.

I kissed her stone and turned to leave. That's when my phone rang. It was Burke.

"Can you get here in the next hour?" he said.

"Depends on where 'here' is," I said.

"My office."

"What's going on?"

"We got the video."

"Anything on it?"

"Sure is. I'll show you when you get here."

Forty-five minutes later, I was sitting in Burke's cramped office. No pictures or anything personal adorned the walls except for a photo of him graduating from the police academy a hundred years ago, sandwiched between the superintendent and mayor while forcing a smile. He was broad at the shoulders even back then, a wide stump of neck shooting out of his stretched uniform. A half-eaten sandwich sat unwrapped on his desk. I was unaccustomed to meeting him in such an official setting. We usually convened in his car or the back table of a restaurant.

He turned his monitor around so both of us could see, then he tapped his keyboard. A black-and-white video began playing. I knew right away it was the alley behind the Manor; it faced east, in the direction of the Warehouse Bar & Pizzeria. Thirty seconds went by before a large truck rolled through the alley, heading east. Another forty-five seconds, then the middle of the three garage doors suddenly opened. A dark car nosed out into the alley. I could tell by the lights it was a Bentley. It pulled all the way out, turned east, then raced away down the alley. It was a late-model Bentley Continental GT convertible. Once it drove out of frame, Burke stopped the tape.

"Three hundred thousand plus," I said. "Or maybe it's a W12, which means another fifty thousand dollars."

"What's that, a model number?" Burke asked.

"Engine."

"I've heard of a V12 but not a W12."

"It's an engine configuration used in airplanes back in the 1920s. The Volkswagen Group, which actually makes Bentley, uses it in some of its cars. But they use a new W configuration that has four rows of three cylinders instead of the three rows of four cylinders they used in the planes."

"What the hell does it matter?"

"The V12 gives you ridiculous power, but the W12 gives you that same level of power and a smooth ride. You buy a Ferrari for sheer power. You buy a Bentley GT for power and refinement."

"Well, now that I've gotten a mechanic's seminar, let's forget the engine and talk about the owner of the car."

"Must be someone with deep pockets."

"That car belongs to Elliott Kantor."

I looked back at the screen and the time stamp on the video. 11:03 p.m. Elliott had arrived a little less than an hour earlier. Jenny Lee had arrived at 11:09, six minutes after the car had pulled out.

"By the time the Bentley left the garage, Elliott was dead, and Jenny Lee hadn't arrived yet," I said.

Burke nodded. "So who was driving the damn car?" he said.

"I guess that's the three-hundred-thousand-dollar question," I said. "Has anyone talked to Simon?"

"We did," Burke said. "He didn't even know his father had the car. He said his dad always had a driver. The last time Simon saw Elliott physically drive a car was when Simon was in college and Elliott moved Simon's car from a no-parking zone so he wouldn't get a ticket."

"And his assistants? Anybody talk to them?"

"Neither of them had been to the apartment in months. They didn't know he had the car either."

That struck me as strange. Elliott Kantor was not a man who walked into a local DMV to register his car or call an agent to buy insurance. Billionaires simply didn't do mundane things like that. They had a small army of people who took care of these nuisances. Why didn't anyone know about this car? And whoever it was driving the car, how did they know about it or even know where to find the key? Had Elliott given it to them?

"We traced the car all the way out the alley, where it takes a right and turns north on Southport Avenue. We have it passing St. Josaphat Church at the corner of Belden and Southport, but then we lose it after that."

"Nothing from any of the nearby PODs?" PODs were police

observation devices—cameras set up on light poles and traffic signals throughout the city.

"Some of the guys are pulling the footage now, but there aren't a lot of PODs in that part of town, so it's not likely to help."

Of course there weren't a lot of police cameras in these upper-middle-class neighborhoods. The city had hung up most of their surveillance on the South and West Sides, where the demographics were predominantly people of color and immigrants, and income levels were glaringly depressed. Now in a bit of poetic justice, a key piece of evidence for a case involving one of the city's wealthiest residents may not be available because of systemic and implicit bias.

"Someone in city hall is going to wake up one day and read the statistics and realize that crime happens all over this city," I said. "Once that happens, *everyone* will actually be safer."

"What, are you running for office now?"

"Not yet. I have to lose my entire soul first to qualify."

"No disagreement from me on that point."

"Simon Kantor is not happy about the lab results," I said. "He insists his father wouldn't use meth. He thinks it's a lab error. He's hired a third-party pathologist to prove it."

"I've talked to him several times," Burke said. "He knows it's not a mistake. He's called everyone up and down the chain. He wants it scratched from the autopsy report. It's worth a lot of money to him."

"Insurance money," I said.

"Exactly. The insurance company won't issue a payout for someone who died from using a recreational drug. There's a hundred and fifty million dollars at stake. He's gonna do whatever he can, but facts are facts."

"I thought insurance companies still paid out for overdoses."

"They won't if they think you lied on your application about your drug-use history. It's a risky technicality to use for a defense of nonpayment, but given the size of the potential payout, it's a technicality they won't be afraid to enforce."

"Any idea where Kantor might've gotten the drugs from?"

"We've been digging. Might be easier finding a dropped earring in the middle of a lake."

"Anything else missing from the apartment other than the Bentley?"

"No way to tell. There were several million dollars still hanging on the walls, untouched. We can't find anyone who knows enough about what was in there to figure out if something else was stolen. Kantor really kept the place walled off from everyone, even from his assistants, who knew all of his secrets."

"Obviously, not all of them," I said. "And if they do, they're not telling."

WHEN I GOT BACK TO my office, I walked up to the dry-erase board that ran the full length of a wall and started jotting down details. It always helped when I could put all of the data points on a board, then start drawing connecting lines as I tried to figure out how everything fit together. As with most cases, the early part of an investigation always meant more questions than answers, and right now, it felt like I had very few answers. Once I had written everything out, I sat back in my chair and looked it over. Was Jenny Lee really as innocent in this as she claimed? Why would Kantor book her, yet have someone else already there or on the way? Was Jenny supposed to be part of a threesome? Dr. Olivia had mentioned that many people liked having a third partner involved. Who was behind the service that gave Mickiewicz the assignments for his angels? Did he really not know their identity?

I picked up my phone and dialed the number of Marlena Benton. She was everything you would expect a hacker not to be. A tall, former college basketball player who had competed in five Ironman contests and placed in two of them, she knew her way around computers and software better than anyone I knew. We met at a museum charity benefit where she was helping run the technology for the silent auction. I had my eye on a pair of signed Walter Payton football cleats, but she told me to save my money. Most of the sports memorabilia was priced at least double the true market value, and I'd be better off going directly to the source or finding it on some of the online sites. She took out her phone to prove it to me. A week later, I got another pair of cleats Sweetness had signed for a third of the price they eventually went for at the auction. I sent Marlena an arrangement of flowers as a thank-you, and she became my go-to when I needed IT help, legitimate and otherwise.

Marlena answered right away.

"You're either calling me from the golf course or stuck behind the computer in your office," she said.

"I wish like hell it were the first," I said. "Is this a bad time?"

"Nope, just got in from a run. What's up?"

"How hard is it to hack into a Cash App account?" I asked.

"It's not the easiest hack, but I'm sure it's been done. Depends on what exactly you're trying to do."

"I have someone's username, but I want to know who actually owns the account and their contact info. I want to speak to them."

"They owe you money?"

"No, they sent money to someone who's part of an investigation I'm running, but that person doesn't know the contact info of the person who sent it."

"If you just have the username and nothing else, hacking into the account is gonna take a little work. It's not impossible, but it'll take some time. But instead of hacking them, try trapping them first. It could be faster."

"How?"

"Set up an account. Once you have an account set up and verified, you can request money from other people's accounts. They can pay the request or decline it."

"How would that help me trap them?"

"Once you set up the account, keep making large requests for them to pay you. Make it for something big, like ten thousand. Obviously, they'll decline the request, but keep doing it. Make it a nuisance. Then you can send them a text message within the app. Tell them they owe you for something, and if they don't pay you, you're going to report them for fraud or something. Leave your phone number. If you bother them enough, somebody will probably call you to tell you that you're crazy and to leave them alone."

"Do you know if this has been done before?"

"I know it's gone the other way. Scammers will call someone and tell them they'll walk them through the steps of transferring money from the app to their bank account. Then the scammer will put their account in there as an intermediary, get the transfer, and disappear. Something else they'll do is call and pretend like they're customer support and they need to verify the account credentials, so people give up all their info. You'd think people would know that play by now, but they still fall for it."

"I'll try to set the trap first," I said. "If it doesn't work, we'll look at plan B."

"No problem. In the meantime, I'll dig around and see what's out there as far as the app's vulnerabilities. If big banks can be penetrated, so can an app that only offers an email address for customer service help."

"I'll let you know how it goes."

I spent the next twenty minutes setting up a Cash App account. I chose the username $goldenwingschi and sent a request for ten thousand dollars to the username Mickiewicz had given me. The trap was set; now all I could do was see if they went after the bait.

12

My father liked alternating where we ate dinner in his rambling Bronzeville house, insisting that we never eat in the same location twice in a row. So tonight we sat at his formal dining room table, which could seat twelve comfortably and squeeze in fourteen if the need arose. He, of course, sat at the head of the table, and I to his right. Pearline had once again flaunted her gastronomic mastery, preparing the salmon with a sublime lemon butter sauce and sitting it perfectly on a bed of thin, vinaigrette-soaked cucumbers on top of creamy mashed potatoes. We now stared at two enormous pieces of warm sweet potato pie, which I had made at my father's request. Our wineglasses were nearly empty for a second time.

My father suggested we retire to the media room in the basement, which he had refurbished last year with large, comfortable reclining chairs and a new 4K projector. He picked up a remote control the size of a computer keyboard, and after he tapped several buttons while mumbling a few expletives, the projector turned on, and we were immersed in the story of Black churches.

It had been a while since I had gone to church, but listening to the old spirituals that our ancestors sang to speak code to each other in the cotton fields and watching the firebrand preachers from small

Pentecostal revival tents in the Deep South to the megachurches in big cities like Dallas and New York, made me feel like a little boy again, sitting between my parents on a hot North Carolina Sunday as my grandfather belted out another fiery sermon. I was enraptured by the images of little children dressed in their Sunday best, walking into cramped one-room churches at the end of a country road. There were big-city choirs, some over a hundred strong, raising their voices to the heavens in praise. First-name singers like Aretha, Whitney, and Patti had all started as young girls in the church, only to become superstars on mainstream radio stations and inside the DJ booths of sweaty discos. For almost two hours, we sat there, mesmerized by the story of our people, the struggles and triumphs, the injustices and the hope. Occasionally, I looked over at my father and caught him dabbing his eyes as the powerful sermons and thunderous voices awakened memories within him that were both joyous and painful. When the show ended, we sat there quietly for a couple of minutes in the still darkness.

"Nice piece of work," he said. "We've come a mighty long way."

"Sometimes we need to hear our stories to refocus our purpose and perspective," I said.

"And context. A lot of our brothers and sisters have lost their way, as have the men of the cloth. Look at Bishop Keegan Thompson. What a shame."

"What happened?"

"Dead at forty-five."

Bishop Keegan Thompson was the pastor of the Bright Tabernacle Church, a megachurch based in Los Angeles that rivaled Joel Osteen's in Houston and T. D. Jakes's in Dallas. His father had started the church in the back room of a laundromat fifty years ago, and then Bishop Keegan Thompson took over, injecting the controversial prosperity theology, a more recent religious belief among some Christians that God has intentions of financial prosperity and physical well-being for all of those who believe. By honoring one's faith, speaking positively, and generously donating to the church, God would return these good deeds by increasing the follower's material wealth. Money and flamboyant materialism, traditionally believed to be symbols of hedonism and the devil at work, were now embraced, and proudly displayed as God's blessings. A couple of years ago, Thompson was the target of criticism by politicians who decried the announcement that the church had purchased a private plane for Thompson on top of the Rolls-Royce and Beverly Hills mansion he already owned.

"What happened to him?" I asked.

"No one knows," my father replied. "I heard it on WVON on my way home from tennis. He was here in Chicago to preach for McCaskill at South Baptist, and they found his body late Saturday night, early Sunday morning."

It made sense that one of Chicago's most successful megachurches would invite Thompson, a religious superstar who had it all, including a beautiful wife who had been a model and young twin daughters.

"Was his family here with him?" I asked.

"The report said he was here alone."

I took out my phone and googled Thompson. I would've expected several headlines announcing his death. Neither the *Tribune* nor the *Sun-Times* had anything on it. Only the *Chicago Defender*, one of the country's oldest Black newspapers, had any coverage. The online article was a single, simple paragraph. They had a photograph of Thompson in a pin-striped suit, leaning against a white Rolls-Royce in front of his massive church. The article spoke mostly about his beginnings and success and the millions of people who followed him on social media and through his various media enterprises. There was no cause of death listed, but it was the last sentence that struck me as odd. Thompson's body had been recovered from an apartment in the northern section of Bronzeville.

"Looks like he was found close to us," I said. "He was in an apartment right here in Bronzeville. Doesn't feel right."

"Stranger things have happened," my father said. "After all, this is Chicago."

I found another photograph of the smiling Bishop Keegan Thompson, his hair trimmed razor-sharp, his two-thousand-dollar custom suit, his Beverly Hills stone-and-brick mansion rising up behind him. All of that gone in an instant, his wife now a widow, his young children fatherless, his thirty-thousand-strong congregation now without their spiritual leader. He would become yet another footnote in the long, fabled history of the Black church.

THE NEXT MORNING, I FOCUSED my efforts on Kantor's apartment building. Burke had given me transcripts of the interviews that had been done with the three other residents. I read carefully through what the detectives had gathered. The other unit on the first floor, 1E, was owned by the Mann family. The husband was a retired DePaul history professor and his wife a music teacher. He was the man from the video who had been wearing a Cubs hat. The interview was extensive. They had seen their neighbor infrequently, usually getting out of his SUV or occasionally being picked up. They hadn't even known his name. He was extremely quiet. They never saw him with anyone, nor did they see anyone going in the direction of his apartment. They had the usual curiosities: Did he have a family? What did he do for a living? Why was he seen so infrequently? The wife had gone to his door several times a couple of years ago to give him slices of cake she had baked for holidays. He never answered the door. They claimed there was a period where they hadn't seen him for at least five months. They thought he might've moved or died, but then they saw him again, getting into the SUV with the man who always drove him. They assumed he had been on vacation. Their final thoughts were that the occupant of unit 1W was a mysterious man who liked to keep to himself and not be bothered with the business of anyone else in the building.

The second interview had been conducted with the owner of unit 2W, Hugo Melzer. Melzer was a stockbroker who worked for one of those giant international financial firms on South Wacker. He was the last of the residents to purchase his unit. He was single, an avid hockey player, and spent a lot of time at work or entertaining the firm's clients. He had never seen the owner of unit 1W, nor had it ever crossed his mind to wonder who lived there. He was too busy with his own life to have any interest in discovering who else shared his address. The second-floor apartments had private elevators, so the only time the building occupants would run into each other would be in the lobby or the garage. Melzer had grown up in New York City, where he had lived most of his life, until he moved to Chicago after college to get his MBA from Kellogg. He didn't own a car, because he never learned to drive, so there was no reason for him to go to the garage. When the detectives showed Melzer a photograph of Elliott Kantor, he was visibly shocked. He recognized Kantor right away and couldn't believe he owned an apartment in the same building as one of Chicago's richest businessmen. He was so surprised that he asked the detectives if they were certain Kantor was the owner of unit 1W. They assured him that Kantor was, and he assured them that he had never seen Kantor anywhere near the building and would've recognized him right away if he had. The detectives were careful not to disclose to any of the other residents that Kantor had died in the building. They looked at Melzer's calendar and other supporting documents and were satisfied that Melzer had been in Dallas visiting clients for a three-night stretch, one of which was the night Kantor had died.

The last interview had been conducted with the Spiewak family, who lived in unit 2E. Craig and Pam Spiewak were a young couple with a four-year-old boy. They were one of the first occupants of the building. Craig worked for a national engineering consulting firm, and Pam had been a paralegal until their son was born. Now she was a stay-at-home mom who planned on returning to work next year when her son was in school full-time. Craig had only seen Kantor a few times, either walking through the lobby or being dropped off by his driver in the black Escalade that Craig noted was always shiny, even in the middle of winter. Craig never had much of a conversation with Kantor, as he spent a lot of time traveling for business. Pam, however, had spoken to him more than anyone else in the building, but never for more than a few minutes. Pam knew him as Mr. Henry. She didn't think he had a family, because one afternoon, she was running bathwater for her son, got distracted, and forgot to turn it off. The bathroom flooded, and she was worried it might get into Mr. Henry's apartment beneath her. She went down and knocked on the door. It took a while, but he finally answered. She told him of her concerns, so he let her come into the front foyer while he went to check the various ceilings. Several minutes later, he came back and told her that everything looked fine. She gave him her number and told him to call her if he or his family had any issues, and she would pay for the repairs. He told her he didn't have a family, thanked her for her concern, and closed the door.

There was another occasion, when Pam was struggling to carry several bags of groceries while pushing her son's stroller and trying to open the door. Mr. Henry's driver was waiting for him outside, but Mr. Henry noticed she wasn't having an easy time, so he helped her get up to her apartment. Mr. Henry asked her why he never saw her with the boy's father, and she explained that her husband traveled a lot for work, and when he got home, he was often exhausted. His response stuck with her. "Sometimes the time spent chasing money isn't worth the time lost with family." She said he seemed very sorrowful when he said that, almost as if he were speaking from experience. She asked him if he wanted to come in and have tea or something, but he declined, saying he had a dinner to attend. Pam said she had never seen anyone go to his apartment, nor had she ever seen Mr. Henry with anyone other than his driver. She thought he was a lonely old man and felt bad for him. While she had not seen him often, each time she did, he was extremely courteous and conversational. He always smiled and said nice things to her son. She was very sad he had died, and she regretted never inviting him up for dinner with her family. He looked like he could've used the company.

I turned on my computer and looked at the video from the night he died. I tried putting together in my mind a story for each of the residents, what they were doing that night, what they had seen or heard that might've been helpful. I watched the Amazon deliveryman with the trunk, and something bothered me. I looked at the time: 9:53 p.m. Wasn't that late for a delivery?

I dialed Carolina's number.

"How often do you get deliveries from Amazon?" I said when she answered.

"No 'good morning, how is your day going, how are you feeling'?" she said.

"I'm sorry. Yes to all of the above."

"I get at least a couple of deliveries every week or so," she said. "Why?"

"What time do they make the deliveries?"

"Depends. There's no set time."

"You've gotten them at night?"

"Sure. You want to tell me what this is about?"

"How late?"

"I don't know," she said. "I never really looked at the time. But sometimes they'll ring the bell after dinner."

"An Amazon driver made a delivery at 9:53 to Kantor's building the night he died. Isn't that late?"

"I don't think so. I've seen their drivers on the road that late. I think it depends on how many packages they have to deliver that day and how fast or slow they go."

"Thanks, I'll call you back."

I called down to my doorman.

"Harold, what's the latest you've seen Amazon deliveries?" I asked once he answered.

"I don't work the night shift often, but I've seen them come as late as ten o'clock," he said.

"You sure?"

"Positive. I remember talking to one of the drivers, and he was exhausted. He was finishing a twelve-hour shift, and ten o'clock was quitting time."

I thanked Harold, then called Burke.

"The Amazon delivery to Kantor's building that night," I said. "Did your guys ask the other residents about that delivery?"

"Give me a second," he said. "I need to open the file."

I heard him riffling through papers and mumbling to himself. When he came back on, he said, "I don't see where they asked. What's the problem?"

"The driver showed up at 9:53," I said. "That's late, but still within their normal delivery time. They shut down at ten. Something about that delivery is bothering me, but I can't call it just yet. Maybe your men can ask around and see if anyone had a delivery that night. Might not amount to anything, but it's worth getting it checked off the list. Speaking of which, any update on the missing Bentley?"

"Negative. We've pulled a lot of video and can't pick it up anywhere."

"I'm still trying to make sense of it. Who had access to the car?

Who even knew he had a car? He was always with his driver, so why or when did he have a need for a car anyway?"

"We have almost every city services agency looking out for that car," Burke said. "We've checked all the chop shops for any of its parts. Nothing."

"What about all the tolls?"

"Nothing."

"Maybe there was a tracking device," I said.

"Negative. We found the dealership he bought it from up in the northern suburbs. Locators aren't installed by the manufacturer. Customers have to make a request, then they install an aftermarket device. Kantor never made that request, so his car didn't have one."

"Of course not. That would be too convenient."

Someone must've seen whoever had taken the Bentley. They might not have known it was Kantor's car, but at some point, whether they passed the person in the building or getting into the car, someone saw the driver. How did the cameras not catch them? Then I had a thought. Maybe I was looking at this wrong. What if the driver never entered the building, but instead gained entry to the garage from outside?

13

Manny Acevedo enjoyed a quiet, comfortable life with his wife and two children in a small, south suburban town called Hazel Crest, about a twenty-five-minute drive from the city. He was a former long-haul truck driver before the hours away from his family became too challenging, and then he landed a job at one of the popular private car services. He had gotten a last-minute airport call almost ten years ago for a passenger whose regular driver had fallen ill. Manny reluctantly took the call, and it was a decision that would change his life. That passenger was Elliott Kantor, one of the richest men in the city.

"Thanks for meeting with me," I said as I took a seat in a chair across from Manny. He wore a loose-fitting black suit and open-collared white dress shirt. His thick black eyebrows were a perfect match for his heavy mop of hair that looked like it had been recently brushed but was refusing to cooperate. I couldn't help but notice his eyes. They were a deep blue.

"Simon said it was important I speak with you," Manny said.

"I'm just looking for some answers," I said. "You worked for Elliott Kantor for ten years."

"And a week," Manny said. "The night he died, it had been exactly ten years and a week to the day."

"You kept track that closely. Impressive."

"Mr. Kantor changed my life," Manny said. "He was the best boss I've ever had. I'm very grateful for what he did for me and my family."

"You were a limo driver before that, right?"

"I was. Five years. The hours were tough, but it was a better job than being on the road, driving a truck and missing my kids grow up."

"What was your schedule with Elliott?"

"Monday to Friday, four o'clock to midnight. Weekends I drove him as needed, but I shared it with Olag, who drove the day shift."

"What were Olag's hours?"

"Six to four," Manny said. "Olag picked him up early in the morning and drove him all day. I took over in the afternoon and drove him around at night."

"He was a busy man," I said.

"Super busy. Mr. Kantor was very important, but I don't need to tell you that. He also liked to be busy. He didn't like sitting at home. My father was the same way. He never knew how to just relax. Always on the go."

"What kept him so busy?"

"My father?"

"I was referring to Mr. Kantor, but you can tell me about your father if you'd like."

"My father put in driveways for a living," Manny said. "Big commercial lots, small residential driveways, he did them all. He worked long hours when the weather was good; then, when it was raining or snowing and the crew couldn't work, he'd find other things to do that had him out all day. He could never rest, but he took care of us and made sure we had everything we needed. He was a great provider."

"And Elliott Kantor?"

"Similar, but with a lot more money," Manny said. "That's what I liked about him. He was never afraid to work, and he enjoyed doing it. He liked to provide for his family and friends. He was generous to a fault."

"Did you ever travel with him when he went on his business trips?"

"Maybe a couple of times, but it was rare. He traveled alone."

"None of his assistants went with him?"

"Not very often. They set everything up for him, but they rarely traveled with him. He liked to go alone and have someone meet him on the other end. That's just how he liked to do it."

"What about the place in the Bahamas?"

"I went there once," Manny said. "He invited me and my family to go down there for spring break. It was the best trip we ever had. My wife had never been out of the country. He really took care of us. We stayed in our own house on the estate. We had people waiting on us hand and foot. He treated us like we were family. It meant a lot to us."

I looked out the window, toward the northern part of the lake. I could see the hundred-foot-tall clock tower on Northwestern's campus rise out of the blanket of green treetops. At night, they would sometimes light up the four clockfaces with a purple light, the school's official color and that of their mascot, the wildcat.

"What kind of social life did Elliott have?" I asked.

"What do you mean by social life?" Manny said. "Events and dinners?"

"I was thinking more along the lines of female company," I said.

Manny's face tightened a little. "Are you asking about women?"

"That's typically what female means," I said. I smiled, as if we were both in on the joke.

"Mr. Kantor had company sometimes," he said.

"Would you mind elaborating?"

"What do you want me to say?"

"I'd like to know what kind of company he had. Girlfriend? Girlfriends?"

Manny moved uneasily in his seat.

"I'm not comfortable talking about Mr. Kantor's private life," he said. "He was my boss. He treated my family well. What he did privately is none of my business."

I understood his reluctance. I also understood that he knew things that others didn't.

"Did you know where Elliott died?" I asked.

"At his house," Manny said.

"Which one?"

"Kenilworth."

"Guess again."

His eyes widened. The shock was genuine.

"Elliott Kantor died in his Lincoln Park apartment," I said.

"This is the first I'm hearing of this."

"And I don't think he died from a heart attack due to old age. I think someone killed him."

"Killed him?" Manny said, leaning forward, his eyes tightening.

"Yes."

"Killed him how?"

"I'd rather not get into that right now, but let's just say I have good reason to believe he was killed, and I have a good idea how they did it. My job is to find out who did it and why. So I need you to tell me what you know, even if you think it might be embarrassing to your former boss or his family."

Manny took in a deep breath, then exhaled slowly. He closed his eyes, then opened them and looked out the windows, toward the lake. A large yacht slid across the horizon.

"Mr. Kantor was an older man, but he was still a man," Manny said. "He liked women, and they liked him. He didn't have anyone who was his girlfriend. He liked different girls. He took care of them and treated them well. They had fun."

"How many girls?"

Manny shrugged. "I don't know for sure. I only drove three or four of them, and I didn't drive them often."

"Do you know their names?"

"Some of them. Serena, Roxanne, and I think one was called Maribel. There was another girl. She was from Vietnam or somewhere in Asia. I forgot her name."

"What kind of girls were they?"

"Very beautiful."

"Young?"

"Late twenties, early thirties."

"Did you ever see him party with them?"

"I always stayed in the car, waiting for him," Manny said. "I never went inside."

"Where did they go?"

"Restaurants, bars, sometimes a nightclub, but not often. The Asian girl always wanted him to go to the nightclubs. He would go, but only with her."

"You ever see Elliott do drugs in the car?"

"Drugs?"

"You heard me correctly."

"Never! Elliott drank when he went out, but he wasn't into drugs."

"How about the girls?"

"I never saw them do drugs either."

"Even though you didn't see them do anything, did they strike you as women who might do drugs? You know, get high every once in a while?"

"I can't say for sure. They were pretty and young and in the scene.

Lots of kids do drugs these days. If they were doing it, I guess I wouldn't be surprised."

"Take me back to the night he died," I said. "What happened?"

"I arrived at the office building a little before four," Manny said. "The front entrance of the building is on Michigan, right near the Apple store. But the rear entrance is on the basement level that lets out on lower Wacker. I always waited for him in the loading dock. Someone from the office would call and let me know what time he was heading down to the car so I'd be ready for him. He got in just after five. His oldest grandson, Lucas, had asked Mr. Kantor to get some Garrett Popcorn. So we drove down to the store on Ohio and picked up a bucket of the Chicago Mix. My wife loves the cheese and caramel, so he bought an extra bucket for me to take home. His dinner meeting that night wasn't until eight, so he had a couple of hours to kill. He decided to go over to the Bulls' practice facility and watch some of the players who were still in town shoot around. He loved sports and hanging out with the players and coaches."

"Did you go into the practice also?"

"No, I stayed in the car and waited for him. About seven thirty, he came out, and we drove over to RPM Steak. He was having dinner with Mr. Min, who had flown in from China. Mr. Min liked American steak. They ate, and when they were done, Mr. Kantor got back in the car."

"Do you remember what time it was?"

"Just after nine thirty."

"How are you so sure?"

"Because my alarm went off at nine thirty. Every weeknight, I have my alarm set for that time, so I remember to call and say good night to my kids. I had just finished speaking to them and my wife when he walked out of the restaurant. He got in the car, and I headed over to the expressway to take him up to Kenilworth."

"Wait, so he had planned on going to his estate that night?"

"Definitely. He hadn't planned on staying in the city."

"So, what changed?"

"He got a call. Had a quick conversation, then told me he wanted to spend the night in the city. I got off the expressway and headed over to the apartment. I asked him if he needed me to pick up anything from the store, since sometimes he wanted snacks or drinks and might not have had anything in the refrigerator at the apartment. He said he didn't need anything, so I drove straight there and dropped him off."

"I noticed in the surveillance video that he seemed to be waving you off when he was getting out of the SUV and you were trying to help him."

"He always did that." Manny laughed softly. "He didn't like being helped. He said it made him feel old, and he wasn't old yet. I still offered to help, because sometimes he might have had a little too much to drink and his balance wouldn't be that good. One time, he fell getting out and almost hit his head. Ever since then, I always tried to help him get out of the car when I knew he had been drinking."

What Manny described perfectly matched what I had seen in the video, and I could imagine Kantor responding in that way. I could also tell by the way Manny spoke that Kantor was more than just someone who signed his checks. Manny genuinely cared about Kantor and had probably spent more time with him than Kantor's own children had. I had come to learn over the years, after dealing with many wealthy people, that while their staff had been hired to serve, they also doubled as confidants—always around, often hearing and seeing things that weren't even shared with family members.

Learning of Elliott's last-minute change to stay in the city forced me to reconsider my hypothesis that his murder was premeditated by someone who knew his schedule well in advance to coordinate his murder and set up the scene as if his death had been an accidental overdose or sexual play gone too far. This reintroduced the real possibility that Elliott wasn't murdered at all. He just got unlucky with dirty drugs that overwhelmed his tired heart.

"Do you think it was that call that changed his mind to stay in the city?" I asked.

"Definitely," Manny said. "Had he not gotten the call, he would've gone home."

"Do you know who called him?"

"Yes. They've talked many times. I've never met him before, but I know his name. Monroe. He's a lawyer."

Could this be a coincidence? Jenny Lee's Maserati was registered to an LLC, and the managing agent was Monroe Connelly, partner in an overpriced law firm.

"Do you know Monroe's last name?" I asked.

"Never forget it," Manny said. "Every time I hear or see it, I think of the mystery writer. It's Connelly. My wife has read all of his books."

14

Mechanic and I arrived at 1425 West Fullerton just after one o'clock in the afternoon. We found a spot in front of the insurance company across the street, which again looked like it wasn't doing too much business. Javier from Kantor's office had given us a building key and the numeric code to Kantor's front door. We entered the building and stood in the lobby.

"Let's figure out the layout of the common areas," I said. "See what access people have once inside the building."

We took a left out of the lobby, which sent us down a short hallway that was connected to another longer hallway in the shape of an *L*. This brought us to apartment 1E, which belonged to the older couple, the Manns. We walked past their door, which had some large preserved floral decoration hanging above its center. The hallway dead-ended at a brick wall. A row of very tall windows that were at least ten feet above the ground ran along the left wall, washing the hallway in bright light. We returned to the lobby, then turned left and walked to the back of the building. Two elevator doors sat across from each other halfway down the hallway. These were the private elevators for apartments 2E and 2W, respectively. There weren't any windows or doors off this hallway, and it too dead-ended at a brick wall. We returned to the lobby.

"Everyone has to have access to the garage from inside the building," I said. "I can't believe they would construct a building where access was only from the outside."

"But there aren't any garage doors here on the first floor," Mechanic said.

"Exactly. Which means access must come from within their apartments."

We walked toward Kantor's apartment. The hallway was identical to the Manns', *L*-shaped and dead-ending at a brick wall. There weren't any other doors except Kantor's, and a similar row of windows was along the opposite wall. I punched the code into the keypad and opened Kantor's door.

"Jesus Christ," Mechanic said as we stepped in. "This place is gigantic. And this was just his city getaway?"

"Welcome to the lifestyles of the rich and famous," I said.

We walked deeper into the apartment, carefully inspecting each room. There were at least twelve rooms on the first floor. Six bedrooms, including the primary suite, as well as a formal library, sitting room, dining room, and family room. The kitchen was the size of an entire one-bedroom apartment. We finally located the garage door in the back of the apartment, off the hallway, between the primary suite and one of the bathrooms. It opened into a cavernous garage. A Mercedes and Porsche SUV sat on the polished limestone. Kantor's now-empty bay was simply marked with his unit number. We walked over and inspected the three garage doors that led to the back alley. They could be activated by either a remote or manually by a keypad along the wall.

"Let's go out and check the external access," I said.

We didn't have a remote or the code, so we had to go back through the apartment, then out the front door. We took a left once we reached the sidewalk, then another left, heading down Janssen Avenue. We turned into the alley and examined the doors. There was no keypad, so external access could only be gained using a remote control.

We were walking back along Janssen Avenue to get to the front when Mechanic suddenly stopped and said, "What's this door?"

Against the building's exterior wall, about a third of the way down, was a small door that I hadn't noticed before. It was camouflaged with the same coloring and texture of the limestone wall, but when you looked at it closely, you could see its edges. There wasn't a handle or lock, just the outline of a door.

"Maybe it's not a door," I said. "There's no way to open it. Maybe it was a door before the building was refurbished, and they just closed it off."

"Possible," Mechanic said. "But then why not just run the stone over it and close it permanently? If you're rehabbing the entire building and you want the door to go away, that would've taken little effort."

We went back into the building and down the hallway outside of Kantor's apartment. I didn't see a door, but that didn't surprise me. It wouldn't have come off this wall anyway. It was at least twenty or thirty feet beyond the end of this hallway, which meant it would've been coming off a wall deeper inside the apartment.

We entered the apartment and examined the first room on the right side, a large sitting room. The side back wall had been covered in orange wallpaper with swirls of fabric throughout. We knocked against various parts of the wall but didn't hear any change in sound that would suggest there had been a door.

The next room was a guest bedroom. The walls and ceiling had been painted a pastel blue. Two large windows ran along the side wall and were also visible from outside the building. A queen bed sat in the center of the room, flanked by two ornate nightstands and lamps. A large dresser with a flat-screen TV sat across from the bed. The room looked as if it had never been used.

"Someone forgot to clip the price tag on this lamp," Mechanic said. He lifted the tag that had been hanging behind the nightstand. "Damn. Who pays seven goddamn thousand dollars for a lamp?"

We searched the wall, tapping and running our hands over it but not finding any indication a door had once been there.

"Stay right there," I said. "I'm going outside to mark this off."

I walked outside the building and started pacing off the point where Kantor's apartment started. Once I arrived at the door, I took out my phone and dialed Mechanic's number.

"I'm gonna bang on the door," I said once he answered.

"Copy that," he said.

I waited for a woman to walk by, and once she was well out of earshot, I pounded on the door several times.

"I hear you banging through the phone, but not against the wall," Mechanic said.

"I'm gonna hang up and bang and then call you back," I said.

I disconnected and knocked on the door several times. A car drove by and slowed down. The driver looked at me suspiciously, then moved along. I called Mechanic.

"Nothing," he said.

I counted the number of strides it took to get from the door to the front of the building, then went back inside and walked the same number of strides. I landed back in the bedroom Mechanic and I were just in.

"It has to be in here," I said. "The distance matches."

I looked in the corner of the room and noticed a closet that I hadn't seen before. I pulled the door open, and there in plain sight, against the right wall, behind a rack of coats, was a lever handle. The door was heavily insulated, and the entire closet had been soundproofed.

"This is why you couldn't hear it," I said to Mechanic.

He joined me in the large closet.

"What the hell was this man up to?" Mechanic said.

I put on a pair of rubber gloves from my pocket, then pushed the handle down. The door opened. However, it didn't take us directly outside, as I had expected. Instead, we stood in a small, dark space about six feet across. I switched on my phone. In the far corner of this space, I spotted the metal panic bar of a door. We walked toward it, and I pushed it. We found ourselves looking out on Janssen Avenue.

I closed the door, and we walked back into the apartment. I dialed Kantor's office number. Pedro answered.

"Who was in charge of the construction plans for Elliott's apartment in Lincoln Park?" I asked.

"An architectural firm we hired," he said. "They drew up the plans for the general contractor."

"Did you see the plans?"

"I did, but I'm not an architect. It was just a bunch of lines and numbers to me."

"Did you know there was a secret door?"

"A secret door? What do you mean?"

"Behind one of the closets, there's a hidden door that goes out onto the sidewalk next to the building."

"How do you know this?"

"Because I'm here at the apartment and just found it. Do you still have the building plans?"

"I'm not sure, but I can check the files. It's been several years."

"Look for them as soon as possible, and if you locate them, let me know."

I turned to Mechanic and said, "I think Elliott Kantor had secrets. Time for you to go to work."

I told him about Manny's recollection of what happened that last night and how plans had been changed by that call from Connelly. Mechanic knew what I was coming to next.

"How many days you want me on him?" he asked.

"Let's start with three or four," I said. "See if we can get an idea why a big-time law partner who works for one of Chicago's richest men is cavorting with a casino cocktail waitress and professional escort."

"'Cavorting'?" Mechanic said, rolling his eyes. "That choice of word necessary?"

"The only SAT word in just over an hour. Thought you'd commend my restraint."

Mechanic looked at me, shook his head, then walked out of the apartment.

I DROPPED MECHANIC OFF AT Hammer's gym, then headed south to the Jackson Park Driving Range. I needed to look at everything through a new lens and hopefully discover new connections. Being out in the warm air and swinging my clubs always had a calming effect. There was something about the repetition of my swing and the crack of the ball hitting the face of the club that allowed my thoughts to settle into better focus.

So far, all roads led to Elliott Kantor; I just wasn't sure how. What was out there that I hadn't learned about him and the expanding circle of people who played a role in his life? All of us, whether we intended to or not, had our secrets. The second series of lab results had come back only to confirm the first results—Kantor had died of a heart attack secondary to an overdose of methamphetamines. Pedro had gotten the architectural prints for me, and there was no plan for a door leading out of the closet. Elliott must have decided to have it installed after the drawings were complete and the renovations had already started.

My phone rang just as I had gotten halfway through my first bucket of balls. It was my father.

"Let me guess," he said when I picked up the phone.

"Your guess is correct," I said. "And my nine iron is popping about ten yards farther than usual."

"If only you had given your tennis so much effort."

"You keep forgetting the small detail that I ruptured my ACL."

"Plenty of players have come back from that injury and gone on to great careers in various sports," he said.

"Did you really call to have our millionth conversation about my tennis disappointments?" I said.

"I called to talk about Bishop Thompson. I heard some things that reminded me of your case with that billionaire. Thought you might find them interesting."

"Such as?"

"For starters, he was found half naked in a sexually suggestive way in a bed that was not his own, his arms and legs tied up to the bedposts."

"Damn. What the hell was he doing?"

"By the sounds of it, too much," my father said.

"Whose bedroom was he in?" I asked.

"Some fitness trainer. He claims to have come home and found the body."

"He?"

"I didn't stutter."

My mind started racing. This was going in all kinds of directions I hadn't expected. How does one of the country's most visible preachers end up dead, half naked, and tied up in the bed of a male fitness trainer?

"How did you hear about this?" I asked.

"Clarence Allen over at the *Defender*. He called to talk about tennis and told me in confidence what he had heard about Thompson."

"Who was his source?"

"These are all questions you need to ask Clarence. I told him you might be interested in knowing more about what happened. He agreed to meet with you in his office."

15

Clarence T. Allen, publisher of the famed *Chicago Defender* newspaper, sat behind an enormous oak desk in a spacious office with walls covered with framed black-and-white prints, an illustrated timeline of African American culture. The steely smile of Shirley Chisholm, the first Black congresswoman, adjacent to the unnerving photo of Martin Luther King Jr. being pelted by bottles and rocks during his march in Chicago. A who's who of civil rights luminaries, from A. Philip Randolph to Julian Bond, Fannie Lou Hamer, and Medgar Evers, had been captured at this most courageous moment, frozen in time and now gleaming behind glass-covered frames.

Allen's great-grandfather had started the newspaper in the early 1900s out of the tiny kitchen in his landlord's apartment and with an initial investment of twenty-five cents. The first press run totaled three hundred copies, but by the start of World War I, it had become the country's most influential Black weekly newspaper, and one of the biggest influences to spark the Great Migration that saw more than six million African Americans flee the oppressive South for better opportunities in other parts of the country.

Allen, barely over five feet and not weighing more than a bag of ice salt, stood as I entered. He offered a firm handshake and wide smile. He wore a light blue shirt, gold tie, and suit pants held up by suspenders. His gray mustache and hair shined against the deep blackness of his skin.

"I haven't seen you since you were knee-high to a grasshopper," he said, settling back into his chair. "Your mother used to bring you to the tennis courts in your stroller, and you'd get out with a small tennis racquet and run as long as they'd let you. You had a great swing, even then."

"Well, it's been a while since I've swung on a tennis court. Most of my swings are on the golf course now."

"So your father tells me. Not exactly his favorite topic."

"My father always thought he'd be sitting in the player's box at Wimbledon, watching me in all whites on the grass. But what can you do? Life happens."

"Fathers can always dream," Clarence said.

I looked at the large photo hanging behind Clarence's desk. He and Harold Washington, Chicago's first Black mayor, stood next to each other at a ribbon-cutting ceremony. Two congressmen stood on Clarence's right, and Reverend G. T. McCaskill, the founder of South Baptist and father of its current preacher, Harlan McCaskill, stood to the left of the mayor.

"Did you know Bishop Thompson?" I asked.

"Not as well as some of the other clergymen, but we were acquaintances," Clarence said. "I actually went to college with his father. Damn good quarterback at Hampton. Should've gotten drafted in the NFL, but back then, they didn't take players from the Black colleges, and they certainly didn't want any Black quarterbacks. Keegan was built just like his father, but he never wanted to play. He was more into the social life."

"How did you hear about his passing?"

Clarence got up, walked over, and closed the door, then sat in a chair next to mine instead of returning behind his desk.

"One of our stringers heard the call over the police frequency," Clarence said. "He didn't know it was Keegan, but he heard there was an unresponsive young male who wasn't breathing and presumed dead in an apartment on Thirty-Fifth Street. The stringer was just a few blocks away, so he got dressed and went to the location. He arrived before the police and got upstairs to the apartment. The guy who lived in the apartment was standing outside, all shaken up. The stringer talked his way into the apartment, took several photographs, then left just as the police and paramedics arrived."

"Did he know it was Thompson?"

"He didn't recognize him but saw the man's pants lying next to the bed and a small envelope sticking out of the back pocket. It had the name Bishop Thompson written across it. When the stringer got home, he looked up Thompson on the internet and realized it was the famous LA preacher. He called my deputy, who called me right away and told me what happened."

"Who has the pictures?"

"I do," Clarence said, getting up and walking to a filing cabinet next to his desk. He opened the top drawer and pulled out a folder, then handed it to me before sitting back down.

I opened the folder and pulled out five photographs. A muscular Black man was lying face down on a small bed. He wore what looked like a one-piece wrestling uniform, except it had only one arm strap, and instead of there being shorts, it ended in a tight bikini that didn't cover the entirety of his bottom. His hands and legs had been stretched apart and tied by leather straps to the bedposts. The next photograph was a close-up of his face. His eyes were open, and his mouth and nose were submerged in what looked like vomit. The third photograph was of a pair of women's high-heeled shoes resting next to the bed. The fourth photograph focused in on his ankles and the leather restraints. I noticed the becket bend knot right away, the same knot used to tie up Elliott Kantor. The fifth photograph was of Thompson's wrists and their restraints. They also had been tied by the same knot.

"Not exactly how you'd expect to find one of the country's most prominent African American preachers," Clarence said. "In a small, second-floor walk-up one-bedroom above a thrift store in Bronzeville."

I nodded. "Whose apartment was he in?"

Clarence reached over to his desk and grabbed a piece of paper sitting on top of a stack of magazines. He put on his reading glasses and said, "Guy's name is Malcolm Boyd. Twenty-eight years old. He's lived in that apartment for just over two years. He declined to give out any more personal information. He said he came home and found this dead man in his bedroom. He denied knowing the man or ever having seen him before. He wouldn't answer any more questions and asked the reporter to leave him alone."

"The story you published didn't have any of this information," I said.

Clarence smiled patiently. "Ashe, let me explain something," he said. "My great-grandfather started this paper because we didn't have a voice, and because the white media either didn't cover our stories or, when they did, they were full of lies and bias. They only wanted to talk about us when it was something salacious to report. They didn't have anything to say about our successful businesses, college graduates becoming doctors and lawyers and teachers. We invented things, and they always found a way to attribute our inventions to someone else. This paper, along with others, like the *Amsterdam News*, was started so that we could celebrate our people and communicate to others across the country what was happening to our community. Yes, we covered crimes and politics and news that wasn't always the most uplifting; we are journalists, after all. But my family has always been sensitive to what we publish and how we publish it, as it can have a deep and lasting impact on the image and psyche of our people. The *Sun-Times* or the *Trib* would've put this story on their front page, embarrassing photographs and all. That's not what our paper is about. Whatever Thompson was doing in that apartment and who he was doing it with is a private matter. There's no public good achieved by airing his dirty laundry."

I nodded. I just didn't know how long the details of Thompson's death could be kept out of the headlines. Malcolm Boyd, the man whose apartment he was found in, knew, as did the officers and paramedics who responded. I was surprised the information hadn't leaked already. Someone had put a lock on it.

"Did your stringer get Malcom Boyd's phone number?" I asked.

"Yes, Darryl has it," Clarence said. "He'll tell you what he knows. I've already authorized him to speak freely with you."

I stood to leave, and Clarence wrote the number on a loose piece of paper, then handed it to me. He said, "Your father says you're working on another case that's similar to this, and somehow this might help."

"I'm not sure yet," I said. "There seem to be a couple of similarities, but I won't know for sure until I dig into it a little more. Might be nothing more than a strange coincidence."

I left the *Chicago Defender* building knowing full well that those becket bend knots and the cross-dressing connected Bishop Keegan Thompson's death to that of Elliott Kantor. I just didn't know how.

16

The next afternoon, Stryker and I were out for a walk in Grant Park. The winter thaw was long over, so the grass was thick and green and ready to be explored, which Stryker could do for hours on end if you let him. He also enjoyed walking near Buckingham Fountain after his exhausting runs, so the mist would spray and cool him down. He was in the midst of eyeing a mini collie with pink ribbons in her hair when my cell phone rang. It was Burke.

"We found the car," Burke said.

"Where?" I said.

"Sitting on four cinder blocks over on South Lafayette in Washington Park."

"Have you moved it yet?"

"No one's touching it til I get there."

"I'll be there in thirty."

WASHINGTON PARK WAS A DEPRESSED neighborhood on the South Side, known for its enormous 372-acre park bearing the same name. Hidden in the shadows of the neighboring University of Chicago, this community of wide, long streets and boarded-up houses had once been a thriving hub for its African American residents who had moved here during the apartment construction boom at the turn of the twentieth century. The process of reclaiming the neighborhood had begun in earnest nearly thirty years ago, but progress had been slow as dirt, and the air of hopelessness still hung above the community like a lingering gray cloud refusing to go away long after the rain has stopped.

South Perry Avenue was a small, one-way, north-south street that ran off the biggest thoroughfare in the neighborhood, Garfield Boulevard. I hadn't been to this area of the city since I was a detective and worked a case where a mother and her two children had been held at gunpoint by an ex-boyfriend in the middle of a drug-fueled mental crisis. He shot and killed all three, then fled, and we eventually found him several weeks later in a crack house on the West Side. The neighborhood looked even worse than the last time I had visited. There were a couple of new buildings along Garfield, but the large grass median was littered with empty bottles, wrappers, and discarded food containers. Every block had large gaps of vacant land between the old buildings, weeds knee-high, and signs posted by the city forbidding trespassing.

I turned onto South Perry. The elevated Metra train tracks, sitting above a long stretch of unoccupied land overrun by wild weeds and dying trees, ran along the right side of the street. I wondered how many bodies had been discovered there over the years. Along the left side of the street were a few dilapidated single-family houses, a couple of them with battered cars parked on the trampled brown lawns. Midway through the block the houses ended, giving way to a great expanse of empty land leading up to a large wooden greenhouse covered by clear plastic tarp. A sign hung on the front door marking it as a project of the Sweet Water Foundation. An enormous garden had been fenced in, and the fresh soil was evidence of a recent planting. Beyond that, the street became increasingly desolate, with more empty lots overrun by wild brush and twisted trees. I imagined few people drove down this street, and those who did were probably lost or looking for a shortcut. This was a perfect location to abandon a stolen car.

I rolled farther down the street. A large brick building rose up behind a concrete wall that had barbed wire running down its entire length. The black rolling gate had been padlocked, and a Maersk shipping container could be seen through the gaps. There were no markings on the building, but a wood sign attached to the concrete wall announced the address and phone number and the name Wah King Noodle Co. It was difficult to tell what was inside, but given the condition of the decaying edifice, I wouldn't eat any noodles that had been manufactured there.

Across the street sat several unmarked cars and one patrol car. A small group hovered over what remained of the Bentley. Burke met me as I got out of my car.

"Almost stripped to the shell," Burke said.

"Most of those parts are halfway down to Texas or on a long drive to California," I said.

Burke handed me a pair of gloves. I recognized one of the detectives, a short stocky guy named Delacorte. Both of his parents had been cops. We had been separated by a year at the academy. He had been a solid detective and widely respected. We nodded at each other. I stepped closer to the frame now sitting precariously on cinder blocks. The seat belts were intact along with the front seats, but the leather was badly ripped and had lots of water damage. I had once read that Bentley sourced its leather from Scandinavian bull cows and dyed it to match any color requested by its customers, then hand-stitched it into its trademark quilted pattern.

I continued my inspection partially for investigative reasons and partially because I was a fan. All of the laminated wood that typically lined the dashboard had been meticulously extracted. My guess was that Kantor had probably chosen the Vavona veneer, the rarest and most expensive of the custom wood assemblies that had been sourced from felled California sequoias. The steering wheel was gone, but the floor pedals had little street value, so they remained like narrow, skinless feet hanging from a skeleton. Surprisingly, the leather-and-chrome gearstick knob with its classic lacquered *B* logo remained where the stripped center console had once shined. I wondered why it hadn't been taken as well, considering they ran north of a thousand dollars.

"Had real problems getting the seats out," Burke said.

"Or they were scared away while trying to do it," I said. "Seats like these have different assemblies and floor mounts than the old cars. You need special tools to break them free. It's not easy, and it takes a while."

"Who the hell puts quilted seats in a car anyway?" Burke said.

"People who have more money than they know what to do with," I said.

I walked to the front of the car and looked in the engine well. The hood had also been unbolted and stolen, along with the entire bay of parts. Only a few hoses and wires remained, but they had been cut to free the more expensive hardware underneath. The front hood latch remained, as well as a chrome placard centered and anchored to the front lip. The number twelve had been stamped on the placard with the words *Twin Turbo* underneath it, indicating the engine had been a rare W12. I continued walking around the body of the car and was surprised by how immaculate it remained. No scratches in the paint or any dents in the metal frame—except for all the missing parts, it looked like it had just rolled out of the dealer showroom.

Two crime scene techs went to work dusting for prints, but I was confident that in the unlikely event they found anything, it would be of little help to the investigation. This car had been chopped up by experts, not a bunch of juvenile vandals getting their cheap thrills destroying property. I walked to the back of the car. They had even stripped the taillights, which, as a pair, could set you back a few thousand dollars.

Delacorte met me behind the car. "You're looking great, Ashe," he said. "Retirement looks good on you."

We hugged each other.

"You should try it someday," I said. "Does wonders for the skin."

"For the bank account too by the looks of your ride," he said. "What is that, early nineties?"

"Eighty-six," I said.

"All original?"

"Only way I like 'em."

"Man, I've been figuring out my own plan B. Another ten years and I can take early retirement."

"What do you have in mind?"

"Been doing a little trading on the side and looking into all this cryptocurrency stuff. One of the sergeants who got me into it just retired last year. Said he was losing too much money coming to work, so he turned in his shield, kept his union benefits, and now he spends half his day on the computer, looking at charts and graphs, and the other half looking at investment properties."

"Better than dodging bullets," I said. "My best advice is to go find a young financial person who's hungry and understands all this complicated investment shit. I was lucky enough to find this little brainiac from MIT. Worth his weight in gold."

"Speaking of gold, nice watch," he said, pointing to my wrist.

"Doesn't tell time any better than a quartz," I said. "But it looks good on a golf course."

"You ever miss this?" he asked.

"All the time," I said. "But not everything. The fieldwork like this, being out and gathering evidence, trying to connect the dots—that's the stuff that charges your adrenaline. But all the politics and hierarchy and inside-outside shit? Don't miss it for a second."

"Is it true?" he said, lowering his voice and leaning into me.

"What?"

"That case against the deputy superintendent last year. Was it you?"

I had taken on a case to protect one of the city's popular evening news anchors, who was also investigating the suspicious killing of an unarmed Black man. What first had been reported as a case of mistaken identity turned out to be the final ruthless act preceded by a web of lies and a vicious attempt to cover them up.

I smiled. "You shouldn't believe everything you hear," I said.

"Word travels," he said. "That anchorwoman is good, but we all know she needed help to piece that together."

I shrugged.

"So Burke has you looped in on this case?" he said.

"Unofficially. Just offering an outside perspective. What does it look like for you on the inside?"

"I'm not the lead on this, but they asked me to come out and take a look. Another set of eyes. But from what I've been told so far, a lot of it doesn't add up. There's something else going on."

"Like?"

"Feels like a setup to me. I can't say what exactly is making me feel that, but it's just strange. One of the richest men in the city goes out like he did, and he's got loads of meth in his system and a prostitute who came by to get freaky with him. Then someone steals his Bentley the same night he dies, and it ends up on blocks way over here, in a neighborhood like this. Something's missing."

"I keep trying to figure out the motivation," I said. "Who wanted him dead and why?"

"That's one perspective," Delacorte said. "Then there's the possibility he was into kinky sex, took some dirty drugs, and his heart stopped. Whoever was with him panicked and bolted from the apartment. Maybe they took his car to escape."

"There's no video of anyone entering or leaving the apartment," I said.

I didn't mention the secret door I had found, because I wanted to process it more before talking to Burke about it.

"We got something," one of the techs called out.

We all walked over to the other side of the car. The tech pulled out a crumpled piece of paper that had been wedged between the seat and the console frame. He opened it and held it up to the sky.

"A gas receipt," he said. "Five days ago. Twelve ten a.m. Just over fifteen gallons for sixty-three dollars."

Burke took a look at it, and then it was carefully passed along by the rest of us who had on gloves. When it got to me, I took out my phone and shot a picture of it.

"Let's go take a ride over there," Delacorte said to me. "It's a gas station. They definitely have video."

17

Falcon Fuel sat in a tough neighborhood on the South Side, at the busy intersection of Vincennes Avenue and Seventy-First Street. It was one of those hardscrabble areas of the city where anything could go wrong at any time. Daylight worked to our advantage, but by no means did it give us a false sense of security. We had been in enough situations in places like this to know that danger was never too far away.

A couple of cars had been parked adjacent to the pumps, their drivers carefully watching the gas gauges roll up near the limit of what they wanted to spend. Delacorte had pulled up in his dented unmarked, which caught more attention than my shiny Porsche. I parked right in front so I could keep an eye on it. We walked through the door and entered an unkempt store with narrow aisles; crammed, disordered shelves; and floors badly in need of a heavy mop. Like any convenience store, the refrigerated units lined the walls, and in the back sat an unattended hot bar of overcooked hot dogs and old pizza. The heavy smell of frying grease hung thick in the air. A couple of teenagers stood at the counter buying Flamin' Hot Cheetos and tall cans of sweet iced tea. They were laughing about something one of them had done at school to a teacher.

Once they had paid, Delacorte and I stepped up to the bulletproof plexiglass cage. A short Indian man with wavy jet-black hair and a thin mustache under a prominent nose stared at us with weary eyes. It looked like he hadn't slept in a week.

"Are you the owner?" Delacorte asked.

"Owner's not here right now," the man replied with little interest.

Delacorte took out his shield, flashed it, then said, "Listen, bud, we need to talk to the owner ASAP."

"We pay on Saturdays," the man said. "I don't have the envelope."

Delacorte and I looked at each other. Some things never changed.

"We're not here for that," Delacorte said. He pointed to the four monitors bolted to the ceiling. "We need to take a look at your cameras."

"Is there something wrong?" the man asked, turning toward the monitors. "I didn't call the police."

"Nothing that you did," Delacorte said. "We're looking for a suspect who might've come in to get gas about five days ago, just after midnight."

"You have to talk to the owner about that," the man said. "I don't touch the cameras. I don't even have the key to open up the case. He's the only one."

"When will the owner be in the store?" Delacorte asked. "This is a top-priority investigation."

"He'll be back this weekend."

Delacorte smiled as a show of patience. "Pick up your damn phone, call him, and tell him the police are standing in front of you, and we need him to come down here right now."

"Won't do any good," the man said with a shrug. "He's out of town with his family. All the way in Michigan, outside Detroit. He won't come back early, but if you want to talk to him, I will call him."

"I wanna talk to him," Delacorte said.

The man picked up his cell phone, dialed the number, said a few words, then opened the exchange compartment at the bottom of the plexiglass and placed the phone in it. Delacorte opened the hinged door on our side and picked up the phone. The conversation was brief. Delacorte opened the compartment and put the phone back in.

"He's the only one with the key," Delacorte said to me. "He'll be back sometime this weekend. He saves the surveillance footage for a month, then tapes over it. If the person or persons drove that Bentley here, we've got them on camera."

THAT NIGHT, I HAD EVERYTHING set for Carolina. I hadn't seen her in a little over a week, and my body was increasingly reminding me at the most inconvenient times that it had been way too long. I decided to try a new recipe I had seen on the *Rachael Ray Show*, a creamy risotto with sun-dried tomatoes, glazed asparagus tips, and cut pieces of grilled salmon. I took out a bottle of pinot noir from New Zealand and set the table so we would be facing the lake.

The lights were dimmed and the candles already lit when she rang the bell. She wore a snug peach dress and lip gloss that matched. Her skin had begun to darken like it always did this time of year.

"It smells so good in here," she said after kissing me. She tasted like sweet fruit nectar.

I followed her down the hall and into the living room, the entire time wondering how I could be the luckiest man in the world.

"This is beautiful," she said after she turned the corner and spotted the table against the window. "This is a perfect gift after abandoning me for over a week."

"Actually, your gift is after dinner and through that door," I said, nodding toward the bedroom.

She turned and pressed her body into mine and wrapped her hands around my neck. "What if I want my gift before dinner?"

"Then you don't need to say another word."

I walked into the kitchen, turned down the heat under the food, and lowered the oven temperature. By the time I had blown out the candles, she had already gone into the bedroom, and her dress was on the floor. I closed the door so Stryker wouldn't bother us, lifted the covers, and climbed on top of her.

"I LOVE THIS NEW RECIPE," she said.

We were halfway through the meal. We had taken a long shower together, and now she was dressed in a pair of my sweats, and I was wrapped in a monogrammed robe my father had given me last Christmas.

"You have that glow," I said. "Are you just saying that because we're postcoital?"

"I'm not that easy," she said, smiling. "I think the sun-dried tomatoes nicely complete the flavor profile."

We clinked our wineglasses and took sips.

"And this wine is perfect," she said. "It's very lively. Similar to the one from California you bought me for my birthday last year."

"Speaking of California, I've been meaning to ask you about a guy named Bishop Keegan Thompson."

"Should I know him?"

"He's the pastor of a megachurch in LA. Well, was the pastor."

"'Was' meaning he retired, or 'was' meaning he's now flying loops with the heavenly angels?"

"The latter."

I explained to her what I had learned from Clarence Allen, as well as the photographs the stringer had taken.

"You think this has anything to do with the billionaire?" she asked.

"I don't see how, but I can't stop thinking about those knots,"

I said. "Both of them tied up to bedposts with leather straps and a special knot that ninety-nine percent of the world doesn't know how to tie."

"And wearing undergarments that I'm sure they wouldn't want advertised."

"I had never seen anything like the outfit the preacher had on. It was like a taut wrestling uniform made out of tights, but half of it was gone. I don't even know where you'd buy something like that."

"Nowhere in the shops on Michigan Ave., that's for sure."

"And how does this multimillionaire with a mansion in Beverly Hills and his-and-hers Rolls-Royces end up in an eight-hundred-dollar-a-month second-floor apartment above a thrift store in Bronzeville?"

"Sounds to me like you need to talk to this photographer who talked to the fitness trainer, who I assumed talked to the police."

"We have a meeting set up for tomorrow afternoon."

I looked out into the blackness of the lake. I could see the distant lights of a single boat floating south. I wondered who was on the boat and where they were going. Could they see us sitting up here, looking at them?

"What's making me suspicious is that none of the local media has really picked up on this story," I said. "The *Sun-Times* had a paragraph on it, and a couple of the TV stations mentioned it on their website, but other than that, no one paid much attention to it, and none of the stories had any of the details I just shared with you."

"If this guy is as influential as you say he is, you'd expect someone to make more noise about it. Someone is keeping it buried."

"My thought exactly."

"But who?"

"That's where you come in," I said. "I need you to dig around and see what's in the case file."

"Perfect timing as always," she said. "You wait until I'm two glasses in, halfway gone, and vulnerable before the ask."

"Don't forget the postcoital part too," I said.

"If I didn't know any better, I'd think you were taking advantage of me."

"That part comes after dessert, when you lose the sweatpants."

She smiled. "Remember, you can only consider it taking advantage when one side doesn't want it to happen."

18

The next morning, after seeing Carolina off to work, I set out toward the lake for a quick three-mile run. The sun was out in all of its glory, and finally the breeze coming off the water was warm, a welcome change from the punishing winter winds. The running path was busier now, which meant navigating all of the distractions—most importantly, avoiding slower runners and being hit by passing cyclists. I turned up my earbuds, ran a moderate first mile, then kicked up the pace. My watch buzzed with a message, but I was in full stride and didn't want to break focus. I had one mile left, and my lungs were starting to burn. I took a few deep breaths, then lost myself in the familiar mechanics of my stride, arms pumping, and my heart racing to keep up with the increased work of my lungs. The last quarter mile I had mapped out so that it would be slightly downhill, and I could give it a full kick. I stopped my watch at eighteen minutes and twenty seconds.

I walked back toward my apartment, enjoying the post-run high, which was typical after a strong run like this. I looked down at my watch and read the message that I had ignored earlier. It was from Emily Kantor, asking if I could meet her for tea at the Peninsula sometime that afternoon. I had a meeting with Darryl Wolcott at noon to talk about Bishop Thompson, so I texted her back and told her I could meet up with her at two.

I had read what little I could find on Emily Kantor, the youngest of the Kantor children. She kept an extremely low profile. I found only one picture of her, from many years ago, and that was at some charity event where she made a million-dollar donation to an Alaskan wildlife conservation group. I couldn't find any extensive biographical information other than that she was thirty-nine years old, went to Yale for her undergraduate studies, and had gotten her pilot's license when she was twenty-five. There was no mention of her ever being married or having children. She had never participated in the family's business and now lived on a 130,000-acre ranch in Montana.

My phone rang as I walked into my apartment. It was Carolina.

"How was your run?" she said.

"Strong," I replied. "A quick three miles."

"I would never put 'quick' and 'three miles' in the same sentence without also including 'airplane.'"

We both laughed. Carolina despised running as much as I loved it. She was the living embodiment of what it meant to have great DNA.

"Anyway, I'm calling about Thompson," she said.

"You already found something?"

"Not the case report, but I put in a call to my friend in the ME's office. She told me Thompson's going on the table today."

"Today? What took so long? It's been over four days!"

"The family didn't want an autopsy. Their lawyer put up a big fight. They lost. First cut happens in a couple of hours."

"Why were they fighting it?"

"She didn't know. But that doesn't feel right to me. Wouldn't you want to know why your husband, who didn't have any medical problems, suddenly died?"

"Assuming he didn't have any medical problems. He was only forty-five."

"And most forty-five-year-olds don't just drop dead."

Carolina's point was well-taken. Families of younger people who suddenly died typically were aggressive in their push for autopsies. They wanted to know how it was even possible their loved ones could suddenly just die without warning. Then there were those who declined to have an autopsy performed. They typically refused on religious grounds or because they already had an idea of the cause of death and didn't want that information exposed. My suspicions about the Thompson family favored the latter.

"Who's doing the autopsy?" I asked.

"St. John," she said.

Margot St. John had been the chief medical examiner for the last several years. She had been an assistant medical examiner for many years before that. She had been hired to clean up the department literally and figuratively after an embarrassing scandal where hundreds of neglected bodies were discovered in the morgue. It was rare for her to do cases. Most of the autopsies were performed by the other doctors.

"If anyone will get to the bottom of what happened, she will," I said. "Anything someone's trying to hide will come out on her table."

"No stone uncovered," Carolina said. "As soon as I finish my morning admin meeting, I'll check into his case file and see what I can find."

I thought about cluing Burke in on my suspicions, but I didn't feel like I had enough information to convince him one way or another. Right now, my best evidence was the becket bend and good old-fashioned statistics. It was simply a game of statistics. What were the chances that within the span of a couple of weeks, two very wealthy men had been found dead, tied up in beds with the same knots, wearing women's clothes?

"Something's missing," I said. "I'm heading to meet the photographer. Maybe he can fill in some of the blanks."

DARRYL WOLCOTT HAD AGREED TO meet me at a Starbucks on Stony Island Avenue, one of the major arteries on the South Side, where Black people lived and white people dared to enter only when they needed to reach the toll road that led to Indiana.

I spotted him the second he walked through the door in his green Chicago State hoodie. I hadn't expected him to be so tall or so young. He looked like he should be playing forward on a college basketball team. His hand wrapped around mine like a catcher's mitt. We took a seat by the window.

"All of the so-called experts never thought a Starbucks would work in this neighborhood," he said, looking at the long line of cars queued up at the drive-through. "Too many gangbangers and drug dealers." He smiled again. "They were all wrong. This is one of the highest-grossing Starbucks in the entire city."

"'It is not in the stars to hold our destiny,'" I said.

"'But in ourselves,'" Wolcott finished. "That's one of my favorite Shakespeare quotes. Should be a mantra for our people. Would do a lot of us some good."

"True, but mantras are useless if people don't believe in them," I said. "We need more believers."

"And more of us looking out for each other. Too many people only thinking about themselves. Sometimes we gotta think about the bigger picture."

"Is the bigger picture why you didn't release those photos of Bishop Thompson?" I asked.

Wolcott smiled. "I can't take full credit for that, but I agreed with Mr. Allen's decision. It made sense when you do the cost-benefit analysis."

"Which is?"

"What greater good would be served by publishing compromising pictures like that of a well-known Black preacher? He was on his own time, doing his own thing. It would get tons of downloads and shares and clicks, but at the end of the day, who really benefits?"

"Those pictures could get a lot of money on the open market."

"Of course they could. Another Black man being torn down. Enough already. Look at what those pictures would do to his legacy and his family's memory of him. At some point, we have to start choosing principle over money."

"Honor is a rare quality these days."

"I don't know if it's honor or the times we're living in. George Floyd's murder wasn't just a wake-up call for racial and social justice. It was also a call to our people that we need to do better, have higher expectations, be more unified. One way they try to keep us down is by dividing us. We don't need to sow our own divisions."

I liked this guy. He represented the real promise of the younger generation that had driven the social unrest over the last couple of years that had given birth to a greater sense of pride in who we were as a people and a fearlessness to stand up and challenge old norms steeped in inequity and systemic racism. These biases had been so interwoven into the societal fabric that those who perpetuated them were often unaware that they were doing so. Thoughtful, determined young people like Darryl Wolcott were the fresh faces and voices for change. I couldn't help but think about the shortcomings of my generation and how the progress of our people had stalled on our watch as we mistook false societal gains for real social change.

"Tell me what you think was going on in that apartment," I said. "I'm interested in your perspective."

Wolcott shook his head and stared out the window. "It was obvious the man was getting his freak on," he said. "He was tied up, half naked, ladies' shoes next to the bed. No doubt he was gettin' it in. Then, I don't know, but something must've gone wrong. Really wrong. The sex got too rough. Maybe he took something that didn't vibe with his system. I don't know what happened, but nothing about what I saw looked natural."

"Such as?"

"I didn't have a long time in there with him, but the place seemed too perfect, almost like a hotel room. It was really clean. Too clean, especially for a guy's apartment. And I know lots of people get into all that tying-up bondage shit, but the way he was stretched across the bed didn't look comfortable. I don't see how that could feel good."

"Did you see any blood or any signs in the apartment that there might've been a struggle or that he was attacked?"

Wolcott shook his head. "Nope. Everything was orderly. It even smelled nice, like someone had burned scented candles."

"Drugs or drug paraphernalia?"

"Nothing I could see."

"Clarence said you heard the call over the police frequency."

"I monitor it from time to time to see if there's anything going on. Usually, it's just a bunch of chatter, but that night when I heard the call, it sounded like it could really be something. Plus, I was already in the neighborhood visiting my girl, who stays over at Lake Meadows, a few blocks away. So I grabbed my camera and hustled over there."

"And Boyd, the tenant who found him, just let you in?"

"I think he thought I was the police. I knocked on the door, and he opened it. He looked really upset. I walked in and asked him what happened. He asked if I was with the police. I told him I wasn't, but the police were on the way. I could tell he had been crying. His eyes were red. The guy was really jacked, muscles everywhere. I asked him what happened. He said he came home from work and found a guy in his bed, and he was dead."

"What time was it?"

"A little after nine."

"Then he took you to the body?"

"I asked him if he was sure the person was dead. He said he was sure. The guy wasn't moving, and he wasn't breathing. I told him to let me see the body to make sure. He took me upstairs to the apartment. The bedroom is straight off the living room. I walked in, and the guy was lying there in the middle of the bed, all strapped up."

"Did you say anything to Boyd when you saw the body?"

"What was I gonna say? It was a really bad situation. I couldn't say anything to make it better."

"How was Boyd acting?"

"What do you mean?"

"What was his temperament like?"

"He was scared as shit. Most people don't come home and find people tied up in their beds, dead."

"You believe that's what happened?"

"Which part?"

"That he just came home and found one of the country's biggest preachers sprawled out in his bed, dead."

Wolcott raised his hands. "Listen, man. I ain't the detective. You are. I just listened to his story. My job wasn't to do an investigation. I wanted to get the pictures and get outta there before the police came."

"Did it seem like he knew it was Thompson in his bed?"

"If he did, he wasn't showing it. He kept saying how he didn't know how the hell this could happen to him, and he didn't understand what had happened."

"Were those his exact words?"

"Verbatim."

"A strange response from someone who says he walked in on a dead body."

"I thought the same thing," Wolcott said. "But once again, I ain't the detective. You are."

19

The Peninsula Hotel stood in all its limestone decadence on East Superior Street, just off the more exclusive section of Michigan Avenue. Tiffany occupied a couple of floors of the same building to the east, and on its western border sat a posh French café aptly named Pierrot Gourmet. When my mother was alive, her sister, Delilah, would visit us once a year, and despite there being plenty of guest bedrooms in our house, Aunt Delilah always insisted on staying at what she regaled as one of the finest hotels in the country. The only one she liked more was the Peninsula in New York City, and that was because she said it was smaller and offered a more intimate experience.

I took the elevator to the fourth-floor Shanghai Terrace, situated outside on the eastern edge of the building with a breathtaking view of the iconic Water Tower building blocks away. Large planters and fresh flowers transformed the space into a Chinese oasis, with red umbrellas and large bronze sculptures dotting the landscape. No more than half of the tables were occupied. I heard my name and turned toward two women seated at a nearby table. One of them wore a turquoise top and oversized sunglasses. She waved me over. I was a little confused at first, because I wasn't expecting there to be three of us. They both stood as I approached. Emily Kantor was taller than her brother, extremely fit, and attractive in a natural way. Her arms were well-toned and her handshake firm.

"Thanks for joining me on such short notice," she said. "Meet my partner, Cecily."

Cecily and I shook hands. She too was tall, with long black hair and olive skin. Her eyes were topaz blue, the same color as her painted nails. She wore a fitted dress that made it very clear she was no stranger to exercise. She had a distinctively South American look about her.

"CC and I are heading back home to Montana tomorrow morning, but I wanted to talk to you before we left," Emily said.

"I've only been to Montana once," I said.

"How long ago?"

"Exactly twenty-five years ago, almost to the month."

"How is your memory so precise?"

"My father was turning fifty, and before that happened, he had set a goal of fifty before fifty. He wanted to have visited all fifty states before his fiftieth birthday. He had four left. Both Dakotas, Wyoming, and Montana. Big Sky Country was the last state we visited. I don't remember much about it, other than I had never seen so much open land in my life. Nothing but mountains and wide-open space."

"That's why we live there," Emily said. "No smog, no congestion. I haven't heard a horn or a siren in ten years. The noises we hear are the winds blowing across the plains."

"And the animals at night," Cecily chimed in. "The rumbling of the bison or the coyotes howling."

Emily placed her hands on Cecily's, and they smiled at each other.

"Montana is a long way from Chicago," I said.

"Long enough," Emily said. "Not too close, not too far. Just right."

"How did the two of you decide on Montana?" I asked.

"Emily was already living there," Cecily said. "We were friends at

Cal Berkeley. Reconnected after grad school. She invited me to come out for a weekend. I never left."

"I always wanted a place in Montana," Emily said. "Growing up under the microscope of Chicago, I felt so closed in and restricted. The pressure was constant, having to go to the right parties and hang around the right crowd. It was exhausting. Even at a young age, I knew that wasn't how I wanted to live. I was looking through a magazine one day and read this story about a family that had acquired a lot of land in Montana, because they loved how open it was and wanted to prevent developers from building on it. This family lived in New York City, but they wanted to be able to escape outdoors, so they bought hundreds of acres and built a working ranch. I cashed in some of my stock and did the same thing."

The waiter brought over several plates of dim sum and announced the barbecued pork buns, shrimp spring rolls, spicy beef pot stickers, and vegetable dumplings. I reached for the barbecued pork buns and vegetable dumplings.

"So, is it true what they say about Montana and fishing?" I asked. "It's illegal for married women to fish alone on Sundays and for unmarried women to fish alone at any time?"

Emily rolled her eyes. "It's true. It's arcane. It's ridiculous. And it's something we're working on getting changed."

"Do you fish?" I asked.

"All the time," she said. "Any day of the week and with whomever I choose, and I dare someone to say or do anything about it."

Cecily leaned in and kissed Emily on the cheek.

"I pity the game warden who makes the mistake of approaching you," I said.

"And so do I." Emily smiled.

We munched on the dim sum and washed it down with orange-infused iced tea and cucumber-and-lime water coolers.

"You said there was something you felt I needed to know about the investigation into your father's death," I said.

"There is," Emily said. "Simon and I have the same parents, but we couldn't be any more different."

"I kinda figured that out already," I said, smiling.

"I love my brother, but there are many things about him that I don't love."

"Such as?"

"His obsession with money. And it's hard to solely blame Simon, because he got a lot of that from my father. I took after my mother. She grew up a poor Jewish girl in Brooklyn, New York. Money was never important to her. We had it. She enjoyed what it afforded us, but she would have been just as happy had we not had any of it. She always taught us that our last name was something we inherited, not something we earned. She also reminded us that happiness should never be associated with things that others controlled. It's important to find it through kindness and personal exploration into our purpose. Simon wants to find out what happened to our father because there's a huge price tag on the outcome. I want to find out what happened because I think he was being taken advantage of, and that pisses me the hell off."

"Who do you think was taking advantage of him?"

"Who wasn't?" she said. "My father was a great businessman who made a lot of money. But just because you're great in business doesn't mean you're also great in making the best decisions in your personal life. I think my father became a target of young women who knew he was an easy mark."

"Do you have any proof of this?" I asked.

"Unfortunately, I don't."

"Do you have any names of the women?"

"I don't, but it shouldn't be difficult for a good detective like yourself to find out who they were."

"Any idea where I might start?"

Emily reached into her handbag sitting on the chair next to her, pulled out a folded piece of paper, and handed it to me. "That's the number for Bernadette Langstrom. She's been the head caretaker of our house in the Bahamas for the last twenty years. She first called me a little more than a year ago to tell me of her concerns."

"What were they?"

"That my father was hosting a new crowd at the house that came and went as they pleased, people that never would've been allowed access had my mother still been alive."

"Did she say what they were doing that made her so suspicious?"

"According to her sources on the island, they were doing lots of drugs and having sex parties, two things I had never known my father to be involved with. After the death of my mother, my father became a man I didn't know."

20

Delacorte had called and asked if I wanted to join him for a return visit to Falcon Fuel. I didn't mind getting an early start to my day since I had a one o'clock tee time at the Flossmoor Golf Club with my father's friend who worked as a lobbyist for AT&T. The gas station was packed with cars as I entered the lot, and Delacorte sat in his unmarked, waiting for me.

We walked into the store together. It looked worse than the last time we were there. A short man with a prominent belly stood behind the plexiglass shield. His heavy mustache covered most of his mouth, and his hair was so thick and shiny, it looked like a wig.

"We're looking for a Mr. Agarwal," Delacorte said.

"Who are you?" the man said in a tone that wasn't exactly friendly.

"The fuckin' police," Delacorte said, flipping out his shield.

"One minute," the man said. "I'll be right back." He ducked through a door adjacent to a wall of cigarettes and condoms, then returned shortly with a slender, bald man who wore wire-framed glasses and an ample smile.

"Good morning, gentlemen," he said. "I'm Rohan Agarwal. Is this related to the call earlier this week about the security footage?"

"It is," Delacorte said.

"I can help you," he said. "Do you want to see it?"

"We'd appreciate that," Delacorte said.

"I'll meet you at the door over there," Agarwal said, pointing toward the corner of the store at the end of a row of coolers.

We walked to the back of the store, and seconds later, Agarwal opened the door.

We followed him down a short, dark hallway and passed what looked like a bedroom on the right, then entered a tiny office. An old metal desk had been positioned in the center of the small room. Several monitors hung on the wall, streaming videos from various vantage points inside and outside of the gas station. Agarwal took a seat behind the desk and started typing on a keyboard.

"What was the day and time?" Agarwal said.

"Seven days ago," Delacorte said. "Twelve ten a.m."

Agarwal ran his fingers over the keyboard and clicked the mouse several times. "The system is a little slow," he apologized. "One more minute."

I looked up at the six monitors. All of the pumps were covered, as were the two entrances to the parking lot and the entire interior of the store. It would have been practically impossible for the driver to have avoided being captured on camera.

"Right there," Delacorte said. "Pause it."

The time stamp read 12:08:15 a.m. The Bentley pulled into the gas station from Vincennes Avenue with its headlights on. The last three digits of the license plate number matched Kantor's Bentley. It was his car.

A red Camaro was parked at one of the pumps with an older man standing beside it, holding down the nozzle. The Bentley pulled in on the other side.

"Do you have a camera with a better angle?"

"I'm sorry," Agarwal said. "But not on that side. This is the best we have."

The tape rolled for the next seven minutes. We could see the door open, and the driver get out and walk to the pump. It was obviously a male driver, but we couldn't make out much other than that. He finished pumping his gas, then got into the car. A few seconds later, his door opened, and he exited the car. He walked toward the entrance of the store. The cameras caught him clearly. He was young with a slender build, wearing a large, shiny necklace and a wifebeater. A long tattoo ran down the left side of his neck and halfway down his arm.

"Stop it there," Delacorte said. "Can you move any closer, so we can see his tattoo better?"

Agarwal tapped a couple of keys, and the video zoomed in a little, but not much. "That's the best I can do," he said.

It wasn't enough for us to clearly see the tattoo. It looked like maybe an anchor and chain, but the picture was too blurry to know for sure.

"Not the greatest," I said. "But it's something." I took out my phone and snapped a picture of the screen.

"Let it roll," Delacorte said.

The video continued to play. It was difficult to make out his face because of his baseball cap.

"Take another camera," I said. "You have one inside the shop, pointing toward the entrance. Let's see him come in."

"Let me find the right one," Agarwal said. He made some adjustments, and the video changed from the outside camera to one of the interiors. A new video popped up on the screen. He fast-forwarded the tape to the point where the driver was entering the store. He let it play. The driver walked through the door, his face still hidden underneath the flat bill of his cap. He walked to the counter and had an exchange with the cashier.

"Who is that working the register?" Delacorte asked.

"Ganesh," Agarwal said. "He only works the night shift."

Ganesh turned and pulled a pack of cigarettes from the shelf behind him. The driver then walked over to one of the coolers and pulled out what looked like a couple of bottles of beer. He returned to the counter. He and Ganesh had another short exchange. The driver made gestures with his hands as if they were having a disagreement, then he turned and walked out of the store. Ganesh watched him.

"Back to the outside camera," Delacorte said.

Agarwal went to work on the keyboard and brought up one of the exterior cameras. He rolled through the tape until it picked up the driver returning to the car. The driver got into the Bentley, then drove away.

"Can you get Ganesh on the phone?" I asked.

"Maybe," Agarwal said. "He's working his day job right now."

"What's that?"

"He drives for Uber and Lyft."

"Call him and see if he picks up," I said.

Agarwal took out his phone and dialed the number. He said something in a language I didn't understand, maybe Hindi, then handed the phone to me.

"Ganesh, we are investigating a stolen car," I said. "We're looking at the video of last Saturday night. You had a customer who came in during your shift. Thin Black guy wearing a baseball cap and white tank top with a large chain. He had a big tattoo on the side of his neck and arm. He came in just after midnight. It looked like the two of you had a disagreement. He was going to buy cigarettes and beer, then the two of you had words, and he walked out."

"I remember him," Ganesh said.

"What happened?"

"He looked really young. I told him I had to see some identification. He said he never been asked that before. I told him it was state law, and if I didn't see it, I couldn't sell it to him. I could lose my job if I didn't follow the rules. He said to me that he was the proper age. He told me to look at his ride. If he wasn't the proper age, would he be driving that? I looked outside. Very expensive car. I only see a car like that once or twice before. But I tell him, no matter how nice the car, I have to follow the rules. He get upset and leave the store and never come back."

"Had you ever seen him before?"

"Not that I remember, but I see so many customers, I'm not sure."

"And he never came back?"

"He drive away and leave for good."

"Did you get a good look at the tattoo on the left side of his neck?"

"It was big," Ganesh said. "It had two chains wrapped around each other, like DNA."

"DNA as in genetics?"

"Yes. Double helix. But I couldn't see what was at the bottom."

"Did you see any writing?"

"No words," he said. "Just letters, like they were base pairs."

"Base pairs?"

"You know, the base pairs for DNA."

"Are you some sort of scientist?" I said.

"Yes," Ganesh said. "I was a doctor back home in India, but too hard to pass the test here. I'm still trying. I knew it was a double helix as soon as I saw it. You can't miss it."

"Had you ever seen it before?"

"The double helix? Of course. Lots of times."

"No, what I mean is, had you ever seen it as a tattoo?"

"Never. First time."

"Thanks for your help," I said.

"Did the owner get his car back?" Ganesh asked. "Very nice car."

"He didn't," I said. "He's dead."

DELACORTE AND I HAD COME UP with a plan to try to identify the driver. He was going to talk to the gangs squad and see if any of them recognized the tattoo. Neither one of us had worked gangs, and there were so many new crews popping up all the time, we would need help from the cops who did this work every day. While Delacorte checked with his sources, I decided to go check with mine.

Lanny "Ice" Culpepper was the widely feared leader of one of the toughest, most murderous gangs in Chicago, the Gangster Apostles. Rumor had it that he had gotten the nickname Ice because he moved more crystal meth on the street in just a month than anyone else in the city moved in a year. I had also heard he had gotten the nickname as a teenager for his ruthless, cold-hearted manner of killing his enemies. Either way, with his vast, complicated network of street soldiers who had built his drug business into a multimillion-dollar empire, Ice knew what was moving on the street better than anyone.

Ice ruled his lucrative kingdom from a suite of offices located above Mr. Knight's Laundromat in one of the deadliest zip codes in the city, a neighborhood called K-Town. I didn't bother calling ahead, because once I pulled up out front, his security team and his phalanx of surveillance cameras would let him know in a matter of seconds that I had arrived. I parked next to a fire hydrant and didn't bother locking my car. The mayor's personal parking spot in front of city hall couldn't be safer.

Two armed men the size of Russian tanks patted me down, then allowed me to pass through the door and up the stairs, where I was met by Dexter Barnes, Ice's head of security, a man who only tipped the scale close to a hundred pounds because a quarter of it was the weight of his jewelry.

"You don't have an appointment," Dexter said, patting me down. "Chairman is busy today."

"I was in the neighborhood," I said. "Thought we might have a little tea."

Dexter smiled an array of gold-capped teeth and shook his head. "Man, you still got that mouth," he said.

"And both eyes and ears."

Dexter nodded for me to follow him. I walked down a short hallway, through a large reception area still helmed by the same well-appointed woman I had met on my first visit a couple of years ago, when I worked a case involving Ice's murdered nephew. She winked at me quickly as I walked by, and I replied in kind.

Ice's door was open, and he sat reclining behind his enormous hand-carved desk, talking on his cell phone. A large Picasso had been permanently centered on the near wall, surrounded by bookshelves crammed with rare editions of literary masterpieces. He ended his conversation abruptly with "I want a fuckin' answer before I take my next shit." He then rested his phone on his meticulous desk and said, "Now, you just think you can come up here anytime you want without making an appointment?"

"I thought maybe we had moved beyond those formalities."

"Assumptions don't always become realities."

"True, but according to Asimov, they are the windows to the world, and if you don't scrub them every once in a while, the light won't come in."

"Well, I got plenty of damn light in here already," he said. "I don't have time for your philosophical shit today. I'm busy. Tell me why you're here."

I took out my phone and pulled up the photo of the driver's tattooed arm. I pushed the phone toward Ice. "I'm looking for that tattoo," I said.

Ice picked up the phone, stared at it for a moment, then said, "I don't run no damn tattoo parlor."

As he continued examining the photo, I studied the new Basquiat hanging on the wall behind his desk. It was a colorful depiction of what looked like a human skull in a style that was unmistakably Basquiat. Heads and skulls had been an obsession of the late painter of Haitian and Puerto Rican descent. A Japanese businessman had paid $110 million at auction for one of the skull paintings. I wondered how much Ice had paid for his.

Ice caught me staring at the painting.

"I own five of his pieces," he said proudly. "I didn't care for his style much at first, then someone told me he was Black, and a lot of his art was about the underground culture. Our painters will never become commercially successful if we always set our goals to buy the old white masters and their protégés. So I also buy our people. That's the only way to drive up the market for them."

Burke had once told me that estimates put Ice sitting on more than a quarter of a billion dollars. No one knew the exact number, and he wasn't publicly flamboyant about his wealth, but the few who had been to his mansion in a gated cul-de-sac in suburban Burr Ridge said it made the White House feel small.

"Have you seen that tattoo before?" I asked. "Maybe it's gang-affiliated."

"I don't know anything about gangs," Ice said. "I run an organization."

"Understood," I said.

"And for the record, I've never seen it before," he said.

Ice nodded to one of his men posted in the corner of the office. The enormous man trudged his way over, and Ice passed him my phone. He looked at it carefully, nodded his lack of recognition, then handed the phone back to Ice.

"What's the business with the tattoo?" Ice asked.

"Less the tattoo and more who's walking around with it," I said. "The guy stole a Bentley Continental from the North Side."

"Nice ride. Business so slow, you're now chasing car thieves?"

"The owner of the stolen car died minutes before the car was taken. I think he was murdered, maybe by this guy with the tattoo."

"And the name of the car's owner?"

"Elliott Kantor."

Ice smiled. "The big kahuna," he said.

"You knew him?"

"Not personally. But everyone knew who he was."

"That tattoo isn't just any midnight special. It's a double helix."

"What the hell is a double helix?"

"The shape of our DNA under a microscope."

"You a damn scientist now?"

"Hardly. But someone who saw it recognized what it was."

"So it's a tattoo of DNA?"

"Or meant to look like that."

Ice picked up my phone and looked at the photo again pensively. "Text the photo to me," he said, returning my phone. "I'll ask around and see if anyone knows anything."

"Between you and me, Kantor really died from a bad dose of Molly that made his heart explode," I said.

Ice raised his hands, proclaiming innocence. "Not my trade," he said. "That was probably some Albanian shit."

"What makes you say that?"

"Because that's the shit they run through the nightclubs."

"Kantor didn't go to nightclubs," I said.

"Maybe *he* didn't, but you need to find out about the people he was partying with. Ten to one, the Albanians were supplying."

21

That night, Carolina and I sat on a bench facing Buckingham Fountain, watching fourteen thousand gallons of water shoot skyward every sixty seconds. Most of the tourists had either gone back to their hotel rooms to sleep off a long day of sightseeing or were finishing up a late meal at one of the popular restaurants they found on Tripadvisor. Several pedicabs lit up by flashing neon lights wheeled through Grant Park, carrying passengers around the fountain for photographs.

"Hard to imagine that just a few months ago, this same ground was covered in three feet of snow," Carolina said.

I ran through the park all winter, and not only had the snowfall blanketing the city been the worst we had seen in years but the fountain's striated basin had been continuously draped by a heavy necklace of menacing icicles.

"How much longer do you think you'll stay here?" I asked.

"Here tonight?" Carolina said.

"No, Chicago."

"I've thought about moving to other cities, but I like my job, I like my apartment, and I'd miss the restaurants. What about you?"

"I could see myself leaving one day," I said. "Not permanently, but maybe during the winter. That trip I took to Arizona last winter made me realize how nice it is to wake up in the winter and not have to wear three layers of clothes when I go outside."

"Would you want a place in Arizona?"

"Or the Sunshine State. I read somewhere that it had four times the number of golf courses as Arizona."

"I think you need to teach me how to play golf."

"Why would you want to subject yourself to that kind of torture?"

"Because I know how much you love it, and when we get old, I don't want to be a golf widow."

I welcomed the implication in her statement. Things had been going so well that I hadn't wanted to complicate the situation. We enjoyed being together and still having our own space to breathe, and I was still nervous as hell about proposing again. My therapist had explained it was important for me not to let the disappointment of my broken engagement to Julia be an obstruction to trying again with someone I loved and trusted.

"I found the case file on Thompson," Carolina said. "It's very thin for such an important person who died under those kinds of circumstances." She opened up her handbag and pulled out a folder, then handed it to me. "I made a copy for you."

I opened the folder. There were only three pages in the file, which immediately raised red flags. Thompson's case was definitely a heater, and it would've attracted a lot of attention and generated a serious amount of paperwork. I read the report. There wasn't much information that I hadn't already learned from Wolcott, other than that he was staying at the Four Seasons downtown and his phone wasn't found either at the apartment where his body was discovered or back in his hotel room. His wife said she had spoken with him a couple of times earlier that day and all seemed fine. Thompson was due to fly back home the next day, but the detectives hadn't been able to locate an airline reservation in his name. They were awaiting the autopsy results.

"There must be a shadow file," I said, closing the folder. "A case like this should have almost fifty pages of notes by now. Someone's gotta be keeping the real file under wraps."

"But who and why?" Carolina asked.

"That's what we need to figure out."

"We?"

My phone buzzed. It was Mechanic.

"I have an update for you on Monroe Connelly," he said.

I mouthed to Carolina that Mechanic was on the phone. "What's going on?" I asked.

"He's a really busy guy once he gets out of work," Mechanic said. "He makes a lot of stops before he heads out to the suburbs."

"What kind of stops?"

"Two consecutive afternoons, he stopped by a townhouse on North Dearborn. The sign on the door says it's the law offices of Eugene Andrade, Esquire. Lawyer work, I guess. Then this is the third night out of four that he's gone to a restaurant, walked out with bags of food, then drove over to a building in River North, parked, and went inside with the food."

"What's the address?"

"Give me a sec. I need to get out and take a look at the front door. I can't see it from where I'm sitting."

I heard the car door open and the rustling of the night breeze. A siren drove by, then faded away in the distance.

"400 West Huron," he said.

"Are you sure?"

"I wasn't a math genius in school, but I know how to read numbers of an address."

The address sounded familiar.

"Is that on the northwest corner of Sedgwick and Huron?" I said.

"Yup. Gray mid-rise building with lots of glass."

I knew why the address seemed so familiar. It was the same building Jenny Lee visited the night I followed her from the casino. She didn't live in that building. It was highly unlikely to be a coincidence that Jenny Lee's Maserati had been registered to Monroe Connelly, and Lee and Connelly just happened to be visiting the same building.

"Do you see a blue Maserati parked anywhere nearby?" I asked.

"Negative," Mechanic replied.

"That's the same building Jenny Lee walked into the night I talked to her."

"Sounds like somebody's up there having a good time."

"Is Connelly still in the building?"

"Yup. It's been just over an hour. He's usually out by an hour and a half, then he drives home."

"Where's his house?"

"Out in River Forest, just past Oak Park. He must be a damn good lawyer, because his house is about the size of an elementary school. And this is the second vintage car I've seen him drive. The other day, he was in a black '69 Mustang. Tonight, he's in an old black Jag. You're a car guy. You'd appreciate his style."

"Take a pic and send it to me," I said, wondering if the cars were fully original or if they had been restored with newer parts. Some guys liked to fully restore their cars. I preferred them untouched and just as they were when they came off the assembly line. An old collector had told me after I bought my first classic, "A car is only original once."

"Want me to stick with him?" Mechanic said.

"Yup, and be on the lookout for Jenny Lee. See if he makes any other stops before he gets home."

I looked down at my watch. It was a little past ten o'clock. If

Jenny was working tonight, she'd still be on her shift at the casino. If she was there with Connelly, then things had just gotten a lot more interesting.

I SAT AT MY COMPUTER in my apartment, reading about Bishop Thompson. There were hundreds of mentions of his unexpected death, but not one story included the details of where he was found or how. In a city where leaks were as common as a cold and deals were made behind bulletproof doors, it was impressive that someone had been able to keep such a tight lid on everything for so long.

I looked for anything on social media or in the gossip columns that might've alluded to a less spiritual side of Thompson, but couldn't find anything. There was no mention of a mistress, domestic violence, or unclaimed children. Except for the complaints about his lavish spending and concerns about whether his church should be allowed to keep its tax-exempt status, Thompson checked out clean.

I picked up my phone and sent another text message to Malcolm Boyd. It had been a couple of days since our last text exchange. Maybe a little nudge late at night might get his attention. Just as I turned my attention back to the computer screen, my phone buzzed with a notification. I was hoping Boyd had responded, but it was Mechanic.

> He left the building alone. No sign of Jenny Lee or a blue Maserati. He just walked into a mansion a few blocks west of the other building.

I dialed Mechanic's number, and he answered right away.

"Where is he now?" I asked.

"Huge house on the corner of North Kingsbury. 701. The front of the house covers the entire block."

"Was he by himself?"

"Yup. Parked his car, walked up to the house, and as soon as he got on the landing, the door opened."

"Could you see who opened it?"

"Not sure, but I think it was a woman. He walked in, and the door quickly closed behind him."

"Has he ever gone to this house before?"

"First time I've followed him here."

"Stick with him. Let me know when he leaves."

I got up from my computer, walked into the living room, and turned on the TV. I would catch another airing of ESPN's *SportsCenter* or see what the Golf Channel was offering up. ESPN was showing the daily top ten, so I stuck there. The countdown was already on number six, and a golfer on the Champions Tour, who had a hole in one the day before, scored another hole in one in the subsequent round, making him only the second PGA golfer in history to score a hole in one in consecutive rounds. Number five was a baseball highlight of a player who had accomplished the rare feat of stealing home, one of the most difficult and rarest things in the game to do. Then it got down to number four. It was during the time-out of an NBA game, and two fans had been selected to compete against each other for a pair of airline tickets. They had to push a trunk that was on wheels for the full length of the court, while at the same time balancing a basketball on top of the trunk. If the ball fell, they had to go back to the starting line and begin again. Once they got to the other end of the court, they had to stop the trunk at a mark about eight feet from the basket, then shoot. The first one to make the basket won the tickets. The competition was between a tall teenage girl and a middle-aged businessman type who took off his suit jacket before the race began. They both made it to the other end without their ball falling off the trunk. They started shooting toward the basket at the same time, and the balls collided in midair, then fell to the ground. They ran and collected their balls and hustled back to the shooting marks and shot again. Same result. They collected their respective balls and raced back to the mark. This time, both balls dropped through the hoop nearly at the same time, and they got stuck in the net, neither ball falling to the ground. It looked like they both had gone through the rim at the same time, but on slow-motion replay, it was apparent the girl's ball went through first. Once the stadium announcer declared her the victor, the lids of both trunks flew open. A star player from each of the opposing teams had been stowed away in the trunks, and they jumped out and shocked the girl and the businessman with big hugs and roars from the crowd. That's what got me thinking.

I went back to my computer and loaded the video from Kantor's building that night. I fast-forwarded to the arrival of the Amazon van. I watched the driver get out of the car, then pull the trunk down the back ramp. I paid closer attention than I had before, and this time noticed that while he had wheeled the trunk, his body movements indicated that he struggled a little with its weight. Then I realized the mistake I had made earlier. I never watched the Amazon driver once he was inside the building.

It took me a while of going through all of the video clips, but I finally found the footage of the driver entering the building. He took a right once inside, which meant he was heading to Kantor's apartment. I cursed myself. I knew better than this. The answer had been right in front of me, but I had missed it because I was so intent on looking for someone else.

I watched the driver return to the lobby several minutes later, then walk out the door and to his van. He had been in and out in less than five minutes, but when he returned, he didn't need to roll the trunk back up the ramp. It was light enough for him to lift and drop it through the side sliding door of the van. I was convinced the Amazon driver had delivered a live person inside that trunk, the same person who had gone into Kantor's apartment and likely left in the Bentley.

My phone buzzed. It was Mechanic.

"He's just leaving," Mechanic said. "By himself. Doesn't look as neat as he did when he went in."

"What do you mean?"

"His shirt looks a mess, half tucked in, like he got dressed really quick. The flap on his left jacket pocket isn't right either. His hair looks like he just woke up."

"Anything else not seem right?"

"He walked the wrong way when he got outside, then turned around and walked to his car."

"Maybe he's been drinking or something. If he stops anywhere else before he goes home, let me know."

"If he doesn't get pulled over by the cops first."

I explained to him my theory about the Amazon driver and delivering the car thief in the trunk.

"Did the cameras catch the plate of the van?" Mechanic asked.

"That would be too easy," I said. "Unfortunately, they were pointed in the wrong direction. Tomorrow I'm going to some of the nearby businesses and see if any of their cameras caught it."

"I know it was a nice car, but it's hard to believe that someone killed him just to steal it, then strip it for parts."

"I agree. I think there was something else going on. I just can't figure out what that something is."

22

Monday morning, I took Stryker for a leisurely two-mile run along the lake. He was a fair-weather companion, only wanting to join me when the weather was just right and there weren't too many people on the path. The sun was well into its ascent, effortlessly burning the haze off the lake. The conditions couldn't have been more perfect. Once we reached the path, we headed south toward Museum Campus. Stryker stayed focused on what was ahead of us, and the cars zipping by on Lake Shore Drive didn't distract or bother him. We made it to the Field Museum in about twenty minutes, then took the tunnel under the drive and emerged in the middle of Grant Park. I took Stryker off his leash in the open field so he could bark and chase seagulls.

My cell phone buzzed with a text message. It was Malcolm Boyd.

> I don't need to speak to you about the situation. I already talked to the police.

I texted back. I know you've talked to them. I just have a few questions. It won't take much of your time.

Stryker ran across the field toward a black Labrador whose

owner had also let run free. The two met toward the middle of the field, stared each other down, nose to nose, then started their game of chase.

Boyd texted me back. Still not interested. The issue is over. I'm too busy for all this.

I thought this was a strange response. If he already talked to the police, how could a five-minute chat be much of an inconvenience? My gut started tingling.

I sent another text. Did you know Keegan Thompson?

A thought came to me, so I dialed the number of my contact inside the ME's office to see if she could help me with the autopsy report. She told me the autopsy hadn't been completed yet, so there wasn't a report. That was all she knew at the moment, but when she found out more, she'd give me a call.

I walked toward the center of the field, where Stryker and the Labrador were on the ground, rolling over each other, having the time of their lives. The other dog's owner met me nearby. She was a tall woman, wearing bright turquoise tights and a Cubs baseball cap with a long blond ponytail coming out of the back. She had the body of a runner.

"Your dog is the cutest," she said. "What's his name?"

"Stryker," I said. "How about yours?"

"Rex."

"No question, they like each other."

"You come here often?" she asked.

"Every once in a while," I said. "When he's in the mood."

"My name is Karla Coe," she said, extending her hand.

"Ashe," I replied.

We shook hands. Her grip was firm. She looked like she was in her early thirties.

Stryker and Rex went chasing after birds. We instinctively walked in their direction. My phone buzzed. Boyd responded, I don't know who the fuck you are. Leave me the fuck alone. This is the last time I'm gonna tell you this.

"Everything okay?" Karla asked.

"Just dealing with someone with a limited vocabulary," I said. "Two f-bombs in one text message."

Karla laughed softly. "My daily life," she said.

"Really?"

"I'm a lawyer. I don't know what a day would be like without hearing an f-bomb."

"What kind of lawyer?" I asked.

"Public defender."

Stryker and Rex chased off one bird, spotted another, and ran toward their next victim, who was also sure to fly away just in time.

"You work with some rough people," I said.

"As rough as the people I worked with when I was doing corporate law," she said. She turned and pointed toward the downtown office buildings towering above us. "Ruthless lives on both sides of the spectrum. Those starched shirts and ties up there are as ruthless as the people in the streets. Maybe worse."

"Facts," I said. "So you went from a high-priced fancy firm to defending petty thieves and drug dealers?"

"Accused murderers and carjackers too," she said, smiling. "No such thing as a boring workday for me."

"How do you feel about defending repeat offenders?" I asked.

"Everyone's innocent until proven guilty beyond a reasonable doubt, right? Everyone has a right to counsel, even those accused of the most heinous crimes. At least, those are the things my law school professors drilled into us. Since joining the public defender's office, most of my clients have been totally innocent of many of the charges filed against them by the State's Attorney's Office. Prosecutors throw the book at my clients hoping they'll take a quick plea, so they won't have to spend time trying the case."

"You ever plea out?"

"Only when my client confides in me that they're guilty, and only after I negotiate the best deal I can get."

We walked toward the dogs, who had now found another group of birds to torment.

"So, what do you do?" she asked.

"Play as much golf as I can."

"My father's a big golfer. He taught me how to play when I was a little girl. I played all the way to my junior year in high school, then quit."

"What happened?"

"I fell in love with the captain of the football team, and nothing else mattered. Gave up golf, my grades tanked, and I was one suspension away from being expelled."

"And who says there's no such thing as redemption? Look at you now. Turned it all around, went to law school, made good coin at a fancy firm, and now you're helping the least of us."

"That's one way of looking at it," she said.

"What's another way?"

"I was really close to losing everything. My parents threatened to disown me. My friends no longer wanted me around. And my boyfriend decided he liked my best girlfriend more than he liked me. I came close to doing something really bad to myself. Then I heard a song on the radio, and it changed my life."

"What was the song?"

"'Independent Women' by Destiny's Child."

"I like that song too," I said. "Anthemic."

"Those three girls changed my life. Even though they broke up as a group, every year without fail, I go to one of their solo concerts."

I looked down at her left hand and didn't notice a ring. I thought about borrowing a line from Beyoncé's "Single Ladies" but thought better of it. Instead, I asked, "What time does your workday start? Shouldn't you be heading down to the County?"

"I take one weekday off every month so I can get caught up on my regular life. Today's that day."

Stryker and Rex chased away the last group of birds, then ran back to us. They stood at our feet and looked up, as if to say they had had enough.

"Well, Karla, nice meeting you," I said.

"You too, Ashe," she said. "Maybe we'll meet here again. Rex usually doesn't get along too well with other dogs, but he's found a friend in Stryker."

"Now that the weather's turned, we'll be getting out more often," I said. I put Stryker back on his leash, and she did the same with Rex.

"So, besides golf, what else do you do?" she asked.

"Search for the bad guys that you end up defending."

Stryker started tugging at his leash. He was ready to go.

"You're a cop?" she asked.

"Used to be. Now I take on cases privately when something interests me."

"You working on something now?"

I nodded. "Supposed to be, but I feel like it's working me."

"I know the feeling," she said. "Maybe we'll meet up for drinks or something and exchange war stories."

"If we don't meet up in court first."

Stryker barked one last time at Rex, then pulled me away.

I SPOTTED BOYD COMING OUT of LA Fitness, all muscle and lots of swagger. He was halfway through a protein bar, and every time he brought it up to his mouth, his biceps blew up like balloons. I stepped up to him as he walked into the parking lot.

"You have a license to carry all that muscle?" I said.

He turned and looked at me dismissively.

"Who the fuck are you?" he said.

"Your vocabulary could use a little expansion," I said. "You find a way to work 'fuck' into every sentence."

"Like I can find a way to work my fist against your wise-ass mouth."

"You'll never get it there," I said. "Too slow. I'll crack one or two of your left ribs just as your punch is badly missing."

I could tell in his eyes that he was considering his options. His body tensed for a moment, then his massive shoulders relaxed. "What the fuck do you really want?" he said.

"To know what your relationship was with Keegan Thompson."

"Who said we had a relationship?"

"You had something. One of the country's wealthiest preachers just randomly decides to break into your apartment, put on some women's lingerie, and die in your bed? You expect me to believe you didn't know him?"

"Why is this any of your fuckin' business?"

"Because I work for a family whose father was found in his bed, tied up the same way. They wanna know what happened to their father. I think the two deaths might be related."

"So you're not working for the cops?"

"Those days are long over."

"Follow me," Boyd said.

We walked away from the building, across the parking lot, and to a small bench facing the cluster of enormous residential towers of Lake Meadows. Cars and buses sped by along King Drive.

Once we had settled, Boyd said, "Man, I ain't tryna get in no shit. My life is on the right track, and I don't want nothing to mess it up."

I nodded.

"If I tell you what I know, will that stay between us?" he said.

"We never had this conversation," I said.

Boyd turned and looked off into the distance. His face tightened.

"I was at a bar about a year ago with my girl," he said. "We were just chillin'. A few drinks, good conversation. She got up to go to the bathroom. This guy comes over and stands next to me and orders a drink. Good-looking guy. Dressed nicely. He spoke, we started talking. Nothing serious. I remember he had on a really nice gold Rolex. He got his drink and said goodbye. Then my girl came back. That was it. I didn't think much of it. The next morning, I was looking for my keys. I checked my coat I was wearing the previous night. I ran my hand in one of the pockets, and there was a business card in it. It was blank, except for a handwritten note that said 'Enjoyed meeting you. Give me a call.' There was a phone number. I didn't know what to think. I put the card in my wallet and tried not to think about it. My girl and I had been dating for about six months, and I had been faithful."

Boyd bit his lip softly and shook his head. I just listened and gave him space.

"Two weeks later, I was taking out my credit card to pay for groceries," Boyd continued. "The card fell out. That night after my girl left my apartment, I called the number." Boyd sighed. "A few weeks after that, KT was back in Chicago and in my bed."

I sat there and looked out onto King Drive as a growing stream of traffic raced by. People were going on about their days, heading to doctor appointments, picking up kids from basketball practices, rendezvousing with secret lovers—all of us scampering around like mice in the never-ending maze of life. Millions of people called the same city their home, yet for most of us, our lives would never intersect in any substantial way other than cars waiting at a stoplight or bodies passing through a closing train door.

"So what happened that night?" I asked.

"It was some strange shit," Boyd said. "KT and I had only been together once before that night. We kept in touch, but he was always busy, and I sure as hell didn't have the money to fly out to LA. But he said he would be coming back to Chicago soon, and when he did, we would get together. So he called me about a month ago and said he had to come and guest-preach at a church on the South Side. We set it up. He was having dinner with the host preacher and the first lady on Saturday night, then preaching on Sunday. We couldn't get together on Sunday because he had to leave right away after he finished preaching to get back to LA. So we agreed to meet after he had dinner Saturday night. I had a personal training session with a client that night, but I left KT a key so he could get into my apartment and be there when I got home."

Boyd closed his eyes and lowered his head. I looked down and noticed his fists balled up tightly.

"When I got home, he was dead," Boyd said. "In my bed, tied up. Dead."

I gave him a moment before saying, "Did you talk to him after he had gotten to your apartment?"

"No, I was in my session," Boyd said.

"This tying-up and cross-dressing is something he liked to do?" I asked.

Boyd nodded. "It was his thing, not really mine. He liked the role-playing. He said it made him orgasm better."

"Did you know he was married with children?"

"Of course I did. He didn't hide it."

"Did you have a problem with that?"

"In what way?"

"In any kind of way. I don't know. Did that make you hesitant, getting involved with him?"

"Not at all," Boyd said. "He was living his truth."

"Which was?"

"He loved his wife and kids. He was attracted to his wife. But he was also attracted to men. Most men are attracted to other men; they just don't act on that attraction. They keep it hidden. But he wasn't gay."

"I don't understand."

"Most people don't. Just because you're attracted to someone of the same sex doesn't mean you're gay. That's a bunch of shit. There was never anything between us more than touching. And it was only me doing the touching. He never touched me. That was part of his deal. He told me from the beginning, he wasn't interested in all of that. He wanted me to dominate him and get him aroused. That's what got him off. I know gay. He wasn't gay. He was just freaky. Lots of people are; they just don't show it."

We sat there for a moment, watching several passengers disembark from a bus that had stopped just a few yards away. I wondered where these people were going, what their houses or apartments looked like.

"What do you think happened?" I asked as the bus pulled off.

Boyd shook his head. "I have no fuckin' clue. It's some crazy shit. All I can come up with is someone had to be there. Can't nobody tie themselves up like that. Not even Houdini."

"You have security cameras?"

"There's one outside and one in the lobby, but they haven't worked for a while. The landlord is too cheap to get them fixed."

"Has anyone ever broken into your apartment before?"

"Never."

"How many apartments in your building?"

"Just two. I'm upstairs, and Mr. Jerome is downstairs."

"Did you talk to Mr. Jerome?"

Boyd nodded. "He says he saw one man, who he hadn't seen before, go up the stairs. He said he didn't say anything, because he heard keys jingling, so he figured it was a friend of mine. He said about fifteen minutes later, he heard voices, then footsteps. He looked out his peephole and thought he saw another man going up the stairs, but he didn't see the man's face. Said he just saw his black boots."

"Did he tell this to the police?"

"None of it," Boyd said, shaking his head. "And he ain't got plans to say anything either. When he was younger, he did a twenty-year bid for armed robbery. Been out for about fifteen years. He doesn't want anything to do with trouble or to get mixed up with the cops. And I don't blame him. You get the wrong cop, and he'll fuck you."

23

After several text message exchanges, Lacey Vinton, Manny Acevedo's ex-girlfriend, and I agreed to meet at the Foxtrot market in Streeterville, a couple of blocks from my building. Everything seemed to be out in full force: the sun, the pampered dogs, and lots of tanned flesh. I had snagged the last outdoor table, next to a woman who looked like she hadn't eaten in a month and should be featured on a billboard for dermatology malpractice. I tried not to stare at her plump lips, but they were too much of a spectacle to ignore.

Lacey Vinton was much younger than I had expected and extremely easy on the eyes. She wore a tight, cropped, backless green halter top and a pair of acid-washed jeans that looked like they would have to be peeled off that night for her to get in bed. Her dark hair had been pulled back into a long ponytail, putting the beauty of her tanned face on full display.

"Thanks for meeting with me," I said as she took her seat. "I won't take up much of your time."

She looked down at her phone. The bejeweled protector shined in the sun. "I still have another hour before I need to leave for work," she said.

"What do you do?"

"I'm a docent at the Art Institute."

She must've read the slight adjustment in my expression, because she said, "Don't worry, I don't dress like this when I'm giving a tour."

"Would be worth the price of admission," I said.

She unleashed a smile that I was certain had crushed at least a thousand hearts. "Kids need to learn it's cool to like art," she said, "and you don't have to be a hundred years old to appreciate or understand it."

"I'm willing to bet that you get more attention than those old masters hanging on the walls."

"You'd be surprised," she said. "But it's not really the kids. It's more the teachers. Kind of creepy when they ask me for my number right in front of their students."

I looked at how snug her top fit and found it completely understandable why they would shoot their shot.

"So you and Manny were seeing each other," I said.

"Only for a minute," she said. "Nothing too serious. One day, I was heading home from work, and we sat next to each other on the train. We had a nice conversation. He was funny. He asked me if I wanted to grab something to eat. He seemed nice enough, so I agreed."

"How long ago?"

"About two years."

"He's been married for six."

"That's why it didn't last long. I ended it once I found out. I didn't have a problem with him being older. I've always liked older men. But I didn't want to get caught up in some entanglement. I have friends who dated married men. It was nonstop drama. I didn't need any of that in my life."

"Did you know he worked for one of the richest men in Chicago?"

"Not at first," she said. "He told me he worked logistics for a private company. I never really pushed him about his job. I didn't care what he did. He was cute and nice and made me laugh. It wasn't like I was trying to marry him, so his job didn't matter."

"How did you find out who he worked for?"

"It was All-Star weekend, and all the NBA players were in town for the game. We were having drinks one night, and his cell rang. He answered it, had a quick conversation, then got up and said he had to go. His boss needed him. I called bullshit on him. What boss needs someone at one in the morning? He said he was on call to the owner of the company, and the owner had just decided he wanted to go to Jordan's party. I told him I wanted to go too. He told me it wasn't a good idea. He had to drive his boss, then take him into the party and stay with him. I figured his boss had to be someone important, so I asked his name. He told me."

"Did you know him?"

Lacey smiled. "Of course," she said. "I walk by his name almost every day. The Kantor Wing of Contemporary Art. He's a legend in the art world."

"Did you ever meet him?" I said.

"Only once," she said. "By accident. He came to the museum for a board meeting. I was filling in for a friend working the morning shift. We were in the elevator together. He was wearing a name badge. He was very nice. Asked me about my work and what my favorite painting was."

"What did you say?"

"*Boy and Dog in a Johnnypump*."

"Basquiat."

"You know his art?"

"Know it but can't afford it. That's the painting the billionaire Griffin bought for a hundred million in the middle of the pandemic."

"It's really disgusting how much cash these guys have," she said. "They have money to burn. You like Basquiat's work?"

"For sure. I like his philosophy and message as much as the art itself. He was the people's artist. Focused on New York City street life. Interested in painting what he called the saints and heroes of the street. I read somewhere that he wanted to put these skeletal male figures in some type of regal history to be admired and remembered."

"I've seen the *Johnnypump* painting a hundred times, and each time I've seen something different in it," she said. "Too bad that's the only piece we have of his. Well, sort of have."

"What do you mean?"

"The museum doesn't actually *own* the painting. It was loaned to us for an indefinite period of time so the public can enjoy it. He's done that with a lot of his collection."

"'Among the rich you will never find a really generous man even by accident. They may give their money away, but they will never give themselves away; they are egotistic, secretive, dry as old bones.'"

"Well done," she said, smiling. "I feel like I've heard that before."

"G. K. Chesterton, English writer, philosopher, and art critic."

"A private investigator who quotes philosophy."

"And plays the fiddle with his teeth."

"Are you serious?"

"No, but it sounded good."

She laughed.

"Did Manny ever talk about Kantor?" I said.

"Not really. He would just say if he was busy with the boss or had to run an errand for him. He said sometimes Kantor could be grumpy, but overall, he was a nice man. Said he treated him more like family."

"Did Manny ever talk about Kantor's extracurricular activities?"

"What kind?"

"The adult kind."

She shook her head. "Never."

"Nothing about the Bahamas or trips on his private plane?"

"Manny said he had a big estate down there, but that's about it. What do you think happened to him?"

"Between you and me?"

She nodded.

"I think someone killed him," I said.

"For his money?"

"High up on the list. Most murders are related to money, sex, or revenge. Did you ever hear Manny talking to Kantor on the phone?"

"Several times," she said.

"Anything catch your attention?"

She thought for a moment, then said, "Not really. But I wasn't paying much attention, to be honest."

Lacey started gathering her belongings. I found myself staring at her, thinking how lucky Manny had been, even if only for a short time.

"You know, there was one thing that was funny, now that I think of it," she said.

"What's that?"

"I remember one time Manny and I were just talking. I don't remember what we were talking about, but Manny was laughing to himself. I asked him what was so funny. He said something I said reminded him of a conversation he overheard. His boss had called someone, and when the other person answered, he spoke in a soft voice and called himself Plutus."

"Plutus?"

"Yup."

"Are you certain?"

"One hundred percent. Because I asked Manny if he knew who Plutus was, and Manny got confused with Brutus from the cartoon *Popeye*. I told him Plutus was a Greek god. I joked that his boss must've had a real ego to refer to himself as a god. But to each his own. I guess we all can be gods and goddesses in our own minds. We have that right."

"Especially you," I said.

She smiled. "You're kinda cute."

"So I've been told."

"And modest too."

"Honesty is the best policy."

"You know, we could have a lot of fun," she said.

"We could, if I wasn't already taken," I said.

"Are you in love?"

"Something like that."

"Is she in love with you?"

"I hope so. Otherwise, the dream is over. Little hurts deeper than the raw death of an illusion."

Lacey smiled and stood up, and the traffic on McClurg Street came to a stop. "I work at the museum from one to five, Monday, Thursday, and Friday. If you're ever in the mood to vibe over some Basquiat, lemme know."

"And if you ever need a mystery solved, I'm your guy," I said. I stood and extended my hand. She grabbed my shoulders instead, pulled me into her, and kissed me on the cheek. She winked, then turned and walked down McClurg. Even the best-in-class Shih Tzus and Pomeranians stood still and admired the view.

THAT EVENING, I SAT IN my office, staring at my evidence wall. I had pinned up Thompson's photo next to Kantor's. I stared at the similarities of their deaths that I had written beneath their pictures. But I didn't have anything that directly connected them. Mechanic walked in, grabbed a cold Sam Adams out of the fridge, and took a seat across the desk.

"Plutus?" he said, looking at the wall.

"Greek god of wealth," I said. "That's what Kantor called himself."

"Like a nickname?"

"I'm not sure. A gorgeous ex-mistress of his night guy, Manny, told me that's how Kantor referred to himself while talking on the phone."

"Did she laugh when he said it?"

"She didn't hear it, but knowing her, she probably would have. Manny told her that Kantor had called himself that."

"Why are rich people so damn crazy?"

"Because they have everything else in the world they want, so they need something different to keep themselves entertained."

"But everybody's got problems, I guess."

We sat there in silence for a few moments, then I explained to him my conversation with the trainer Malcolm Boyd.

"You believe him?" Mechanic asked.

"I do."

"You don't find the whole situation a little weird?"

"I do."

"You think there really was a third guy?"

"I do. And maybe something didn't go as planned."

"Or maybe it did."

"Which is why finding the third guy could help fill in some of these gaps," I said. "Let's take a little field trip."

"Where?"

"Back to the scene of the crime. Kantor's apartment building. Let's do some old-fashioned detective work."

"Which means?"

"Knock on some doors and ask some questions. People know a lot more than they think they know."

AN HOUR LATER, WE STOOD on the porch of a salmon pink brick home just a few doors down from the Manor on Janssen Avenue. Two planters full of purple and red petunias lined the railing leading up to a fire-engine red door. A heavy brass knocker in the shape of a boar's head hung prominently below the number 2334. I pulled it back and tapped softly, trying not to scare whoever might be inside. Seconds later, we heard the lock slide back and the door creak open. A short, older woman with a mash of silver hair welcomed us with a friendly smile.

"How can I help you gentlemen?" she said.

She had a trace of an accent. Maybe Slavic. I wasn't sure which country.

"We're canvassing the neighborhood, trying to find information about the apartment building a few doors down at the corner of the street," I said.

"Are you looking to buy?"

"Nothing like that," I said. "I'm a private detective."

I took out one of my cards and handed it to her. She studied it, then looked up at Mechanic.

"He works with me," I said. "He just doesn't speak much."

"Did something bad happen?" she said.

"There was a car stolen from the building several weeks ago. We're trying to identify who might've stolen it, so we're just asking the neighbors to see if they saw anything suspicious."

"This is the first I'm hearing of it," she said. "I'm surprised such a thing could happen here. This is a really quiet street. I've been here longer than you are old. Never any problems."

I pulled out my phone, brought up a photo of a Bentley that looked like Kantor's, and showed it to her. She stepped closer, tilted her head back slightly, and adjusted her large glasses as she examined the photo.

"I'm afraid I'm not going to be of much help," she said. "I don't know anything about cars. I couldn't tell one make from another. I don't pay much attention to them. What night was it stolen?"

"May second."

She shook her head. "I'm sorry, gentlemen. I can barely remember what happened two days ago, let alone a couple weeks ago. But I know someone who might be able to help. My neighbor Emily, four houses south of me, tends to stay on top of these things. And she's a lot younger, with a much better memory."

"Thanks for all your help," I said. "We'll go and talk to Emily now before it gets too late."

"Unfortunately, you won't find her there," she said. "Her mother broke her hip a few days ago and had to have surgery, so Emily flew out to Phoenix to be with her. But when she comes back, I'll give her your card and have her call you."

"We'd appreciate that," I said. "And if you think of anything or hear from any of the neighbors, please give me a ring."

"Will do."

She smiled again and closed the door. Mechanic and I spent the next half hour walking up and down the street, knocking on doors, talking to people, approaching neighbors who had just come home and were parking their cars. They all said mostly the same thing: This was a very quiet street, and they were shocked someone had their car stolen. Did this mean they should be worried about more crimes coming to the neighborhood? It wasn't until we were almost two hours into our search that we got a hit. Miles Carthew lived at the opposite end of the street. He was a divorced software analyst who worked long hours downtown and lived alone with his pug, Felix. He had never seen the blue Bentley, but he did remember something strange one night a couple of weeks ago.

"I was walking Felix up to Fullerton," he said. "I typically walk up the west side of the street, but Felix had gotten neutered earlier that day, and the vet didn't want him getting excited and jumping around. There was another dog about ten yards away, heading in our direction. Felix is really friendly, so I knew he'd want to jump all over the other dog. I crossed the street to stop that from happening. We were walking along the side of that apartment building, just a few yards from reaching Fullerton, when we almost got hit by a door I didn't even know existed."

"What do you mean?" I said.

"I've walked by that building a thousand times, and I never knew there was a door on the side of it. Suddenly it swung open out of nowhere and almost hit us. A small man rushed out and headed south on Janssen."

Mechanic and I locked eyes without saying anything. We both knew it was Kantor's secret door.

"You remember what he looked like?" I asked.

"Not really," Carthew said. "He was wearing all black. Jeans, hoodie, boots—everything was black."

"Did you see his face?"

"Not much of it. He was moving so fast. I do remember he had a small diamond nose ring. It shined under the streetlight."

"Did he say anything?"

"Nope. He just put up his hand to apologize, turned around quickly, and kept going. And he had a funny walk."

"What do you mean?"

"He had a limp, like his hip was hurting." Carthew closed his eyes for a moment. "He was leaning to his left side."

"Do you remember the specific night this happened?"

"Not off the top of my head. Wait. Hold on for a minute." He pulled his phone out and slid through a couple of screens. "One second." He tapped the screen a couple of more times, then said, "May second."

I looked at Mechanic, then back at Carthew. "Are you sure that was the date?" I said.

"A hundred percent." He turned his phone so I could see the

calendar he had brought up. "Felix had his neuter appointment that morning."

"Do you remember what time it was that you saw the man leave the building?"

"Not exactly, but I know it was after ten and before midnight. I was at a dinner that night with one of our clients, and we left the restaurant just before ten. So I figure, by the time I got home and got Felix out, it had to be after ten o'clock."

"Did you see anyone else enter or leave the door that night?"

"Nope. Felix and I walked up to Fullerton, turned around, and went home."

Nothing like good old-fashioned detective work. Carthew had just helped confirm the timeline.

24

The next day was a momentum day, something that—if you're lucky—happens when the pieces you've been studying, turning, and scratching your head about suddenly start to fall into place. I had just picked up my '86 Porsche Turbo from storage when my cell rang. It was Ice.

"Sounds like you're on a racetrack," he said. "Surprised you're not on the golf course, weather like it is."

"I'm supposed to be playing tomorrow," I said. "And I'm not on a racetrack. Just picked up my car for the summer."

"A car for the summer," Ice said. "Pretty damn fancy for a private detective."

"A private detective whose parents both went to Ivy League schools."

"Which makes you a flunky, since you broke tradition and went to a regular school."

"True, but a flunky who can hit a golf ball three hundred yards."

"And I can shoot an apple from the same distance."

"Mediocre," I said. "I've seen Mechanic hit a seedless grape at that distance."

"Bullshit," Ice said. "The man is good, but ain't nobody got gun skills like that. Not even them damn snipers in the army. Anyway, I'm calling about your kid with the tattoo. I found him."

"Took you long enough."

"I got an organization to run, man. Playin' cops and robbers ain't high on my list. His name is Jalen Duncan. They call him Puddin'. He's a twenty-three-year-old knucklehead out in the streets, trying to make a name for himself."

"Is he affiliated?"

"Nope. Don't know which gang would want his sorry ass. Used to work at an auto parts store til he got caught selling shit out the back of the store."

"You have an address for him?"

"He lives with his girlfriend, LaShonda Brooks, over in Chatham. But he's in and out most of the day and night."

Ice gave me the address. I could hear babies in the background.

"Sounds like you're in a nursery," I said.

"My great-nieces are with me for the day. Their mother dropped them off an hour ago, and they already tore up half the damn office."

I smiled, imagining Chicago's biggest gangster babysitting twin babies, the daughters of his nephew who had been murdered because he and his girlfriend had discovered the deceptions of her wealthy family.

"Are they talking yet?"

"And talking back. Smart, just like their father."

"You still miss him."

"Of course I do. Every day of my life."

"Thanks for the info. I'd like to see the girls one of these days."

"They spend a day with me once a month. Next time I have 'em, I'll let you know."

As soon as I got off the phone with Ice, I called Burke and told him about Duncan. He looped in Delacorte, and we agreed to put a team together and head over to the girlfriend's house to see if we could find him. Just as I was unlocking the door to my office, my phone rang. It was Kantor's assistant Pedro.

"You asked about the flight manifests for Elliott's plane," Pedro said. "I know you wanted six months, but I was able to get the last three months. They changed their computer system or something and can't find the other three months, but they're working on it."

"How many pages?"

"About twenty."

"Did you look at them?"

"Not really. I just got them in a few minutes ago."

"Can you send them to me right now?"

"They're on the way."

I walked back to my computer and found Pedro's email sitting at the top of my inbox. I opened it, then downloaded the attached manifests. I quickly scanned through the pages. There were twenty-two total. Each page represented a different flight. There was lots of information at the top of the page, including the flight date, departure, destination points, and times, as well as the pilots, crew, and passengers. I took each flight separately. Kantor was on board for at least half of the flights. I took out three colored highlighters. Any name except for Kantor's that I saw twice, I marked in blue. If a name appeared three times, I marked it in pink. If it appeared four times, I marked it in yellow. The most passengers a flight had was ten. That was on February 4, going from Chicago to Albany in the Bahamas. The plane came back to Chicago on February 12. All of the passengers returned. There were plenty of flights without Kantor. I already had the former football player Lance Greene on two of them. He went down both times with a woman named Fiona Manheim. I knew he wasn't married. Maybe it was his girlfriend. I kept reading and marking.

I made it to the seventh page. It was a flight from Chicago to

London. There was only one passenger: Monroe Connelly. He had flown over in March and turned around and flew back home the next day. I checked the other manifests. Connelly had taken three flights in the last three months. His last flight was in April. There were eight people on the plane, including Kantor. All men. The plane left April 4 and returned April 7. Connelly's name, however, was not on the manifest of the return flight. There could've been lots of reasons why he didn't fly back with everyone else, but I starred the flight anyway, just to follow up on it.

I had combed through half the flights when my phone rang. It was Delacorte.

"You want a ride to the party?" he said.

I thought about driving myself, then remembered I had the Porsche.

"I'm at my office," I said. "I'm ready to go."

"I'll be there in fifteen."

I took one last look at the manifests where I had highlighted Connelly's name. Something bothered me, but I couldn't put my finger on it. I put those manifests to the side. I'd take another look at them first when I got back.

WE PICKED DUNCAN UP WITHOUT incident. Of course, he tried running out the back door of the tiny bungalow-style house, only to run into six cops who had their guns raised and were itching for any small reason to pull the trigger. Duncan now sat alone in a small interview room in the Third District. Burke, Delacorte, and I stood in the observation room, watching him. He tried to look confident, but I could tell he was nervous by the way he was tapping his foot. Even the most hardened criminals try to play it tough, but they all have apprehensions before the initial interview.

"You go in first," Burke said to Delacorte. "We'll roll tape just in case he confesses. Push him as hard as you can, but don't back him into a corner screaming for a lawyer. Let's get as much as we can out of him right now."

"Plan B if he doesn't cooperate?" I said.

"Then you take a spin at him," Burke said. "You can be the good guy. Delacorte softens him up; you come in to close it."

"I'm getting nostalgic," I said. "The interview tag team. I miss the repertoire."

Burke rolled his eyes. Delacorte bumped my fist and left. We watched as he entered the room. Duncan remained slouched in the chair, seemingly unfazed.

"So, how did you get the name Puddin'?" Delacorte said, taking a seat across from Duncan. I already liked his style. Conversational. Disarming.

"Same way you got the name asshole," Duncan sneered.

Delacorte absorbed the jab and smiled. Professional. "So much for small talk, I guess," he said.

"I don't want no kinda talk," Duncan said. "Big or small. I ain't did shit. Let me the fuck go."

"You answer a few simple questions, and you'll be on your way."

"What kind of questions?" Duncan said. "You tryna set me up. I know how you crooked cops do."

"Not at all," Delacorte said, raising his arms in a surrender gesture. "You answer my questions truthfully, everything checks out, and you'll be good to go."

Duncan smirked and tipped his head back.

"Do you know a man named Elliott Kantor?" Delacorte asked.

"Nah. Never heard of him."

"You ever visit 1425 West Fullerton up in Lincoln Park?"

"What the fuck for? You must got bad eyesight." Duncan lifted up the back of his hand and pointed to it. "I ain't got no business on the North Side. Everything I need is south of Soldier Field."

Delacorte got the message and nodded. "You ever drive a Bentley before?"

"A Bentley? How the fuck I'm gonna get a whip like that? Maybe you ain't ever been to Chatham, but you ain't ever gonna see a car like that on our streets."

Delacorte smiled. Congenial. "Have you ever stolen a car before?"

"Man, what kinda questions is these? Fuck nah, I ain't stole no car."

Delacorte looked up from his notebook. "I'm sorry. We're looking into a burglary, so I need to ask these questions. I'm not trying to get you upset."

"Well, you are, because I was minding my own business, and you dragged me down here without telling me what was going on. Now you asking if I stole some damn car. What the fuck? I look like a car thief to you?"

"Just doing my job and covering all the bases," Delacorte said.

"Then do your job right and get the muthafucka down here that really stole the car. I ain't stole shit."

"I hear you loud and clear," Delacorte said, closing his notebook. "Anything else you wanna say?"

"Yeah. Can I get the fuck outta here now?"

Delacorte pushed his chair back from the table as if he were about to get up. Then he stopped and said, "Oh, one more question before I go. That tattoo on your neck and arm. What is it?"

"What the fuck that got to do with a stolen car?" Duncan said.

"Just curious," Delacorte said. "I've seen a lot of tats before, but nothing like that."

"A ship anchor wrapped with DNA," Duncan blurted out. "Ain't nuthin' out there like it. It's my original creation."

"Mean anything special?"

"Remain true to who you are, and that will always keep you anchored."

"Poetic," Delacorte said.

"Turn off the camera," Burke said to the officer at the controls. He nodded at me.

I left the observation room and entered the interview room. Duncan sat up in his chair when I entered. I took a seat next to Delacorte, opened up the thin folder I had carried in with me, then pulled out the photograph of Duncan in Falcon Fuel with his tat showing. I slid it across the table. Duncan looked at the photograph, and the cockiness quickly drained from his face.

"How about we have a little chat?" I said. "Toi et moi."

Duncan scrunched his face.

"My French is a little rusty," I said. "Translation: just you and me."

"Who the fuck are you?" Duncan said.

"Maybe the only person standing between you and a long trip downstate."

Delacorte stood up. "You've answered my questions," he said, "for now. As far as I'm concerned, you're free to leave." Delacorte walked out of the room.

Duncan looked at the open door, then back at me. He was calculating his next move.

"You walk through that door, and the second you step foot outside of it, they're gonna arrest you for burglary and suspicion of first-degree murder."

"Man, you talkin' some bullshit. I ain't murdered nobody."

"I know you didn't, but it's not me you need to convince. It's those guys outside with those shiny stars hanging around their necks. I can help you convince them."

"You ain't a cop?"

"Not anymore."

"Then what are you?"

"The closest thing you got to a savior without going to church. You tell me what really happened that night, and I'll talk to some people I know and see if we can work something out."

"Alright, man, fuck. I stole the car. Drove it a little and got rid of it. That was it. I didn't touch nobody. Didn't hurt nobody. Just took the car."

"How did you get it?"

Duncan sighed audibly and tilted his head to the side. "It was all a setup," he said. "I got paid to take the car and leave it."

That wasn't what I was expecting him to say. "Someone hired you to steal the car for them?" I asked.

"Pretty much."

"Who hired you?"

"I don't know."

"How can you not know who hired you to commit a crime?"

"Because that was the deal. I wouldn't know who hired me. I was supposed to get the job done, get paid, and that was it."

"Help me understand how this works."

"I got a message on Snapchat. It said if I wanted to make some quick cash, to call this number. I called the number and spoke to some girl. She told me she was pulling a prank on her friend's father. She wanted me to steal his new Bentley, drive it to the South Side, and leave it in an abandoned lot near Washington Park. Once I dropped the car off, I would get paid."

"How much?"

"Three stacks."

"That's a lot of money just to pull a prank. That didn't make you suspicious?"

"Man, I wasn't even thinking like that. I figured she rich. The other family rich. Rich people do crazy shit."

"No argument from me there," I said. "But how did you get the car?"

"She gave me the address and simple instructions. I had to be there exactly at eleven. I couldn't be late. She left a side door open so I could get straight into the apartment. The door took me into a bedroom, and I walked from there straight to the garage, just like she said. I didn't touch anything. I didn't go into any rooms I wasn't supposed to. I went to the garage fast as I could and got in the car. I used the remote to open and close the garage door. Then I drove it where she told me to and left it."

"That's it?" I said.

"That's it."

"What about the stop at the gas station?"

"That wasn't what I was supposed to do. She told me to take it straight to the parking lot so it had a full tank of gas. Ain't every day a bruh gets to drive a Bentley, so to be honest, I took it for a little ride. I drove the tank down to half, so I needed to get some gas. She said if I didn't leave it full of gas, then I wouldn't get paid."

"How did you get paid?"

"Cash. All hunnids."

"Did you see her when you picked up the money?"

"Nope. She left it in a shoebox near the train tracks over in Washington Park. I took the money and left."

"You still don't know whose car you stole?"

He shook his head. "No idea."

"Elliott Kantor," I said. "The richest man in Chicago."

"Goddamn," Duncan said. "What the hell I get myself caught up in?"

25

I left Delacorte with Duncan for a second interview. His story was strange, but I believed it. I didn't fill in Burke on all that I had gleaned over the last couple of weeks, because I wanted things to be more cohesive before I presented them to him. I also didn't want him to feel the need to rein me in, as if that were possible. I decided to rush back to my office to take another look at the timeline. I had just gotten into the car when my phone rang. It was a number I didn't recognize, but I answered anyway.

"This is Mrs. Graves," the caller said. Clarinda Graves had been a friend of my mother's for as long as I could remember. They had gone to the same church and sang in the choir together. Mrs. Graves had been working in the ME's administrative office for over forty years and had no intention of retiring.

"A voice for sore ears," I said. "Do you have anything for me?"

"They got the preliminary autopsy results back yesterday," she said. "The report was just uploaded into the computer. I have a copy for you."

"Did you read it?"

"I did. Didn't seem too remarkable to me, but I'm not a doctor. You can form your own opinion."

"What took so long for the autopsy?"

"The family out in California didn't want it. They didn't feel like it was necessary. They even hired a local lawyer to stop it. Didn't work. By law, we have to do an autopsy on all cases like this."

"Which family member was fighting it?"

"The wife. She was adamant."

"You have a contact number for her?"

"An address too. I'll put it on the back of the report."

"I'll swing by to pick it up tonight."

"That's what I figured, honey. I'll have a slice of peach cobbler waiting for you and one for that beautiful lady friend of yours who you need to make an honest woman of."

"I'm working on it."

"Well, you take much longer, and they'll have to bring me to the wedding in a wheelchair."

I entered my office and went straight to the evidence wall, where I had printed out a timeline for the night Kantor had been found. At 9:53, the Amazon driver showed up in front of the Manor. At 9:59, the driver returned to the van, loaded the trunk, and took off. Kantor arrived at 10:05. The Bentley pulled out of the garage at 11:03. And now I could add that Duncan arrived at the building and entered precisely at 11:00. It fit perfectly. He wasn't in the apartment too long, followed instructions, went to the garage, and left. Miles Carthew had been walking his dog that night. He saw a man leave the building, but he wasn't sure what time that was. He knew it was sometime after ten but before midnight.

I stared at the timeline, then at the photographs of Kantor and Thompson. All of this made sense, except for the woman who hired Duncan. Who was she? Why did she want Duncan to steal the Bentley? Maybe she wanted it to look like a burglary gone bad. But if it were a simple burglary, then why tie Kantor to his bed while he was wearing panties? I couldn't make the sexual nature of the scene match the car being stolen.

I studied the similarities between the cases again. Carthew saw a man leaving through Kantor's secret door. Duncan said the door was left open for him. So the man entered Kantor's apartment first. He killed Kantor, then exited through the secret door and left it open enough for Duncan to enter. Duncan entered the apartment and followed the instructions he had been given to get to the garage and take the Bentley. The woman who gave him the instructions must've been familiar with the apartment to know the layout. She knew Kantor had a Bentley, something that his own kids hadn't known, and she knew where the car key was kept. She and the man who left through the side door and almost hit Carthew and his dog had to be working together. She set it up, and the man completed the job.

I looked at Thompson's case. No one was in Boyd's apartment when he got home except for a dead Thompson strapped to his bed. His neighbor said he had heard footsteps and looked out his peephole and saw a man's black boots going upstairs. Could that have been the same man who left Kantor's building? Even if the man did kill both of them, that left the biggest question on the board unanswered: Why?

I CURBED THE PORSCHE ON LaSalle Street, just outside of city hall. On the dash I slid the police credential Burke updated for me every year, then walked into the gigantic rectangular building. Just in that two hundred square feet of lobby space, the entire demographic kaleidoscope of Chicago was represented. Lawyers and businessmen waited at the enormous bank of elevators, next to hardened contractors making the always inconvenient trek to renew permits, intermingled with angry homeowners en route to the assessor's office, fuming about yet another property tax hike.

I exited the elevator on the fifth floor and walked to the entrance of the mayor's suite of offices. A police officer seated at a desk in front of the door checked for my name on a clipboard, then allowed me to pass. Another officer sat next to an older woman, who was barely visible with all the flowerpots on and around her desk. She called me by my name as I approached her and told me to go ahead into the office. The boss was expecting me. She had a bowl of mints on her desk, which reminded me of the mints my grandmother would carry in her purse to church on Sunday mornings. The older woman saw me looking at them and offered me one, which I gladly accepted.

Bailey sat behind an enormous desk that looked like it must've been carried in with a forklift. He was leaning back, talking on his cell phone. His French-blue shirt was open at the collar, and his sleeves were rolled up to his elbows. His tie and suit jacket sat on the back of a chair at his enormous conference table. Like most Chicagoans, I was accustomed to seeing the mayor in front of microphones, in complete control as he sparred with journalists. Seeing him like this actually humanized him. He ended his call and slid his phone into his shirt pocket.

"I appreciate you taking the time to come and see me," he said, standing and offering his hand. I took it and waited for him to let me know where he wanted to sit. He chose two comfortable chairs in front of an enormous window with views of downtown and the lake.

This was only the second time I had been in this office. The first time hadn't gone so well. I had been a detective in the Second District. An unarmed young Black kid had been shot sixteen times while walking away from the police. The entire tragedy had been hidden from the public for over a year. I got wind of what went down and started making noise about this rogue cop being a murderer and how he needed to be held accountable. Bailey knew the case would be a powder keg in a city that had always been operating on the precipice of an all-out race war. He sent messages through intermediaries, trying to convince me to go along with the department's official position. When he had gotten word that I wasn't exactly the cooperating type, he summoned me to this office. His polite suggestions quickly turned to threats, then a full-on screaming match that prompted his security detail to rush into the office to make sure we weren't throwing hands. I made a few phone calls to a journalist friend, the bodycam footage was finally released to the public, and the officer was charged, tried, and found guilty of second-degree murder and sixteen counts of aggravated battery. I reached a hefty settlement with the city as an agreement for my resignation. Bailey survived the political blowback, and I was destined to be his eternal adversary.

Once we had settled into our seats, he said, "I know this is a busy time of year for you. With all the rain we got last month, I hear the courses are in great shape."

"The fairways are lush," I said. "The rough is thick and treacherous."

"Not sure why I never took to the game," Bailey said. "Had plenty of opportunity, but just didn't suit me. Too genteel, maybe."

"Takes a certain mindset," I said. "Discipline. Calm. Patience."

"Well, that must be why I'm not cut out for it. Patience isn't my strong suit."

"Neither is subtlety," I said. "Burke told me you were the one who referred me to the Kantor family."

"I did. Elliott Kantor was a good man. He and his family have been great for the city and great to me personally. I want them to get the answers they deserve."

"You have over eleven thousand men and women under your control who can help get those answers."

"That's true," Bailey said, smiling wryly. "But you're good at what you do. Very good. And you operate differently."

"'If any man doubt that, let him put me to my purgation,'" I said.

"'I have trod a measure. I have flattered a lady. I have been politic with my friend, smooth with mine enemy.'"

"You're still quoting Shakespeare," Bailey said.

"Wole Soyinka too."

"Who the hell is that?"

"One of the most acclaimed playwrights and poets in Nigerian history."

Bailey nodded softly. "I know about the good work you did for Gerrigan and his family a few years back, when his daughter went missing."

"Good work until they fired me for it being too good."

Bailey shrugged. "Sometimes it can get complicated with rich people," he said. "They tend to see the world differently than we do."

"Which is why we're sitting here right now, trying to be civil to each other, though I know the sight of me makes your innards boil."

"'Forgive your enemies, but never forget their names,'" he said.

"President John F. Kennedy," I said. "Not bad."

"I called you in to help because I know that, in your new line of work with clients, you value discretion," he said.

"That's definitely something my clients expect and pay for," I said.

"That's what the Kantors need more than anything," Bailey said. "This is traumatic on many levels. So, what have you learned so far?"

"Hard to say. There are times during an investigation when you feel like you're learning a lot, then there are times you feel like you don't know anything at all."

"Which time are you in right now?"

"Nothing at all," I lied. I had no intention of telling him anything substantive with regards to the case. It didn't matter how philosophical and complimentary he was being; I didn't trust him or his intentions.

"You must have some thoughts about what happened," he said.

"I have a few."

"Care to share?"

"I think he got caught up in some extracurriculars that didn't favor a man of his advanced age," I said.

"You think the drugs killed him?"

"Old age and street drugs are not the most perfect union."

"Is it possible he wasn't using drugs and he just died from natural causes while he was doing whatever he was doing?"

It was clear he and Simon were reading from the same script and wanted the same ending. Made sense. Beyond the inheritance, there was a lot of insurance money riding on the cause-of-death determination, and I was certain a financial windfall for Simon also meant some generosity thrown in Bailey's direction.

"Not sure how you can reason he wasn't using drugs," I said. "They found drugs in his system. No one can magically put them there."

"Unless he had a drink that was spiked or something like that."

"Possible," I said. "But given how he was found and what he was wearing, it's not too far of a stretch to believe he might've also popped a pill or two to get himself in the mood. Drugs can make the most rational people do the most irrational things."

Bailey groaned. "Jesusfuckinchrist. This is a real fuckin' mess. Of all people, how does this happen to Elliott?"

I didn't have an answer, so I didn't offer one. Bailey stood, walked up to the window, and leaned against it. He quietly surveyed the skyline crammed with towering steel and shiny glass. I could see the admiration in his eyes. His city. His destiny. I also took in the view and appreciated the fact that with as many dreams that had been built in our complicated city, just as many had come crashing down. A sliver of the Ferris wheel on Navy Pier could be seen in the distance. He pointed toward it.

"No other family has been more instrumental in building this great city than the Kantors," he said. "Whether it was adding a wing to the Art Institute, funding programs for students at Science and Industry, or refurbishing the asphalt for hundreds of city basketball courts, they have helped make this city great. Take Navy Pier. That Ferris wheel is standing over the lake along with Festival Hall and the Children's Museum in no small part because of Elliott's old man, who ran the family business when my father sat in this office. When the city couldn't afford to totally refurbish the pier, old man Kantor reached into his own pocket and wrote an enormous check. What once was a training facility for the US Navy back in World War II is now the biggest tourist attraction in the entire Midwest. Last year alone it attracted over nine million visitors. The Kantors have given a lot to this city."

"And the city has given them a lot in return," I said.

"It has," Bailey said. "That's why this is so tragic, and why Elliott and his family deserve to be treated with dignity."

"With all due respect to the family and what they've done for the city," I said, "but every Chicagoan, regardless of their zip code or the size of their checkbook, should be treated with dignity."

"Of course," Bailey said, turning back around and facing me. "The last thing my father said to me before he died was 'At the end of the day, the city always belongs to the people.'"

"*All* of the people," I said.

Bailey extended his hand. "My door is always open," he said. "Whatever you need from my office to help you help the family is fully available to you."

We shook hands firmly, and I turned and left the office feeling like I had just made a deal with the devil.

26

That night, I sat in my apartment with the TV turned to the Golf Channel, a large slice of peach cobbler that Stryker kept eyeing and Keegan Thompson's autopsy report sitting on my lap. I read the report quickly in the car before heading home from Mrs. Graves's. Now I could study it more closely. It was a fairly straightforward affair. There had been no signs of trauma. One small erythematous area had been found in the right buttock, around what looked like a tiny puncture wound. Two old, linear scars had been found spanning both buttocks. Remnants of blue fingernail polish had been found along the rims of the cuticles of digits two and three of the left hand and also on one and four of the right hand. There were no other significant findings, as his major organs appeared in good health and noncontributory to his death. The cause of death had been listed as indeterminate. The lab tests on his blood had not come back yet. I picked up the peach cobbler and leaned back on my couch. As I watched an early round of the US Open at Pinehurst, I couldn't help but wonder why the wife had fought against the autopsy. Was there something she didn't want to know? Better yet, was there something she knew but didn't want anyone else to know? I made a mental note to try to contact her.

My phone rang. It was Mechanic.

"You busy?"

"Watching the Open and looking at Thompson's autopsy."

"You still think he's connected to Kantor?"

"Can't prove it right now, but it's too hard for me to believe two rich, powerful men were found tied up in bed with the same type of knot the average person doesn't know how to tie, with women's lingerie on, and suggestions of sexual foreplay."

"Anything in the autopsy?"

"Nothing that would make me think there's a connection. He had a small puncture wound in his ass. Maybe the sex got a little rough, and he was being beat with something, like a spiky belt. They found some old scars across his ass. Maybe he was a sub and getting beat was his thing."

"Who the hell are these people?"

"Rich people do crazy things."

"Well, speaking of rich people, I was bored tonight, so I decided to see what our man Connelly was up to."

"Without me even asking. How enterprising of you. What happened?"

"I followed him from work. He stopped at a taco restaurant over on Lake and came out with two large paper bags. He drove straight from there over to River North."

"Back to the same house on North Kingsbury?"

"Yup. He walked up to the front door and rang the doorbell. You're not gonna believe who opened the door."

"Who?"

"Look at the text I just sent you."

I opened up the message app on my phone and tapped on Mechanic's text. I stared down at a photo of a shirtless Lance Greene standing inside the doorway, smiling at Connelly.

"It really is a small world," I said. "A lawyer, a shirtless future Hall of Fame football player, and two bags of greasy tacos."

"And a tall, beautiful Asian woman in thigh-high boots."

"How is she involved?"

"I'll get to that in a minute. About an hour after Connelly arrived, he and Lance left the house and jumped into his car. I followed them all the way east to the lake. They drove behind Soldier Field, then took a right turn in front of the planetarium. I stopped there and waited."

"Why didn't you follow them?"

"Because at that point, I was the only other car around, and where they were driving was really dark. They would've known I was behind them. So I waited. I knew they would have to pass me to come back out."

"How long were they gone?"

"About ten minutes. They came flying back out and drove away from the lake. Not sure why, but Greene, not Connelly, was behind the wheel."

"He was driving fast?"

"Fast as a fuckin' cheetah. I ran two red lights and a stop sign to keep up. Not sure what got into them, but something happened."

"They went back to the house on Kingsbury?"

"After they stopped at a liquor store. Connelly came out with three bottles of champagne. Dom. I could tell by the bottle. About twenty minutes after they got back to the house, another visitor showed up at the front door. Look at your text messages."

I tapped on the new message he had just sent. A tall, curvaceous Asian woman stood at the door, being greeted by a cute, young white woman in a bathrobe.

"Where was my invite?" I said. "How long did this party last?"

"It's still going on."

"How long has it been?"

"Approaching three hours."

"Any new arrivals?"

"Nope, just the Asian goddess."

I thought out loud. "Just so I'm clear. Connelly and Greene, who we didn't even know knew each other, drive over to the lake in Connelly's car and disappear for about ten minutes behind the Soldier Field complex, then reappear driving like a bat outta hell but with Greene driving instead of Connelly. They stop and pick up some expensive champagne, then go back to the mansion, which I'm assuming is Greene's, since he answered the door without a shirt on. Twenty minutes later, a tall Asian woman dressed in thigh-high boots appears at the mansion. This time, the door is opened by a cute white girl in a robe. And for the last three hours, all four of them—or more, if others arrived before you got there—are inside, drinking and partying in an indeterminate state of dress or undress."

"Sounds about right," Mechanic said.

"So, what's your plan?"

"I could knock on the door and see if they'll let me into the party."

"And when they decline?"

"I don't have anything else to do tonight, so I'll just wait in my car and see what happens next."

"How about you forget about inviting yourself to their private party and just wait in the car? I want to see if anything else unusual happens."

"I'll call you if anything changes."

I ended the call and turned my attention back to the golf tournament. The player I had been rooting for just hit his ball from a deep greenside sand bunker, and it miraculously landed on the green and rolled straight into the cup. He now shared the lead with a kid from Australia I had never heard of before. All of the other players were already in the clubhouse, so the round was over. I took another big bite of the peach cobbler and pushed the remote to see what was on ESPN's *SportsCenter*. As I flipped through the channels, Morgan Shaw, the prime anchor for WLTV and a former client who used me in ways I would never forgive nor forget, popped up larger than life on my screen. She said that a body was found hanging on Northerly Island, a large, finger-shaped landmass sitting in the lake, just east of the Field Museum and Soldier Field. I'd only been there once, and that was a while ago. I didn't remember there being much on the island other than vast and empty parkland, a small beach, a venue that hosted musical events, and a yacht club.

Shaw tossed it to a stone-faced reporter standing at the entrance of the island, a bright light making his dark skin look sweaty. He matter-of-factly explained that the body had been found about an hour ago, hanging on a statue in an area called Daphne Garden. The reporter said they were calling her Daphne because of a tattoo found on the side of her right hip. The reporter went on to point out the irony that a woman named Daphne chose Daphne Garden to hang herself. The police were asking anyone with any information about a missing woman in her late thirties with a small build and *Daphne* tattooed on her right hip to reach out to them to help fully identify her.

Strange story, I thought to myself. *Daphne goes to Daphne Garden and hangs herself.* Maybe she had a sense of ironic humor at the end. I turned to *SportsCenter* just in time to catch the top ten plays of the day. On play number seven, my phone buzzed. It was Mechanic. I hit the pause button on the remote and answered the phone.

"The party's over," he said.

"What happened?" I asked.

"The goddess came out first," he said. "She got into the back of an Uber and took off. About fifteen minutes later, Connelly walked out and headed to his car."

"Anyone else leave?"

"Nope. Greene and the girl are still inside."

"Anyone else join them?"

"Negative. Everything's quiet."

"It's midnight. You can call it quits."

"What are you thinking?"

"I need to find out more about Monroe Connelly. He's connected to Kantor; Jenny Lee, who showed up at Kantor's apartment the night he died; and now Lance Greene. Connelly appears to be the X factor. I just don't understand why."

27

Nothing much happened over the next couple of days. Thompson's lab tests weren't back yet. Duncan had been interviewed a third time and then released. I finally got ahold of Keegan Thompson's wife, Veronica, via text. She was unwilling to talk on the phone or via text but would talk to me in person if I made the trip to LA. Simon was pressing me harder to prove anything else other than drugs had killed his father. I hadn't played a round of golf in almost a week.

Carolina and I made plans to meet up for dinner. I put Stryker on his leash, and we headed for some exercise in Grant Park. We hadn't been there for five minutes when he found his friend, Rex, the Labrador he had met. They tackled each other and rolled around on the ground. Karla stood twenty yards away, admiring the bromance, which was in full force. I walked over to her.

"We have to stop meeting like this," she said. "These trees will start talking."

Karla wore a pair of pink leggings and a matching crop top that showed at least four of her very defined abdominal muscles.

"I'm sure these old trees know a lot of secrets they could share and get a lot of people in trouble," I said.

"There's something different about you," she said, narrowing her eyes. "I can't put my finger on it."

"I haven't shaved in a few days."

"It's a good look," she said, smiling. "You should shave less often."

"Unfortunately, I'm not a connector," I said.

"Connector?"

"I can't grow a full beard. Can't get the sides to connect at my jawline."

"You have a great jawline," she said. "And you don't need a full beard. What you have right now completely works."

"So is all that," I said with a nod. "You're a lawyer *and* a fitness buff. Deadly combination. How's the defense business going?"

"It's going," she said. "Too many clients. Not enough public defenders. Lots of innocent people being forced to plea out because there's such a logjam in the system."

"What's the solution?"

"Well, there's no one solution, but it could start with better training for cops, and not just in the academy but those who have been out for a while. Mandatory retraining every five years to fine-tune their skill set and introduce them to new policing methods and de-escalation techniques. Too many nuisance arrests for trivial misdemeanors that are just clogging up the system. Too many people getting hurt or dying while being taken into custody."

"Retraining every five years? Good luck with that. The union would never agree to it, even though it would make it safer not just for the citizens but the officers as well. 'Mandatory' is a fighting word when it comes to unions."

"Well, something needs to be done, because the way things are right now, nothing is being accomplished except a waste of taxpayers' money and everyone's time."

"You having second thoughts?"

"About?"

"Leaving that fancy law firm and the big bucks to help keep the common man from getting eaten up by the system."

"Not at all." She nodded toward the skyline hovering above us. "The lawyers up in those office buildings are the ones who engineered the system. It's just that no one knows their names, because they're cowards and they do their work behind closed doors."

"Speaking of names," I said. "Have you ever heard of a lawyer by the name of Monroe Connelly?"

"Doesn't ring a bell," Karla said. "Should I know him?"

"Not necessarily. I'm working on a case, and his name has come up. I know he has a pretty high-end clientele. Just thought your paths might've crossed at some point, or you might've heard of him."

"What kind of law does he practice?"

"No idea."

"Is he a good guy or bad one?"

"That's what I'm trying to figure out."

"Can you tell me more about your case?"

"I wish I could, but discretion is one of the big reasons why my clients hire me. Being the great lawyer that you are, I'm sure you can relate to that."

"How do you know I'm a great lawyer?"

"You reek of confidence and success."

"Are you always this charming?"

"'It is a great mistake for men to give up paying compliments, for when they give up saying what is charming, they give up thinking what is charming.'"

She smiled. "Shakespeare?"

"Oscar Wilde."

"You quote poetry, you solve cases, and you seem to always have the right thing to say. Is there anything you can't do?"

"Square dance and break par on an eighteen-hole golf course."

"I'm sure you could do both if you tried hard enough."

"I'll take a pass on the square dancing, but the breaking-par business is high up on the bucket list."

Rex and Stryker found another dog and welcomed him to the party. They chased each other in zigzags for almost a hundred yards, then made their way back.

"I'll ask around to see if anyone knows anything about this Monroe Connelly," Karla said.

"I'd appreciate it if you could do it discreetly," I said.

"Not my first time at the rodeo," she said.

Seeing the sudden glint in her eyes, I completely believed her.

THAT AFTERNOON, I DECIDED TO focus on the unknowns, and at the top of the list was the Amazon driver. After two hours of phone calls and several Google searches, I quickly learned that the key to Amazon's operations and booming success was its supply chain—most notably, the fulfillment centers and its delivery fleet. The fulfillment centers were located all over the world. These enormous buildings contained Amazon's operational guts. Customers placed an order online, and that got sorted and received by a fulfillment center. Workers picked, packed, and shipped the orders. That was when the distribution started. Packages were flown or driven to the sorting centers, where the packages were distributed based on final destination and speed of delivery required. The packages finally arrived at gigantic delivery stations. The next stop for the packages was the customers, something Amazon called the last-mile delivery. Amazon finally decided they could deliver their packages more efficiently and less expensively themselves rather than using the US Postal Service or carriers like UPS, so they built up their delivery network by partnering with thousands of small delivery companies around the world, who had their own vans and just slapped the

Amazon logo on them. That was as far as I could get. I was about twenty calls and ten hang-ups in, and no one wanted to answer any specific questions about the third-party company that would've made a delivery to the Manor on May 2.

I dialed Penny Packer.

"I'm only picking up because it's you," she said. "I'm on the twelfth tee at Augusta."

"What's your club selection?"

"There's a lot of wind today, so I'm going with my five iron."

"Did you say a prayer?"

"Of course I did," she said. "Before I teed off on the eleventh."

The eleventh, twelfth, and thirteenth holes at the famed Augusta National Golf Club, home to the Masters Tournament, had been collectively dubbed "Amen Corner" because of how treacherous they could be for golfers. They were the three hardest holes on the course, and many green champions' jackets had been won and lost on these holes. The twelfth was considered by many to be the most difficult, even though it was by far the shortest of the three.

"I need help on something," I said. "You have any contacts at Amazon?"

"Of course. My godfather is on the board. What do you need?"

"I have a question about logistics."

"What the hell do you care about Amazon's logistics?"

"I'm looking for a delivery driver."

"Is this part of Elliott's case?"

"Yup. I need to find out who delivered a package to his building."

"Are you getting any closer to figuring this mess out?"

"I'm making progress."

"Well, I wanna hear all about it when I get back. Shit, it's my turn to tee off. My partner just dumped his ball in Rae's Creek. I gotta go. Don't worry, I'll get you a contact number."

"Pick your club, look over, and check to see how the trees are blowing on the thirteenth fairway, then wait for the right wind before you swing."

"If I didn't know any better, I'd think you've played here before."

"Not yet," I said. "But I'll be ready when I do."

While I waited for Penny to finish her round and get back to me, I decided to tackle the next unknown on the list, the connection between Jenny Lee and Monroe Connelly. Why was Jenny Lee driving his Maserati? It had to be more than a coincidence that she had been hired to entertain Connelly's biggest client, Elliott Kantor. I pulled out the report submitted by Block, the owner of Cash App. The $Cashtag @friendlypartners69 was connected to a man by the name of Aleksander Wojcik. After an exhaustive search, the CPD Cyber Crimes Unit determined no such person existed. They had used a fake name. The unit was, however, able to track the banking information that had been attached to the account, and that had been tracked to an LLC that had been formed in Delaware just over five years ago. It was a Bank of America account. A subpoena had been issued to the bank by the lawyers to force them to release the customer's name and personal information, but there was some legal technicality with the way the subpoena was served, so the bank insisted a new subpoena be issued directly from the court. That was currently in process, but like everything else in the backlog of Cook County, expedited still meant things moved at a glacial pace. I had an idea.

I locked up the office, grabbed a wad of cash from the safe, then jumped into my car and headed deep into the South Side. I found a branch at Eighty-Fourth and Stony. I parked as close to the door as possible so I could keep an eye on my car. There were three tellers working and a line that seemed to be moving quickly. I scanned for the youngest teller and set my sights on a thin young man wearing a suit that was ill-fitting, but he had a smile you could spot a mile away.

Unlike the older tellers, who appeared somber and bothered, his affability was an indication that he was still new, and the grind of the job hadn't yet crushed his enthusiasm. As luck would have it, when I was next up in line, his window wasn't free, so I told the customer behind me that she could go ahead. Mr. Energy called me next. I looked at his name tag as I approached the counter. Elgin.

"I need to make a deposit, Elgin," I said, pulling out the envelope.

"No problem," he said. "I'm happy to help. Just slide your ATM card in the keypad and enter your PIN."

"I don't have a card for this account," I said. "It's a business account. My name should be on file."

"That's not a problem," he said. "Can I get your ID?"

I handed him my license. I also handed him a small piece of paper on which I had written the bank account number.

"Ashe Cayne," he said. "Cool name."

He started typing on his keyboard. I decided to chat him up, maybe distract him a little.

"You ever hear of Arthur Ashe?" I said.

"I think so," he said. "Can't remember where."

"That's who my parents named me after. He's the most famous Black tennis player. Well, *was*, before Serena came on the scene."

"I know her of course."

"Well, Ashe was the first and still the only African American man to win Wimbledon, the US Open, and the Australian Open."

Elgin looked up from his monitor. "Are you serious? The only one?"

"Wimbledon was the last major he won, and that was in 1975. Your mother wasn't even born yet."

"Crazy stuff. Why can't we win these tournaments?"

"Longer conversation for another day," I said.

He nodded and went back to the monitor. After a few moments, he wrinkled his brow. "I'm sorry, Mr. Cayne, but I don't see your name on this account."

"There must be a mistake," I said. "Can you check again? Maybe it's on a different screen."

He shook his head skeptically and tapped the keyboard a few more times. "I'm sorry," he said. "Nothing's coming up. Are you sure you have the right account number?"

"A hundred percent. Silver Lake Industries, right?"

"Yes, that's the business name."

"There should be four of us listed on the account."

He looked back at the screen and softly read the names to himself. "Fitz Darcy. Leslie Funk. I'm sorry, I don't see your name."

"There must be some mistake," I said, pretending to be perturbed. "I've never had this problem before."

"When was the last time you made a deposit?" Elgin said. "I can look that up."

I definitely didn't want him to do that. "It's been so long, I don't even remember," I said. "Can I just make the deposit anyway? I don't want to keep carrying all of this cash on me." I opened the envelope and flashed the bills.

"Unfortunately, I can't make a deposit into someone else's account. You would have to be listed on the account and authorized to make transactions. It's all legal. Way above my pay grade. But I can have you talk to my manager, see if she can do something."

I slid the money back into the envelope and into my pocket. "No need," I said. "I don't have a lot of time, and I don't want to be a hassle. I'll just have someone at the office make the deposit later today."

He slid my ID back under the glass. "You know, I was named after a famous Black athlete too," he said. "Elgin Baylor, the basketball player. He was my grandfather's favorite player."

"Your grandfather knew basketball," I said. "Before there was

Jordan, there were guys like Elgin Baylor. He's one of the greatest players to never win a championship. Took the Lakers to the NBA finals eight times and never won a ring."

Once I had gotten to my car and pulled onto Stony Island, I called Carolina.

"You better not be calling to cancel on me," she said.

"Au contraire," I said. "I'm calling to tell you how excited I am to see you."

"That's more like it."

"And to tell you that I have a couple of names and a business I need you to check out in one of your fancy databases."

"That's gonna cost you an upgrade on the wine tonight."

"If you can get me an answer in the next fifteen minutes, there will be a surprise upgrade after dinner too."

"These aren't the kind of things you should say to a girl who's still at work and hasn't been intimate in over a week."

"Trust me, that was the PG version. I'm saving the adult version for later tonight."

"Working on this case with all of its sexual undertones has made you frisky."

"That's one way of looking at it."

"So, what am I looking up?"

I explained to her the Cash App payment and the subpoena and my trip to the bank on Stony Island. Then I told her the two names and the name of the business.

"Anything you can find on those two people and the business would be a big help," I said. "I need to talk to someone at the company and find out who actually made the request for Jenny Lee to visit Kantor."

"I have a staff meeting in about an hour," Carolina said. "I'll jump on it right now and get you as much info as I can."

"It never gets old, feeling like I'm the luckiest man in the world."

"And it never gets old, making you feel that way."

Just as I got back to the office and turned on my computer, my phone chimed. I looked down to find a text message from Penny.

Andrew Thorndyke is expecting your call. He runs the delivery station over in McKinley Park. 773-555-0105.

I dialed the number right away. Thorndyke picked up on the second ring and announced himself.

"I was expecting your call," he said. "How can I help you?"

"I'm trying to track down a delivery that was made the night of May second at 1425 West Fullerton," I said.

"I was told this was an urgent situation," he said.

"Extremely."

"Was the package lost?"

"Not exactly," I said. "The package was delivered, but there were complications. I'm trying to sort through what happened."

"Can you give me the name of the recipient?"

"Elliott Kantor. But I need that kept between you and me."

"Understood," he said. "I was told this was a discreet inquiry, so I won't ask too many questions. If you have a few minutes, I can check on this right now."

"That works for me," I said.

I could hear him typing on his keyboard. "Let me try another way," he said to himself. He typed more. "You said the address was 1425 West Fullerton, right?"

"Yes."

"I'm not seeing anything in the system for a scheduled delivery there on May second," he said. "Are you certain that was the date?"

"Absolutely."

"Is it possible the delivery was made through USPS? We don't ship as many packages through them as we used to, but they still do a decent number of deliveries for us."

"I'm certain it was an Amazon van. I saw the vehicle and driver on surveillance footage taken from one of the building's cameras."

"Okay. Let me try something else."

I heard him typing on his keyboard again, then he said to someone else, "1425 West Fullerton. What zone is that?"

I couldn't hear the other person's response, but I heard Thorndyke say, "That's what I thought. Who has that route?"

More tapping on the keyboard, then he came back on the phone. "Can you give me another couple of minutes?" he said. "I want to call our delivery partner and have them check their database. Any chance you got the license plate of the van?"

"I wish," I said. "It was out of view of the cameras."

"Of course. Did you get a look at the driver?"

"Tall Black guy, kinda heavy, with a thick beard."

"Okay, give me a minute."

Thorndyke picked up another phone and made a call. I could hear only fragments of the conversation. He was obviously familiar with whoever was on the other end. He said something about Bears tickets and the quarterback Justin Fields. They talked for about a minute, then Thorndyke returned to me.

"Approximately what time was the delivery?"

"The van arrived at 9:53."

He relayed this answer to the delivery company, then he asked me, "Was there anyone else with the driver?"

"The driver arrived, carried a trunk inside the building by himself, and returned to the van by himself. He was alone."

Thorndyke repeated my answer to the delivery company. He listened for a moment, said thank you, then ended the call.

"Some things aren't matching up," he said. "First of all, our partner who handles that route says they had no delivery for that address on the second of May. Second, I gave him a description of the driver. Two problems there. One, they don't have any driver on that route who fits that description. Two, when drivers are dropping off extra-large packages, they have an assistant come along with them because of the weights and sizes of those packages. You said you were sure there was just the driver. Dispatch said that is not how they staff those deliveries."

I wasn't surprised to hear his responses, nor was I disappointed. This information could be very useful.

"Thanks for your help," I said. "This all makes sense."

"Really?" Thorndyke said. "I wasn't able to track down the delivery or the driver. I don't feel like I helped at all."

"You did, but not in the way you're thinking."

"Okay, well, if you need anything else, you have my cell phone. Feel free to call."

I didn't have all of the answers I wanted, but I confirmed my suspicion that the man with the trunk was not an Amazon driver at all. He was part of the team that night that had targeted Kantor. I suspected he delivered the killer in the trunk, who then murdered Kantor, escaped through the secret door, and left the door unlocked for Duncan to enter and steal the car as a distraction. Kantor was in his bed, already dead, when Duncan entered, which was why he had been given strict instructions to take the specified route from the guest bedroom to the garage. That route had been mapped out so he wouldn't enter Kantor's bedroom and find him dead and strapped to his bed. He also had been told to wear gloves so that his fingerprints wouldn't be left in the apartment. Kantor had drugs in his system, but it didn't mean he wasn't murdered.

28

Carolina called me as I stood before the evidence board, examining the list of important questions that remained unanswered. I was hoping she would have enough information that would resolve the issue of who had requested that Jenny visit Kantor.

"I don't have the best news," she said.

"Not the words most people want to hear at the start of a conversation," I said.

"How about I'm wearing that black pencil skirt you like and my new pair of red bottoms to dinner tonight?"

"That's a lot better," I said. "If you didn't have that staff meeting in five minutes, I'd sit down, turn off the lights, and ask for more of a preview."

"It's not the preview you should be thinking about. The encore is always better."

She giggled softly, and I wanted to reach through the phone and kiss her.

"Now for not-the-best news," I said.

"Silver Lake Industries LLC was formed as a Delaware corporation five years ago. It was registered to a Fitz Darcy with an address at 333 North Green Street in Fulton Market. He's listed as the managing partner. The other partner was Leslie Funk, whose address was listed as the same as Darcy's."

"So they were cohabitating?"

"Possibly. But no more. Leslie Funk now lives in a nursing home way up in Skokie. Fitz Darcy died ten years ago at the age of eighty-two in a hospital in Sarasota, Florida."

"How can a dead man start a business? Are you sure it's the same Darcy?"

"I am. I cross-referenced his Social Security number. The Fitz Darcy who died in Sarasota is the same Fitz Darcy who founded Silver Lake Industries."

"Unless someone lifted his Social Security number and used it in the LLC filing with the state of Delaware."

"Wouldn't be the first time," Carolina said. "But there's more. Fitz Darcy still owns a three-bedroom apartment at 333 North Green Street. He's also listed as a current tenant of the building."

"The reincarnation of one Fitz Darcy," I said.

"And quite a handsome one at that," Carolina said.

"Meaning?"

"I did a quick search on social. Fitz Darcy is very easy to look at."

"I'll be the judge of that," I said. "Send me the link."

"Already done."

I tapped on the link in her text message, which brought me to an Instagram page with the handle @therealfitzdarcy. A young guy in his early to mid twenties, with a chiseled jaw and shoulder-length sandy blond hair, was living the dream. Sunning on yachts, partying in Ibiza, and sitting courtside watching the Chicago Bulls; beautiful women were always within arm's reach.

"I concur with your assessment," I said. "Fitz Darcy has a first-rate gene pool."

"And according to his posts, his pick of skinny-waisted models around the world," Carolina said.

I had several hours before dinner with Carolina, so I called Mechanic, who had just finished sparring at Hammer's, and scooped him up on my way to Fulton Market. We rode mostly in silence, as we tend to do, with the radio tuned in to the classical station WFMT. They were in the midst of a tribute to Chopin.

"You got me actually liking some of this shit," Mechanic said.

"I've never heard Chopin's work being described as shit," I said. "But I get the point."

"It's actually good music to relax to," he said. "I sometimes listen to it on my way home from the gym."

"You better not tell anyone," I said. "You'll end up losing your tough-guy card."

"No worries in that department," he said. "I could listen to lullabies all day and still go out and put someone in the hospital."

"Well, let's not put anyone in the hospital right now," I said. "Or at least let me get the information from the guy first, then you can put him in the hospital."

Mechanic looked straight ahead and nodded almost imperceptibly.

We entered the trendy Fulton Market District with its array of expensive restaurants, overpriced bars, and luxury apartment buildings where there had once been foul-smelling meatpacking shops that quartered, chopped, and sold prime beef during the day while prostitutes traded their wares by night. Now 333 North Green Street was an enormous building full of all the stylish architectural appointments that amounted to nothing more than marketing fodder for developers to charge outrageous prices for living spaces the size of most people's walk-in closets. I parked next to a fire hydrant in front of the building, and then we made our way through the shiny glass doors.

A young Black kid who had eaten one too many Italian beefs and not enough quinoa sat attentively behind a black granite desk. His fancy gray-and-gold uniform looked like he could use it in a pinch for a wedding on the weekend. He stood as Mechanic and I approached.

"Can I help you?" he said.

I looked at his badge. "Freddie, we're trying to catch up with Fitz Darcy."

"Is he expecting you?"

"Maybe."

Freddie smiled. "Which means?"

"We have mutual friends."

"And?"

Aware of all the cameras in the lobby, I discretely slid a hundred out of my pocket and kept it hidden in my hand. I laid my hand on the counter and opened it just slightly so he could see it, which he did.

"We'd like to discuss mutual interests with him," I said.

"Well, you just missed him," Freddie said. "Left about twenty minutes ago."

"Any idea when he might be coming back?"

"Probably not til the morning sometime. He had company." Freddie winked. "Really nice company."

"What time does your shift start?" I asked.

"Tomorrow, I start at five. I'm covering half a shift for the guy who works the overnights."

"His last name wouldn't be Shaw, would it?"

Freddie looked at me, confused.

I looked at Mechanic, who allowed a hint of a smile before he said to Freddie, "Forget it. The overnights. Morgan Shaw. It's an inside joke."

I reached out to shake Freddie's hand and slid the hundred into his. Then I gave him one of my business cards. "Text me when our boy Darcy gets home in the morning."

"First thing," he said.

Mechanic and I left the sterile lobby and walked toward the car.

"What are you going to do if he won't talk?" Mechanic said.

"Turn and look the other way while you convince him."

BAVETTE'S BAR & BOEUF SAT in an unmarked brick building across the street from Merchandise Mart in the River North neighborhood. Its drab, nondescript exterior belied the culinary and atmospheric greatness on the other side of the otherwise ordinary brick façade. In a city where there was a steak house on practically every corner, Bavette's stood not just head and shoulders but half a body above the rest. Its atmosphere had always been as rewarding as the food. With its dimly lit wood-paneled interior, exposed brick, and tufted maroon banquets, it combined classic French elements with that of a New Orleans speakeasy, creating an anti-corporate environment, which meant the restaurant and the rest of us were spared the testosterone- and alcohol-fueled crush of banker outings that too often tarnished the appeal of the other steak houses.

The hostess sat us at a coveted table near the back wall on the other side of the bar, granting us the best views of the room. Our waiter, dressed in a crisp white shirt, black vest, and jeans, allowed us time to get familiar with the menu before coming to take our order.

"We'll share the Shrimp de Jonghe," I said. This was one of my favorite dishes on the menu.

"He'll be eating the bread and the shrimp," Carolina said. "I'll only be eating the shrimp."

I ordered the ten-ounce filet with classic béarnaise sauce and steak frites. Carolina opted for the broiled salmon. We decided to split the truffle mac and cheese and the caramelized Brussels sprouts.

"And I haven't forgotten about the wine upgrade," I said.

"Even though I didn't have the best news?" Carolina said.

"I'm a man of my word." I turned to the waiter. "Let's get a bottle of that 2005 Spanish cab from Rioja."

"Excellent choice," he said before collecting our menus and leaving.

"So, what did you find out about Darcy?" Carolina said.

"Not much more than we already knew. He lives in one of those overpriced buildings in Fulton Market, and he's spending the night romping with one of his model groupies. He'll be home in the morning."

"Will you go back?"

"The doorman will text me when he returns from his evening exploits."

"How did you manage that?"

"The way these things are always managed in Chicago. A little wink, a little grease."

"What's your plan?"

"Ask him why the hell he's impersonating a man who's been dead for a decade."

"And if he won't answer?"

"Introduce him to Mechanic, then turn my back."

"Jesus Christ. Mechanic will hurt the kid."

I smiled. "The debonair Darcy might not be making any Instagram posts for a few weeks."

The waiter delivered a basket of warm bread, the way bread is supposed to be served.

"I don't understand how you can eat an entire loaf of bread and not gain an ounce of fat," Carolina said. "All I have to do is look at bread, and I feel like I go up a size."

"It's all psychological," I said, dipping a large piece of bread in olive oil and taking a healthy bite. "You have to embrace the process and believe that the bread will just disappear once it goes down your throat."

"Oh, so that's the trick?"

"And then run three miles the next morning," I said.

"And that's why I can't eat bread. I hate running."

"That's where the psychology enters the picture. You have to tell yourself you love the bread more than you hate the running."

"Then I won't be eating bread anytime soon."

Our waiter returned with our wine. I swirled, smelled, and tasted. I wasn't the biggest wine drinker, but I knew a good wine when I tasted it. This was worth every penny of the exorbitant price tag.

"What shall we toast to?" Carolina said.

"How about our trip to Paris over Thanksgiving?"

"I didn't know we were going to Paris."

"Well, now you do."

"I need to go shopping."

"Is that always the first thing you think of when it's time to travel? Nothing about the sightseeing or travel logistics. Clothes are always first."

"And the shoes are a close second."

"And that right there explains the difference between men and women," I said.

"I'm going to the capital of fashion," she said. "Damn right I think about shopping. I'm not gonna fly all the way over there to be eaten alive by a bunch of fashionista piranhas."

"To la Ville Lumiere," I said, holding up my glass and tapping it against hers. "The City of Light."

"You're already practicing your French."

"I need to be able to tell all those Parisian men of mystery that you're unavailable."

"Speaking of mystery, what's the latest with the Kantor case?"

Our appetizer was served, and in between bites of the shrimp, I dipped the toast that came with it in the garlic butter sauce with a touch of herbs and sherry. I brought her up to speed on all that was going on.

"Plutus?" Carolina said.

"Not to be confused with Pluto," I said.

"Well, I know that's a planet," she said.

"Not like it used to be. Several years ago, it got downgraded from a full planet to a dwarf planet."

"Why would they pick on a poor planet?" Carolina said.

"Not only pick on it, but every year, they celebrate its downgrade. They have something called Pluto Demoted Day."

"You're not serious."

"I am."

"Don't these people have anything better to do?"

"I guess your sense of humor takes a turn after looking through a telescope most of your life, trying to identify stars, asteroids, and planets."

"I can't tell Pluto from Jupiter," she said. "But maybe when we get back to your place tonight, we can open the curtains, jump under the covers, and turn off the lights. We'll search the sky, and you can help me identify her."

I started to say something, but before I could get the words out, I froze.

"You okay?" Carolina said.

"You just did it," I said.

"Did what?"

"Made the connection I've been looking for. Holy shit. What would life be without serendipity?"

"You care to let me in on the secret, or are you gonna just sit there looking all handsome, keeping it to yourself?"

"It's the last thing you just said. 'Help me identify her.' That's exactly what that reporter said to Morgan Shaw the other night."

"Wait, you were with that Shaw woman the other night? I didn't know anything about that."

"Not like that," I said. "I had finished watching the golf tournament and was turning the channel to *SportsCenter.* I just happened to catch her giving a report on a woman who they suspected killed herself on Northerly Island. The reporter was doing a live shot close to where the body was discovered. He was saying how ironic it was that this woman—who they were calling Daphne, because that's the name they found tattooed on her hip—hung herself on a statue in Daphne Garden."

"Slow down for a second," Carolina said. "I've never even heard of this place Daphne Garden. And the woman goes there to hang herself? Not to speak bad of the dead, but I'd call that more than ironic."

"I'd never heard of Daphne Garden either until the reporter said that."

"What is it?"

"I have no idea. But what just got me thinking is talking about Kantor and Plutus, then thinking about Daphne. It's all a Greek mythology connection."

"The only thing I remember about the Greek mythology I learned in high school was the almighty Zeus. Everything else is a blur."

"I actually liked Greek mythology," I said. "Not necessarily because of the course, but because I had a secret crush on the teacher and wanted to impress her. Who knew that teenage hormones could be an academic stimulant? Anyway, Daphne was also part of Greek mythology. From what I remember, she wasn't a goddess or anything, but she was a dryad, a tree spirit. She was the daughter of Peneus, the river god."

"Geez, you really must've had the hots for that teacher," Carolina said. "All these years later, and you can remember what she taught to that level of detail."

"You'd have to see Ms. LaCava to understand," I said. "To a class of hormonal boys, she was everything. And we weren't the only ones crushin' on her back then. I heard that several of the male teachers had taken their shots a few times in the teachers' break room. Anyway, hearing about Daphne makes me think about Kantor, because he once referred to himself as Plutus. Well, Plutus, not Pluto, was also part of Greek mythology. He was the god of wealth, who was blinded by Zeus and was well-regarded because he liked to share his wealth with others."

"That fits Kantor," Carolina said. "One of the richest men in Chicago, with his family's name on almost every important building in the city."

I pulled out my phone and googled Daphne Garden. I read aloud what I found on the Chicago Park District website.

"'Artist Dessa Kirk created the artwork that features three female figures entwined with lush flowers and plants. Chicagoans and visitors had such positive reactions to Daphne Garden that the Chicago Park District decided to move the installation to Northerly Island in 2006.... For the Daphne Garden project, Greek mythology served as the inspiration. In an ancient myth, the nymph Daphne was pursued by Apollo, the archer god. To protect her from Apollo's advances, Daphne's father turned her into a laurel tree. By highlighting Daphne, Kirk wanted to explore the theme of the exploitation of women. The three figurative Daphne Garden sculptures are made of welded automobile parts. Kirk's decision to use dismantled car parts is based in her interpretation of older Cadillacs as a symbol of materialism and self-destruction. The winglike arms of the figures emulate leaves, with vines serving as skirts for the three women. These natural elements reinforce the imagery of the mythological Daphne transforming into a tree.'"

"Interesting, but I can't say I remember that story," Carolina said.

"I remembered Daphne because of one of my classmates, Iris Gilbride," I said. "She went off in class one day about it. She said that this was the typical plight of women, even today. When a woman says no to a man, and he won't leave her alone, she's the one who has to suffer, because a man's pride won't allow him to accept rejection and move on."

"Iris was a precocious one," Carolina said. "Men refuse to accept that sometimes women simply aren't interested, and pursuing us harder isn't the way to change our minds."

"Some men," I said.

"Yes, present company excluded."

"This gives more context to why this woman decided to hang herself at that location, beyond the similarity with her name."

"What do you think she was trying to say?"

"Maybe someone was after her, an ex or spurned lover. She felt like the only way to get away from him was taking her own life."

"And she did it in Daphne Garden for its symbolism. Makes you wonder what was troubling her."

"I'm curious."

"So, what are you going to do?"

"Call Burke and ask him about this mysterious Daphne."

"And then?"

"Take you back to my place, jump under the covers with you, and teach you about all those galaxies up there."

Carolina pushed the dessert menu to the side. "That sounds a lot better than the crème brûlée right now. Let's go play solar system."

29

I had just finished the first quarter mile of my morning run when my watch vibrated. I looked down, and it was a message from Freddie the doorman.

He just walked in.

I stopped running and typed back, On our way. Let me know if he leaves before we get there.

I called Mechanic and arranged to pick him up on my way over to North Green Street.

The lobby was mostly empty when we arrived. A couple of women and self-important men in suits walked out of the elevator, nodded at Freddie, then pushed through the revolving doors, on their way to work.

"What's his apartment number?" I said as we approached the front desk.

"I'm supposed to announce all visitors," Freddie said. "I have to call him and let him know you're here to see him."

"The cameras are on you, right?" I said.

"They are," he said. "Two of them cover the front desk."

"Is there audio?"

"No audio, just video."

"Good. That makes it easier."

"But if I let you up, and Fitz doesn't know it, and he complains to management, I'll lose my job. Man, this gig doesn't pay much, but I need it."

"Don't worry, we're not gonna cause you to lose your job over something like this," I said. "Is there a mail or package room nearby?"

"Yes, right behind me."

"So here's the plan. You're gonna walk into the package room as if we asked you about a package. You're going to stay in there for two minutes. We are going to go to the elevator and go upstairs without you knowing we did that. No one can blame you for something you didn't see."

Freddie looked at me, then at Mechanic. "Are you going to do something bad to him?" he said. "Fitz is a cool guy."

"We just wanna have a little talk," I said. "We come in peace."

A young woman in spandex hustled through the lobby with her earbuds in and gave Freddie a quick wave before she pranced through the revolving door and down the street.

"Apartment 2120," Freddie said, then he turned and walked into the mail room.

Mechanic and I quickly made our way to the other side of the lobby, around the marble wall, and into an open elevator. We got off on Fitz's floor and made little time getting to his door. Mechanic stood to the side so that he couldn't be seen through the peephole. I rang the bell. Seconds later, the door opened, revealing a bare-chested Fitz Darcy in a pair of black biker shorts. Hours of tanning had turned his skin almost the color of mine. He wasn't exactly muscular, but he wasn't scrawny either. He stood about an inch shorter than me.

"I think you've got the wrong apartment," he said. "I didn't order anything."

I almost punched him in the face for saying that, but instead, I smiled and said, "You're Fitz Darcy, correct?"

"I am," Fitz said. "Who are you?"

Mechanic stepped into view.

"Batman and Robin," I said. "Your pick who you want to be Batman."

I pushed past him and walked into the apartment.

"What the fuck?" he said. "Get the hell outta my apartment before I call security."

"I hope you can dial with your front teeth," I said. "Because by the time he finishes with you, that'll be all you have left that can push anything."

Mechanic pressed Darcy into the apartment and closed the door behind him. Mechanic leaned against the wall. The three of us stood there while Darcy made some serious calculations.

"We just want to have a little talk," I said.

"About what?" Fitz said.

"Your name, for starters."

"My name?"

"You have a very famous name," I said. "Or at least a derivation of a famous name. So I was wondering about the etymology of it."

Fitz wrinkled his brow, then looked at Mechanic for help.

"The man likes big words," Mechanic said. "What can I say? It turns him on. I like to put people in the hospital. That turns me on."

"So back to the name," I said. "Were your parents being coy when they named you?"

"I don't know," he said. "This was the name they gave me."

"You know who Fitzwilliam Darcy is?"

"No idea."

"You study literature in high school?"

"Of course."

"Then you must've been absent during the class on *Pride and Prejudice.*"

"I read that book."

"Then you weren't paying much attention. Fitzwilliam Darcy was the rich guy in love with Elizabeth."

"Okay. I remember something like that."

"Well, you seem to be the rich guy in love with escorts."

He looked at me quizzically but didn't say anything. He didn't have to. The expression said it all.

"But we'll get to that in a second," I said. "First, tell us your real name."

"You already know it," he said. "You just went through the history of my name."

"The history of the name you stole," I said, "from a man who died ten years ago in a hospital in Sarasota, Florida."

"Are you the fuckin' police or federal agents or something?" Fitz said.

"None of the above."

"Then why the fuck do I have to answer any of your questions?"

"Because if you don't, that quiet guy standing over there is gonna hit you so hard, you'll be pissing blood for a week."

Fitz looked at Mechanic, whose eyes were half-closed by now. His pulse was probably somewhere in the low fifties. He liked to slow everything down before he went to work.

"I really don't know what's going on right now," Fitz said. "Just level up with me. Are you undercover cops? IRS agents? What are you?"

"Listen," I said. "We're not here to get you in trouble, if that helps. I know you run an escort service. I know you have an account at Bank of America. I know you use the $Cashtag @friendlypartners69. The sixty-nine part is actually pretty clever. So let's not do the whole denial bullshit. I don't give a fuck that you're able to afford this lifestyle because a bunch of old rich guys will pay through their nose for a hand job. I just want to ask you about one of your girls and a job she did on May second."

Darcy considered my words for a moment, then said, "And this stays between us?"

"You give me the information I need, and you can keep on being the fake Fitz Darcy and poppin' bottles at the club."

"Okay," he said. "Follow me."

Mechanic stayed posted against the wall as I followed Fitz down a long hallway and into an office that had a full western view of the city. The United Center, home of the Bulls, wasn't too far off in the distance. He sat in front of an enormous, curved computer monitor, tapped a few keys, shuffled through several screens, then said, "Okay, what's the date again?"

"May second."

"Do you know the name of the friend?"

"Vernon."

Fitz tapped his keyboard a few times, then a chart popped up. It had all of the details about the assignment. Very professional.

"So, what do you want to know?"

"Who made the request?"

"You mean Vernon's real identity?"

"Do you have that information?"

"No. The reason why people like our service is because we never ask for the friend's real name."

"How do they make a request?"

"They send an email or text with the address and the specifics of what they want. We take the request and check to see if it's a new or returning client. We do our due diligence, then when everything looks okay, we assign the friend a name. We then send the information to another service that provides the girls."

"Which service do you use?"

"Depends on the request."

"Which service did you use for this assignment?"

Fitz moved the cursor across the screen, then stopped. "This one went to Karol's Angels. We use them when the client has more upscale tastes."

"So you send the client's name, address, and their preferences to Karol's Angels? That's it?"

"That's all they need to know."

"And who does the friend pay?"

"He pays us directly. We don't set up the appointment until we get payment in full. Once the girl completes the appointment, we pay the service provider their percentage of the fee. In Vernon's case, we paid Karol's, because they provided the girl."

"And how much information do you have on the people who make the request for a friend?"

"Not a lot," he said. "We make it a point to be as minimalist as possible. Clients prefer it that way. So we just ask for the essentials—email or the number they texted us from and the form of payment. No one uses a credit card for obvious reasons, so they typically send a wire or Zelle or bank transfer."

"If you have their email address or phone number, then theoretically you could discover their identity."

"I've never tried doing that, because it's not likely to work. These guys use burner phones or fake email addresses."

"Was Vernon a new customer or returning?"

"New."

"Can you tell if his request came in via email or text?"

Fitz tapped a few keys. "Email."

"What was the address?"

"VintageBlackOnly@gmail.com."

"Can you tell if he made any requests after the second?"

Fitz typed the name *Vernon* in the search bar. No results. Then he typed the email address. Still no results.

"Looks like only that one request," he said.

"Was that assignment on the second completed?"

"Yup."

"How do you know?"

"Because we only release the funds to the service provider once the girl has contacted the service provider to report it's complete, and we match that with a confirmation from the friend that they received their services."

This told me a lot—most importantly, that Kantor might've requested Jenny Lee, but a dead man couldn't send a confirmation that the visit was complete. Someone had to have done it for him. Who was VintageBlackOnly@gmail.com?

30

I arrived in LA late in the afternoon on the first day of June. It had been several years since I'd been to the City of Angels, but judging by the passengers who had been sitting in first class, not much had changed. I hopped into my rented BMW M8 convertible, because of course, only in LA could you throw down your plastic and rent cars that carried a six-figure price tag. I avoided the endless parking lot on the 405 freeway, instead retreating to surface streets, where I carved my way up La Cienega and north toward the Hollywood Hills. Sunglasses on, drop-top down, sun with an occasional breeze—I was in LA.

My phone buzzed. It was Burke.

"Where the hell are you?" he growled. "Sounds like you're stuck in a damn wind turbine."

"City of Angels," I said.

"In the middle of all this shit, you decide to go to Hollywood?"

"I'm out here to talk to the wife of that preacher who was found tied up in another man's bed."

"I heard something about it," Burke said. "He died having sex in some trainer's apartment over in Bronzeville."

"There's a lot more to it than that," I said.

"You think it has something to do with Kantor?"

I brought Burke up to speed on my conversation with Malcolm Boyd. When I finished, he said, "You knew all this and didn't say anything to me?"

"I was waiting to fill in some of the gaps," I said. "I needed to chase some leads down first as delicately as possible, before your boys come in with a wrecking ball."

"You're not the only one who knows how to work a case, hotshot," he said.

"That's true, but there are lots of people out there who will talk to me and not to some guy in a blue uniform and Kevlar vest."

"I had a chance to look into that Daphne case," he said. "Not really a lot there. They still don't have a confirmed identity. They've gotten some missing person calls from out of state, but none of them have checked out."

"Nothing on the cameras?"

"Zilch. Believe it or not, there aren't any cameras back there."

"Well, there have to be cameras closer to Soldier Field and the planetarium."

"There are, and they've been looked at. Not a lot of traffic going in and out of Northerly unless there's an event out there. And nothing has happened there for over a month. The body was fresh when they cut her down. They figure less than eight hours."

"How did they find it?"

"Someone's dog."

"Is that a place where people walk dogs?"

"Not really. It's pretty much out of the way. But some guy was on his boat late that night and took his dog out to take a shit. The guy said the dog started acting agitated and took off. By the time he caught up with the dog, the dog was standing underneath the body, barking and running in circles."

"Anything on the guy?"

"Nothing much. He's a retired former president of Northwestern Hospital. He keeps his boat docked over there. Checks out clean."

"Well, the body didn't just magically appear on that statue," I said. "Someone had to bring it there."

"Or she went there on her own and killed herself."

That was still a possibility, at least officially, but it just didn't ring true to me. I considered telling him about Daphne Garden, but decided I needed more clarity and direction. Right now, it was just a suspicion and a lot of Greek mythology he wouldn't understand.

"I wonder what they found at autopsy," I said.

"Nothing. They haven't done it yet. They're backed up."

"More confirmation of what I always say."

"Which is?"

"Death is a big business in Chicago."

"Sure in hell keeps a lot of people employed," he said. "Including you. So you flew all the way to LA just to talk to the guy's wife?"

"And see the Hollywood Sign from the Griffith Observatory."

"You'd save a shit ton of money and time talking on the phone or doing one of those Zoom meetings."

"She was only willing to talk to me in person, so I agreed to meet at her house. She said it was easier to trust someone sitting across the table."

"She might regret that decision," Burke said. "She doesn't know what she's getting herself into with you."

"Just doing my job," I said. "By the way, any chance you can dig up whatever they have on Thompson's investigation?"

"Not my jurisdiction. And what would I say if they ask about my interest?"

"You're still a cop," I said. "I'm sure you won't have any problem making something up."

The last thing I heard him say was "Asshole!" before the phone went dead.

I checked into my hotel in West Hollywood, then jumped back in the car and headed over to Thompson's church. I didn't have any specific plan in mind other than to get a better feel for what Thompson's day job might've been like. His church operated out of what used to be called the Forum, an enormous circular arena built in the mid-sixties and most famously the former home of the Los Angeles Lakers. Once the new Staples Center, now Crypto.com Arena, opened its doors, the Lakers vacated the Forum for their new age digs, and after several years of vacancy and deterioration, Thompson and his ministry purchased the building and its surrounding property at a steep discount.

After a twenty-five-minute drive straight south of the hotel, I entered Inglewood, a tough working-class city just minutes east of the airport and a few exits away from the notorious Compton. I wasn't expecting there to be much going on at the church on a Saturday night, but the parking lot was bustling with activity. Three large tents had been set up at the end of the parking lot closest to the building. Two semis were parked next to the tents, their back doors open, supplies stacked from floor to ceiling on pallets. Several men in each truck worked at a feverish pace to unload the inventory and transfer the items to the volunteers on the ground, who distributed them between the three tents. Three long lines of cars had queued up in front of the respective tents. Volunteers in purple-and-gold shirts moved quickly, carrying bags and cases of water to the cars, passing them through the window or placing them in the open trunks. This was a well-coordinated operation. Several armed security guards stood around the perimeter, keeping watch. I took a moment to scan their faces before finding my target. I slowly pulled around the other cars and eased along the perimeter toward a large man with short salt-and-pepper hair and aviator sunglasses. He had the look.

"Everyone needs to wait in line," he said firmly as I got closer.

"I'm not trying to pick up anything," I said. "My first time here. Mind if I ask you a few questions?"

I pulled out my retired CPD star and ID. He looked at it and nodded. His body posture relaxed slightly.

"You're a long way from the Windy," he said. "What brings you out this way?"

"Just in town to meet up with a couple people. Heard a lot about this church, plus I have an uncle who was a big Lakers fan when they played here. Wanted to take a picture of it so he could see it."

"The team's been gone from here for a while," he said. "But this is where they did all that work during the eighties."

"Five titles in nine years."

"Damn right, and they could've won more. Made it to the championships three other years in that decade, but Bird played lights out for the Celtics in '81, Malone led the Sixers in '83, and Dumars with Detroit killed 'em in '89."

"Magic and Kareem," I said. "Jack Nicholson in his shades sitting courtside. Prettiest cheerleaders in the league. Showtime."

"At that time, the greatest show on Earth," he said. "Nosebleed tickets practically on the roof ran you a thousand dollars. But let's not forget, y'all had a nice little run yourself when Jordan and Pippen won all those rings."

"Unstoppable," I said. "You guys had the eighties. We owned the nineties. Six rings. I was a little kid then. That's all anyone talked about. Jordan and the Bulls. But now we're struggling to win the first round in the playoffs."

"We were down for a bit too," he said. "Then we got Kobe, may his soul rest in peace, and Shaq. And now Bron and Davis are trying to put it together before Bron retires."

"Bron said he's not retiring before he gets a chance to play with his son."

"Bronnie has to get into the league first. Easier said than done, even if Bron is your dad. These boys are playing some ball these days, and not just a few. Lots of 'em, names you don't even recognize, are putting up big numbers."

I extended my hand. "Ashe," I said.

"Roland," he said, swallowing my hand with his mitt.

"I won't even ask you the question," I said.

"Don't need to," he said, smiling. "Jordan, then LeBron. No player has done some of the shit MJ was doing back in the day. And I say that with all due respect to Kobe and Bron."

"You won't get any argument from me," I said. "But I give LeBron some credit I can't give the others. A player of his stature and all he has, and he's a real social activist. Unafraid. Speaks his mind and doesn't care what it may cost him in sponsorship or endorsement deals. He's the real deal."

"Amen, brutha."

I felt like I had him softened up enough. Sports and food were always effective weapons. Even enemies could find common ground.

"This is a pretty big church," I said. "What's it like?"

"You mean what it looks like inside?"

"No, the congregation. The vibe."

"Good, God-fearing, God-loving people," Roland said. "I mean, look at this. Today they'll give out over five thousand bags of groceries and ten thousand cases of water. Cars will be driving up here well after midnight."

"'For I was hungry, and you gave me something to eat. I was

thirsty, and you gave me something to drink. I was a stranger, and you invited me in.'"

Roland finished without missing a beat. "'I needed clothes, and you clothed me. I was sick, and you looked after me. I was in prison, and you came to visit me.'"

"Matthew 25: 35–36. All churches should stand on those principles. They take in a lot of money on Sunday mornings, but are they giving some of it back to the needy?"

"Well, they do a good job of it here," he said.

"What are you all gonna do now that you lost your minister?"

"To be honest, this isn't my church. I just work security when I'm off duty. I live and work down in Torrance. When I get some extra time, I come up here and help out. So I don't really know about the inner workings of the place."

"You hear anything?"

He shrugged. "You know how it is," he said. "You always hear things. Difficulty is figuring out what to believe."

"What do you think happened?"

"Best I got is, he was cheating on the first lady, and the husband of the woman he was cheating with wasn't too happy about it. Found 'em in bed together and killed him."

"I've seen pictures of his wife and daughters," I said. "Not to covet thy neighbor or anything, but she's a real nice piece."

"Shit. Fine as she wanna be. Body for days. But you know how it is. You rollin' up to the same thing night in and night out, I don't care how fine she is, that shit starts getting a little old. Especially when you look like he looked and had all he had. Single and married women threw themselves at him. Sometimes he'd come out here and help give away the bags. One night we had to separate two of the volunteers. They were about to throw hands, arguing about who should work in his tent."

"The wife must've known about all the attention he was getting."

"Please. She'd have to be blind as Stevie not to know. But she's not new to the game. This shit comes with the territory. When you take that robe and collar off, a preacher is still a man."

"Did they get along?"

"I heard they were cool. She got a huge mansion up in the hills, a garage full of cars, and more money than she can ever spend. They're not regular people like you and me. When it comes to relationships, these people have agreements."

"He was a young guy to lose all of that so suddenly."

"Life in the fast lane," Roland said.

"Tomorrow is promised to no one," I said. "So, who will take over now that he's gone?"

"I heard there's a scramble going on right now. Lot of money and power at stake. She wants it, but not everyone is on board with that."

"You think she'll get it?"

"I've only met her a few times, but I learned real quick. Don't let her good looks and those fancy clothes fool you. That woman got a brain like a computer and the heart of a lion."

31

The next morning's forecast called for a temperature in the triple digits and a humidity level not too far behind. I got up while it was still dark and ran north to Sunset Boulevard, turned west, and headed toward UCLA. A few other runners had the same idea, but the streets were mostly deserted, and the slight wind was much cooler than I had expected on a day that was predicted to turn into an oven. I made it to the lush campus of UCLA, something I had always wanted to do after watching their basketball and football teams and constantly hearing how beautiful the campus and coeds were. The sun had just started to lift as I stood there, surveying the scrubbed brick buildings and tree-lined walkways. Just this view alone made it abundantly clear why almost 150,000 high school seniors applied for entry into the freshman class.

I walked around the campus for a few minutes, grabbed breakfast at a coffee shop in Westwood, then caught a rideshare back to the hotel. By the time I had showered, changed, and talked to Carolina, I was in the car with the top down and on my way to the Thompson manse.

I worked my way through the wide, palm-tree-lined streets of Beverly Hills with multimillion-dollar mansions partially hidden by tall privacy hedges and painted concrete walls. European cars sat in all of the driveways—at least the few that were visible from the road. I finally left the flat area of Beverly Hills and started climbing into the actual hill portion of the town's name. The roads climbed and curved and were sometimes so narrow that oncoming traffic had to stop at times to coordinate alternate passing. After several near accidents, the road widened, and I arrived at the gated entrance to Beverly Park. A uniformed security guard stepped out with a clipboard and asked for my name and identification. He went back to his booth, got on the phone, then returned with my ID and instructions on how to get to the Thompson house.

If the security guard and ivy-entwined gate weren't enough to indicate that I had entered an extremely exclusive part of Beverly Hills, the fact that as I drove up to the Thompsons' none of the houses were visible from the road was confirmation that this was the land of Hollywood elite. I finally reached the top of the hill and the entrance to the Thompsons' driveway. As I pulled up, the gate slowly rolled back, and a wide, immaculate driveway constructed of large rectangular pavers came into view. I slowly climbed the curving driveway lined with enormous trees and an assortment of lawn sculptures. As I neared the top, a gigantic brick Georgian manor swelled above the landscape. A black Rolls-Royce Phantom sat in the middle of the driveway, its chrome grille shining like a lighthouse against a dark sky. I pulled behind it and walked up to the portico. Just as I was about to ring the bell, the door opened, and staring at me was Veronica Thompson in a white silk pantsuit. Describing her as beautiful would be insulting. She was breathtakingly flawless, with honey-colored skin, her perfectly coiffed hair falling to her shoulders, and a sculpted body that could put a mannequin to shame. She offered me a restrained smile, but not her hand.

"Please come in," she said. "Abigail has us set up in the sky room."

After stepping into a vast foyer of Italian marble, I followed her through a maze of large, opulent rooms until we reached what felt like the back of the house and entered an enormous space with floor-to-ceiling windows occupying the entire fourth wall. I could see planes approaching and departing LAX, as well as the downtown skyscrapers to the east shrouded in gray smog. This view alone was worth a couple of million dollars.

We took a seat in two comfortable chairs that were separated by a marble coffee table and perfectly positioned in front of the windows. A tea service and glass pitcher of lemonade had already been set up for us, the handiwork of Abigail.

"Tea or strawberry lemonade?" Veronica asked.

"I've never been much of a tea drinker," I said. "Especially when it's a scorcher like today."

She poured both of us a glass of lemonade.

"How was your trip in?" she said.

"Without incident," I said. "By the time I finished my second movie, the pilot was activating the landing gear."

"Where are you staying?"

"The London."

"That's a fun hotel," she said. "Not as pretentious as the Peninsula or the Four Seasons over on Doheny."

"Not as expensive either," I said. "And breakfast is included."

"Very economical of you," she said.

I wasn't sure if she was being condescending or just stating facts. I gave her the benefit of the doubt.

"This is a beautiful home," I said. "Very impressive."

"Thank you," she said, taking a small sip of lemonade. "We bought this from the Zanucks."

"Excuse my Midwest naivete, but the name doesn't ring a bell."

"The father, Darryl, was a studio titan. Formed 20th Century

Pictures. He was one of the pioneers of the studio system. His son, Richard, followed in his footsteps and became a big producer. You might be too young to remember *Driving Miss Daisy* with Morgan Freeman. It won the Oscar that year. *Planet of the Apes*, *Jaws*, *Charlie and the Chocolate Factory*, Dick Zanuck produced them all. He built this house and lived in it until he died."

"I guess that's what they mean when they say Hollywood royalty," I said.

"Old school," she said.

We both quietly looked out of the windows. I could see the rooflines and swimming pools of other mansions perilously hanging above the cliffs.

"It's very peaceful up here," I said. "A world of its own."

"That's what we liked about it so much," she said. "Isolated in some respects but still convenient. We can get down to the church in thirty-five minutes or so depending on traffic, and if we want to go to the valley, that's just minutes away on the other side of the hill."

I couldn't help but wonder how many of the parishioners who dug in the bottom of their handbags on Sunday morning to find money for the offering had ever seen where their pastor and first lady called home.

"I don't want to take up too much of your time," I said. "I just had a few questions, if you wouldn't mind."

"You said you were working a case similar to my husband's."

"Very similar," I said.

"And you think they're connected?"

"I'm not sure, but there's a strong possibility."

"Can you tell me about the other case?"

"Not as much as I'd like," I said. "Confidentiality issues. But the deceased was a very prominent man, like your husband, and his death was very unexpected, also similar to your husband."

"That's all that's connecting them?"

"I didn't say that was all. I was just giving you a couple of similarities."

"Was this man found in bed also?" she said.

I smiled.

"Was it his or someone else's?" she said.

"So you're aware of all the details of your husband's death?"

"Aware of as much as I need to know."

"I just wasn't sure how much you were told."

Veronica smiled, and the room's brightness instantly increased by about five thousand lumens. "You seem like a man who appreciates directness," she said.

"I am."

"Then we'll get along well. Keegan was my husband of fifteen years after five years of dating. There's very little a police officer in Chicago can tell me about him that I don't already know."

"Well, since you don't mind me being direct, were you aware of your husband having relationships outside of your marriage?"

"I take it you've seen photos of my husband," she said.

"I have."

"Then you're aware of how handsome he was."

"I am."

"I also take it that you're aware how much he was loved by his followers not just here in LA but around the country."

"I am."

"And being the good investigator that I have every reason to believe you are, I'm sure you're aware that we paid twenty million dollars for this house."

"I am."

"So, given all that you know, would you find it surprising that someone like Keegan would entertain relations outside of our marriage?"

"Well, considering what's sitting across from me right now, I would certainly question his need for doing so."

She smiled. "They told me you are as charming as you are handsome."

"'They'?"

"I do my homework too."

I took a sip of lemonade. "How are you doing?" I said.

"It's extremely painful to know my husband, who I loved deeply, died the way he did in that small, strange room. But I have to keep it together for our two daughters. They motivate and anchor me. I stay strong on the outside while my heart aches on the inside."

"'Smooth runs the water where the brook is deep,'" I said.

"You read Shakespeare," she said.

"When I'm not catching bad guys or trying to reach the green in regulation."

She looked confused.

"I'm a bit of a golf junkie," I said. "Difficult for me to go an entire day without some kind of reference."

"Keegan was too busy flying around the country to be any good at the game," she said. "But he did belong to the Los Angeles Country Club."

"Not as pricey as Riviera, but a lot more difficult to get into. Lots of old families and a no-movie-star policy."

"You would've liked Keegan," she said. "And he would've liked you. You're similar in many ways."

I nodded. "I'm curious as to why you didn't want an autopsy performed. That didn't make sense to me, especially given the circumstances."

"Because it wouldn't have brought him back, but it could've

brought me a lot of aggravation and public humiliation from annoying journalists, who always find a way to get their hands on leaked information that was supposed to be confidential."

"Do you think your husband was murdered, Mrs. Thompson?"

"Keegan might've had his critics, but he never had enemies. Do you think someone intentionally killed him?"

I thought for a moment before answering. "I don't know what happened," I said. "But I'm a firm believer that in most cases, anything is possible."

I heard footsteps descending a staircase adjacent to the room. A gorgeous and very curvaceous olive-skinned woman who was barely wearing anything appeared, then quickly returned up the stairs when she saw me.

Veronica Thompson stood up calmly and smiled. She then said, "'Women may fall when there's no strength in men.'"

"*Romeo and Juliet*," I said.

"You certainly do know your Shakespeare," she said, smiling. "How much longer are you here?"

"I leave tonight."

"Well, if you're ever back in LA, you have an open invitation to come visit."

I walked out of the mansion and toward my car that had been carefully washed and dried. Nice touch. I couldn't help but think about what Roland had said. *Brain like a computer and the heart of a lion.*

32

I left Veronica Thompson and went directly to get some lunch at the Ivy on North Robertson, not far from my hotel. I had been told that this was the buzzy place to see LA in all its Tinseltown glory. I wasn't much of a celebrity hound, but I figured, since I was in LA, I might as well do LA. So I took a small table outside on the raised white-picket-fenced veranda, with an unobstructed view of the entrance. I was perfectly situated to see all of the arrivals and air-kissed departures. It was not even noon yet, and the restaurant was already half-full, and the plastic surgery quotient was in overdrive.

I noticed an actress who played in a movie Carolina and I had watched on our flight to Morocco a couple of years back. She was extremely attractive on the screen, but in person, she looked no better than ordinary. I only recognized her by her hair. She had the brightest red hair I had ever seen and a smattering of freckles that spread across the bridge of her nose. She sat talking to a guy who had that slick look of an agent: sports coat with a black T-shirt, designer jeans, and riding loafers without socks. As soon as I placed my order of spicy fresh corn chowder and the fusilli with bufala mozzarella, tomato sauce, and diced chicken, my phone buzzed with a text message.

Are you still in LA?

I didn't recognize the number, but I responded anyway.

Who is this?

Flavius Bechet. I got your number from Roland.

Any relation to Sidney Bechet?

Never heard of him.

Are you in LA?

Yes. I want to talk to you.

Lakers or Clippers?

I don't follow basketball.

Tiafoe or Aliassime?

Who are they?

The best Black tennis players in the world.

Nice, but I don't follow tennis either.

What do you follow?

Scripture.

I surrender. You found my Achilles' heel. How can I help you?

I used to be Bishop Thompson's personal assistant. I want to meet with you if you're still here.

I'm heading home on the red-eye tonight. Can you meet before then?

I'm down in Long Beach at a youth ministry conference. I'll be back first thing in the morning.

Can we talk on the phone?

I prefer not to.

Is this important?

Yes. I want to tell you about Bishop. I think there were other things going on.

Like?

I prefer not to do this over text.

I thought about it for a moment as I watched an actor, whose name I couldn't remember but whose face I couldn't forget, come strolling in with a girl young enough to be his granddaughter. She carried a tiny dog in her tote bag. He carried an unlit cigarette in his mouth. The hostess greeted them effusively, then guided them into the restaurant. I looked down at my phone. Another twelve hours wouldn't hurt.

After several more exchanges, we agreed to meet early the next morning at the Urth Caffé on Melrose. I continued my people-watching and quickly came to the conclusion that you had to be a certain type of person to live in LA, and I simply was not that type.

I ARRIVED AT THE EUROPEAN-STYLE café a little early and secured an outdoor table. Flavius Bechet pulled up in a candy-apple red 560 SL Mercedes. He was of average height, with free-form dreadlocks and a sharply trimmed goatee. He wore a powder blue polo shirt, fitted jeans, and a pair of blue-and-white Air Jordans that matched his shirt. He walked with confidence.

"Nice ride," I said, as he sat at the table. "'88?"

"Close," Flavius said. "'89."

"How many miles?"

"Just under twenty-five thousand."

"All original?"

"Just like it rolled off the showroom floor."

"Where did you pick it up?"

"My grandfather left it to me."

"Your grandfather knew his cars."

"Better than he knew his own children, but that's another conversation. I really wanted to tell you the truth about Bishop."

"I'm all auricles," I said.

"You work for the software company?" he said with hesitation. "I thought you were a private detective."

"Different auricle," I said, pointing to my ear.

"Why didn't you just say the word 'ear'? A little pretentious, don't you think?"

"Pretentious would've been me calling it 'pinna.'"

"Which is?"

"Another name for the outer ear, just not as well-known."

"I thought you were a retired cop."

"I am."

"I've never met a cop who uses words like 'auricle' and 'pinna,'" he said, laughing.

"And I bet you never met a cop that quotes both Giovanni and Dostoevsky."

"Giovanni as in Nikki Giovanni?"

"Precisely."

"Wait, what's going on here?" he said. "I feel like I'm suddenly in some literary version of *The Twilight Zone*."

"Not a bad place to be sometimes," I said. "I felt the same way driving up to the Bishop estate yesterday."

"You went to their house?"

"And had Abigail's strawberry lemonade while watching planes land at LAX."

"I've only been there once, but never inside the house. Bishop invited me to a reception in the yard. How was she?"

"She?"

"Veronica."

"I thought you church folks used the term 'first lady.'"

"She's a bitch."

I lifted my eyebrows.

"A bad bitch, but a bitch nonetheless."

"When did you leave the church?" I asked.

"It'll be exactly eight months tomorrow."

"You're counting the days?"

"And the hours too."

"I take it you're not missing your old job."

"Bishop had a lot going on," he said.

"I'm starting to figure that out."

"He had a way of dividing up his life and sequestering the parts in different rooms."

"Sequestering," I said. "Nice word."

"Thought you'd appreciate it," he said, smiling. "Anyway, once he put his life in these rooms, he only allowed certain people access to a limited number of rooms. No one had access to all of his rooms."

"Not even the bad bitch?"

"You're funny. No, not even Veronica."

"Which rooms were you allowed to enter?"

"Only the ones pertaining to the business of the church."

"But you were his personal assistant," I said. "Didn't you need access to other parts of his life?"

"There were three of us," Flavius said. "Belinda handled the family business, kids, school, dry cleaning. Ayanna handled the social stuff, like appearances, galas, golf, et cetera. I only handled things related to the ministry. The three of us had to coordinate to make everything work, but we each had our own domain."

"And Veronica?"

"She had two of her own assistants. The three of us would have to coordinate with the two of them when she and Bishop needed to do something together."

"I'm getting a headache just hearing you describe this."

"Imagine what we got actually doing it."

"Is that why you quit?"

"That's what I told Bishop."

"But it was something else."

"I felt betrayed."

"That's a big word."

He looked at me quizzically.

"Not in the sesquipedalian way," I said. "'Big' in the implications way."

"You're entertaining to talk to," he said.

"Wait til you hear me sing gospel."

Flavius smiled. "'Betrayal' is an accurate word for what I was feeling. Bishop recruited me from the youth ministry to become his personal assistant. He sold it to me as a big promotion from what I was doing. I didn't want to do it at first, because I really liked working with the youth and all the new energy they brought. But Bishop was persistent. He wouldn't take no for an answer. For two weeks, he filled my head up with conversations about virtue and this being my calling to serve God in a higher way. Then he added another twenty-five thousand to my salary and two extra weeks of paid vacation."

"An offer you couldn't refuse."

"And he knew that," Flavius said. "So I accepted it and started working in his office. It was challenging keeping up with all he had going on, but I enjoyed it, and I was damn good at getting things done. Then one night, I left work and forgot a bag that I was supposed to drop off at one of the deacons' house. I went back to get it, thinking everyone had already gone for the day, but Bishop was in his office with his door cracked, talking on the phone. I was about to knock to see if he needed anything else, but then I heard him talking like I've never heard him talk before. He was talking about hair color, height, ass, the tit size he liked. I just froze. It was like he was putting in an order for a woman. I was furious."

"Because the man likes a certain kind of woman?"

"No, because of the hypocrisy. All the sermons about fidelity. All the things he talked to me about being virtuous in the eyes of God. It was all bullshit. The man I was listening to was not the same man who had convinced me to join the church and then become his personal assistant."

"Not to get into a debate about morality, but maybe you were being a little tough," I said. "Preachers are human too."

"But they should be held to a higher standard. They're supposed to lead by example, not just words."

"Maybe you were reading too much into the conversation," I said. "He could've been just having guy talk with one of his friends. Men who wear robes and quote Scripture from memory still have a certain organ between their legs."

"Having a dick is one thing but using it outside of your marriage is everything the Bible teaches us not to do. What was even more sickening was how he was talking about what he wanted, like he was ordering food at a steak house. She couldn't be more than twenty-five, and she had to have a dominant personality. I didn't hear everything he said from that point on, but he did say something I never expected to hear."

"Which was?"

"He wanted a guy to come with the girl, and he wanted him to be about his height, muscular, very masculine, and as young as the girl. I missed some of what he said next, but then he said the words 'Eagle Rock.'"

"What did he say about Eagle Rock?"

"I don't know. I just heard those words. I don't know why he said them or what they meant."

"And you have no idea who the guy he was talking to on the other end was?"

"I know it wasn't a guy."

"How can you be so certain?"

"Because before he hung up, he said he was looking forward to the weekend. Then he called her Daphne."

I drove the short ride back to the hotel to think about my next move. The legend of Bishop Keegan Thompson had grown significantly over the last twenty-four hours. His widow had definitely not been completely straightforward, which made me curious about the kind of relationship they had really had. Had they had an open marriage? I knew that was becoming a more common arrangement, but would a megachurch pastor and his wife risk public exposure of such an alternative lifestyle? Who was the scantily clad woman who had started to descend the steps while I was talking to Veronica? Was that her girlfriend? It certainly felt that way. And now Flavius Bechet had come forward with a conversation he overheard that sounded like Thompson was arranging a tryst with a young woman and man, ordered to his specifications. By the time I arrived at the hotel, I had made my decision. I needed to talk to Veronica Thompson again. I dialed her number as the valet drove away in the BMW.

"Afternoon, Ashe," she answered. "I'm about to head into a meeting. Is this urgent?"

"This will be quick," I said. "I remember there was something I forgot to ask yesterday, and it has me a little confused."

"I'm listening."

"What is Eagle Rock?"

She paused, not long, but enough to let me know she was

calculating her response. I had learned a long time ago from interviewing thousands of witnesses and suspects that the words they speak might provide answers, but how they communicate those words and their body language can sometimes speak louder than the words.

"Where did you hear that from?" she said calmly.

I found that to be a curious response. No quick explanation or denial, but rather, questioning the question. Another tell.

"Came up in a conversation I was having, so I was wondering if you had heard of it."

"Who were you talking to?"

"Just someone familiar with my case."

"I understand," she said. "It's an interesting name, but unfortunately, I've never heard of it."

I didn't believe a single word coming out of her mouth, but I played along. Give them enough rope and let them finish the job.

"Well, sorry to bother you," I said. "Thanks again for the lemonade and aerial view of the city. When I hear the words 'Hollywood Hills,' I will always have that image in mind."

"You're welcome," she said. "But now I'm a little confused."

"Why's that?"

"You called to ask me about this Eagle Rock. Are you suggesting this is something I should know?"

"Only if you do," I said.

"You're very quick," she said. "And annoyingly clever. Sorry I couldn't be more helpful. Safe travels back to Chicago."

I hung up the phone and looked around suspiciously. She had just wished me safe travels back to Chicago. I had told her I was leaving last night. How had she known my plans had changed? I was now convinced that the alluring Veronica Thompson definitely knew a lot more than she was letting on.

33

A few days later, I was back in the real world, racing down Lake Shore Drive to hit some golf balls at Jackson Park. I sat in standstill traffic near the Museum of Science and Industry, because the construction of the nearby Obama Presidential Library was in full swing, and while the South Siders were excited to honor the country's first Black president, the traffic it was causing had become a living hell. My phone buzzed. It was Mrs. Graves.

"The lab results for Bishop Thompson are back," she said.

"Did you look at them?"

"I did."

"Anything in there?"

"There's something about findings of a sedative. I can't pronounce these fancy names, but it's in the report."

That raised a big flag. A sedative had been found in Kantor's blood also. I quickly swerved and took the next exit, then started driving back north.

"Do you see any mention of recreational drugs?" I said.

"You think a celebrity preacher like Bishop Thompson would do drugs?" she said, sounding offended by the suggestion.

"I'm open to all possibilities, no matter how unlikely they are,"

I said. "No offense, but if preachers can put hands on little boys and drink alcohol, doing drugs isn't exactly a stretch. And I'm not saying Thompson touched little boys or did drugs. I'm just saying, men of the cloth have been found guilty of much worse."

"I don't see any mention of recreational drugs," Mrs. Graves said.

"How soon can I get the report?"

"How soon do you need it?"

"Now."

"I take my lunch in half an hour. Meet me at Chipotle, at the corner of Ogden and Damen."

I SAT IN MY OFFICE with Kantor's and Thompson's reports sitting beside each other on my desk. They both had significant levels of the potent sedative midazolam. What were the chances this was coincidental? Very low. According to what I could find on the internet, midazolam was a drug used as part of the anesthesia for surgical patients and for people experiencing severe seizures.

I picked up my phone and called Dr. Barry Ellison, a retired pathologist and medical school classmate of my father's. He had helped me last year with the Morgan Shaw case and the evening news anchor who had mysteriously died in her sleep. Now he spent most of his time playing golf and teaching science a couple of days a week to underserved high school students on the South Side.

"Ashe, is that you?" he said as soon as he answered.

"The one and only," I said.

"How ya hitting them these days?"

"Long and straight, when I can get out there."

"You must be on another case."

"I am, which is why I called. I wanted to talk to you about a sedative that might be used as a sleeping medication."

"Are you having problems getting to sleep?"

"No, my girl is very good at taking care of that."

We laughed.

"The drug is called midazolam," I said. "I read that it's typically used in anesthesia before medical procedures, and it's also used to treat severe epilepsy."

"Yes, status epilepticus," Dr. Ellison said. "It's a severe type of seizure where there's more than one seizure within five minutes. But I wouldn't exactly describe midazolam as a sleeping medication."

"Why?"

"People can take it to fall asleep, but it's certainly not something a doctor would prescribe for that purpose. It's in a class of medications called benzodiazepines that belongs to a group of medicines also referred to as central nervous system depressants. In effect, they slow down the central nervous system."

"Is it easy to get a prescription for it?"

"Not at all. Just the opposite. It's a controlled substance, because it can be fatal if you take too much or mix it with other drugs or alcohol. Most people don't understand that alcohol is a CNS depressant also. If you take a medication that slows your system down, and you drink alcohol, which also slows down your system, then you potentially have a big problem, especially with breathing. These drugs and alcohol can slow your breathing, and you can imagine that if you slow it too much, well, you stop breathing altogether, because you're not getting enough oxygen into the body."

"How common would it be to find levels of midazolam in the body at autopsy?" I said.

"Hard to give a simple answer to that," Dr. Ellison said. "It really depends on the person and their situation. The person could've died during surgery or some other medical procedure. If the doctor used midazolam, then you'd expect to find some on board at autopsy."

"Any other reasons you would expect to find it?"

"Not any reason that would adhere to standard medical care. But as you know, people get their hands on all kinds of drugs that they shouldn't."

"How would this drug be taken?"

"Two ways: either via pill or injection."

I turned the pages on Thompson's autopsy and read the conclusion. Small erythematous area in the superior aspect of the right gluteal muscle, suspicious for a puncture wound.

"Could the drug be injected into the ass?" I said.

"It could," he said. "Not how it's typically administered. A doctor will usually inject it intravenously. However, it can be injected intramuscularly. Or into the ass, as you describe it."

"This is a big help," I said. "I owe you a round of golf."

"Have clubs, will travel," he said.

I disconnected the call and dialed Simon Kantor.

"I heard you were in LA," he said. "Business or pleasure?"

I figured he must've spoken with Burke. Otherwise, how would he have known?

"Pleasure for me would've been standing on the tee box of the first hole," I said.

"Fair enough. So, are you any closer to figuring this out?"

"I'm making progress," I said. "Lots of moving parts with investigations like this, but things are starting to fall into place."

"That's good to hear. The sooner I get some answers, the better."

Which I interpreted as *The sooner you can tell me my father didn't die from taking drugs, the faster I can collect that big insurance payout.*

"I called to ask you about your father's health," I said. "Was he an epileptic?"

"No."

"Did he ever have a seizure that you know of?"

"Not to my knowledge."

"Did he ever complain of having difficulty falling asleep?"

Simon laughed. "Just the opposite," he said. "Dad could fall asleep sitting in the middle of a tornado."

"I'm the same way," I said. "I've come to learn from some of my insomniac friends how special of a gift that is."

"Can you tell me why you're asking these particular questions?" Simon said.

"Just trying to follow a thread," I said. "Everyone describes your father as being so energetic and robust. I just wanted to confirm that again from you."

"It's confirmed," Simon said. "I'm actually glad you called. I'd like to give you an added incentive to find who's responsible for my father's death."

"I already have all the incentive I need," I said. "If someone killed your father, I want to find out who it was and make sure they pay for it. Might sound old-fashioned, but that's incentive enough for me."

"I respect that about you," Simon said. "But in my business, we believe in rewarding good results."

"A thank-you and the balance of the retainer is reward enough for me," I said.

"One million dollars," Simon said.

I laughed.

"Why are you laughing?" Simon said. "That's not enough?"

"I'm laughing because you could say ten million, and it wouldn't change how I work, Simon. When I take a case, I see it through to the end. How much money is on the table doesn't move me one way or another."

"Understood. Well, look at the million dollars as my family's way of expressing our deepest gratitude."

"If that's the way you choose to thank me, who am I to refuse?" I said.

"You can get a lot of rounds of golf with that," Simon said.

"And enough left over to buy a small island on the Maine coastline."

After I finished with Simon, I immediately dialed Flavius out in LA. He answered right away.

"How's the ministering business going?" I said.

"We're growing every day, saving lives, and spreading positivity," he said. "I'm blessed to be doing the work God has called me to do."

"It's good to see you didn't lose faith after your experience with Thompson."

"I lost faith in him, but never in our Lord."

"Good man," I said. "I have a couple of questions I want to ask you."

"Shoot."

"Was Bishop Thompson an epileptic?"

"Not that I'm aware of. He was very healthy and very fit. I was around him ten or twelve hours a day. He never complained of any health issues."

"He ever complain about falling asleep and needing some help?"

"Help in what way?"

"Sleeping pills or sedatives to calm the nerves and help him settle in."

"Bishop never complained of a lack of sleep. He was a real good sleeper, actually. Sometimes he'd come back to his office and take a quick thirty-minute nap between services and wake up like he'd been sleeping for hours. As busy of a schedule as he kept, sleep was never an issue."

After I finished the call with Flavius, I was about to leave the office when there was a knock on my door. I stuffed my gun behind my back out of habit and looked through the peephole. It was my father, dressed in a suit and tie as if he were still going to his medical office. I opened the door.

"Dad, what are you doing here?" I said.

"That's your version of a warm welcome?" he said imperiously.

"I'm sorry, I'm just surprised to see you here."

My father had only been to my office one other time, and that was to tell me that my mother had died.

"Are you gonna leave me standing here or invite me in?" he said.

"Of course." I stepped to the side to let him in. Then he did something he hadn't done since I graduated from college. He grabbed and hugged me. And not just a quick nice-to-see-you hug, but a firm squeeze that brought me into his body and forced me to adjust my breathing. I wasn't sure what to say, so I said nothing and invited him to take a seat by the window.

"Nice view you have here," he said. "I suspect not too many private investigators can sit in their office and see the boats gliding on Lake Michigan and the Ferris wheel spinning on Navy Pier."

My father always preferred to call me an investigator. He said the word carried more heft than *detective*.

"I do okay for myself, even if I didn't play professional tennis," I said.

"I wanted you to play professional tennis because you were so gifted," he said, "and I thought it could give you special opportunities in life."

"The problem is, I played tennis not because I loved it," I said, "but because I knew it made you happy."

We sat silent for a moment, staring out the window. I must've looked out that window five thousand times, but it never got old, and each time I found something new and interesting. At that moment, I noticed how the lights along Lake Shore weren't fully coordinated and caused traffic to back up unnecessarily.

"I'm sorry," my father said.

I turned and looked at him. He kept his gaze out of the window.

I was speechless. *Sorry* was not a word I often heard come from my father's mouth. Apologies didn't come easy to him. They never had.

"What are you sorry for?" I said.

"For pushing you so hard at times when I should've been hugging you instead. I wanted it so badly for you that I didn't know when to back up and give you space. I'm afraid my tenacity is what chased you from tennis."

"Partially," I said. "And it wasn't that I didn't like the sport, but I just didn't love it as much as you did. I needed to find what worked for me."

"And I should've given you that opportunity."

"I was thinking about playing again," I said. "As much as I love golf, I miss being out on the court."

"For what it's worth, I miss seeing you out there. You were such a joy to watch." He stood to leave. "I'm meeting the dean for lunch," he said. "They want me to be more active with the medical students."

"I thought you were enjoying retirement."

"I am. But teaching the students a couple of times a week might fill some of the gaps in my days."

My father was lonely. He would never admit it, and I would never say that to him, but I knew. He turned around once he got to the door and reached into his jacket pocket.

"This arrived in the mail for you today." He handed me a small envelope that looked like an invitation.

"Someone sent it to *your* house?" I said. "That's strange. Who would even have your address or know that was a way to reach me?"

My father shrugged. "You haven't been over for dinner in several weeks," he said. "It would be nice if you could make some time for me."

"Let's do it next week," I said.

"Toward the end of the week," he said. "I'm leaving for London tomorrow afternoon. The grass season has started over in Europe."

"I forgot Wimbledon was coming up."

"And I'm hoping Tiafoe and Aliassime or Eubanks will make it to the quarters. First time ever that two Black men would be in a quarterfinal in a major."

"Who are you rooting for?"

"I like all of them," he said. "I'd be happy if any of them took it. Ashe was the only and last one to do it. I just want to see us hold and kiss that trophy again in front of the royal box before I leave this earth."

He shook my hand, then left the office. I walked back to my chair by the window and sat down. I wasn't exactly sure how I was feeling at that moment—partly relieved, partly sad. Everything had taken me by surprise, starting with his arrival at my door, the embrace, and then the apology. I lost track of how long I had been sitting there, but it had been a while. My phone's ringer jolted me from my haze. It was Burke.

"They ran fingerprints on that Daphne woman," he said. Burke always dispensed with pleasantries. It felt like he was forever in a rush. "There was a hit in the national database. Her name isn't Daphne. It's Bianca Wembley."

"Anything come back on her?"

"Nothing yet. They're working on it now. Nothing so far in our databases. We'll see what they turn up. Still no idea why she chose to go to Northerly Island to kill herself."

"Assuming it was her decision to go to Northerly Island. And assuming she took her own life, and someone didn't kill her."

"You know something we don't?"

I don't know what it was that pushed the thought into my head, but I suddenly remembered what Mechanic had said about the night he followed Greene and Connelly to an area behind Soldier Field. They disappeared for a while, then returned with Greene driving instead of Connelly, and he was driving fast. They stopped and picked up champagne, then went back to Greene's house to what seemed to be a party. Where had they gone? And why had they been driving so fast?

"What was the night her body was found?" I said.

"Hold on," Burke said.

I cursed myself for not making this possible connection earlier. How could I miss this?

Burke returned to the phone. "They found her on May twenty-third. That was two weeks ago. They think she had been hanging there for no more than four or five hours before she was discovered."

"I gotta go," I said.

"Wanna tell me why so many questions about this woman?"

"I do, and I will. But I need to confirm some things first. Once I do, I'll get back to you."

Before he could protest, I disconnected the line and dialed Mechanic. At the same time, I did a search for Northerly Island on my computer and pulled up an aerial view on Google Maps.

"You told me that you followed Connelly and Greene from Greene's house in River North to the area behind Soldier Field."

"I did."

"What day was that?"

"Not sure, probably a week or two ago?"

"Any way to nail down the exact day?"

"Hold on, I gotta think for a sec. The night they did that was the same day I had lunch with Lana."

"Wait, you and Lana are back together again?"

"We had lunch," he said. "I wouldn't call that being back together."

"Just lunch?"

"Well, you know how those things go. Anyway, I just looked at my text messages with her. We were together on May twenty-third."

"Are you sure?"

"I'm looking at the text messages right now with the date on them. Unless the phone suddenly screwed up the date, that was definitely the day."

"You ever hear of Northerly Island?"

"I don't think so."

"I think that's where Connelly and Greene went that night. When you followed them east toward the planetarium, which way did they turn?"

"They took a right in front of the planetarium and drove into the darkness. I sat there and waited for them to come back out."

I looked at the map. He was describing Northerly Island. "You were there and didn't even know it."

"Where?"

"On Northerly Island, where they found that woman who hung herself on a statue. They know her real name now. Bianca Wembley. Connelly and Greene were on the island at the same time her body was hanging."

"Are you trying to say what I think you're saying?"

"I'm not really sure what I'm saying, but the date and times are matching up. That gives them an opportunity. But I can't even guess the motivation for why or how a former NFL player and big-time lawyer could be connected to this unknown woman hanging from a statue."

"I don't see it," Mechanic said.

"Neither did I, but it's sitting here, right in front of us. We can't ignore it."

Once Mechanic got off the phone, I looked up at Connelly's name on the board. What was the real deal with this guy? I texted Karla to see if her contacts had come up with anything yet. I rested the phone on my desk and saw the envelope my father had dropped off. I opened it, expecting to find either an invitation to a fundraiser or some type of spam mailer telling me I could claim my million-dollar prize if I called a hotline. Instead, it was a small piece of white paper with two simple sentences typed across it.

> LEAVE THIS ALONE.
> WE KNOW WHERE YOUR FATHER LIVES.

I sat there staring at the note for a moment, in some ways hoping that with the more I looked at it, the words would read differently or disappear altogether. But after several minutes alternating my gaze between the piece of paper and the view outside of my window, the words were still there, and it began to sink in that my father had just been threatened. First I got worried, then I got angry.

I picked up my phone and dialed my father's number.

"Where are you?" I asked.

"About to walk into the restaurant to meet the dean."

"Which restaurant?"

"Nella, on Fifty-Fifth Street."

"Are you outside or inside the restaurant?"

"I'm just getting out of my car. Why are you asking me all of these questions?"

"I'll explain later. Walk into the restaurant."

"That's a ridiculous thing to say to me. Of course I'm walking into the restaurant. How would I meet the dean if I don't go inside?"

"Are you inside yet? I want to be on the phone until you get inside the restaurant."

"What the hell has gotten into you, boy?"

"I'll explain everything later. Are you inside yet?"

"Yes, I just opened the door and walked in."

"Is the dean there?"

He paused momentarily, then said, "Yes, I see her."

"Is the restaurant crowded?"

"Pretty busy. It's their lunch crowd."

"Once you get to the table and sit down, then you can hang up."

"What the hell has gotten into you? Why are you doing this?"

"Just let me know when you've reached the table."

"Okay, fine. I'm at the table. I'm hanging up now."

He was gone before I could tell him what to do after he was finished eating. I dialed Mechanic.

"Where are you right now?" I said.

"Down at Hammer's, about to ease underneath three hundred and fifteen pounds on the bench press," he said.

"I just got a letter threatening my father," I said.

"What the hell are you talking about?"

"Someone sent a letter to his house, addressed to me. It said, 'Leave this alone. We know where your father lives.'"

"Where's your father right now?"

"Having lunch with the medical school dean in Hyde Park. I'm walking to my car to drive over there. I need to make sure he gets back home okay. Could you run over to his house and make sure it's clear?"

"I'm on it. Some fuckin' coward had the nerve to threaten your father? I can't believe this shit. I'll be waiting and ready."

I jumped into my car and drove south at speeds reaching triple digits. I kept racking my brain, trying to figure out who would send a threat like that, and the only answer I kept coming back to was someone related to the Thompson case. But why with Thompson and not Kantor? I was certain their deaths were connected, and both were murdered but made to look like they had died before having rough sex. Whoever killed Kantor had also killed Thompson, or at least they were coordinated in some way. But why hadn't they felt threatened when I was investigating Kantor? I flew to LA, had a couple of conversations about Thompson, and all of a sudden, someone wanted to take a run at my father. I must've hit a nerve in LA, and this was the response.

I made it to the restaurant in Hyde Park and pulled up in the bike lane close to the front door. I got out and looked through the window. My father sat at a table in the back of the restaurant, talking to an Indian woman who looked too attractive and too young to be a medical school dean. My father's back faced the door, so he couldn't see me staring through the window. I stepped into the lobby, near the host stand, and surveyed the other diners. A couple of tables were full of college students splurging on a decent meal, and the rest looked like faculty members, with a sprinkling of locals. Comfortable that the restaurant was clean, I went to my car, pulled away from the door, and waited. I had dealt with some of the toughest criminals in Chicago, from gangbangers to the Russian Mafia to dirty cops. Plenty had taken a run at me, but no one had ever threatened my father. I wasn't afraid, but I was uncomfortable because of my father's vulnerability and his stubbornness. He was from another time, and as a retired psychiatrist, he lived in a different, more civilized world than the one I was often dragged into with these cases. He would never understand or appreciate the danger.

After ten minutes, Mechanic called in.

"All's clear here at the house," he said. "Door was locked. None of the windows had been messed with. Doesn't look like anyone was here."

"Outside?" I said.

"All of the cars parked on the street are empty. I'm sitting about half a block away with clear sight of the front door."

"He hasn't finished eating yet, but when he does, I'll drive him home and spend the night with him. He's flying over to London tomorrow afternoon to go to some of the grass tournaments leading up to Wimbledon, so the house will be empty."

"I can take a shift in the morning so you can go home and shower and stretch your legs," Mechanic said.

"Then I'll have Carolina come over and pick him up and take him to the airport," I said. "Once we get him out of here, I'll feel much better."

"You have any idea who's behind this?"

"None, but I think it's connected to Thompson."

"You ruffle some feathers while you were out there?"

"And obviously pinched some nerves too."

34

That next afternoon, Carolina pulled her tinted-window Jaguar into my father's garage. In the event someone was watching his house, we secretly loaded his suitcases into the trunk and him in the back seat, and she pulled out and headed to the airport. Mechanic sat in his car at the end of the block to see if anyone pulled in behind her. No one did. She got him to the airport without incident, and he was safely on his way to London. Mechanic planned to watch over the house the next couple of days to see if there were any visitors who showed up without invitation.

By the time I got back to the office, a large, unmarked envelope had been slipped under my door. I opened it and pulled out the autopsy report of Bianca Wembley. I immediately went to my desk and read through it. The ME's report was largely unremarkable. There were no signs of trauma. She had impressions on both wrists, which could've been from bracelets worn too tightly. She had a piercing in her left nostril, but no nose ring present. Ligation marks were found around her neck consistent with the body being hung on the statue. The cause of death was listed as suicide.

My curiosity was getting the best of me, and I couldn't help but wonder about the circumstances surrounding this woman's suicide. One of the deficiencies of an autopsy was that there was no way to assess the mental state of the deceased, and in cases of suicide, what brought the person to the point where they felt no other option was viable other than to end their own life. The ME only had the physical evidence to work with to describe the how of death, not the why.

I called Dr. Ellison, who said he would take a look at the report, but per the information I relayed to him, it sounded like a straightforward suicide, of which he unfortunately had seen many in his career. But he would give the report a full vetting and see if there was anything that might've been missed. He cautioned me that in cases like this where the decedent had not yet been identified, and given the volume of cases the ME's office was struggling to clear, these exams tended to be superficial and highly prejudicial toward the actual findings at the scene of discovery. In other words, if the evidence in the field strongly indicated a manner of death, most autopsy reports in cases like this were going to support those findings.

KARLA COE FINALLY GOT SOME information on Connelly, so we agreed to meet at the Eleven | Eleven bar on Lake Street that was owned by Nazr, a former player for the Chicago Bulls who I had met in the Meinsdorf's owner's suite a few years back. It was one of my favorite bars, because the vibe was low-key, it was never too crowded, and Nazr hired a Michelin-worthy chef who turned out creations worthy of some of the city's finest restaurants. I arrived a few minutes before Karla and was seated on the small roof-deck almost eye level with the "L" train above Lake Street.

The bartender personally brought over an old-fashioned as compliments from Nazr, who had told me when we first met that it was his favorite drink. The other tables were full of fashionable, hip patrons who spoke quietly while enjoying the warm breeze. I had just put my drink down when Karla appeared. She wore a sleeveless pink silk top that showed her toned arms, and a snug skirt that accentuated her commitment to the gym. She had her hair down and her face made up lightly with some color in her cheeks and eyeliner that made her hazel eyes pop.

"Sorry I'm late," she said, sitting. "I was at a celebration for a law school classmate who just made partner."

"You have fun?" I said.

"I survived it," she said. "It reinforced the reasons why I decided to leave the world of big firms, overly entitled clients, and supersized egos. Complete shit."

"You don't miss the big salary?"

"Not enough to sell my soul again," she said. "Besides, I did pretty well for myself, and I'm not a big spender."

"You just look like one."

"That's where the art lies." She smiled, and I couldn't help but wonder how many of those Randolphs who were senior partners got a little randy with her.

"What are you drinking?" I asked.

"I really shouldn't," she said. "I'm already at my limit. What are you having?"

"An old-fashioned."

"I love a good old-fashioned," she said. "But I shouldn't. Maybe a glass of wine."

Our waiter came, and she ordered a glass of Chardonnay from Carneros, the southernmost tip of Napa Valley.

"I see you still have the stubble working," she said.

"I got back from LA a few days ago and haven't been inspired to shave," I said.

"Maybe it's best you don't find that inspiration. This look really works for you."

I had a response but thought better of it. Instead, I said, "So your sources have come back on Monroe Connelly."

"In a big way," she said. "When you told me his name, I figured him for just another corporate type sitting on top of the bloodsucking law-firm pyramid. But this guy's a real doozy."

"Sounds fun."

"First of all, he's a named partner, makes a shit ton of money, but doesn't have that many clients."

"So how is he making so much money?"

"The clients he does have are all big and always in need of his services."

"He's running a margin business and not volume. I can't be mad at how he's playing the game."

"'Game' is the right way to describe it. He did a lot of work for the businessman Elliott Kantor, who died recently."

"What kind of work?"

"Mostly real estate deals and any work that other attorneys turned down. He's the kind of guy you call for dirty work, things that need to be done off the books. An alderman needs a little encouragement to sign off on a project in their ward. Someone files a nuisance lawsuit, and you need the plaintiff to quietly go away. He's super connected, and a lot of people in this town owe him favors."

"Family? Wife? Kids?"

"He's been married to the same woman for thirty years. They have one son, who's in college. No one ever sees the wife. They live out in River Forest, and supposedly she's happy being a suburban wife and not getting mixed up in all his activities here in the city. But speaking of family, he's the brother of Eugene Andrade."

"I've heard that name before," I said. "'Love is urgent. A boat at sea is urgent. It is urgent to destroy certain words, hatred, loneliness, and cruelty, some sorrows, many swords.'"

"I'm impressed," she said.

"Don't be. Those weren't my words. They belong to Eugénio de Andrade."

"So you know him?"

"A different Eugene. He was a twentieth-century Portuguese poet. One of his famous poems was 'É urgente o amor.' 'Love is urgent.'"

"You're the first private investigator I've ever met who can solve crimes *and* quote poetry."

"And juggle three bowling pins while blindfolded."

She laughed.

"But in all seriousness," I said, "I know I've heard the name Eugene Andrade somewhere else. I just can't place it."

"First deputy administrator of COPA," she said.

COPA was the Civilian Office of Police Accountability that had been established by a city council ordinance in 2016 in response to the public anger over the long-standing and ineffective police review infrastructure known as the Independent Police Review Authority. The city had suffered from a rash of police-related incidents where civilians were either injured, killed, or their civil rights had been brazenly violated. COPA members were appointed by the mayor and were charged with investigating complaints made against police, as well as specific incidents, such as the dangerous discharge of a firearm, the death of a detainee in police custody, and when a civilian was killed during the course of a police officer performing law enforcement duties.

"This COPA connection adds a new wrinkle," I said.

"In what way?" Karla said.

"That means Connelly has access to the inner workings of certain police information and activities. And in this city, access equals power."

Hearing about Andrade's appointment to COPA made it likely that Connelly and Bailey had some kind of relationship, the nature of which was still in question. The waiter brought Karla her Chardonnay, as well as the tuna tartare and caprese salad I had ordered.

I thought out loud. "So you have two brothers who are lawyers. One does real estate work and has a moonlighting gig in COPA. The other does real estate too, but he moonlights as a legal fixer for rich clients. They must have some relationship to the mayor, because the COPA position is his appointment."

"What do you think all of this means?" she said between small bites of tuna.

"I have no idea, but I'm thinking that Andrade's work with COPA could easily become part of Connelly's sphere of influence."

"Can I ask what specifically your interest is in Connelly?"

I thought for a moment. She had been nice enough to help me without asking many questions. The least I could do was give her an outline, even if it was vague.

"I'm working on a case right now, and I'm not sure if Connelly is involved. I'm trying to get a better understanding of who he is and what he does to see if he's connected in some way. What you've told me is a big help."

"How?"

"Because I think he might have knowledge or access to knowledge that would make him party to what's happening with my investigation."

"Have you ever met him before?"

"Never."

"It's certainly not for me to tell you your job, but have you thought about just approaching him and asking him your questions?"

"I have. But with someone like him, your timing has to be almost perfect when you approach. Sometimes you only get one shot, and if you haven't done your homework, you can blow it all."

"There was also talk about him being very social," Karla said. "But I never know how much stock to put into rumors like that."

"Social in what way?"

"Stepping out of his marriage. He's supposed to be quite the ladies' man."

"Any names flying around?"

"I wasn't given any. I was just told he likes to be out there. He considers himself an operator. Wears expensive bespoke suits. Drives a lot of vintage cars."

I was just about to shovel in a piece of mozzarella, but that stopped me. "What did you just say?"

"He's an operator. He considers himself a ladies' man."

"No, the car part."

"Supposedly, he's got this big car collection. But he's very specific. He only collects vintage cars, and all of them are black."

That put a big smile on my face. Sometimes in the course of an investigation, the heavens open up, and a gift falls from the sky and finds its way right into your lap. This was one of those moments.

"Everything okay?" Karla asked.

"More than okay," I said, raising my glass.

"What are we toasting?" she said.

"Good goddamn luck," I said. "That's what you are to me."

I now was certain that Monroe Connelly was VintageBlackOnly@gmail.com. He was the one who requested Jenny Lee visit Kantor that night, and he was the one who confirmed the appointment had been completed. He was also in the vicinity of Northerly Island when Bianca Wembley's dead body was hanging from that statue. It was way past time to have a sit-down with Esquire Connelly.

35

I was awakened by my phone vibrating across my nightstand. It was Mechanic, at one o'clock in the morning.

"We had company," he said.

"Where?"

"Your father's house."

"How many?"

"Two."

"Are they still there?"

"No, but the bone fragments from one guy's left shoulder are."

"What the hell happened?"

"I was sleeping in a chair in your father's bedroom when I heard the chime. I could tell it was from one of the windows and not the doors. I grabbed Betty, flipped off the safety lock, and waited for them to find me. Took a couple of minutes, but they finally arrived."

"What did you do?"

"Shot the first one."

"In the shoulder?"

"Anywhere else and there would've been blood all over this Egyptian rug your father has in here. I was trying to be considerate."

"So, where are they now?"

"At least one of them is in some emergency room thanking God for skin, because that's the only reason his arm is still attached right now. The other one is probably kneeling in the back of a church somewhere."

"Did they fire back at you?"

"No, I don't think they were prepared for that kind of party."

"Did you follow them out of the house?"

"I did. They jumped inside of a dark truck before I could reach them. Of course, the truck didn't have a license plate."

I gathered my thoughts for a moment, then said, "I don't know who's behind this, but I think I know why."

"Care to share?"

I told him about my conversation with Flavius Bechet and his mentioning of Eagle Rock and my subsequent call to Veronica Thompson.

"You think she knows what Eagle Rock means?"

"By the way she answered my questions, I'm certain."

"You think she's sending these assholes after you?"

"No, I think she told someone that I was asking about Eagle Rock, and *they* decided to send the assholes with a message."

"Well, we just sent a clear message back," Mechanic said.

"Yup. Tag, they're it."

After my walk with Stryker later that morning, I got on my computer and searched for Bianca Wembley. There was nothing on any of the social media platforms and nothing on LinkedIn. The closest thing I could find on the internet was a drag queen with the same first name, who was the first to headline at Wembley Stadium in London. I searched for a good hour, trying various combinations of search terms and even spelling her name several different ways. Nothing came up. I was on the twentieth page of results and about to give up when I stumbled across a potential hit. I found a link to a research article that was published over fifteen years ago in a political science journal. It was titled "America Has Outgrown the Two-Party System." She was one of several co-authors of the article, and they all were part of the Colgate Department of Political Science. I read the article, and while it was short, it was well-written and extremely convincing that the fault in our politics was the limited number of options we had to select our political leaders. Other parties had been formed over the years, but they were always never more than a brave idea, and never taken seriously enough to threaten the two establishment parties. At the end of the article, it had Wembley listed as a student. I then spent the next half hour searching her name in combination with *Colgate* to see if anything else would come up. Nothing. I figured there would at least be a picture of her, maybe a high school yearbook or college sorority photo. Nothing. In these times of mass exposure, viral videos, and endless information sharing, it took a concerted effort to have an almost nonexistent digital footprint. Bianca Wembley had done just that.

A COUPLE OF DAYS LATER, I sat in the customer waiting area at Cephus's Car Joint, a car wash at the corner of State and Fifty-Eighth Street, whose previous owner—whom the wash had been named after—had been forced to surrender the business. My Porsche was on the receiving end of a meticulous hand-washing and fresh coat of wax. The old guy working on her was slow, but he was damn good, and I let him take his time without complaint.

My cell phone pinged.

> This is Pedro. I finally got the other 3 months of manifests. Emailing them now.

A few seconds later, my phone's email notification sounded, and I opened the attachment Pedro had sent. There were only twelve pages, each representing a flight. It would've been much easier to deal with all of this on my computer, but at least I could scan the pages and see if anything caught my attention. It wasn't until I got to the seventh page that I found something. A flight from Chicago to Belize. Kantor, Connelly, Lance Greene, and Keegan Thompson were the listed passengers. The next page was their return flight three days later. I dialed Pedro.

"You ever hear of a man named Keegan Thompson?" I asked.

"Never," Pedro said.

"How about Bishop Thompson?"

"Not that name either."

"On November fifth, Elliott took a flight to Belize with Monroe Connelly, Lance Greene, and Keegan Thompson. Do you know what they were doing?"

"Elliott owns a farm down there," Pedro said. "They must've been going down there to visit."

"A farm?"

"Elliott owns the biggest cattle farm in Belize," Pedro said. "He bought it from a friend of his who had run into some financial trouble. He needed the cash, and Elliott offered to buy the farm until he could get back on his feet."

"Did he ever sell the farm back to the guy?"

"The guy committed suicide a week after he got the money from Elliott."

"Have you ever been down there?"

"No, but I've seen pictures of it. It's huge. Over three thousand acres. The farmhouse is the size of a factory."

"Any idea what they did when they went down there?"

"Not sure, but I've heard the Belizean women are not only beautiful but very friendly, especially to American guests."

Connelly, Thompson, Kantor, and Greene seemed like an odd group. If they were standing in a crowd, you'd never pick them out as acquaintances. But I couldn't stop thinking mostly about Connelly. It seemed like every time I turned a corner, he was sitting there, waiting for me.

THAT EVENING, I WAITED OUTSIDE of Monroe Connelly's gargantuan house in River Forest. The brick mansion sat far back from the road, with a sweeping lawn that had been landscaped to perfection. I was surprised that there was no imposing gate surrounding the property, but then again, this was a zip code where the biggest crime was someone not putting enough change in the parking meter. I arrived a little after six o'clock and parked several houses down, behind a pair of white HVAC contractor vans. I was hoping that would make my position less noticeable on the lightly traveled street. I had been sitting there for just over an hour and only counted ten cars that had passed and a single old couple on an early evening stroll. The silence was deafening, so I turned on the radio, leaned my seat back, and let my mind run through the various parts of the case. I closed my eyes softly and imagined all of the faces and scenes and how they might eventually be connected. I also ran through the conversations with Simon and his sister, Clarence Allen at the *Chicago Defender*, Malcolm Boyd, Veronica Thompson, Flavius Bechet, and Karla Coe. Sometimes when you strung the interviews together in the right order, you could start seeing the shape of a narrative forming.

At a little after eight, Mechanic called in.

"We're just getting on the expressway," he said. "He's driving a black 250 SL Mercedes. Thing is no bigger than a shoebox, but it's sharp as hell."

"This guy's a player," I said. "How far away are you?"

"Probably thirty-five if traffic's not too bad."

"I'll follow him into the driveway," I said. "You stay on the street. If I need your help, I'll put my hand behind my back when I'm out of the car."

"You think he's really going to talk to you? The guy's a lawyer."

"That's exactly why he'll talk. Once I tell him what I know, he'll make quick work of calculating his legal jeopardy. And you don't even need a fancy Juris Doctor to do that."

The sun had fallen low enough that the tree-lined street had finally welcomed darkness. A few cars passed and pulled into the various driveways of the elegant manses. Almost thirty-five minutes on the nose, a pair of headlights approached from behind. As they got closer, I could see the outline of the old Mercedes. The top was down, Connelly's hair blew effortlessly in the wind, and the car's chrome accents glistened under the streetlights. She was a beauty for sure.

Mechanic was at least fifty yards back. He slowed, and I waited for Connelly to turn into his driveway before pulling out from behind the vans and following him onto the property. I could see Mechanic turn off his lights and come to a stop at the foot of the driveway. Connelly pulled his car into the semicircular part of the driveway in front of the house. A detached garage, which I hadn't been able to see from the street, sat a little farther back from the house. It was a mansion of its own.

Connelly got out of his car, either unaware that I had been behind him or unconcerned because he was on the property of his kingdom on a street of other kingdoms, and bad things just didn't happen here. He stopped when he noticed my car and offered a friendly lift of his hand. I got out and met him halfway between the cars. The first thing that struck me was how unbelievably quiet it was, except for the occasional cricket having a moment somewhere off in the woods.

"How can I help you?" he said as we stood a few feet apart. He had the build of an ex-athlete, and his chestnut-colored hair had started to gray near his temples. His suit was perfectly tailored, and the gold Rolex hanging on his wrist had just enough diamonds to be taken seriously but not too many to be flamboyant.

"Monroe Connelly, attorney-at-law," I said. "Nice to finally meet you." I pointed to the car. "What year is she?"

"'68."

"Don't see many of them on the road these days. If I remember correctly, it has a 2.8 liter, straight six under the hood, right? Those oval lights and chrome lip were a real upgrade from the previous models."

"You know your cars," Connelly said. "Who are you?"

I offered my hand, and he accepted it. "Ashe Cayne," I said.

"Do I know you?"

"I'm not sure. But you might know some of my work."

"What kind of work do you do?"

"Help the cops catch the robbers."

"You won't find many robbers in these parts," he said.

"Carjackings and purse snatchings aren't the only forms of robbery," I said. "Lots of people living in these big houses steal all the time. But since they also control the system, Lady Justice tends to look the other way."

Connelly smiled. "We all have a right to our own opinion. It's been a long day, I'm tired, and I want to get into my house. Mind telling me why you're really here?"

"We work for the same family," I said. "The Kantors."

Connelly's expression changed. That had gotten his attention.

"Are you an attorney?" he said.

"No, I'm a private investigator looking into what happened to the old man. His son hired me. Do you know Simon?"

"Not personally, but I know of him," Connelly said.

"It's a little strange that with as much work as you've done for the father, neither the son nor his assistants know who you are."

"Elliott had professional relationships with a lot of people," he said. "I'm sure Simon and his assistants didn't know everyone he worked with. So if that's all you've come to check on, then there's not much more I can say."

The front door opened, and a woman in a relaxed-fitting dress stood in the doorway. She was tall, with long blond hair that had been pulled behind her ears.

"Everything okay, Roe?" she said.

As he started to walk in her direction, I said, "Maybe we can talk about Jenny Lee when you get a chance."

That stopped him midstride. "I'll be there in a few," he said to his wife. "Just finishing up this conversation."

His wife looked at us for a moment as if making an assessment, then closed the door behind her.

"Let's go for a walk," he said.

I put my right hand behind my back and followed him down the driveway. He stopped in front of the garage, whose exterior lights had been activated as we approached.

"What exactly are you trying to accomplish?" he said. "I need to understand the scope of what you're trying to do."

"That's pretty easy," I said. "I'm just trying to figure out why one of the richest men in Chicago was found hog-tied to a four-poster bed in his multimillion-dollar secret apartment on the evening of May second, wearing only ruby-colored women's panties. And why Jenny Lee, formerly Su-Wei Hsiah, no relation to the great doubles tennis player from Taiwan, who spells her last name with an *e* instead of an *a*, was visiting Kantor, your client, the same night he died, and was driving a blue Maserati that's registered under your name. How's that for scope?"

Connelly smiled confidently. "Don't take this the wrong way, but I think you're getting yourself into something that's way above your pay grade," he said. "Sounds like you have a bunch of disparate pieces of information, and you're trying to make it all fit together."

"Not sure how disparate they are," I said. "They all seem pretty close and connected to me. But I'm willing to accept your interpretation. So why don't you indulge me a little and explain how I've got this all wrong? Then I'll be on my way."

"You probably should just be on your way, because, unfortunately, any information I have relative to Elliott Kantor is protected under attorney-client confidentiality. And that protection remains in force even after the client dies."

"Yes, but suppressing information in a police investigation has nothing to do with attorney-client privilege."

"I have no idea what you're talking about."

"Let me explain to you my idea," I said. "I think you asked your brother, Eugene Andrade, who's the first deputy administrator of COPA and ironically shares the same name with a great Portuguese poet, to keep a lid on the investigation of Bishop Keegan Thompson, who was found similarly to your client, hog-tied in bed, wearing women's accessories, and who was not only wealthy but also a friend of Kantor, and who joined you, Kantor, and Lance Greene about seven months ago on a trip to Kantor's cattle farm in Belize."

"Sounds like you've been working hard and doing a lot of digging," Connelly said. "Or creating."

"That's why I get paid the big bucks," I said. "Well, not the kind of bucks you make, obviously, with a place like this and the collection of cars you own, but I find a way to scratch out a decent living."

"I also think you have a very active imagination," he said.

"I think you have a lot of explaining to do."

"I have nothing to explain. Especially to you."

"No problem," I said. "We'll do it your way. You don't have to talk to me, but you can explain to someone at CPD who's not in your brother's pocket why you and a future Hall of Famer were on Northerly Island the same night Bianca Wembley was found hanging from a statue there."

"I've never heard of a Bianca Wembley."

I believed him.

"But you've heard of Daphne," I said.

"I appreciate that you're trying to help the family get some answers for what's obviously a difficult situation. I was very fond of Elliott. He was a good man who did a lot of good things for tons of people. Losing him like this has been difficult for all of us. He was more than just a client. He was also a friend."

"Is that why you sent Jenny Lee to his apartment that night? Except by the time she made it there, he was already dead."

He shook his head dismissively as he smiled nonchalantly.

"You can deny it as much as you want, but you're the one who made the payment for her visit," I said, "and you're the one who confirmed the visit was complete."

"Listen, I'm going inside my house to have dinner with my wife," he said. "It's been a long day."

"VintageBlackOnly@gmail.com," I said.

Connelly turned and walked toward his front door, never once looking back at me to see what I was doing or about to do. He calmly opened the door, walked inside, and closed it behind him. I'd come to learn that when people turn their back on a perceived threat, they are either completely confident no harm will come to them, or they're stupid. Monroe Connelly might've been many things, but stupid was not one of them.

36

The next two days were surprisingly quiet. I convinced my father to extend his overseas trip an extra week, so he decided to take a train down to Paris and attend the famous Paris Jazz Festival. I had an entirely new security system installed in his house, with cameras that could be controlled remotely via my phone. Burke reported that the CPD finally got an address for Bianca Wembley in Lakeview. Connelly had gone quiet and hadn't been to his office since the night we talked. Simon had called, looking for an update, and Bailey had sent a message wanting to arrange another meeting. Penny and I hit a round at Medinah Country Club, where I played the front nine like I had never been to a golf course before, then turned around after lunch and amazingly shot even par on the back nine.

I had been sitting at my desk doing an internet search on Eagle Rock and coming up with little that seemed connected to Thompson, except for the fact that there was a small neighborhood located in Northeast LA between Glendale and Pasadena with the same name. I made a note to look into that. Maybe in that conversation Flavius overheard, Thompson was making an arrangement to meet the woman and man in Eagle Rock. I had just clicked on a link about the neighborhood when my phone buzzed. It was Dr. Ellison.

"I thought you had forgotten about me," I said.

"Not at all," he said. "I wanted to make sure I had my thoughts sorted out correctly before getting back to you."

"You found something?"

"For sure, but before I give you my impressions, can you give me a little more background about this young woman?"

I told him about the circumstances surrounding Bianca's death and how she had finally been identified. I didn't mention Connelly or Greene or anything to do with Kantor.

"And the pathologist who carried out this exam, is she new?" he said. "I don't recognize her name."

"I'm not sure," I said. "But I can check it out and get back to you. I know they recently had a mass hiring to help them get through the backlog of bodies they always seem to have."

"Well, I'm going to be honest," he said. "I don't like to criticize someone else's work, but this report you sent me is badly missing the mark. It almost strikes me as the work of a young pathology resident just learning the trade."

"What's bothering you?"

"I don't have a problem with the exam itself, but the conclusion doesn't match the findings. I've listed five areas of concern. Do you have the time now to discuss them?"

"Absolutely." I grabbed my case pad, turned to a blank sheet, and wrote *Bianca Wembley autopsy* at the top of the page.

"Let me start with the big picture," Dr. Ellison said. "This appears to be an otherwise healthy young woman who had a few incidental findings, like a small mitral valve in her heart, a slight lateral curvature of the spine, and a one-inch leg-length discrepancy."

"Could any of these things contribute to her death?"

"Not at all. That's why these kinds of findings are called 'incidental.' You just happen to find them at autopsy; otherwise, you might never even know they existed."

"Don't most of us have one leg that's longer than the other?" I said. "Or is that just one of those urban myths?"

"No, it's very true. Some estimates are that between forty to seventy percent of the population has some degree of limb discrepancy. But those are typically small, an eighth or quarter of an inch. When the difference is half an inch or more, and in her case, an inch, then that could start presenting problems with walking, and if that's not addressed correctly, it could eventually lead to joint or spine issues from the constant imbalance. That might explain the slight curvature they found in her spinal column. This discrepancy is also enough to cause her to noticeably limp if her shoes aren't properly adjusted or fitted with a prosthetic. But once again, that was just an incidental finding. Let's go through the things that raised red flags for me. Let's go in descending anatomical order from the superior aspect of the body to inferior. Were you able to see the body yourself either at the scene or in the ME's office?"

"No."

"Do you have any photographs of the deceased?"

"I've searched online but can't find any images of her."

"I ask because the description of her face coloration caught my attention but doesn't surprise me. Her skin was a darker hue, and that's likely from what's called venous congestion, where the veins in the neck have been blocked and the blood can't flow freely, thus leading to congestion, which can manifest in the skin becoming a darker color."

"Does that indicate hanging or something else?"

"It indicates she died from asphyxiation, which is basically a death from interruption of breathing or inadequate oxygen supply. But hanging is not the only way to develop this discoloration;

strangulation can do it also. That's something to keep in mind as you go through the possible mechanisms of death."

I took copious notes so that when I reviewed everything in the file, I had the reference information I needed to make a well-informed assessment of the facts.

"My next area of interest is the eyes," Dr. Ellison said, "particularly the conjunctival surface of the eyelids. Both eyelids had petechiae, which are round pinpoint red spots resulting from localized bleeding. This happens for two main reasons. When a person is hypoxic, or not getting enough oxygen, and when there's an acute increase in the blood pressure inside the veins of the neck and head. This is commonly found in both a hanging and manual or ligature strangulation."

"So just to be clear, this could be another sign that it wasn't a hanging?"

"Precisely. Next on the list, the periorbital abrasions."

"Which means?"

"Several areas around her mouth showed skin irritation and translucency that had clear lines of demarcation. This is significant, because let's say it was something like an allergic rash, then you might not expect the borders to be so well-defined. They tend to be irregular. But in this case, there's such a clear definition of the affected areas, it makes me think of some type of adhesive covering."

"Like a Band-Aid," I said.

"Or duct tape," Dr. Ellison said. "But unfortunately, the pathologist doesn't list this as a possibility for the periorbital abrasions. In fact, she never addresses this at all."

"What do you think the skin changes mean?"

"That her mouth was duct-taped."

"Why would someone who's about to commit suicide duct-tape her own mouth, remove the duct tape, then hang herself?"

"When you put it like that, it doesn't make much sense at all," Dr. Ellison said. "Which leads me to her wrists. The pathologist reports that several markings consistent with bracelet impressions were found on both wrists."

"You don't like it?"

"What I don't like is that she seems to have rushed through the possibilities. It's rational to think that a young woman might've been wearing bracelets. And depending on the type of bracelets they were, they could've left the marks that were seen around the wrists. But restraints could've left similar marks too. Why doesn't she even consider that in her conclusion? She took what was the most convenient explanation, put blinders on, and stuck with it. Too expedient for my liking. I would've liked to see her give it more thought."

I continued taking notes.

"My third and most significant item is the neck dissection she performed," Dr. Ellison said. "She noted hemorrhage in several of the neck muscle layers. That's an equivocal finding, meaning it could be the result of a hanging, or it could be the result of strangulation. But that's not what has my interest. It's the hyoid bone fracture that's giving me pause."

"What's the hyoid bone?" I said.

"It's a small horseshoe-shaped bone in the front of the neck along the midline. It sits just above the much larger thyroid cartilage that protects the larynx, or voice box. The fact that it was found to be fractured makes me think this was an incomplete or rushed exam."

"Why?"

"Because a fractured hyoid typically means some type of strangulation, either manually or by ligature," Dr. Ellison said. "In the vast majority of cases when someone dies from hanging, the hyoid bone is rarely fractured, because there's not enough sudden pressure on the bone to cause it to break. The exception is judicial hangings."

"By judicial hangings, you mean hanging executions, like in the old days?" I said.

"Correct," he said. "Back when they used hanging as a form of capital punishment, in almost all of those cases, if those bodies were indeed autopsied, they would've seen a fractured hyoid bone, as well as a fractured thyroid cartilage and one or more of the cervical spinous processes. That's because the gallows they used to hang those sentenced to death were at least a story high. They would tie a noose around the neck, then let the body free-fall until it was violently jerked to a stop by the rope. That motion and sudden catch about the neck caused lots of fractures throughout the neck. But you don't typically see these fractures in a simple suicide hanging. Not enough force to do that kind of damage."

"So, what are you suggesting?"

"In some cases of hanging, examiners will order an MRI of the neck to look for things they can't find at regular gross inspection at autopsy."

"Which means?"

"When the pathologist does a regular autopsy, there's only so much level of detail that can be seen with the naked eye. That's called a gross inspection. When more detail is needed, then the pathologist can use imaging studies like a CT or MRI to get a closer look at the tissues in question."

"I don't remember reading anything about an MRI or CT scan," I said.

"That's because they weren't done," Dr. Ellison said.

"Was that a mistake?"

"I don't know if I'd call it a mistake. It's really up to the discretion and suspicions of the pathologist."

"So if she had a high suspicion that the cause of death was something other than hanging, she might've ordered one or both of the studies."

"Exactly," Dr. Ellison said. "There are a lot of protocols in forensic pathology, but there are plenty of gray areas where the examiner needs to make decisions based on their findings, evidence presented, and their working narrative of what likely happened."

"Would you have ordered an MRI?" I said.

"I would have, but that's easy for me to say, sitting in the comfort of my living room and not in a cold lab."

"What do you think happened?"

"I think someone restrained and strangled this woman, then hung her up to make it look like a suicide," Dr. Ellison said.

"Would you be willing to bet on that?" I said.

"Not everything I own, but a damn good chunk of it."

37

A few days later, Burke called and informed me that Bianca Wembley's older brother, Oscar Wembley, had called to report that the woman who was initially thought to be Daphne was indeed his sister, Bianca. He was flying in early the next morning to identify and claim her. Now that she had undergone an autopsy, he planned on having her cremated, then taking her ashes back with him to San Francisco. Burke gave me his cell phone number, and after exchanging a couple of missed calls, we finally connected. Oscar seemed hesitant to meet at first, but when I explained my serious doubts about his sister's suicide and my suspicions that the autopsy might've been misdirected, he was eager to help figure out what really happened to his baby sister. Once he took care of business at the medical examiner's office, he and I would sit down for a chat. I knew virtually nothing about Bianca Wembley, so I was encouraged that her brother might be able to provide some answers to the many questions I had.

OSCAR WEMBLEY WAS A LARGE man with curly brown hair, bright blue eyes, and a slight coloration to his skin. His grip was strong, and he had a voice to match. He carried a large envelope in one hand, which I assumed were papers from the ME's office.

"Sorry to meet you under these circumstances," I said as he got settled into his seat. "I know this must be tough for you and your family."

"There's not much family," he said. "It was only Bianca and me left. We had a couple of cousins, but we saw them sparingly growing up."

"Where did you grow up?"

"Oswego, New York, a small town upstate on Lake Ontario. We were adopted by two teachers who couldn't have children on their own. Bianca and I weren't biological siblings. I was ten years older."

"Are your parents still alive?"

"Unfortunately, they're both gone. They were older when they adopted us. My father had a heart attack while running along the lake one morning. My mother was hit by a drunk driver a few years ago."

"I'm sorry to hear that," I said.

"They were good people," Oscar said. "They took me in when it wasn't popular to adopt biracial kids." He smiled. "Bianca and I would get a kick out of telling people we were brother and sister. She was barely five feet and pale as the moon. I was always tall and clearly had at least one Black parent. It was always fun to see people struggle to hide their surprise."

"I can only imagine the looks the two of you must've gotten."

"Especially in a small, sterile town like Oswego." Oscar smiled at the memory.

"Was your sister suffering from depression or anything like that?"

"Not that I know of," Oscar said. "Bianca and I weren't so close the last five years. I had moved out to San Fran and started a family. She had moved out here after school. We talked occasionally, but it's tough when you're so far apart, and then we lost Mom, so we didn't have that connection back home."

"Did she have lots of friends?"

"Not sure about that either. She never talked about boyfriends or anything to do with her social life. I know she liked to travel a lot, but I never saw many pictures. I assumed she was going with friends or a partner."

"When was the last time you spoke to her?"

"My oldest daughter's birthday, May seventeenth. She and Bianca FaceTimed each other. Bianca bought her a Gucci backpack. Bianca always bought the girls expensive gifts. But I could never figure out how she could do that from the small online arts-and-crafts business she ran."

"Lots of people took up arts and crafts during the pandemic," I said. "If she was good at what she did, then she could've done really well."

"I guess," Oscar said. "But buying a fourteen-year-old girl a two-thousand-dollar backpack is excessive. But Bianca insisted. She said they were her only nieces, and she didn't have her own kids, so she had the right to spoil them. The girls really loved Bianca."

"What was the name of her business?"

"The Crafty Magic," Oscar said.

"When you last talked to her, how did she sound?"

"Perfect. Like her usual self. Funny. Upbeat. She was planning a trip to South Africa this Christmas."

"No signs at all that she might be sad about something or worried?"

"Nothing. She was happy."

"I'm going to shoot straight with you, Oscar," I said. "I don't think your sister committed suicide. I think someone killed her and tried to stage it as a suicide."

"The medical examiner is saying it's a suicide."

"I know. But the medical examiner has bodies coming through the doors every day, and it's hard for them to keep up. They're humans like anyone else. If you have a long list of cases on your desk and you have an unidentified, unclaimed body and the police report describes what looks like a suicide, that could influence how quickly you make the same determination."

"What makes you think someone killed her?"

"I have been working on another case that had nothing to do with her. But just by chance, I heard about your sister on the evening news. Something struck me as odd. I was more curious than I was suspicious. But as I looked more into my case, I started seeing some similarities with your sister's. I couldn't find out much about your sister, but from what I was able to gather, something just didn't sit right with me. I was able to get my hands on a copy of the autopsy report, and I had an outside pathologist take a look at it, because I definitely don't understand all of the medical lingo. He's pretty certain your sister didn't hang herself."

"What does he think happened?" Oscar said.

"He thinks she was restrained at her wrists, duct-taped, and strangled. When she was dead, they hung her on that statue to make it look like a suicide."

Oscar blinked to fight back tears. "I just can't imagine who would do that to her," he said. "And I'm surprised she didn't fight back. Bianca was small, but she was feisty as hell. She wouldn't let anyone just walk over her. She spent almost every summer fishing and hunting with our grandfather. She was pretty, but she was a real tomboy. They would go camping in the woods for several days at a time. Just the two of them. Catching fish and shooting small game, then bringing their kill back to the campsite to clean and cook it on the fire. If Bianca could've fought, she would've."

That made me think that they had immobilized her somehow. I wondered if she had a sedative on board like Kantor and Thompson had. I made a mental note to look into it.

"Was she still in touch with your grandfather?" I said.

"No, he died about fifteen years ago. Broke her heart. Like I said, our dad was a teacher, so he was more into the academic stuff. But my grandfather was one of those outdoorsy guys. I remember the smile on her face one summer when they had come back from camping. She was thrilled that he taught her how to shoot a rifle and tie a proper knot to secure the animal on the hood of the old Jeep my grandfather drove. She spent an entire week that summer walking around the house tying knots, so she'd be ready that weekend when they went back out."

"Your sister's life feels like a mystery," I said.

"Meaning?"

"Well, she just seemed so reserved, keeping to herself."

"Well, I don't want to give you the wrong impression. Bianca wasn't some introverted loner who was incapable of socializing. She could be very social, but she did like her privacy. Oswego was not exactly the most exciting place to live. Most of the townspeople didn't get us. And to be honest, we really didn't care. We got us, and that was what mattered. But when she went to college, that's when I think she came into her own. She enjoyed the freedom, the bigness of it all. Her world opened up at Colgate."

"Speaking of college, that's the one thing I was able to find," I said. "She co-authored a paper in a political science journal about our political party system. It was a really convincing argument. Not typically my type of reading, but I enjoyed it."

Oscar smiled. "Bianca was deceptively smart. People would see this pretty little girl and think she might be a cheerleader or something, but Bianca had a huge brain. She knew something about everything and wasn't afraid to let you know it." Oscar laughed to himself. "She took after our father in that regard. You got him wound up, and he could debate a dead tree."

"So, what are you going to do next?" I said.

"Have her cremated and bring her back with me," Oscar said. "Bianca was never into funerals and things like that. She always thought they were sadder than they needed to be. She always thought there should be a celebration of life. Problem is, I don't know how to reach her friends to celebrate."

"Have you been to her apartment yet?"

"I'm going there now," he said.

"Would you mind if I joined you? Maybe there will be something there that will give us a clue as to why someone would do this."

"Let's do it," Oscar said.

After stuffing his enormous frame into the passenger seat of my Porsche, we raced up to an address in Lakeview that Oscar had written on a piece of paper. The quiet residential street looked like it was more suited to young families of means or retired couples who had downsized from larger homes and opted for something smaller to remain in the city. Bianca lived in a slim, three-floor limestone house with a small front yard surrounded by a tall privacy fence. Two cameras on both corners of the house pointed in our direction. Oscar produced a key that let us in the gate, then in the front door of the house.

We stepped into the foyer and stopped to make a visual inspection. Everything was immaculate, almost as if it were a staged home and no one actually lived there. The furnishings were sparse but well-appointed, and the rooms felt cold in the way overly designed homes could be when functionality became secondary to aesthetic.

"I never knew Bianca was doing this well," Oscar said, his head slowly swiveling to take it all in. "This is a pretty spiffy place."

"Makes me feel like I'm in the wrong business," I said. "Who knew Popsicle sticks, yarn, and glitter could add up to all of this?"

"Where should we start?" he asked.

"The bedroom," I said. "If there's any room that can tell you most about a homeowner's character, it's usually the privacy of their bedroom." I had flashbacks of seeing Kantor tied up to his bedposts. "The bedroom is where people can be who they are without judgment."

We walked through the first-floor rooms, a formal dining room, a large living room, and a marble-tiled kitchen in the back. We scaled the carpeted steps to the second floor, where we found the primary bedroom sitting alone, at the opposite end of the hall from two large guest bedrooms. Stepping into the room was the first time I felt like a woman really lived here. There weren't any pinks or pastels or framed boards preaching *Live, Laugh, Love*. But the attention to detail in the curtains, the comforter, and even the pillowcases was clearly the discriminating choice of a woman.

"What a TV," Oscar said.

The bed faced a massive TV screen hanging on the opposite wall.

"*Sunday Night Football* would look really good on a screen that big," I said.

I slowly walked around the room, looking for anything that might give me a clue as to who Bianca was and what her interests had been. I didn't see any electronic devices—no tablet, phone, or computer. How could a thirty-six-year-old woman exist and not be connected? Even more confusing, how could she run an online business without a computer?

I walked into her closet, which was the size of a small bedroom. Just like the rest of the house, everything was in perfect order. One entire wall had been lined with shelves to house her extensive shoe collection. Based on what I had learned from Carolina, these looked to be the designer brands sold at the luxury stores on Oak Street. I noticed a shelf that had various types of plastic moldings, which must've been the orthotics Dr. Ellison said she had probably used to even out her leg-length difference. I left the closet and entered the bathroom with its floor-to-ceiling marble and double-steam shower. I opened the cabinets of the vanity and found standard female accessories neatly organized. Her toothbrush and other items rested neatly in silver cups on the polished countertop. I opened the drawers and found combs and brushes, as well as a recent birth control prescription.

I walked back into the room and looked at her nightstand. In front of a stack of political biographies sat a framed photograph of three beautiful girls with their hands around each other as they stood on a bright beach, with the water at their backs.

"Your daughters?" I asked Oscar.

He walked over, picked up the photo, and smiled. "Charlotte, Cayden, and Camden," he said. "We were down in Cancún over winter break a couple of years ago. Bianca was supposed to go with us on that trip, but she had some last-minute work situation."

"By the looks of the gene pool, you're gonna have a lot of problems on your hands very soon."

"Soon? Boys are already texting Charlotte nonstop and sending her messages all night on Snapchat. And she's only fourteen."

"I guess in the scheme of things, that's not the worst problem to have," I said. "Kids are into a lot of bad things these days. A little flirtation and pursuit are manageable. The alternatives, not so much."

"Couldn't agree more," Oscar said, resting the photograph back on the nightstand. "We've heard the nightmares from other parents."

We walked into the guest bedrooms on the same floor, but finding nothing out of order or interesting, we went back downstairs, where we found an office at the back of the house. I turned on the light and stepped into the dark-paneled room. Two of the walls were lined with floor-to-ceiling bookshelves, and the third wall was a gigantic fireplace with a large oil-on-canvas painting of a mermaid framed above the mantelpiece. Against the fourth wall, which was just windows, sat an oval black walnut desk. An orange orchid plant sat on one end and a slender crystal lamp on the other. What really caught my eye, however, was that there wasn't a computer. There was a stack of papers neatly arranged in a letter tray, a recent issue of *Vanity Fair*, and a copy of Michelle Obama's autobiography *Becoming* resting on top of Hillary Clinton's *Hard Choices*. A Montblanc pen rested on top of a blotter, and the desktop was so clean, I got the feeling it was never used.

I walked behind the desk and pulled the chair back. I opened the top drawer. It was mostly empty, except for a calendar and old copies of a few fashion magazines. The other drawers contained basic office supplies and a folder of receipts that I opened and flipped through. Nothing stood out. She had gone to London a couple of months ago and stayed at Brown's Hotel. She was only there for three nights. I put the folder back in the drawer, then looked down at the floor. That's when I found what I had been looking for: an HP computer charging cord, which meant at some point, there had been a computer on the desk, before someone decided to take it. The reason why everything seemed too perfect and there were so few of her personal effects was because the place had been cleaned. All traces of what she was doing and who she might've been connected to had been carefully removed.

We went down and inspected the basement. She had installed a small gym with a stationary bike, a treadmill, yoga mats, an adjustable bench, and a rack of dumbbells. I looked for some type of DVR machine for the cameras but didn't find anything.

When we got back upstairs, Oscar said, "So what do you think?"

"Did the medical examiner give you any of her personal effects?" I said.

"They told me she didn't have any. Just the clothes she was wearing."

"While I was walking through the rooms, I kept asking myself, 'Where's the computer? Where's her cell phone? Where's anything that indicates a pretty, active woman in her thirties actually lived here?'"

"Are you saying you don't believe she lived here?"

"Just the opposite. I believe she lived here, but I think someone did such a meticulous job of covering their tracks, they left the house in a condition that seems unrealistic, too sterile. Who really lives this cleanly and this perfectly?"

"I saw two cameras outside when we came in," Oscar said.

"They won't do any good. If they were recording video to a DVR, the machine is probably in the bottom of Lake Michigan right now. If it was recording to the cloud like a lot of these new surveillance systems do, then that's a lost cause too. They were probably controlled remotely via her phone, which we don't have, and it would be almost impossible to access her account without any of her security information."

"So, what do we do next?"

"Do you have anything of hers at your house in California?"

Oscar shook his head. "I really doubt it. Maybe some pictures when we were kids, but that's about it."

"Do you have any pictures of her on your phone?"

"I should," Oscar said. He opened his phone and scrolled through the gallery. "Here she is in London. The girls had never seen a real palace before, so they asked her to take a photo of one when she last went over to the city for a meeting. This was her standing in front of Kensington Palace."

He handed me the phone. Bianca stood in front of an enormous wrought-iron black gate with large gold-leaf ornamental inlays. The roofline of the palace could be seen towering behind her. Bianca had long dark hair and bright hazel eyes. A small diamond nose ring added a sparkle to her face. She had a petite frame but was built well. Getting attention, both desired and undesired, must have come easy for her.

"I think she sent us another one while she was there," Oscar said.

He swiped across the screen to the next photo. Bianca was wearing a different outfit, this time a knee-length skirt and a matching jacket covering a light blue blouse. Unlike in the previous photo, she wore just a touch of makeup and soft pink lipstick. She was no longer wearing her diamond nose ring. She looked happy and vigorous. She was standing in front of a cube-shaped avant-garde building that had full-length columns of what appeared to be crystalline structure that formed the entire wall. I handed the phone back to Oscar. He took one more forlorn look at his sister before sliding the phone back into his front pocket.

"She's beautiful," I said. "I'm very sorry this happened to her. Can you text this photo to me?"

"No problem," he said. "But I just don't understand any of this. Why would someone do this to Bianca? What could she have done to deserve this?"

"I don't know the reason," I said. "And even if I'm able to find one, it still might not make any sense."

"I still haven't told the girls yet," he said. "Every time I try, I can't find the right words."

"It won't be easy," I said. "But after doing this for so many years, I've learned that kids are a lot more resilient than we adults give them credit for."

"I'm going to spend some time alone here, if you don't mind," he said, walking me to the door. "I just want to be in her space."

"I completely understand," I said, opening the door. "And do me a favor. I know you might not have much from her, but if you could dig around a little when you get back home, I'd appreciate it. Sometimes what we think is insignificant can be surprisingly relevant and helpful."

I walked down the stairs and to my car, thinking how vicious and unpredictable life could be.

38

After a frustrating morning of trying to make some progress on the investigation but getting nothing accomplished, I began feeling restless, but not in a way where I wanted to exercise. My head was feeling clogged with facts, suppositions, and open questions regarding these three deaths that I was becoming more convinced were connected. I needed to clear my head, so I walked over to the Art Institute. I called Lacey Vinton, who informed me that she had thirty minutes to take me to see the Basquiat before she started her shift. We made a plan.

Lacey met me in the lobby, dressed more modestly than she had been when we first met. Her hair was tied into a bun, and she wore a pair of horn-rimmed glasses that completed her transformation to full geek hotness.

"How's the case going?" she said as we walked back toward the modern wing of the museum. Foot traffic in the galleries was light but steady.

"It's going," I said. "I need a break, so no thinking or talking about investigations or crimes. I need the next thirty minutes to be all about Basquiat."

"Well, I can deliver on that," she said. "Have you seen *Johnnypump* in person yet?"

"Nope, only online."

"Then you're in for a treat. Seeing a Basquiat in person is a much different experience than seeing photographs online. He painted with such energy and emotion that you have to be in the room with it to fully appreciate all that he brought to his work."

"What attracts you to him the most?"

"His art, obviously," Lacey said. "But also his story. There really wasn't anyone like him in the world. He was part of the Neo-Expressionist movement in the eighties with other experimental artists like Julian Schnabel, Susan Rothenberg, and Francesco Clemente. Not to take anything away from the other great artists, but Basquiat stood out from the rest. And part of that might be his story."

"I remember reading that he died really young," I said.

"Twenty-seven. Overdosed in his apartment on Great Jones Street in New York City. His story is as fascinating as his art. He was born in Brooklyn, New York, to a Puerto Rican mother and Haitian father. He got his start tagging graffiti on subway trains. Dropped out of high school a year before he was supposed to graduate and made a living selling one-dollar postcards and sweatshirts with his artwork on them. He was even homeless for a while. But like most art icons, he finally got the break he needed when some of his work was featured in a group show. He was only twenty. The art world was blown away by how he creatively fused words, stick figures, animals, and symbols. There really had been nothing like it before, and so he went from selling postcards for a dollar to original artwork for fifty thousand dollars."

"Gotta imagine that for a kid on the outs for several years, suddenly making that kind of money must have been a total mind fuck."

"Like many great artists, he struggled to handle his fame. Drugs were his liberation but also his prison. He knew he needed help, so he went to a ranch in Hawaii to get away from it all and deal with his addiction. He returned in less than a week, claiming he had kicked his habit. Just a few weeks later, he died of an overdose in the East Village apartment he rented from the estate of Andy Warhol, one of his mentors and friends."

Hearing her describe Basquiat's ending made me think of Bianca Wembley, even though I was supposed to be avoiding any thoughts or conversations about work. Had she still been alive when they hung her up on that statue, left alone to die in the middle of the open parkland? I imagined she had been duct-taped when they hung her, but then maybe they removed it because she was already dead. I hoped she died before they hung her. Being hung to death seemed so cruel and painful.

We walked through an airy court then finally into the gallery. The painting hit you as soon as you entered the room. The first thing that got your attention was its massive size, eight by fourteen feet. The vibrancy of the colors and images jumped off the canvas. I stood there for a moment to just take it all in. A skeletal stick figure of a Black boy next to a skeletal black dog baring its teeth stood in the center of flashes of red and strokes of white and gray that represented an open fire hydrant. The background was all bright, hot colors that represented summer.

"Jesus Christ," I finally whispered. "Sheer genius."

"This is why I tell people that it's nice to be able to see art online, but it still remains a medium where, if you want to get the true essence, you really have to see it in person."

We stepped feet away from the painting for a closer inspection. The freneticism of the brushstrokes was even more impressive up close.

"The way he drew the boy was how he liked to represent Black figures in his art," Lacey said. "But look at the dog. Notice how strong and rapid the brushstrokes are. This was a technique at the core of Neo-Expressionism, and no one did it better than Basquiat, especially when he added the primitive forms."

I stood there, just looking at the colors and the images. Everything was so loud and restless. There was beauty in the grotesque depictions.

"It's so strong," I said. "It just screams at you, and no matter what part of the painting you look at, the screaming doesn't stop."

"Vintage Basquiat," Lacey said. "Not just with the symbols and the colors and the stick figures but also the messaging. He was very upset about the country's disgusting history of slavery and racism and the events that were still happening in the eighties, with innocent Black people being beaten and killed for no reason. The boy's hair is three-pointed, something he did in other works. This represents Black people as being kings even while living simple lives, because they enjoy freedom. Many critics gave him a hard time his entire career, but he didn't give a shit and told them so. He was always Jean-Michel Basquiat."

"It's humbling just to think how much the guy did in such a short life. So much success at such a young age, then gone like that."

"Like many of the other great artists in history," Lacey said. "Modigliani at thirty-five, Van Gogh at thirty-seven, Seurat at thirty-one. Basquiat at twenty-seven. It's almost like the blessings of their gifts were also curses. Makes you appreciate even more how productive they were for such short lives. Basquiat created a collection of over six hundred paintings and fifteen hundred drawings in less than a decade. Imagine how much more he could've done had he lived."

I took one last look at the painting and thought about the photos I had seen of Basquiat on the internet.

"And then you look at pictures of him," I said, "this eccentric-looking Black kid with free-form hair, casual, unimpressed, a rebelliousness in his eyes. Had you not known who he was, just looking at him, you never in a million years would imagine he was such an artistic genius."

"But that's life, isn't it?" Lacey said. "Often people aren't who you think they are or who they pretend to be."

When I got back to the office, I kept thinking of Basquiat and his short life, about his fearlessness in the face of battering criticism from the art world elite to be true to himself and his ideals. Then I thought about Lacey's final words: *Often people aren't who you think they are or who they pretend to be.* That prompted me to wake up my computer and type *The Crafty Magic*, Bianca's online store. No results for a store came back. The top results were for a glue stick. I checked page after page. Nothing about an arts-and-crafts store. I searched Facebook and Instagram and TikTok. Nothing. Had I written the name down wrong? I texted Oscar to make sure. He texted me back within minutes and confirmed that was the name. He was certain. I checked Delaware's database of corporations, and still nothing came up. I sat back in my seat and stared out the window at the scattered clouds sliding over the lake. Rain was definitely on the way. Bianca Wembley hadn't owned an online arts-and-crafts store, but how had she made a living, and how could she have afforded such expensive trips and gifts for nieces? I was certain Bianca was not who she had pretended to be.

I printed out the photo Oscar had sent me, then took it, along with the first page of the journal article she had written, to the board and taped them next to Kantor's and Thompson's photos. Then I remembered how Oscar had mentioned she would've fought off anyone attacking her. I looked at her autopsy report, hoping to find the same sedative that had been found in Kantor's and Thompson's blood. That would be an important link between the three deaths. Unfortunately, the lab results only showed her birth control medication. I stood there for a moment, looking at Bianca's picture, then wrote underneath her name, *Daphne, who are you?* I looked into her vibrant eyes. It was no coincidence that her killer had taken her to Daphne Garden. They had wanted her body to be found at that specific location for a reason.

MECHANIC AND I WERE IN the middle of a sparring session at Hammer's, working up a good sweat. It was a back-and-forth type of battle, neither one of us willing to give an inch. Some of the other boxers had gathered around to watch. Mechanic delivered a nice one-two combo, jabbing me on my right flank harder than I was expecting, then landing a cross that grazed the right side of my head. I ducked and rolled and threw a left uppercut to his solar plexus, not hard enough to put him down, but with enough power to back him up a couple of steps against the rope, which is exactly where I wanted him. I delivered a rapid succession of jabs that elicited a collective groan from those watching. Mechanic raised his gloves in defense to cover his face, and I continued to work his body.

"Enough already," I heard Hammer yell. Then a strong tug on my shoulder pulled me back. "What, are ya trying to kill the man? Jesus Christ. You're friends."

Mechanic popped up from the ropes, took out his mouthpiece, and smiled. "That the best you got?" he said.

"Okay, tough guy," Hammer said. "You know you can't talk shit once I've gotten you out of a jam. Low-class." He then turned to me and said, "Go answer you damn phone. It's been ringing for the last fifteen minutes. It's giving me a damn headache."

I stepped down from the ring, walked over to the bench, and fished my phone out of my bag. I had two missed calls from Oscar Wembley. I dialed his number.

"Sorry to blow up your phone," he said. "When you asked me last week if I had anything of my sister's, like a school yearbook or other mementos like that, I told you I didn't have anything. But then a few days after I got home, I thought about my mother's emergency box."

"Emergency box?" I said. I slung my bag over my shoulder, left the gym, and jumped in my car. I needed to get back to the office.

"Yes, my mother had this walnut box about the size of a small drawer. It had also been her grandmother's emergency box. Her grandmother had escaped the Nazis, but her father and mother hadn't made it out in time. My great-grandmother used the box to keep all of her most important possessions and papers. She taught my mother the importance of having a portable emergency box. I hadn't looked at my mother's box since she died. Truthfully, I had put it off all these years, almost like if I didn't look through it, then her death was less real, and she was still with us in some way. I know that sounds weird, but that's how I felt."

"Not weird at all," I said. "I lost my mother too. I get it. There are things I still do and don't do after all this time, because I'm still dealing with it in my own way."

"Well, I decided to look through the box just to see if there was anything there, and I think I might've found something. I don't know if it means anything, but I figured it was worth a shot. She mostly kept papers in it, as well as her marriage license, our birth certificates, her and my father's passports, my grandfather's watch, and a couple of pictures of my grandparents over in Germany. I went through everything, but nothing seemed useful to your investigation. Then, when I was about to put all of the papers back in, I noticed there was a flap at the bottom of the box, like a secret compartment. And that's where I found it."

"Found what?"

"A small envelope with a letter inside that Bianca sent to my mother about four years ago."

"Had the envelope been opened?"

"Yes."

"What did it say?"

"At the top it says 'Don't tell anyone you have this information. But if something happens to me, make sure you give this to the police.' She then wrote some words and numbers, but they don't make any sense to me."

"What are they?"

"The first line says 'Eagle Rock.' The second line says 'Apollo.' Then there are two rows of numbers and letters."

I almost dropped the phone when I heard the words *Eagle Rock*. I had one of those dissociative moments, when my mind felt like it didn't belong to me, and Oscar's voice sounded distant and hallucinatory. I don't know how I got the words out, but I said, "Please say those words that were on top of the rows of numbers again," I said.

"'Eagle Rock,'" Oscar repeated slowly. "'Apollo.'"

The second hearing made it real.

"Listen very carefully to what I'm about to tell you," I said. "I need you to take a picture of the letter, then text it to me. Then I want you to put the letter in a big envelope and send it to me overnight."

"Not a problem," Oscar said. "I can do that."

"Who else knows of this letter?"

"No one, except me."

"Do you think your mother shared it with anyone?"

"I doubt it. She hadn't even told me."

"Oscar, you can't tell anyone about this letter or what Bianca had written. Not even your wife."

"What about the police?"

"No one," I said firmly.

"Does this mean anything to you?" Oscar said.

"It means a helluva lot. Your sister was so worried that something was going to happen to her that she did all of this just in case her fears became a reality. I don't know who knows what or who can be trusted. But what I do know is that your sister's killer or killers are still out there, and sooner rather than later, I'm going to find them."

A couple of minutes after we finished the call, my cell phone buzzed. I opened up Oscar's text message and saw for myself exactly what he had just read to me. I attached the photo to an email, sent it to myself, then opened it up on my computer. I printed out two copies, posted one on the board, and placed the other on my desk.

Don't tell anyone you have this information.
But if something happens to me, make sure
you give this to the police.

Eagle Rock
Apollo
+44 20 7499 9000
1766645689
CNATKYKY

I carefully studied the two rows of numbers. I was certain the first row was an international phone number by the plus sign; however, I didn't recognize the country code. I took out my phone and dialed the number. It rang several times before a woman answered.

"Good evening, United States Embassy," she said.

"Where am I calling?" I said.

"You've reached the US Embassy in London," she said. "How can I help you?"

"Is this a private number inside of the embassy?" I asked.

"I don't understand your question, sir," she said.

"The number I called, is it someone's direct line?"

"No, you've reached the switchboard."

"Thank you for your help," I said before disconnecting the call.

I wrote *US Embassy* next to the first row of numbers. I studied the second row of numbers for several minutes but couldn't make any sense of it. I dialed the number but got an automated message telling me that my call couldn't be completed as dialed.

I shifted my attention to the row of letters. Was it an acronym? I sat at my desk and wrote the letters out on a piece of paper and tried different combinations of words, but nothing made sense. I called my father, who could finish the *New York Times* crossword puzzle with a pen, but he too was stumped.

"What were you trying to say to us, Bianca?" I said to myself.

My phone buzzed as I stood there, studying the note. It was Mechanic.

"Connelly finally returned to the office," he said.

"It's been over a week," I said. "Makes you wonder what he's been doing this entire time."

"I'm not sure, but he looks confident."

"What's he driving today?"

"A '69 or '70 Cadillac coupe. Black."

"Jesus, this man's got some rides."

"And he parked next to a blue Maserati," Mechanic said. "Maybe it belongs to that girl Jenny Lee."

I racked my brain, trying to make sense of it. Connelly took a week off from the office, but when he returned, he invited his mistress to the office for everyone else to see?

"Can you get the license plate on the Maserati?" I said.

"Yup. JWC568."

"Give me a sec," I said. I scrolled through my text messages with Carolina. She had run the plate for me after that first night I followed Jenny. I found it. "It's her," I said.

"What do you want me to do?"

"Sit tight. I'm gonna see if I can rattle the cage a little."

I found the number to Connelly's firm and dialed it. A woman answered the phone.

"Could I speak to Jenny Lee?" I said.

"No one by that name works here," the woman said.

"Are you sure? Her car is sitting outside of your building."

"One moment, please."

A few seconds later, another woman got on the phone. She had a slight Chinese accent.

"How may I help you?" she said.

"I'm looking for Jenny Lee," I said.

"What's this regarding?"

"I need to make an appointment with her."

"Appointment? What kind of appointment?"

"Is Jenny there?"

"Who are you?"

"A client."

"Then why are you trying to make an appointment with Jenny? You need to speak to one of the attorneys."

"So you know Jenny?"

"Of course I do. She's my daughter. Would you like to speak to one of our attorneys?"

"I would. Is Monroe Connelly available?"

"Who should I tell him is calling?"

"Ashe Cayne."

The line when silent for a while, then Connelly's voice came on next.

"You're very persistent, Ashe," he said. "You're either courageous or foolish."

"Well, you know what Maya Angelou said."

"Actually, I don't."

"'Courage is the most important of all the virtues because without courage, you cannot practice any other virtue consistently.'"

"But sometimes courage can make even the wisest of men do the stupidest of things," Connelly said. "All actions have consequences, intended and unintended."

"Are you threatening me, counselor?"

"Never. Just sharing facts."

"How about sharing your relationship with Jenny Lee and explaining why she's driving that pretty hundred-thousand-dollar Maserati registered in your name."

"I've had a chance to catch up on some of your work," Connelly said. "You tend to play outside the lines."

"That's where all the fun is," I said.

"And a lot of danger too," Connelly said before disconnecting the line.

39

At four o'clock the next morning, I woke up to Van Pelt on *SportsCenter* going through the top ten plays of the day. I had fallen asleep on the couch. Stryker was stretched out on the floor beneath me. I had been dreaming about London, maybe because in an earlier playing of the top ten, Van Pelt had mentioned a corner-kick goal by the Chelsea Football Club. This gave me an idea. I grabbed a bottle of water out of the fridge, then pulled Bianca's note out of my back pocket.

It was ten o'clock in the morning in London. I dialed the US Embassy. A different woman answered this time. She sounded like an American.

"Can I speak to Apollo?" I said.

"Excuse me?"

"I'd like to speak to Apollo," I said.

"Is this a first or last name?"

I took a guess. "First," I said.

"Hold for a moment," she said.

It took her quite a while, which made me think she had located the person. However, when she got back on the line, she said, "I'm sorry, but we don't have anyone who works here with the first or last name of Apollo."

"Would there be anything related to the embassy that would be connected to Apollo?"

"Such as?"

"The name of an office or meeting room? Anything like that?"

"Not that I'm aware of, sir, but if I could get your name and number, I could have someone look into it and get back to you."

I gave her my name and cell phone number and thanked her. I walked over to my computer and woke it up. I took Bianca's note and did a Google search for acronyms, typing in the series of letters that she had written. In just a matter of seconds, I got a hit. The letters weren't an acronym. They were the SWIFT code for the Cayman National Bank. SWIFT stood for Society for Worldwide Interbank Financial Telecommunication, and its purpose was to identify banks and financial institutions globally. I went on to read that these codes were used when transferring money between banks, in particular when it came to international wire transfers. Banks would also use these codes when they wanted to exchange messages between each other. If anyone would know more about this, it would be Balzac, my whiz-kid financial adviser. But it was only five o'clock in the morning. I'd have to wait a couple of hours before calling him. I put on my running gear and headed outside for a slow trip along the lake.

By the time I had finished my run, showered, and walked Stryker, it was a little past seven o'clock. I dialed Balzac.

"Early bird catches the criminal," he said upon answering.

"With your help, that might be the case," I said.

"Seriously? You're calling me to help with a case?"

"What do you know about Cayman National Bank?"

"Not much, other than a lot of Americans like to park their

money over there when they don't want to pay taxes. When I worked at JPMorgan, several clients had accounts down there."

"I have what I think is an account number, but I'm not sure."

"You want me to check and see if it's legit?"

"That would be a big help."

"Text me the number. Give me an hour. I'll make a few calls."

"What happened last quarter?" I said. "The returns on my portfolio were the best I ever had, but some of my friends got crushed."

"That's because *I'm* not managing their money," Balzac said. "You collect the bad guys, I collect the dividends. Both of us at the top of our game."

I went back to my computer and looked at the website for the US Embassy in London. Maybe I could find Apollo mentioned somewhere. I searched through several links, checked out the leadership that was listed, but didn't see any mention of Apollo. Then I found myself on a page describing the embassy building and its historic move from Mayfair, where it had been for most of the twentieth century and into the early 2000s before it relocated to a revitalized industrial area near the center of London in 2017.

The post talked about the timeless design of the building, created by a Philadelphia architectural firm. It was described as a translucent crystalline cube giving form to the core democratic values of transparency, openness, and equality. Intrigued by the description, I clicked a link to the image. When the building popped up on my screen, I knew right away that I had seen it before, and I knew where I saw it. I looked up at Bianca's photo posted on the board. There she stood smiling in front of the embassy.

My phone rang. It was Balzac.

"I have your answer," he said. "The numbers you gave me definitely belong to an account at Cayman National."

"How can I find out who owns the account?"

"That's gonna be tough. One of the big reasons why clients open these overseas accounts is the privacy they offer."

"What if I have an idea of who the account belongs to?" I said. "If I have the name and the account number, could I get that confirmed?"

"Is the person dead or alive?"

"Dead."

"How recent?"

"Within the last few weeks."

"I'll call you right back," he said.

I went back to looking at the embassy website. I clicked the link to the ambassador. A photo and bio of Ambassador Raymond Sanferd popped up on the screen. I had the feeling I had seen this name before, but I just couldn't remember where. He was a middle-aged man with close-cut dark hair, a receding hairline, and large ears that made me wonder if he had been teased as a kid. He looked confident and diplomatic. I had never met an ambassador before, but this was what I always imagined one looked like.

Sanferd's bio read like a winding road map through the upper echelons of academia and the State Department. He sat on numerous philanthropic and academic boards and was a member of the Visiting Committee of the Kennedy School of Government at Harvard University. Over the last twenty years, he had held various positions in the State Department, where he last served as the assistant secretary of state for European and Eurasian affairs for the under secretary of state for political affairs. He had been named the UK ambassador two years ago.

I had an idea. I called Alicia Gentry, a friend of mine who was an FBI agent in the Chicago Field Office. I asked her to run a check on all employees working for the US Embassy in London and cross-reference their names with the word *Apollo*. She said she should have something back within the next twenty-four hours.

Balzac called back.

"That was fast," I said.

"Helps to have friends in low places," he said.

I really loved this kid.

"I have confirmed that the account number belongs to a Bianca Wembley," he said. "She opened it March sixth, 2015. The account is still open. That's all I was able to get."

"You think there's any way to see the transactions in her account?"

"My friends aren't in places that low," he said. "In order to get that, you'd need either a really corrupt bank officer, proof of ownership transfer as a result of death, or a court order."

"Which route would be the fastest?" I said.

"A corrupt banker doesn't require paperwork," Balzac said.

"My next question is theoretical."

"I already know what it is," he said. "I can call and find out, but my guess is it will have at least three zeroes at the end of the number, and maybe even four. How soon do you need it?"

"Yesterday."

THAT NIGHT, I DECIDED TO get a quick workout at Hammer's before turning in. It had been a productive day, and a good sweat would be the perfect beginning to my unwind. All the parking spaces along Madison were taken, so I turned into the back alley to take Hammer's spot, since he was never there past seven. I grabbed my gym bag and stepped out of the car. I turned to close the door when suddenly I felt like my head had just collided with a brick wall. I fell forward against the car. I took another shot behind my right ear. That really hurt. I turned just in time to duck under a swing that would've put me on the ground, had it connected.

I stepped away from the car to give myself some distance between the car and my attacker. He wasn't a big guy, but he was wide and determined. He stepped in to take another swing, but I caught him first on the side of his rib cage. It felt like I had hit a steel plate. I was lucky if I hadn't fractured my wrist. The punch was enough to slow but not stop him. He kept coming and threw a punch that caught me on the left side of my chest. The force of the blow sent me stumbling backward. He then launched his full body at me, which was his first mistake. I took half a step to my left, lifted my right leg, pivoted on my left leg, and snapped my foot against his charging head with a roundhouse kick. I could hear his nose splinter. A stream of blood and saliva squirted all over my car. He bent down to rest his face in his hands, and I swept his legs to put him on the ground. Just as I was about to jump on him, another guy appeared from the shadows. He was a foot taller and several inches wider. He stepped forward with his arms by his sides, which is what most big guys mistakenly do. Because they have such a height advantage, they don't feel the need to be overly prepared. I moved in a semicircle away from the guy on the ground and negotiated my spacing with the behemoth standing in front of me.

"This isn't fair," I said. "There's only two of you."

"Mr. Badass," the big one said, smiling a mouth full of crooked and rotten teeth.

He kept walking toward me slowly. I kept circling. I knew I had to strike first, but the question was where he would be most vulnerable. Anything I landed between his waist and neck wouldn't do anything to him. I needed to get to his head or his groin. I decided I had a better chance of landing a kick to his groin than reaching his head, but he moved just before I launched it, and I connected with his enormous right thigh, which had about as much impact as a rabbit jumping on the leg of an elephant. He laughed, took a wild swing, which was slow and predictable, and I ducked under it and quickly delivered the hardest punch I could to the side of his face. He turned, grabbed me in a bear hug, and lifted me off the ground as I tried wrapping both of my hands around his massive neck. My chest was collapsing and my energy dissipating underneath his pressure, so I summoned what strength I had left and headbutted him as hard as I could against his nose. He let me go and backed up a couple of steps to tend to his splintered nose. Just as I was about to move on him, I felt my feet being tugged away, and I looked down at the other guy grabbing at my ankles. The big guy took advantage of my distraction and delivered a blow to my chest that felt like I had gotten hit by a wrecking ball. I was dazed, hurt, and in trouble.

"Not so tough now," the big guy said.

Just as I was bracing for him to hit me again, I heard, "There's a party back here and no one invited me to it?"

We all turned toward the voice. Mechanic stood hidden in the darkness. I could only make out the vague outline of his body. Next, a thunderous gunshot exploded, and the muzzle flash lit up Mechanic's stoic face for a split second. The big guy let out a scream as he collapsed to the ground and wrapped his right knee with his hands.

"The next shot will make you infertile," Mechanic said, walking over and pointing the gun at the guy's groin. "Now I'm gonna ask you this question once and once only: Who sent you?"

The two guys looked at each other as they considered their options. Mechanic's finger tightened on the trigger.

The smaller guy said, "We don't have a name."

"It was Connelly," I said. "Monroe Connelly sent you."

"We don't take names," the big guy said, grimacing. "Jesusfuckinchrist, man, you blew my knee off."

"It doesn't work the way you think it does," the smaller guy said.

"How does it work?" I said.

The smaller guy took over as the big guy groaned in pain. "We get a text from a number. We call the number. We get told the name of the target and the action they want. We give a price. We don't negotiate. If they accept our price, we take the job."

"And what was the job?" I said.

"Rough you up a little. Scare you."

"I'm petrified," I said. "When do you get paid?"

"After the job is done."

"In what form?"

"Cash. All small bills. Twenties and tens."

"Where?"

"We have a pickup spot."

"Always the same?"

"Never. That would be stupid."

"It was stupid to take a job to come after me," I said. "Now your partner won't be walking for three months, and you won't be blowing your nose for two weeks. So where's the pickup location?"

The smaller guy looked at the big guy, who nodded his head. "Garbage can on North Clinton, outside the French Market," the smaller guy said.

"If you don't know who's behind the job, how do you know you're not being set up?"

"Set up how?" the smaller guy said.

"Undercover operation by CPD, FBI, whoever."

"We have a code name that changes for each job. Only three of us know what that name is. Before you get the code, we have you checked out to make sure it's legit. When we talk to a customer, if they don't use the code name right away, then we know something's not right. We hang up."

"Il ne faut rien laisser au hasard," I said.

The two guys looked at each other. The big guy was able to squeeze out between groans, "What the hell?"

"In French it means 'Nothing should be left to chance.' And since you're not gonna make it to the French Market to collect that payment, I figured I'd bring some French to you. What time is the pickup?"

"Night after tomorrow. Seven o'clock."

"How will they drop it?"

"Pink plastic bag."

I dialed Burke to have his team come and collect the garbage. Once they had been carted off in an ambulance, I cleaned the blood off my car, then went into Hammer's and had the best damn workout I'd had in months.

40

Alicia Gentry called me back the next morning. There were no matches between *Apollo* and anyone who worked in the embassy, past or present. They even ran a search on maiden and middle names, and still nothing turned up. This wasn't exactly the start to the day I had imagined.

Burke had the two guys who jumped me last night locked up in a holding cell. He would only be able to keep them for forty-eight hours, so the clock was ticking. He was still assembling a team that would stake out the drop-off location the next night and hopefully catch whoever it was behind all of this. If we were lucky, this would lead us to Apollo.

My father had gotten back from Paris and was being his obstinate self, refusing to curtail his activities. He insisted that he was too old to be afraid of some low-life thugs. He argued that appearing scared was exactly what they wanted, and he wasn't going to give them that. He was determined to go on with his normal routine of playing tennis, lunching with friends, and in his words, "doing whatever the hell I want to do." I was still concerned, so I asked my friend Ruqsania Begume to quietly keep an eye on him. Rox had been one of the best female boxers England had ever produced, before she hung up her gloves and moved to Chicago to run her own flower shop in Roscoe Village. Pound for pound, she was the toughest woman I had ever met; my father couldn't be in safer hands than hers.

I went back to the board again to see if there was something I was missing. I had learned many years ago that sometimes the same evidence could say different things if you were patient and consistent enough to keep coming back to it with an open mind. Three people killed within several weeks of each other, with no obvious motivation for any of the murders. I couldn't wrap my head around how they were connected. Where did their lives intersect? I focused on Bianca Wembley. I still didn't know much about her. It was as if most of her life had been erased. How much of it was by her design, and how much was by someone else's intention? As I looked at the questions I had written under her name, my eyes drifted down to the research article she had helped write. That's when I saw it. I couldn't believe my eyes. The name had been staring at me the entire time. Raymond Sanferd. His name was among several that had been listed as co-authors of the article. How the hell had I missed this? I leaned my head back and closed my eyes. Raymond Sanferd had been Bianca's professor while she was a student at Colgate. I couldn't know if their relationship went beyond that of teacher and student, but it obviously extended beyond her graduation, because she was in London recently and had gone to the embassy. She must've had the red carpet rolled out for her, because she was connected to the head honcho, Ambassador Raymond Sanferd.

I went to my computer, pulled up Sanferd's headshot, printed it out, and posted it in line with the others. Kantor, Thompson, Wembley, and Sanferd. Sounded like an expensive accounting firm.

I kept looking at their faces. Three men and one woman. How were they connected in all of this? There had to be a through line. I just couldn't see it yet.

THAT NIGHT, MECHANIC AND I devised a plan. I went out to Connelly's house again and waited while Mechanic picked up his trail at the office. He called me when Connelly got into his car and drove over to Greene's house in River North. Connelly stayed there about an hour, then jumped back in his car and turned onto 290, heading home.

Half an hour later, I saw their headlights. This time, I sat facing the driveway, so he could see my car. As he was about to turn into his property, I pulled in front of him to block the entrance. Mechanic pulled in behind him so he couldn't back up. Mechanic and I both got out of our cars and walked over to him. He rolled down the window of an old Mercury Cougar.

"A new old car every day," I said, standing next to his open window. "The law business has been really good to you."

"Can't complain," he said. He moved his hand toward the passenger seat.

Mechanic stepped forward, his gun against his thigh. "Keep your hands where I can see 'em," he said.

"Whoa!" Connelly said, raising his hands.

"We need to have a serious talk about the other night," I said.

"What happened?" Connelly said.

"You know damn well what happened," I said. "Next time, don't send boys to do a man's job."

"I swear, I have no idea what you're talking about. I didn't send any boys or men or anybody to do anything."

Mechanic lifted his gun.

"Jesus Christ, man!" Connelly said. "Put that thing away. No need for violence. We can be civil about this and come to an understanding."

"Here's the understanding," I said. "I need to have some answers. Some real answers. Playtime is over."

"I hear you. But let's do this someplace more discreet. Let me make you both a drink. Follow me up to the house."

I nodded at Mechanic, who walked back to his car while I jumped in the passenger seat next to Connelly. We pulled up the long, winding driveway and all the way to the garage with Mechanic following. Connelly tapped his remote, and the garage door slowly opened. We pulled into the massive garage with Mechanic falling in behind us. Cars were parked everywhere. I lost count at twenty. All black. All vintage. All exceptionally beautiful. A car lover's dream. In the center of the cars was a red-carpeted area with a bar, several stools, and a couple of pool tables. Two large-screen televisions hung on one wall, and the other wall had been plastered with framed autographed jerseys from various players and sports. A kitchen, bigger than what most people have in their homes, was off to one corner, with a long table that could seat ten. Connelly walked behind the bar.

"What are you drinking?" he said.

"A perfect Maker's Manhattan up," I said.

Connelly smiled. "A man who not only knows a good drink but also how to order it." He looked at Mechanic, who declined with a slight tic of his head.

Connelly went about making my drink, adding the bourbon first, then dividing the proportions of vermouth evenly between sweet and dry, inserting a couple of dashes of bitters, and finishing it with a lemon twist.

"Where do you want to start?" Connelly said, sliding the drink to me.

"The beginning is just as good of a place as any," I said.

Connelly started fixing himself a Manhattan. "Elliott and I first met many years ago, when we were on opposite sides of a transaction," he said. "He badly wanted to get the deal done. My client was being difficult just to be difficult. We all stood to make a lot of money. Elliott called me personally off the record, man to man. We talked it out without all the ego and bluster and got the deal done. Two months after we closed the deal, Elliott called me. He said he liked the way I did business. He wanted to know if I'd work for him. That's how Elliott Kantor became my biggest client."

"Was setting up escorts something you did for all your clients or just Elliott?" I said.

Connelly sat across from me at the bar. "Elliott loved his wife tremendously. They had been married over fifty years. When she died, it broke him. He was beyond distraught. He wouldn't talk to anyone. He could barely eat. He didn't leave his house for two months. No matter what his friends or family tried, nothing worked. I finally got him on the phone and convinced him to go down to his place in the Bahamas. I told him to relax and get away from it all. His wife knew he loved her more than anything, and she would want him to keep living and making the most of his remaining years. I had a friend of mine some years back, similar situation. Wife was his best friend and unexpectedly died. He was so depressed, he almost took his own life. You know what the antidote to sadness is?"

"Lots of things," I said. "But why don't you tell me?"

Connelly took a long sip of his drink, then said, "A good time."

"That's an antidote for almost everything," he said.

"So that's what I did for my friend. I had a contact help me arrange some female companionship. After two weeks down in Ibiza, my friend came back better and stronger than ever. He had a new lease on life."

"So you did the same for Elliott?" I said.

Connelly smiled. "About six months after my friend came back from Ibiza, I got a random call from an unknown number," he said. "The woman knew who I was and what I had done for my friend. She told me about an exclusive club that she had formed. It was called Eagle Rock. A limited number of male members had access to the most beautiful girls in the entire world. Italian, Brazilian, Swedish, Russian, Ethiopian, she had them all. Any shape or size, hair color, or accent. She could deliver whatever flavor you wanted."

"Sounds like an expensive club," I said.

"Two-hundred-fifty-thousand-dollar initiation fee. Fifty-thousand-dollar annual fee. Twenty-five-hundred dollars per hour per visit, and the price went up from there depending on the specifics of what you wanted. So I got Elliott to join when he was down in the Bahamas. He came back to Chicago a changed man."

"Nothing more magical than a little tata," I said. "So where does Jenny Lee fit in all of this? Is she part of Eagle Rock?"

"Jenny has nothing to do with it," Connelly said. "She doesn't even know it exists. Only an exclusive group of people know about Eagle Rock."

"Such as Lance Greene?"

Connelly nodded reluctantly.

"And Keegan Thompson?"

Connelly nodded again.

"So what happened the night Elliott died?"

"I don't know how he died," Connelly said. "But I know what happened before he died."

"I'm listening."

"Eagle Rock's membership terms were simple. Everything was built on privacy. Everyone was supposed to be anonymous. Members were not to know the identities of other members. The escorts were not supposed to know the identities of the members. And the members weren't supposed to know the true identities of the escorts. All communication went through one person—Daphne."

"The same Daphne who was killed and hung on Northerly Island?" I said.

"She was the only point of contact," Connelly said.

"So, what happened?"

"Elliott broke the rules. He started asking the women their names. And that got back to Daphne. She told him to stop, but when he kept doing it, she finally called him and told him his membership was revoked. The rules applied to everyone, including one of Chicago's richest men. Well, Elliott didn't take that too well. Understandably. Elliott was a man who always got what he wanted. He wasn't going to let some young girl boss him around. So he started learning the identities of other members, like Lance and Keegan. He began calling the girls directly and arranging for private appointments, flying them down to his place in the Bahamas and his farm in Belize. Daphne found out and went ballistic. Elliott told her to fuck off. He threatened her. He told her that he would find out her real identity and ruin her. I tried to calm him down. I told him to just let the dust settle for a while. Things had gone to a place they didn't need to go. So he took my advice and tried to make peace with Daphne. The night he died, he called me and told me he and Daphne had made amends, and as a show of good faith, she was sending over a new girl for no charge. When he told me this, I told him not to do it. Something didn't feel right about it. Elliott liked Asians, and he liked to be whipped. I told him to forget about Daphne's offer. I had the perfect girl for him who I could send, and she had nothing to do with Eagle Rock."

"And that was Jenny Lee," I said.

"It was," he said. "So I called the service Jenny worked for and made an appointment for her to visit Elliott. But I didn't tell Jenny that I had done it. I didn't want her to know I was behind it."

"So she shows up at Kantor's apartment not knowing who he is. And when she gets into the apartment, he's already dead."

Connelly nodded. "I got a message from the service later that night asking me if the visit was complete. I called Elliott's cell phone, but he didn't pick up. I tried him several more times, but he still didn't answer. I figured he had fallen asleep. I called the service and told them the visit had been completed. I didn't find out until the next day that Elliott had died."

"And you didn't say anything?"

"What was I gonna say? That Elliott Kantor, Chicago's most beloved billionaire, liked dressing up in women's panties and died when he was just about to get his ass whipped? There was nothing I could do or say at that point. It was too late. He was gone."

"At the very least, you could've spoken up and cleared Jenny," I said.

"I didn't need to. Jenny's a tough girl. She knows how to take care of herself."

"Why were you and Greene on Northerly Island the night Daphne's body was found?"

"I got a call that night from a blocked number. The caller told me that he knew I was trying to figure out Daphne's true identity."

"Was that true?"

"Of course. I wanted to find out who she was to stop her from fucking with us. When Elliott died, I wanted to put an end to it all."

"As in kill her?"

"As in talk to her calmly to reach an understanding."

"And if that didn't work?"

"If you're asking if I would have killed her, the answer is probably. But I didn't."

"So what did the caller say that got you to go to Northerly Island?"

"He said that the threat was over and to go to Daphne Garden at that precise time for confirmation. I wasn't comfortable going by myself, so I took Lance with me. We hadn't heard of Daphne Garden before, but we finally found it. We saw the body hanging on one of the statues. We got the hell out of there as fast as we could."

"Then you bought champagne, went back to Greene's house, and partied like it was 1999."

Connelly looked at me quizzically.

"Partied hard and wild," I said. "It's from Prince's song '1999.'"

"Can you blame us?" he asked. "We were scared to death. She knew too much. She knew things that, if they got out, would've caused a feeding frenzy. Daphne had us by the balls."

"Figuratively and literally," I said.

"And whoever called me knew that," Connelly said. "He wanted it to be clear to the rest of us in Eagle Rock that the threat had finally been eliminated."

Everything he had said made sense, but it also complicated things. I would have to expand my theory from one killer to two or more, and looking for multiple killers was much more difficult than looking for one.

"Why did Elliott call himself Plutus?" I said.

"That was his Eagle Rock code name," Connelly said.

"And Thompson?"

"Eros."

"The god of love and attraction," I said. "Greene?"

"Kratos."

"Clever. The god of strength. Fitting for an ex-football player. Who was Apollo?"

"I have no idea. I don't even know if someone has that name."

"Do you think the same person killed Kantor, Thompson, and Daphne?"

"Your guess is as good as mine. But as long as whoever did it is still out there, we're all still in jeopardy."

41

Everything had been set up for the drop. Twenty undercover officers had been scattered around the building that housed the French Market while Burke and I, along with three other officers, manned operations inside of a blue Ford Transit work van with the name *Windy Electric Group* painted in white letters on both sides. We sat inconspicuously among other work vans that were parked along North Clinton Street. The cameras that had been set up yesterday gave us a full 360-degree view of the building. The garbage can of interest was only half a block to our north.

The drop had been scheduled to take place at seven. Everyone was in place by three. Burke and I joined the control center at five. Several monitors in the van gave us visuals on all sides of the building, in all four directions. We watched quietly as people exited the market and walked casually by the garbage can. Some dropped in empty bottles, but nothing suspicious and no pink bag.

At 5:33 p.m., a young couple leaving the market walked by the garbage can. The woman tossed in a white Styrofoam food container. At 5:50 p.m., a middle-aged man finished his soda and tossed the empty bottle into the garbage can. Eight plainclothes officers were positioned around the building, two with direct sight to the garbage can and only yards away. One was seated on a nearby bench eating, while the other was walking up and down the street, dressed as a meter guy writing parking tickets.

At 6:08, I noticed a homeless man in large, baggy clothes and a dark hoodie slowly walking in the direction of the garbage can. He had a slight limp, as if he had hurt his knee or hip. Before reaching the can, he veered off unsteadily and headed to the curb, where he started drinking from a water bottle he pulled from underneath his sweatshirt. When he tipped his head back, the hoodie fell off, and his long hair fell out. I realized it was not a man but a woman. I suddenly thought about what Miles Carthew, the neighbor who lived down the street from Elliott's apartment building, had told us about what happened the night Kantor died. He had described a small man with a limp, dressed in dark clothes, escaping through the door on the side of the building. I sat back and smiled. It wasn't a man leaving Elliott's apartment that night. It was a small woman dressed in men's clothes. The Amazon driver had transported her in that trunk, dropped her off inside, and left with the empty trunk. She had killed Kantor. That man was Daphne, otherwise known as Bianca Wembley, a petite woman with a one-inch leg-length discrepancy and a diamond nose ring that Carthew saw shining under the streetlight that night. Bianca had also killed Thompson and, just as she had done with Kantor, tied him up using that becket bend knot, one she had learned from her grandfather as a little girl.

At 6:43, a tall man in a gray pin-striped suit walked to the garbage can, opened a briefcase, and appeared to be throwing away a folder. He stopped himself, paused momentarily, then changed his mind, put the folder back in his briefcase, and walked away. No one went near the can again for another thirty-one minutes. At 7:14, a short older woman in a blue sleeveless dress was walking a small dog and heading toward the garbage can. She dumped a bag into the garbage, but then she did something none of us expected. She pulled the bag back out, but it was empty.

"Keep an eye on her," I said.

"Check the can now," Burke said into his radio, instructing an officer sitting at a table. "But casually. Don't look like you're searching for anything."

The guy got up and calmly walked over to the garbage can. He stood over it, wiped his mouth with a napkin, then tossed it in the can. "Pink bag is in," he said into his hidden mic. "And it's full. Either her dog shits like an elephant, or she just made the drop."

"Old woman heading north on Clinton," Burke said into his radio. "Blue sleeveless dress. Walking a small dog. Wait until she's another block away, then take her."

Within seconds, an unmarked van raced the wrong way up Clinton Street. It stopped a few feet away from the woman on the sidewalk. She stopped when she heard the doors fly open. Six guys jumped out of the van, quickly carried her and the dog into the back, closed the door, and sped away. The entire apprehension took less than ten seconds.

"YOU WALK YOUR DOG NEAR the French Market often?" the officer said.

The old woman sat in the interview room with her arms folded defiantly across her chest. She seemed more annoyed than she was angry. She didn't appear scared in the slightest. Burke and I, along with two other detectives, watched the interview from the adjacent observation room.

"I walk my dog everywhere," she said.

"But you live five miles north of that location," the officer said.

"I didn't know it was a crime to walk your dog in neighborhoods you don't live in," she said.

"No crime," he said. "Just curious as to why you chose that location."

"My dog is a papillon," she said. "French. She likes the smell of the French Market. Comes naturally to her."

The detective smiled. "Where did your dog stop and take a shit?" he asked.

"It's a she," the woman said. "And I have no idea. I wasn't looking at the addresses when she did it."

The detective looked down at his notes, then said, "What did you put in the garbage can in front of the market?"

"Is this a serious question?" the woman said.

"It is."

The woman glared at him for a moment, then said, "Shit. I put shit in the garbage can. Where else am I supposed to put it?"

"You have a strange way of throwing shit into a garbage can," he said. "I've never seen anyone open the bag, pour the shit out, then take the bag back with them."

"I'm a conservationist," the woman said, "and economical. Bags are reusable. Is that a crime too?"

"No, it's not," the detective said calmly. "Who asked you to drop the pink bag in the garbage can?"

"What pink bag?"

"The pink bag with all the cash in it."

"I don't know what you're talking about," the woman said. "If I saw money in a garbage can, I'd take it. I'm an old woman on a fixed income. I could use the extra cash. And I know my rights. If you're not going to charge me with anything, then let me go. I'm not answering any more of your ridiculous questions." She pushed back from the table for dramatic effect.

The detective closed his notebook, stood up, and left the room.

He joined the rest of us. As they conferenced on next steps, I got a call from Balzac.

"I'm going to be sending you an email," he said. "This Bianca Wembley could've used my services."

"In what way?" I said.

"She had a lot of money sitting in an account, doing nothing."

"How much?"

"Just over five million."

"That's a lot of money for an online arts-and-crafts store," I said.

"What did you say?"

"Just thinking out loud," I said. "What was her account activity like?"

"Busy. She deposited just over two million in the last year. She also had at least one major expense that she needed to pay."

"What do you mean?"

"On the first of every month, she made a fifty-thousand-dollar payment to the same account."

"Every month?"

"Without fail."

"Any way to find out who owns the other account?"

"I knew you'd ask," Balzac said. "Spruce Mountains LLC, which is registered to a Raymond Sanferd."

"Raymond Sanferd?"

"That's the name on the corporate paperwork."

"Can you send all of this to me?"

"Already sent. It's in your box."

I exhaled slowly. The missing piece had finally fallen into place.

"I'm going to have something for you in about a week," I said. "Be on the lookout."

"A surprise?"

"If that's what you want to call another million dollars for you to invest."

Burke was still conferencing with the detectives, trying to figure out their next move. I caught his attention and nodded for him to join me on the other side of the room.

"Let her go," I said. "You're wasting your time."

"What the hell does that mean?" Burke growled.

"She didn't put the money into the can. The pink bag was already in there before she arrived. Remember that couple who dumped the Styrofoam food container. Inside of the container was the bag. The old woman was hired to open up the food container and rearrange it so the pink bag was visible for the pickup."

"Jesus Christ!" Burke exclaimed. "We have to locate the couple."

"You don't," I said. "Even if you found them, it wouldn't matter. You'd just be slipping down a rabbit hole. There would be more names and people you'd have to track down."

"Why are you so confident about this?"

"Because that old woman has no real information that's going to help us. Bianca Wembley killed Kantor. And while I can't prove it just yet, she probably killed Thompson too."

"What the hell are you talking about?"

I explained Eagle Rock to him.

"I get it, but why would Wembley kill her golden goose?" Burke said. "She was making money hand over fist with them."

"She was, but Kantor and Thompson had broken the cardinal rule of membership. They struck out on their own and interacted directly with the women. They also started talking about the identities of other Eagle Rock members, and that was the most egregious violation, because sooner or later, the hidden identity of the person at the top of the chain would be in jeopardy."

I explained to Burke the Greek mythology story of Daphne, her rejection of Apollo, and her ultimately turning into a laurel tree so that he couldn't have her.

"So if Wembley killed Kantor and Thompson, then why would she kill herself?"

"She didn't."

"Who did?"

"Apollo."

"And who the hell is that?"

"Raymond Sanferd. Our esteemed ambassador to the United Kingdom."

"An ambassador?" he said. "Are you fuckin' kidding me? Why would an ambassador get caught up in all this shit?"

"Fifty thousand dollars a month adds up to a lot more than a hundred and eighty thousand dollars a year, which is the most an ambassador can be paid."

"You understand you're accusing a United States ambassador of running a high-end escort service?"

"And murder."

"You got proof of all this?"

I pulled out a folded copy of Bianca's letter to her mother and handed it to Burke.

"Follow the money trail," I said. "Ambassador Sanferd will be waiting for you at the end of it."

42

I like this place," Carolina said. "It really feels like we're in three countries at once."

Carolina and I sat on an ornate daybed flown in all the way from Bali, underneath an elaborate crystal chandelier in a restaurant in West Town called Beatnik. The atmosphere was everything. Antique carved wooden façades lined the room, as did elaborately designed Persian rugs. A DJ in the corner spun reggae music mixed with bursts of Afrobeat and French pop. The owner's intention had been to create an aesthetic that fused Morocco, the Mediterranean, and Italy. He had succeeded wonderfully.

A plate of smoked baba ghanoush and another plate of fried eggplant in a vinegar mustard sauce were almost entirely devoured. We had ordered different cocktails. She chose the Easy Rider, which consisted of a mix of rum, fernet, passion fruit, strawberry, lime, and mint. I was currently working on a combination of Japanese gin, ginger shochu, rhubarb falernum, watermelon, Thai basil, lemon, and black salt. It was called Immoral High Ground. I thought it appropriate for my thoughts about what awaited us later that evening.

"So how do you feel?" Carolina said, taking a sip of her Easy Rider.

She wore a low-cut blouse and her hair down. Her eyes sparkled from the glow of the candelabra.

"Conflicted," I said.

"How?"

"The deaths seemed so senseless. They were all adults and decent people. At the end of the day, it was about sex and privacy. No one should've died over that."

"The ambassador didn't die."

"Unfortunately. The ones who most deserve to die are the ones who end up living."

"Why did he have to kill her?"

"Because she went way off script and was going after two of their most prominent members. Ultimately, that was putting him at risk, and he figured that silencing her for good was the best way to protect himself."

"What will happen to him?"

"Nothing."

"You're being cynical again."

"I'm being realistic. High-ranking government official. White middle-aged man. Connections all through Washington. Holder of who knows what and how many secrets in that incestuously corrupt town. He shielded himself well enough. Nothing will happen to him. He'll be allowed to resign, then disappear into some million-dollar corporate job or in the back office of some political action committee."

"But if it had been you?"

"Ha. I'd be buried under the jail somewhere in steel pants."

I took a sip of my drink. It felt good going down my throat. The DJ turned up the volume a little. A few people got up and danced next to their tables.

"Lots of losers in all this," Carolina said. "But lots of winners too."

"Oscar will have to fight for it, but he'll eventually get the five million. Which is the right thing. Veronica Thompson inherited everything, but they wouldn't let her take over the church. They reached a settlement with her somewhere north of ten million. She and her friend and those beautiful girls won't have anything to worry about. Simon gets his insurance payout worth tens of millions. Bailey gets another big donation to his political campaign just for telling Burke to get me on the case."

"And you got a million dollars."

"That Balzac promises he can double in a year."

"What will you do with it?"

"Try to impress you."

"That's a tall order."

"How about a week on the beach in Seychelles?"

"And endless margaritas watching the sunset."

"You're a helluva negotiator."

"And endless nights under the covers hearing the waves outside of our cabana," she said.

"Maybe I should pay the check so we can get back to my apartment and start practicing."

"Practicing what?"

I took a small sip of my drink, leaned over, and slightly opened her lips with my tongue, then said, "The immoral high ground."

Acknowledgments

Writing my novels is a lot more pleasure than it is work, and the work that it requires is all part of the fun. While I create the content, it is certainly made better by those who answer my endless questions, entertain my ideas for characters and plot points, and support me in ways that help give me the drive, space, and creative freedom to simply go for it. Thanks first to Tristé, Dashiell, and Declan, who inspire me in countless ways and never tire of me talking about books and characters and plot twists I want to execute. I love you beyond measure.

Thanks to the crack team at Amistad and HarperCollins, especially Patrik Bass and Judith Curr, who totally get Ashe Cayne and share a vision of where the series can and will go. Your support and cheerleading help keep the fire burning. My agents Mitch Hoffman and Lisa Gallagher keep my publishing train on the track and on time, and while I know my writing goals are often nontraditional and audacious, you never back down and you never try to snuff any of my light. Your encouragement and brainstorming are a writer's dream.

Lastly, to all of the Ashe Cayne fans who send me messages asking for the next installment, I deeply appreciate you joining me for the ride. I hope you have as much fun reading about his adventures as I do creating them.

About the Author

Ian K. Smith is a #1 *New York Times* bestselling author. His Chicago-based Ashe Cayne series is currently in development to become a streaming TV series, and his novel *The Ancient Nine* has been optioned to become a motion picture. His acclaimed novel *The Blackbird Papers* was a Black Caucus of the American Library Association fiction honor award recipient. Many of his books have been number one bestsellers and have been translated into more than ten languages. He remains a health and fitness enthusiast, and rarely turns down a round of golf or a good workout. He is a graduate of Harvard and Columbia, and did his first two years of medical school at Dartmouth, finishing his medical degree at the University of Chicago.

For more information, you can visit:

www.doctoriansmith.com
Instagram: @doctoriansmith
X: @DrIanSmith
TikTok: @theofficialdrian